FARRAR
STRAUS
GIROUX

ALSO BY DOUG MARLETTE

The Bridge

Magic
TIME

Magic TIME

Doug Marlette

SARAH CRICHTON BOOKS
Farrar, Straus and Giroux
New York

Sarah Crichton Books
Farrar, Straus and Giroux
19 Union Square West, New York 10003

Distributed in Canada by Douglas & McIntyre Ltd.
Printed in the United States of America
First edition, 2006

Grateful acknowledgment is made for permission to reprint the
following previously published material:
"The MTA," written by Jacqueline Steiner and Bess Hawes. Copyright
© 1956–1984 by Atlantic Music Corporation. Used by permission.
International copyright secured. All rights reserved.
"The Fourth Man," written by Arthur Smith. Copyright © 1955 by Arthur
Smith and Clay Music (BMI). Used by permission. All rights reserved.

Library of Congress Cataloging-in-Publication Data
Marlette, Doug, [date]
    Magic time / by Doug Marlette.— 1st ed.
      p.   cm.
    "Sarah Crichton books."
    ISBN-13: 978-0-374-20001-5 (alk. paper)
    ISBN-10: 0-374-20001-7 (alk. paper)
    1. Journalists—Fiction.   2. Mississippi—Fiction.   I. Title.

PS3563.A6729 M34 2006
813'.54—dc22

                                    2005036396

Designed by Cassandra J. Pappas

www.fsgbooks.com

10 9 8 7 6 5 4 3 2 1

For my father,
Elmer Monroe Marlette,
who helped search for the bodies
of Goodman, Schwerner,
and Chaney

Forsan et haec olim meminisse iuavibit.

A joy it will be one day, perhaps, to remember even this.

—VIRGIL'S *AENEID*
translation by Robert Fagles

Magic
TIME

Troy

CARTER RANSOM AWOKE curled up in the backseat of his sister's Mercury Grand Marquis. The metronomic ticking of tires against scored pavement penetrated the pharmaceutical fog, and he pushed up on his forearms to look out the window. They were speeding along the interstate that flatlined across the Black Belt of southern Mississippi.

"You slept good," said Sally. He caught her anxious glance in the rearview mirror. He raised himself up until he could see his own reflection. There were dark circles under his eyes, and his jawline was shadowed with stubble, his thick brown hair matted. He still had on the black and gold Vanderbilt sweatshirt his sister had found in a chest of drawers in his apartment in New York and brought to the hospital for him to wear on the trip. It was a present Emily had gotten him for his birthday.

"How close are we?" Carter asked.

"Just north of Meridian," said Sally. "We're almost home. Go back to sleep if you want."

He stretched and looked around. One leg was still numb, and his back muscles were tight from the long ride south. He felt thirsty but was too weak to open the ice chest on the floorboard beside him to see if there were Cokes inside. Instead he retrieved the pillow he had been resting his head on, gathered it up close to his chest, and sank into the

backseat vinyl to stare out the window. The medication made his throat
dry and his brain furry. Nausea overcame him as a profound agitation
blossomed again in his stomach.

"Sally, what's going on?" he said. He leaned forward and placed his
forehead against the seat back, turning slightly to squint through the
glare of the side window at the barren Mississippi landscape whizzing by.

"You passed out in the newsroom, remember?" Sally spoke in a con-
scientiously neutral tone, as if she were describing the weather.

Carter stared out at the scrub pine, the red clay, and the heavy equipment of highway construction, trying to focus on what his sister was
saying.

"You were in the hospital a few days but checked yourself out. Your
editor, Mr. Dennehy, offered you some time off, but you insisted on returning to work." Carter had not missed a deadline for a couple of weeks.
Then, Sally explained, one day he did not show up for work or answer the
phone. His colleague Gelman found his bicycle unlocked on the stoop.
When Gelman's knock on the door got no answer, he called a couple of
his police buddies and they broke in. "They found you passed out on the
floor in your bedroom and took you back to the hospital," Sally said.
"The doctor said it was nervous exhaustion and malnutrition." She hesitated. "He also mentioned symptoms of post-traumatic stress disorder."

Carter looked back into the rearview mirror, knowing his sister
would be watching for his reaction. He felt a jab of indignation. "Fuck
that," he said under his breath. The thought that his condition might
have a diagnosis made him feel even worse.

When he surfaced again from a dreamless highway slumber, the car was
stopped at a gas station. He could see Sally inside paying. She returned
with some peanuts and Nabs and seemed grateful when he tore them
open. Back on the road, Carter sipped a Coke and looked out on the
increasingly familiar landscape. He sat up fully for the first time. "This
is a bad idea, Sally."

"You don't need to be by yourself, Carter," Sally said with a quiet
finality.

"You should have left me in the loony bin," he said.

Sally said, "Ashland is not a loony bin."

"You're right. Troy is the loony bin."

The last time Carter had been back to his hometown of Troy, Mississippi, was a couple of years earlier, when he had taken Josh and Emily on the grand Southern tour. They spent one night in Troy. Carter had seldom returned since his mother died ten years before and he had left the Atlanta paper and moved to New York. On the rare occasions he visited, he had calculated to a science the length of time he and his father could spend under the same roof. Forty-eight hours, max, before one of them uttered the words *I have to take a walk.*

"You need to rest, Carter. You need to be around people who love you and can take care of you."

"But I've got a life, Sal. Responsibilities. I've got deadlines—"

"Dennehy said he could manage without you for a while."

As much as Carter cringed at the thought of recuperating in Troy, he knew that once Sally had set a plan in motion, she saw it through. She offered him a bit of her Hershey bar.

"Daddy's excited you're coming, Pross," Sally said. Pross, short for Prosecutor, was a pet name his father called him when he was a boy. The name remained current among only a handful of people.

"How is the judge?"

"Not bad for a seventy-year-old." Since retiring from the federal bench for health reasons, their father had rallied and returned to his law practice. "The firm's having a fortieth anniversary party in a few weeks," Sally said. "Don't tell Daddy, but the new connector's going to be named after him. The Mitchell T. Ransom Expressway."

"What is it, a dead end?"

Sally laughed. "You can come to the party if you feel up to it."

Carter forced a smile. "I don't know how you take care of him."

"Oh, he's no bother. He's dialed it back a lot in recent years. You'll be surprised. He's a good grandfather to Willie, and Willie's devoted to him." Sally's ex, a tax lawyer, had run off with his paralegal when Sally was pregnant with their now six-year-old son. "Besides," she continued, "when you're a bookseller in a town that doesn't read, having no house payment is a godsend."

"Thought of hiring a nurse?"

"Oh, Mr. Primary Caregiver's offering advice now."

Sally had turned on her signal and was moving into the right lane. Carter felt an involuntary pang of love/hate when he saw the green exit sign, TROY HISTORIC DISTRICT.

"How's business, Sally?" He knew how hard it was for her to be away from the shop. And although she would never complain, he felt guilty for being the reason she had to take off.

"Could be worse. The town's changed considerably. You're not going to recognize it."

"That's reassuring."

"The college is Troy University now, you know. Our generation's finally grown up and taken over. The mayor's black, and a couple of council members. There's even an artists' collective in Troy."

"Black-velvet Elvises? Popsicle-stick birdhouses?"

"Ha-ha. There's also a clique of writers developing."

"Ah, Mississippi. Where they write more books than they read."

The conversation had exhausted Carter. He reclined in the seat. Sally had turned off the interstate onto old U.S. Highway 17, the narrow two-lane blacktop that was the only route north out of town in his youth, before the interstate. It was the road he had traveled with his family on vacations, with his basketball team to games in Meridian or Columbus, with church groups to gospel sings in Jackson, and it was the road that took him away from home to college and law school back when the future had seemed knowable.

Except for a few stray billboards promoting products and companies that had not existed in the 1960s, the scenery along the highway remained much as it was during his boyhood—a corridor of unbroken green cutting through incipient hills of pine forest, giving way occasionally to sunbaked farmland, open fields of soybean, corn, and watermelon, or pastures occupied by melancholy herds of humidity-stunned cattle. The relentless sun seemed to have drained the fields of all vitality and through some perverse photosynthesis transmuted an excess of chlorophyll to the lush kudzu, which crept up guy wires and draped telephone poles.

The highway grew clotted with slow-moving trucks hauling lumber, forcing an adjustment of speed and expectation for miles before one reached the city limits, as if returning to Troy required a slowing of metabolism to the velocity of molasses. As they passed the old Troy Casket Company and its sprawling new facility, Carter caught his first whiff of the changes that had come to his hometown. The company's whimsical contemporary logo seemed suited more to a wine emporium in Jackson than to the sides of the parked trucks that would deliver their sad cargo all over the Southeast.

"Lige has been in town a lot campaigning for reelection," Sally said as they pulled into view of the town square. "I'm sure he'll be coming by to see you."

In Mississippi the past had a way of superimposing itself on the present, and Carter experienced that familiar twinning of realities as he made out the old Kress's logo bleeding through the whitewashed brick on the building rising before them: a personal landmark. It was now abandoned, a sign on its soaped windows announcing its next tenant, an organic foods market.

As they circled the courthouse, Sally said, "Look, Pross. See anything different?" She pointed toward the street on the south end of the square. Carter scanned the intersection he had known so well as a child, and he spotted the statue erected on a traffic island in the distance, a small cast-bronze figure of a man with one hand lifted heavenward in a gesture of command. "Guess who that is."

"The Imperial Wizard of the Ku Klux Klan."

Sally laughed and groaned. "Oh, Lord, it's going to be a long convalescence. No, it's Hugh. Remember how he used to direct traffic in front of the Starlite Cafe?"

Hugh Renfro, the retarded son of a respected local physician, had been a well-known town character, sort of like a gregarious Boo Radley. Hugh was always engaging drivers and pedestrians on the streets in conversation and speaking for the most part in rhyme. "Hey, pretty girl in your new spring dress, I'll ask you to marry me and hope you'll say yes."

"Hugh got hit by a pulpwood truck a couple of years ago," Sally said. "The whole town turned out for his funeral. The city council voted to put up a statue to him, and I think Dad kicked in some money. They even commissioned the sculpture in Memphis."

Carter took a slow, deep breath. Troy had been the birthplace of at least two world-class athletes—an Olympic runner and a pro football great—as well as a famous mezzo-soprano with the Metropolitan Opera. But those local achievers were black, and it had been decades before the hometown named streets after them—in the historically black district. When the city finally got around to erecting a statue to a native of distinction, it was to a certifiable idiot, who happened to be white.

Welcome home to Troy, Mississippi.

I

CARTER RANSOM WAS STANDING on the sidewalk in front of the grand art deco *New York Examiner* building on lower Park Avenue, smoking a cigarette and lamenting the Knicks' loss the night before with a couple of guys from the mailroom. A taxi pulled to the curb, and out stepped a long-limbed fashion model, dressed in black and carrying a black leather portfolio. Carter would later think of this dark-haired cover girl often, as a harbinger of doom. One of his smoking buddies jabbed an elbow in his side to acknowledge this perk of working at Two Park Avenue and having the Ingénue Modeling Agency ovulating one floor above the *Examiner.*

Carter drew on his Winston as the stunning Amazon walked by them. "That's your column for tomorrow, mon," Billy said to Carter in his West Indian accent.

Carter stubbed his cigarette in the ash can by the news rack and pulled another from his breast pocket. "I already got my column. Hence, my hanging out with you two perverts." He had just finished up his last phone interview for a piece on the Reverend Charles Lloyd drug scandal. The story was in his head; all he had to do was write it down.

Even after years of turning out newspaper columns three times a week, Carter rarely found himself on top of things so early. Usually he

had to brood and torment himself right up to his six o'clock deadline—
a routine that he had lately begun to suspect was a hedge against mid-
career burnout, to convince himself that the remorseless obsolescence
of daily journalism was worth suffering for. Billy offered Carter a light
as the woman disappeared through the revolving doors. "Why don't you
put the moves on her 'fore she hit the elevator, mon?"

"Yeah, bro," said Billy's sidekick, pooching his lips and making
smacking noises. "Show her what you got."

Carter laughed. Spring fever was an affliction men never outgrew.
"Why don't you?"

"She a foot taller than my boy, that's why," said Billy.

"I bet she worth the climb, though. Come on, Ransom."

"He already got a woman," said Billy. "He's getting married. Right,
Ransom?"

Carter winced slightly. Twenty-four hours earlier he would have said
yes. He and Emily Lerner had been seeing each other for nearly three
years and had reached an understanding, theoretically—which was to
say the question had not actually been popped—that it was time to get
married. But the night before, they had had a fight so serious that there
hadn't really been much fight in it, and now he couldn't answer Billy's
question. He took a last drag off his Winston. The butt hit the gutter in
a spray of sparks. Time to finish his column.

He was heading for the revolving doors when he heard the explosion. The blast echoed off in the distance, perhaps twenty blocks away.
The air shuddered. "Jesus H. Christ!" said Billy. "What was that?"

"Felt like a motherfuckin' earthquake!" said his buddy. The three
men looked north toward the MetLife Building towering over Park Avenue. The reverberation seemed to shake the skyline.

Seconds later, spectators spilled from the entranceways and vestibules
of nearby buildings, looking over the street traffic for the source of the
rumble. Since the start of the war in the Persian Gulf some months earlier to remove the Iraqi army from Kuwait, the city had been on edge.
Warnings of possible retaliatory terrorist attacks appeared in the morning headlines and insinuated themselves into cocktail chatter at night.
The evening news broadcast images of the U.S. aerial assault on Baghdad,

accompanied by reports of Iraqi civilian casualties. News footage from Israel, always accompanied by wailing air-raid sirens, showed people lowering their gas masks, old men and women and schoolchildren scurrying into shelters, the streets of Jerusalem and Tel Aviv swarming with panicked citizens preparing for Iraqi Scud missile attacks.

Carter had done columns about how this new strain of urban anxiety was exposing the inadequacies of the city's emergency preparedness program and the kind of doomsday scenarios the authorities now had to anticipate. He wrote about the possibility of chemical or biological attacks, and how contaminants from weapons detonated downtown could be borne through the subway tunnels in the slipstream of moving trains. Though Carter usually rode his bike to work from his Brooklyn Heights brownstone, or from Emily's brownstone on the Upper West Side, he depended on the subway to get him quickly around Manhattan when he interviewed sources. But recently he found himself questioning the safety of riding the train.

More people poured onto the sidewalks, creating that classic urban tableau of strangers bonding briefly around some experience of catastrophe or mass frustration. Carter listened to the murmuring and speculation rising around him, then moved to the curb to peer again up Park Avenue over the heads of onlookers. He saw nothing. He lit another cigarette and returned to his companions. "Maybe a water main break?"

"Not with that kind of noise," Billy said.

"Maybe a demolition team dynamiting a building," Carter said. But he knew he was reaching. He reflexively thought about his friends and loved ones, surveying a mental map of Manhattan for their whereabouts. Most lived or worked downtown, away from where the blast had originated. Emily's design firm was in SoHo; her son's school was on the Upper West Side. He put morbid thoughts out of his mind. New York was a big city. It could absorb anything.

"Hey, Carter! Ransom!" Carter's editor, Ed Dennehy, was heading toward him, huffing and puffing, as if he had run down the entire nine flights of stairs. "We've been looking all over for you, Ransom. You got to get over to the Institute of Modern Art. There's been some kind of bombing. Picked it up on the scanner. Maybe terrorists. There's a shit-load of casualties. Gelman's already on his way from the cop shop. We got shooters on assignment nearby heading over."

"I'm there," said Carter. He checked his breast pocket for his note-book and headed for the crosswalk at the corner leading to the uptown subway entrance across the street.

"What have you got for tomorrow?" Dennehy shouted.

"The Lloyd drug scandal."

"Can it hold?"

Carter knew the shelf life of each column before he wrote it. The city, which had the attention span of a fruit fly, had taught him how long the news stayed news. Fortunately, his piece on the cocaine-abusing mayoral candidate Reverend Charles Lloyd was a perennially hot topic. "It'll have to."

"Come up with something decent, and we'll tease you on the cover," Dennehy called after him. "Unless Flynn turns in something better."

Carter's adrenaline was already kicking in. He might bitch and com-plain about the pressures of three columns a week, but he embraced deadlines the way a three-point shooter wants the ball at crunch time.

Inside the subway station, he went to a pay phone on the 6 train plat-form to call Emily, but then he hesitated. She had canceled their plans until further notice. He went ahead and dialed the number. Whenever his job brought him into contact with the essence of New York, whether it was its brute downside or its thrilling peaks, Carter always checked in with Emily. He had called her from the station in Hoboken when the gunman opened fire on the commuters on the New Jersey PATH train, and from the lobby of the Belasco Theater when he had been part of Václev Havel's entourage at a Broadway show following Prague's Velvet Revolution. The call went to Emily's voice mail. He knew she had a big meeting that afternoon with potential clients. She had been preparing for the meeting all week, but he hadn't expected her to leave so early. He felt guilty about provoking a relationship crisis before her important career move.

A voice crackled incomprehensibly over the subway public-address system. Any residue of the hangover Carter had incurred at last night's dinner party was gone. He wondered how much damage the bomb had caused. He hated to think of any harm done to the Modern. Emily would be especially crushed. What kind of lunacy or fanaticism would drive someone to destroy such priceless works of art?

Strangely, in all of Carter's time in the city before he met Emily, he had never once visited the Institute of Modern Art. He had been to the Met and the Whitney and the Guggenheim, but never to the magnificent museum designed by Mies van der Rohe. Emily took him there on their first date. Or rather, that's where she agreed to meet him for coffee when he asked her out the first time. He realized later that it had been a test to see if he was a culturephobe like most political journalists. Also, since her divorce, she had had her fill of blind dates, and she wanted to try a safe meeting first, with a visual conversation piece in case they ended up having nothing to say to each other. On a rainy Saturday afternoon, in the museum cafe next to the sculpture garden, they had ended up talking and talking, until Emily realized it was Carter's first visit to the Modern and insisted on "showing him around," in true New Yorker fashion, as if the museum were her personal property.

When they got to the Cézannes, Emily said, "I was in college when my mother died. I was lost and depressed, and I used to come here every day after my classes at NYU. I would sit and stare at *Turning Road at Montgeroult* for hours. Then one day it all opened up for me. It was as if I finally had the eyes for it."

Before that stroll through the Modern with Emily, Carter had never considered that art might be as vital and transformative to someone's life as news and history had been to his. It had not only helped Emily through the crisis of her mother's death but had led her to a career and identity of her own. Her father had been what they called a "legendary" TV producer, a pioneer in the early days of live television, and while Emily's brother strove in his shadow at a network newsmagazine show, Emily had become a partner in one of the downtown boutique commercial design firms.

Emily's sentimental favorites at the Modern were the vast canvases of Monet's Giverny bridge series. As with many a budding young art appreciator, Monet had been Emily's first love, and eventually she grew a bit bored with French Impressionism. But over the years, juggling parent-hood, work, and the burden of a deteriorating marriage, she would come often to the Japanese bridges arching over the lily pad–speckled pond at Giverny to remind herself of who she had once willed herself to be, in another time of trial and upheaval.

Smoke billowed from the black hole that had once been the second-story galleries that housed the Giverny series. That was one of the im-ages that Carter had jotted into prose in his notebook as he took the 6 train from the crime scene back to the office at around five o'clock. What other city, he had to ask himself, could keep the trains running af-ter taking a hit like this? His deadline was tight, but he would make it. Once he was seated at his desk, his hands hit the keyboard and the story poured out of him. The news guys were handling the developing inves-tigation. The Pakistani extremist group, Allahu Akbar, claimed re-sponsibility within minutes of the bombing with a call to CBS Radio and a prerecorded statement by the suicide bomber, a young woman, describing in detail what she did and how she did it and why: to join the heroic martyrs of the cause of Islamic Jihad. She had joined a tour group and set off twelve kilos of dynamite in her backpack, killing her-self and those around her in the great hall of the Impressionists.

Covering such disasters usually had the effect of making reporters go literal, so that they could wall off their emotions. To keep them from being overwhelmed by the horror, all their energy was directed into getting the facts right, every sense invested in the precision of the de-scriptions. Carter flipped efficiently through his notebook for the de-tails he needed. A survivor still wearing her museum docent badge had wept as she described the agony of van Gogh and how long it had taken him to complete the asylum-at-Arles series. The ash-covered bodies arranged in the rubble were almost indistinguishable from the statues that lay broken around them; Carter thought he had spotted the re-mains of one of Rodin's *Burghers of Calais*. But one of the images he recorded induced a swoony feeling somewhere between depression and hallucination. It was a woman's hand he had seen dangling from a covered stretcher; she wore a ring whose stone had been blown from its casing.

Carter went back over the lede to make sure it worked with the ending. The column would run off the *Examiner*'s front page alongside the news article, reaching half a million readers in a few short hours. His imagining the effect that the story would have on the city brought on a ripple of guilt. How had I. F. Stone put it? The building's on fire and you're so excited about having a fire to cover that you forget the building's really burning. But now, reading his copy one last time, Carter had an unwonted charge of emotion, existential emptiness replacing the journalist's default detachment. Carter knew that all the bigfoot columnists around the country—the pontificate, a colleague of his called them—would be doing "It Can't Happen Here" stories, ringing laments of America's "loss of innocence." But Carter would not be joining the stunned chorus. His column would question the very concept of national innocence, an idea he had gotten in part from the strange turn of the conversation at the dinner party the night before, the topic that had led to his fight with Emily. For the aftermath of this—the worst terrorist attack on American soil—had seemed sickeningly familiar to Carter, recalling the bombed-out ruins of his home state from a time when the Americans who lived under threat of terrorism were black Southerners. "The shadow of death," read the last line of his column, "has now fallen on all Americans."

When he checked his voice mail, he was surprised to hear there was a message from Emily. It was time-stamped 9:17 a.m. It must have come through when he was on the phone reporting the Lloyd column, and then he had left the newsroom on his late-morning nicotine break without clearing his messages. She was letting him know that the meeting with the Houston clients had been pushed back to four. "I don't know what to say about last night," she said. "We should talk when we're less stressed, but I don't think this is going to be resolved anytime soon." She then said she was on her way to join Josh's kindergarten class on their field trip. "They're studying Picasso's Blue Period," she said with a little laugh, "so they're going to the Modern. If you're in the neighborhood, I'm sure Josh would love it if you showed up." Her voice dropped to the ritual whisper, but there was a touch of regret when she said, "I love you."

2

C ARTER, IN HIS THIRTIES, HAD BEEN an award-winning columnist with a national reputation when Ed Dennehy recruited him to
the *New York Examiner*. At the time Carter arrived from the *Atlanta Constitution*'s Washington bureau, the city's three tabloids, along with the
stately broadsheet the *New York Tribune*, were in a torrid battle for Manhattan's tough newspaper-reading customers. Dennehy offered Carter the
chance to vent on all the big-city dramedy. Ransom Notes was what they
called his fourteen inches of prime newsprint on page 3 every Tuesday,
Thursday, and Sunday. "The Tabloid with a Heart" was how they touted
Ransom in rack cards and subway posters and TV spots.

Although Carter was comfortable with the liberal politics of the
Northeast, his style reflected the fierceness, undercut with self-mockery,
of the conservatives he had grown up with. His familiarity with the gothic
intricacies of power and how it worked in his native South put him at ease
analyzing the brute forms it took in New York City. His feel for the have-
nots came less from a bleeding heart than from his dismay at the cunning
of the haves. A contempt for any party line distinguished him from other
phyla of columnists—the Irish fraternity of sob sisters, the well-meaning
but mealymouthed liberals who had ideals but no experience, and the
nasty-trickster conservatives who threw facts around like grenades. Carter

was a one-man journalistic subspecies, unpredictably blending reportage, attitude, and a respect for the irony of history.

He had discovered upon his arrival that to be a single heterosexual male in New York City in the 1980s was a pleasant demographic circumstance. It helped that he retained the tall and lanky physique of the high school quarterback he had been, and the summer of acne that plagued him as a teenager had left him with a rugged look that seemed to appeal to grown women. Although his accent was subdued for a Mississippian, he understood his fellow Southerners' urge to self-caricature. Carter didn't know how many times he had run into compatriots in Manhattan with thicker and juicier accents than any he had ever heard growing up in Mississippi. He got a lot of mileage those first couple of years with stories of his home state, which loomed in New Yorkers' collective unconscious as the Heart of Darkness. He regaled them with yarns of down-home eccentrics and charming grotesques, never anything that challenged their assumptions or revealed much about himself.

His entrée into the social scene had also been assured by the *Examiner*'s restaurant critic, Marcy Kennamer, who invited him along as a taster on her high-calorie beat. Between her friendship and his high profile, Carter found himself a favored guest at parties and premieres and dinners given by friends, often the wives of colleagues, who considered his bachelorhood an ailment to be cured. He had missed that premature first marriage, the one that had left friends his age with grown children, first wives, and histories as unrecognizable as the long hair and facial foliage of their twenties. By the time he hit forty, marriage seemed like something that happened to other people. Then, at a Parks and Recreation benefit he was covering at Gracie Mansion, Marcy introduced him to Emily Lerner. Emily was a New Yorker born and bred—a recently divorced dark-haired beauty, with a young son, Josh. She reminded Carter of someone he had known long ago.

On his computer terminal in the newsroom, Carter had taped a quote from E. B. White about the "three New Yorks." White said that "commuters give the city its tidal restlessness; natives give it solidity and continuity; but the settlers give it passion." For Carter—"the person who was born somewhere else and came to New York in quest of something"—the city was a jailbreak from the South, in peril of coming to an end if he ever let down his fugitive guard. Emily had finally brought some long-stunted solidity to his life, as well as a "place" in the social order being Joseph Baum's daughter, a member of a family with that incalculable New York commodity, cachet. But embracing that continuity felt like compromising the quest, abandoning the passion. His ambivalence stranded him between what had been left behind and what was no longer out there. Knowing that he risked losing Emily by failing to act, Carter flashed often on that much-quoted Woody Allen remark about relationships being like sharks: they have to keep moving forward or they die. He had always hated that line, probably because it was true.

Just the night before, hoping that marriage might be contagious, Marcy Kennamer had used the approaching third anniversary of her introduction of Carter to Emily as an excuse to throw a dinner party in the Fifth Avenue co-op that she shared with her husband, Boz Epstein, acquired after years in the outer darkness of Manhattan spinsterhood. Carter and Emily arrived later than expected, their departure having been delayed by a flash indulgence of passion after he beheld her in the sleek black Calvin Klein dress he had given her for her thirty-fifth birthday. They approached the building's canopied entrance giggling like teenagers. Carter pointed out some crack vials lying in a gutter nearby and grinned wickedly. "Marcy sure knows how to party." On duty, Carter might have extracted a column idea from the Dickensian contrast between the opulence of Marcy's prewar building overlooking Central Park and the litter of social dysfunction. But this night was to have been strictly for pleasure.

"The lovebirds have arrived," Marcy announced in her hearty Texas drawl as she flung wide the enormous mahogany double doors of her ninth-floor apartment. Marcy Kennamer was a big-boned honey-blond belle, a former majorette for the Texas Longhorns who had headed straight for New York following graduation. After she gave up her dream of dancing on Broadway, and before she took up food writing full-time, she had been a chef and for years had run a restaurant on Martha's Vineyard.

"You're in luck." Boz, a short, balding man, greeted them. "Marcy's making crab cakes. Can I get you something from the bar?"

Jim and Louise Lassiter were standing in the foyer with their drinks. Jim, an architect, clasped Carter's shoulders and congratulated him.

"For what?" asked Carter.

"Louise tells me you and Emily have been together three years." He gave Carter a "meaningful look." Carter offered to refresh his drink.

Besides being Emily's business partner, Louise was her closest friend and confidante, a plump, self-assured woman who was the managerial brawn behind Emily's creativity. Louise and Emily hugged and then exchanged a brief pep talk about the big meeting the next day with the clients from Houston who were opening an office in New York.

Out on the terrace, the other guests mingled under cirrus clouds streaking the sky's last light in a calligrapher's delicate brushstrokes. Traffic hummed along Fifth Avenue in counterpoint to the Duke Ellington melodies leaking from speakers that Boz had hidden among the trellises and flowerpots of narcissus and primrose. Marcy, who had recently left the *Examiner* to write a food column for the *New York Tribune*'s Sunday magazine, interrupted a group to introduce Carter to the man who had hired her, the paper of record's much-gossiped-about executive editor, Haynes Wentworth. He was talking with Anthony Lyon, discussing a *Tribune* editorial on the president's decision not to march into Baghdad. Lyon was a Civil War scholar and historian at Columbia, whose study of slave narratives, *Mine Eyes Have Seen the Glory*, had been short-listed for the National Book Award. Carter's small-town sensibility still reeled at the city's blasé attitude toward fame and accomplishment, how much exponentially higher the bar of achievement was for anyone to get noticed. He knew that at this very moment there were scores of gatherings such as this one occurring without fanfare all over the city.

"Carter Ransom, you've met my boss, Haynes Wentworth," said Marcy.

Wentworth was a tall, elegant man with blond hair, graying temples, and a thick gray mustache, incongruous among his otherwise fair markings, lounging like a chinchilla across his upper lip. "Please, Marcy," Wentworth demurred, "nobody is your boss."

"Hello, Haynes," said Emily.

"Emily"—he took her hand, holding it a little too long—"you look lovely as ever. I hope your father is well." Then he turned back to Carter. "You're a lucky man."

Carter, though he cringed a bit at the B-movie dialogue, found himself resenting Wentworth's familiarity. Marcy then indicated the tall blond woman at Wentworth's side, with cheekbones that could cut diamonds. "And have you met Colette Merceau, media liaison for the French embassy?"

Colette offered her hand to Carter. " 'Allo," she said.

Speculation over the bachelor editor's love life had been a parlor game in the *Tribune* newsroom since he dumped his wife of twenty years after being promoted to executive editor. Within the austere *Tribune* corporate culture, Wentworth, though a bit of a stuffed shirt, probably seemed like Zorba the Greek.

"Say, you two are both Southerners," Boz said to Carter and Wentworth, his eyes bouncing between the two of them. "Did you know each other there?"

"Don't mind my husband," Marcy interjected. "He's a New Yorker. He thinks the South is one small town like Mayberry and that everybody is related."

Wentworth said, "Yes, it is likely we would know each other. But we've never met officially."

Carter had, in fact, been introduced to Wentworth a couple of times over the years, but being a white Southerner in New York with ties to the civil rights movement had given Wentworth a certain mystique, which he didn't want to share with anybody.

"Say, Haynes, why don't you hire Ransom here." It was the historian Anthony Lyon, an intense man with steel-rimmed glasses and wild white hair. He had served in the newspaper's Washington bureau before moving to academia and was still a bit of a *Tribune* Kremlinologist. "The *Trib* could certainly use a columnist who can write *and* report. You know, most columnists seem to feel that they have no need to actually leave their desks."

Before Wentworth could respond, Marcy chimed in. "Not bloody likely."

"Why not?" asked Boz.

"They couldn't control him." She laughed and downed what was left of her wine spritzer.

Carter gave Emily's elbow a squeeze. One's foibles always sounded more benign when described outside the romantic unit.

Wentworth took a sip of his bourbon, then made eye contact with Carter. "No offense, but we already have a columnist who does what Carter does."

"Lawrence Rogers?" Marcy scoffed. "He's not a columnist. He's a sneer with a word processor." Rogers was the Washington bureau's man with the Rolodex, sort of a bitchy Scotty Reston.

"Maybe my sensibility is too"—Carter smiled as the word came to him—" 'Southern' for Haynes."

"On the contrary," Wentworth said. "There's a great Southern narrative tradition at the *Tribune*, which I like to think I may have even contributed to back in my reporting days."

"Yes, indeed," Marcy intoned on her way to the kitchen to check on dinner. "The *Tribune*'s rich tradition of diversity and multiculturalism is something we can all be proud of, as long as it remains in print rather than in the newsroom."

Marcy returned, pinging a wineglass with a fork, and summoned the party to the dining room, where an enormous table in a blunted oval shape enabled all twelve guests to participate in everything going on around them.

Carter felt Emily press close and slip her arm through his. "You okay?" she asked.

"Yeah," he said, "fine. What happened between you and Wentworth?"

"Nothing. Years ago he had a crush on me."

"That would explain his hostility toward me. How come you never told me?"

"There's nothing to tell. It's ancient history." She shot him a look. "So ancient that he was still married."

As they moved toward the table, Emily whispered under the rising din, "The party's warmed up over cocktails."

Carter took a deep breath as he held her chair. "Maybe defrosted to room temperature."

Carter was seated beside Bunny Hardeker, a playwright, whose monumental self-absorption worked like a stun gun. Carter, caught unawares, was taken without struggle.

"I was saying to what's-his-name on the terrace," Bunny said as the first course—arugula salad garnished with walnuts, mandarin orange, and Gorgonzola—arrived. "I'm just the kind of person who colors outside the lines." Especially when applying lipstick, Carter noticed, taking in the Max Factor Rorschach overlaying her lips. And then it was on to the next non sequitur, something about her new play about to open on Broadway. Carter thought she said the name of it was *The Pubic Triangle*.

"Brilliant," he replied.

Such a flattering review from a male she barely knew unleashed a description of the intra-womb procedures she was undergoing in order to conceive a baby by a donor she described as a "laureate." Each sip of wine Bunny drank increased the graphic intimacy of her revelations. At one point he was shocked to feel her hand grazing his thigh under the table. It was quickly withdrawn when Marcy, after the main course had been served, rose with glass in hand and toasted.

"Here's to my dear friends, Carter and Emily, whom I introduced three years ago this week. To true love."

"Here, here," said Boz.

Louise said, "It certainly took you long enough to settle down, Carter."

"Your sexual adventurism aside, I must say I read your columns with interest." It took Carter a moment to realize the comment was being addressed to him. All evening, first during cocktails, then as they sat across from each other at the dinner table, he had grown increasingly aware of the brooding presence of the poet/essayist and critic Arden Duplain. If her high-end résumé—Yale Law, the Sorbonne, Fulbright, Guggenheim, *The New Yorker*, the American Academy—was not enough to intimidate, her peasant-blouse ruffles and unadorned but pretty-in-a-Radcliffe-kind-of-way features, wreathed by a thick shock of prematurely gray hair pulled back into a single waist-length braid, left no doubt as to her bohemian/intellectual bona fides. He felt it between his shoulder blades—her predator gaze. "Although I was quite disappointed in your columns on Reverend Charles Lloyd and the drug allegations."

"Well," Carter said, spearing a clump of crabmeat, "it wouldn't be the first time I disappointed a reader." The *Examiner* had covered a very public brawl between the mayoral candidate Charles Lloyd and his wife of twenty years, which began when she burst into the local police precinct shouting that her husband was smoking crack with his mistress in their apartment at that very moment. The mistress was his supplier, she told the policemen, and had assaulted her in her own home. Then she gave them the address and demanded that they do their civic duty. She had already reported the situation twice to black officers, and they had done nothing. This time she insisted on speaking to a white officer because she believed the black policemen were protecting her husband. Though a subsequent search of police records turned up no incident report, a black reporter from the *Examiner*, covering another story at the precinct, witnessed the uproar and told his editors about it. Lloyd's cocaine addiction was already a joke in the newsroom. Initially, editors had regarded it as an unfortunate lifestyle choice, but now that he was a leading candidate for mayor, the drug charges seemed newsworthy. Still, they sat on the story until the current, outgoing mayor, a friend of Lloyd's as well as his political sponsor, issued a statement while on a trip to Japan, saying he didn't believe the allegations against Lloyd. That's when the *Examiner* ran with the story and put it on the cover. Carter wrote that Lloyd needed to withdraw from the campaign, and the paper caught a load of flak, especially from the black community.

"Charles Lloyd is one of our city's authentic heroes," Arden said.

"He's a con man and a liar," Carter replied. Ordinarily he was not one to defend himself or his columns or debate them over dinner. But something about his inquisitor's sanctimony vanquished his reserve.

"He's a man of God."

It amused Carter that the only churches white New Yorkers seemed to get misty-eyed over were the ones up in Harlem. "I rest my case," he said.

"You're holding a black man to a higher standard than you would a white," she said. "That's racist." Silence enveloped the table.

"Why is that racist?" asked Marcy. "Atheist, possibly, but racist?"

"Ah, yes, the R-word. The N-word of the nineties," Carter said, surprising himself by warming to the discussion. "Charles Lloyd is a phony and a crackhead."

"Why is it that blacks are crackheads and whites have substance abuse problems?" Arden persisted.

"Okay," Carter said, "he's also an adulterer."

"Charles Lloyd was a Freedom Rider," Arden said. "He risked his life in Mississippi."

"Charles Lloyd was a member of the Student Nonviolent Coordinating Committee, true," Carter said. "But he never boarded those buses. He never took part in the Freedom Rides."

Arden Duplain seemed shocked at Carter's conviction. "How do you know?" She turned on Carter. "Who are your sources?"

"I'm my source."

"Were you there?" asked Wentworth, who had been silent on the Lloyd debate. There was a note of competitive anxiety in his voice.

"Yes, I was. Troy, Mississippi."

"No kidding!" Anthony Lyon looked excited. "Ellis County. Home of the infamous White Knights of the Ku Klux Klan?"

Boz Epstein, suddenly all ears, said, "White Knights?"

"The most militant and violent wing of the Klan," Lyon said. "Responsible for more murders, more church bombings, worst terrorism of that era. You name it. Schwerner, Goodman, Chaney. Vernon Dahmer. Shiloh Church bombing. They made Robert Shelton's United Klans over in Alabama look like choirboys."

"You're quite the scholar of that era, Anthony, to know about the White Knights," Carter said.

"Civil rights history—the second American civil war—is my subspecialty. Plus, I was a baby reporter in the Washington bureau during the Kennedy administration."

Arden Duplain was regarding Carter as though he were an insect. "These Klansmen were from your hometown?"

"I was not myself a member, if that's what you're suggesting."

"A Freedom Rider, then?"

"No."

"So where is your story in all this?"

"There was a Judge Ransom presiding over the Shiloh Church case, if memory serves," said Anthony Lyon. "I hadn't made the connection until you mentioned Troy. Any relation?"

"My father."

"I understand they're reopening that case," Haynes said, trying to reclaim his turf. "Terrible crime. The most casualties of any racial atrocity of that time."

Carter said nothing: the act of true one-upmanship.

Emily spoke up for the first time. "How many people were killed in the bombing?" She addressed her question to Carter, but it was Wentworth who jumped in with the answer.

"Four," he said. "All quite young."

"Tell us, Haynes," Marcy said, retrieving the thread of the conversation. "Why didn't the *Tribune* run the Lloyd story?"

"We ran it. We put Rasheed Lovelace, one of our best young reporters, on it. We just exercised more restraint than the tabloids." Haynes continued, "Without an arrest warrant against Lloyd, it was just a 'he said–she said' story."

"You ran it two days after everyone else," Carter said pleasantly. "And then you buried it."

"The *Tribune*, to its credit, did not consider the story very newsworthy," Duplain said. "I don't see why the *Examiner* did—other than a desire to sell newspapers."

Carter didn't much mind this woman criticizing him, but he wasn't going to allow her to insult Ed Dennehy and the others who bent over backward to be fair to the Reverend Charles Lloyd. "You don't know what the hell you're talking about—ma'am," he said.

Emily looked startled at Carter's ferociousness. Duplain pressed the attack. "Reverend Lloyd is a civil rights hero and a national treasure."

"People died in the movement, Arden. Are you telling me they gave their lives for the Reverend Lloyd's right to have his ass kissed by the media?"

The mood at the table had grown as heavy as the atmosphere on planet Jupiter. Arden Duplain was stone-faced. Wentworth assumed a sober parental expression and spoke with therapeutic concern. "Our city hall bureau says Charles Lloyd has a dependency issue and needs rehab."

"Haynes," Boz said, "were you involved in the civil rights struggle?"

"It was a little before my time. I was in high school during the Freedom Rides. But I was there the day the Freedom Riders pulled into the Greyhound station in Montgomery. I'll never forget, it was a Saturday morning, and I had decided to cut baseball practice. I sensed history was in the making, but I was just an onlooker."

"Wow," Arden said. "Was that a conversion experience for you?"

Before Wentworth could answer, Carter said, "An onlooker, huh?" He sipped his wine and smiled. Haynes, like many Southern liberals, had been a wallflower at the defining moment of his generation. Not that Carter held that against him; he just couldn't bring himself to let Wentworth know he didn't. "That really must have reassured those Freedom Riders," he continued. "I can just imagine John Lewis looking out the bus window into that crowd and saying to the other Snick kids, 'It looks like an ugly mob waiting for us. But relax—some of them are just onlookers.'"

"Are you suggesting I was part of that mob?"

"No. I'm just wondering how anyone could tell you weren't."

"Oh, Haynes," said Marcy, "we all know you were always pure and pristine in your politics. Carter's teasing you—aren't you, Carter?" She shot him a chastising look.

Carter winked over the table at Wentworth.

Anthony Lyon asked Carter, "Were you involved with the civil rights movement?"

"No."

"Come on. Yes, you were. Congressman Knight and I were reminiscing at a fund-raiser in Washington. Your name came up."

"The moon's out, everyone," Marcy announced, trying to rescue her dinner party from the dilemma of race. "Dessert's on the terrace."

Emily squinted at Carter as the others rose. She knew about the hate mail and death threats he had gotten for taking unpopular positions in print during his early years writing for newspapers in the South. But he had never talked about coming of age in Mississippi during the 1960s, at least not as a phenomenon of historical significance. Carter looked back at Emily and saw gathering recognition on her face. He had not intended to withhold secrets from her. Like any real journalist, he simply did not know how to tell the story when he was its subject.

3

CARTER SAT in his cubicle with his head between his hands, staring at the phone. The message from Emily on his voice mail had set off his pulse. Could she and Josh have been in the explosion? The acrid odor of the museum site clung to his hair and clothes. He reviewed in his mind the casualties he had seen there; though most were concealed under sheets, none seemed to have been children. He craved a cigarette.

He dialed Emily's home number. No answer. He called her office. Nothing. He stood up and surveyed the newsroom for a sign as to what he should do. His surroundings had taken on the vibrating intensity of a hyperrealist painting, as if each molecule had a life of its own; yet Carter felt he was in some other, solitary dimension. The office was alive with the static of disaster—the crackle of a police scanner by the photo desk, the ringing of phones unattended in the deadline rush. CNN's coverage of the museum bombing on ceiling-mounted TV monitors was ignored by reporters battering their keyboards and shouting at editors as everyone kicked into breaking-news overdrive: self-celebration.

Carter's eyes searched for Dennehy. The smell of pizza and Chinese takeout reminded him that it was dinnertime. His stomach turned. He dialed Emily's parents. Her stepmother answered, in obvious distress.

"We picked up Josh at school, but we can't reach Emily," she said. "I was hoping she was with you. She hasn't called or anything."

Carter could hear the anxious voice of Emily's father, Joseph Baum, coaching her. "Ask him if we should call the police."

"Did she go to the Modern?" Carter said.

Miriam reported what Josh had told her: Emily had met the kids that morning at the museum but didn't go back to school with them on the school bus. "His class got out before the blast, thank God," Miriam said, "but the last he saw of his mother was in the lobby of the museum." There was a catch in her already quavering voice. "Louise said their meeting was canceled. Emily never came back to the office."

The words hit Carter like a hammerblow. Emily was as dependable as they came. He put Miriam on hold, looked up Louise's number, and dialed her office. The call went straight to voice mail. He hung up and switched back to the Baums.

"Nobody answers at work—" He paused, unsure how to proceed. Then he heard Miriam sob. There was a rustling sound, and Joseph got on the phone.

"What's going on, Carter? What do your sources say?" he said. "The TV news people seem to be working harder on their animated graphics than on getting the story."

"I was there this afternoon. It was—" Carter stopped at the sound of Miriam weeping in the background.

Then, through a muffled mouthpiece, the sound of Joseph trying to reassure her. "Maybe she stopped somewhere. Maybe . . ." Joseph's voice faded. If Emily had escaped the bombing, she would have already phoned them and Carter. He wondered if Emily had told her parents about their falling-out.

"I need to check some things," Carter said. He suddenly had an urge to see Josh. "I'll come by in a while. Maybe I'll know more by then."

"Carter, call us the instant you learn anything," Joseph said, "no matter what it is."

After Carter hung up, he grabbed his jacket and caught a cab back uptown. He had been heading to the museum, but a police roadblock had cut off access ten blocks south. Though he probably could have used his press credentials to get through, his journalistic instincts capitulated to an overwhelming need to get far away from the bombing scene. He directed the driver to Seventy-ninth and Riverside, where the Baums lived in an ornate prewar apartment building.

Carter found Josh stacking his Legos on the floor in front of the TV in his grandfather's study. When Carter walked in, the boy jumped up and hugged him around the legs. The Baums, watching the news reports, looked gaunt and mortal, sitting amid the mementos of Baum's privileged view of his era's great events: a supersized microphone from the Kennedy-Nixon debate; a news clipping on the Army-McCarthy hearings, autographed by Joseph Welch. The adults exchanged updates. Carter spoke more positively than he felt, amazing himself with the fanciful scenarios, such as amnesia blows to the head, that could be conjured from duress. He wondered if he would have to post a picture of Emily on the missing persons bulletin boards that had already been set up around midtown.

Carter felt a touch of pride that Josh seemed so amenable to returning with him to Emily's place, and that the Baums were willing. After a short cab ride, the two of them pushed open her front door. Josh tested the empty apartment, shouting, "Mom!"

The boy managed to get through his evening routines until Carter helped him into his pajamas. Then he fell apart, burying his head in Carter's chest and crying for his mother.

"I know, buddy," Carter said. He extended his pinkie finger for Josh to link with his, a routine that mother and son practiced whenever danger threatened—during a thunderstorm or a bumpy airplane ride. When Josh set his jaw valiantly, Carter almost broke down.

Emily did not allow Carter to stay overnight when Josh was with her. She was fastidious about parental protocol. But before departing, Carter usually handled the bedtime story—tall tales involving magic swamp bats and lucky sno-cones, or harrowing epics of frog gigging from his Mississippi youth. Tonight Carter simply lay down beside Josh in his small single bed and linked pinkies with him till he fell asleep. Then Carter got up and checked in with the newsroom for updates on the casualty count: twenty-four by ten o'clock. He thought about asking Dennehy to have their guys at the morgue check for Emily's body, but he wasn't ready to make his fears official. His sister called from Mississippi. The bombing was all over the news down there. When he got off the phone, he walked out on the terrace and smoked the last of his cigarettes. The unbelievable thing was, the Upper West Side, with the trees beginning to leaf in, looked perfectly normal.

He went back inside and called his office voice mail to replay Emily's last message to him. He couldn't tell if it was an overture to end the hostilities or a reminder that they were entering the final and most delicate phase of negotiation.

After Marcy's dinner party the night before, Carter and Emily had walked home instead of getting a taxi. It was their ritual after a night out—weather and distance permitting—to take a leisurely stroll back to her apartment, working off a heavy meal or an extra glass of wine while performing the party postmortem. But this time they were both quiet as they made their way around the park and up Broadway. For months they had been avoiding the big question about their future, and now the bombshell, disguised as a chance remark at a dinner party, had slipped past all their strategic defenses.

"Were you ever going to tell me?" She had broken the silence a few blocks from her apartment.

"About what?" he stalled.

"What Anthony Lyon brought up—your connection with the Shiloh Church case. I remember my dad going down to cover that."

"You can see why I was reluctant to—"

"No, Carter, actually I can't." She seemed more mystified than vexed. "Your father was the judge in that case. Why would I have to learn something like that from a historian?"

Carter hesitated, then exhaled.

She stopped walking and turned to look at him. "Something's not adding up here," she said with a hint of alarm.

"I also knew the four victims."

"That must have been terrible." Emily plunged her hands into the pockets of her jacket and resumed walking. "So terrible that I can't understand why you wouldn't have told me about it."

"I wasn't purposely hiding anything. I mean anything that you needed to know about me."

Emily's irritation surfaced for the first time. "I didn't realize our relationship was on a need-to-know basis," she said.

Carter flared. "Hey, you didn't tell me about your little flirtation with Wentworth."

"Um," she said, looking him in the eye, "you're putting those on the same level?"

Carter had felt embarrassed and childish the minute the comment about Wentworth was out of his mouth. "I was a kid," he said. "It was a long time ago." He could hear himself sounding defensive, and he felt her bristle. What he sensed was the tautness of possession. But he knew on some level that he would feel the same way if he suddenly found out Emily had had another life she hadn't bothered to mention.

Carter stopped to light a cigarette. She walked on ahead. They reached her brownstone in silence. Carter paid the sitter and put her in a taxi. Josh had long been asleep, but Carter went upstairs to tuck him in. The boy awoke briefly to implore Carter to tell him a story before burrowing back into the pillow. When Carter came downstairs, he found Emily standing at the door with her arms folded.

"Do you want to talk?" he asked. She had her shut-down, "end of story" expression that was intended to convey "no" but sometimes meant "yes." Carter knew from experience that she was more hurt than mad, but he could never be sure whether there was a chance of getting through once she crossed her arms. For all her compulsion to "discuss," Emily was endowed with impenetrable pride.

"I'm going to need to think about all this," she said. "Maybe we need some time off."

"Fine. Tomorrow's a column day for me anyway."

"I don't mean just for a night. Carter, you need to go and figure out why you haven't told me what it is you haven't told me. I'm too old and life is too short for me to be 'bringing guys out.' I fulfilled my quota in high school."

"That was a bit gratuitous," he said, but when he saw she was about to cry, he added tenderly, "Shall we invoke the no-heavy-conversation-after-midnight rule?" He drew her head onto his chest, kissed the crown, and then drew back to try to look at her face. When she averted her eyes, he said, "Let's sleep on it," then turned and trundled down the steps of her stoop as the door closed behind him. He wondered what had just happened.

Now he couldn't allow himself to think that those wounded words might turn out to be the last they would ever speak to each other. He paced through the apartment striking bargains with a God retired long ago in his Baptist youth. If Emily was spared, he would stop smoking, he would file his tax returns on time, he would do volunteer work with cancer patients, he would ask her to marry him.

His sleep was fitful, his dreams wild and retro, filled with images of wagon-rutted roads and tar-paper shacks. He kept seeing a girl's hand with a ring. The sound of gospel singing flattened into a police siren keening louder and closer until it segued into the insistent ringing of a telephone. Coaxed into consciousness, Carter looked at his watch. It was after one. He had fallen asleep on the sofa with his clothes on and the lights on. He fumbled for the phone on the end table and answered.

"Carter."

He sat bolt upright on the sofa. Was he still dreaming? "Emily. Where are you?"

"I'm at my parents'. I'm fine. Just wiped out."

"What happened? Where were you?" Carter did not inhale for fear that she might vanish.

"I was stuck on the subway all day. It was a nightmare. There was a bomb threat called in to the transit authority, and they stopped the train. We were under the river between stations. They wouldn't let us off."

"We thought you were at the museum." Carter still couldn't believe that his worst fears were not faits accomplis.

"I know. Is Josh okay?"

"He was devastated. He finally fell asleep."

After the field trip with Josh, Emily, in her conscientious way, had decided to take one last look at the prospective clients' new office space in Brooklyn Heights, to psych herself up for the meeting that afternoon. She had left the museum and caught a southbound number 2 express train. The transit authority command center halted the train deep under the river between Manhattan and Brooklyn after a bomb threat was phoned in to the Clark Street station, the first stop in Brooklyn. Since the Atlantic Avenue Muslim community was only two stops beyond Clark Street, the train was held on the tracks for hours while the bomb squad scoured the station.

Carter had heard the news reports on the Clark Street bomb scare, but he hadn't imagined that Emily was anywhere near there. "All I knew was that the meeting was at your office in SoHo," he said.

Emily hadn't learned about the Modern until they were out of the train that night. She lowered her voice and repeated the mantra Carter had been hearing throughout the day. "I just can't believe this could happen."

"Come home," Carter said. Tears welled as he spoke. He assumed that the conversation of the night before had been superseded by this act of Allah. But she hesitated just long enough.

"I'll be there before Josh wakes up in the morning."

Carter felt his throat constrict. "Emily, I—"

"Yeah?" she said softly.

"I was so worried."

"I know. We'll talk tomorrow."

"No, wait, don't go yet. I thought I'd lost you."

"You didn't, sweetie. Thanks for helping my parents through this."

Carter was slightly offended by her gratitude, with its implication that he had been doing something outside what was expected. "You're welcome," he said. For all his relief, Carter felt that the wait was not yet over.

The next morning, Emily and Carter took Josh to an everything-is-back-to-normal French toast breakfast at their neighborhood diner. After dropping him off at school, they returned to Emily's apartment. While they were making love, she looked at him with a hint of mischief and said, "It's still you." Carter felt a surge of optimism, and they arranged to meet after work for drinks at the Mark. But his apprehensiveness was restored by her refusal to commit to dinner.

When Emily appeared at the entrance of the small, elegant hotel bar late that afternoon, there was a subtle set to her jaw that Carter had not seen before. After they ordered drinks, she filled him in on the reentry: how her clients had rescheduled, how Josh seemed to be processing the trauma. Carter listened for a while before reaching out for her hand to silence her. "I'm ready to get married," he said.

Emily started but met his gaze and softened for a moment. She breathed audibly through her nose. "Don't it always seem to go that you don't get what you want till it's gone."

Carter refused to hear her. An outpouring of words stopped her from proceeding. He wanted to be with her and Josh. He admitted he had left out some pieces of his life. He had put them in a mental file, figuring he would pull them out someday. But not ever "now." To talk about what happened to him back then felt like a betrayal. Yet that was the very position that made him disloyal to Emily now. The only thing he knew to do was to promise to get help.

"I went through therapy before," he said. But he had never gotten around to finding a new shrink after leaving Atlanta. He was willing to do anything to get relief from this moment, which promised more loss, more pain. He even offered to go into couples therapy.

An array of expressions passed over Emily's face. He caught flashes of love and optimism, the promise of spring, but they subsided into cool conviction.

"Carter, I talked to your sister today." Emily dabbed with the corner of her napkin at the ring of moisture left on the glass tabletop by his beer mug. When she looked up into his face, her eyes were brimming. "And after what Sally told me, I'm beginning to wonder if our entire relationship was really nothing more than a reaction to your secret past. One you would have kept from me for God only knows how long, if history hadn't almost repeated itself." She gave a little shudder. "This is the strangest impasse, Carter," she said. "I've never felt closer to you, but at the same time I feel like you're someone else. I feel sucker-punched. I mean, who have I been with? More to the point, who have you been with, me or her?"

Even in their raggedy passages, Emily and Carter had always maintained a certain wry objectivity about their relationship, the unsentimental aplomb of people who have been through too much to have any illusions. And now, as Carter was feeling his life pass before him and out of him, Emily fixed him with a look of mock long-suffering that drew him briefly back to that realm of hope and endurance memorialized in the casual intimacy of couples.

"If we should ever get into therapy," she said, "you might want to work on your proposal technique."

In the days afterward, Carter lost his appetite, and his face broke out for the first time in decades. He was possessed by a sense of hypervigilance, as if he had to be on guard all the time. He threw himself into work, covering the aftermath of the museum bombing. Even on the days when he couldn't muster enough initiative to brush his teeth, he still reported to the office. The new, ambiguous status of his relationship with Emily somehow embarrassed him. The concern in his colleagues' eyes was unbearable. But he clung to the protocols of the job. He wrote follow-ups on the Modern story—the cleanup, the national security implications, the impact on the art world—without any further reference to his own youthful brush with loss.

After a week, Dennehy pulled him into his glass office off the newsroom and said, "You look awful, you know that?"

"Thanks, Ed. I'll get a makeover when you stop drinking."

"Hey, don't be such a dick. I'm just worried about you, is all."

"Is this why you called me in here? To take my temperature?"

"What are you going to write about tomorrow?"

Carter searched his face, wondering why he was asking. "I don't know. The memorial service, I guess. Who wants to know?" Carter saw Dennehy's tough-guy, *Front Page* bravado melt away.

"I do. Is there something you need to take a few days to take care of?"

Carter looked away. "I don't need time off."

"Look, you think you're invisible, but you're not. You've been be-having erratically, you know that?"

"Says who?"

"You look like you slept in your shirt, for starters. The copydesk said you never responded to their fact-checking queries the other day. They should've killed the column. You missed the appointment with Senator Pothole's chief of staff I set up for you. That's not like you, Carter."

Carter felt a chill run through him, but he refused to let Dennehy see that he hadn't even been aware he was screwing up. He realized how alien the city had suddenly become without Emily as its medium.

"I'll give you one more chance, but I'm watching you, Ransom. I know your type because you're like me. You bottle things up, and it comes out in high blood pressure and heart attacks. I could send Flynn to the memorial service."

Carter looked down at Dennehy's desk. It was scattered with newspa-pers and souvenir artifacts Ed had collected over the years—a Knicks Nerf basketball, a bobblehead toy of the mayor, a naked Statue of Liberty. Then Carter stared out the window at the top of the Chrysler Building rising in the distance. Finally, he turned to his friend and said, "No way."

After returning from the museum bombing memorial service honoring the twenty-seven declared dead so far—a somber spectacle attended by New York's senators and the vice president of the United States—Carter was seated at his desk off the newsroom, eating saltines to settle his stomach. The phone receiver was pressed between his ear and his shoulder. He was following up on rumors that a computer with plans for future terrorist attacks had been found in the bomber's hotel room. While on hold with an FBI source, he scrolled through his notes on the computer screen. Glancing up from his terminal, he saw an old man talking to the young woman who answered the phones at a workstation in the center of the newsroom.

Carter was trying to place the slight white-haired gentleman in the Windbreaker when both the visitor and the news aide looked over in his direction. The woman nodded and pointed toward his cubicle. Carter looked down. Oh, no, he thought, another lame column idea or story suggestion from some guy off the street. How in the hell did he get past the receptionist? Carter glanced furtively toward the reception area on the other side of the glass entrance to the newsroom and saw that there was nobody manning the desk. Cynthia must still be at lunch.

Carter did his best to look preoccupied, but he could feel the man staring as he approached in a way that made Carter feel he should know him. He racked his brain for a name but came up with nothing. He leaned back and tried to ask Henican at the desk outside his cubicle if he knew who the guy was, but Ellis was on the phone, with his back to him. Carter loosened his collar. Heat radiated from his forehead. He had not felt well at the service and had left early. Maybe he was coming down with a fever.

Carter again made eye contact with the white-haired man. His expression of urgency was unnerving. Finally he stood before Carter and extended his hand. Carter rose and took it.

"I saw you at the memorial service this morning but couldn't get to you," said the man, looking up at him with pale blue eyes beneath dense charcoal eyebrows.

"Thank you for coming by." Carter hoped he would say his name.

"You don't recognize me, do you, Carter?"

"I know I know you."

"Herbert Solomon. I read your story about the Mississippi"—he paused to search for the right word—"terrorism."

Carter continued to stare at him.

"I've been meaning to get in touch with you. I've been reading your columns since you came back to New York."

Carter glanced around his desk for an open cigarette pack. What did the man mean by "came back"?

"I am here today on behalf of my daughter," he said.

Carter looked into his face. The air seemed hard to take in. The room began to swirl, and his knees wobbled. The last thing Carter heard before everything went black was the voice of the old man saying, "Sarah."

4

TROY, MISSISSIPPI, once the sawmill capital of the world, was situated on a bend in the Chickasaw River among the hardwood and dense pine forests that stoked the only industry that mattered in Ellis County—the Graysonite Manufacturing Company, producer of wood paneling for the dens and family rooms of middle-class America. Even before Sally's Mercury had crossed the bridge over the Chickasaw into downtown, the pungent aroma of Graysonite took Carter's breath away. On windless days the effluent from the factory smokestacks settled on the town like a fever. The chemical odor permeated Sally's climate-controlled car and cut through the meds in Carter's body, bracing him for the fact that, for better or worse, he was home.

Downtown Troy had undergone reconstructive surgery of sorts. The live oaks still sprawled majestically over the courthouse square, but the shrubbery was as meticulously groomed as theme park topiary. Banners with childlike designs of butterflies and rainbows hung from antique lampposts at regular intervals along the streets, which had been repaved with brick. Flowers grew from brick planters that were surrounded by concrete benches, giving the once comatose commercial district the look of calculated spontaneity Carter associated with shopping malls.

The Confederate war memorial stood guard over the shady green of the square, and behind it rose the Corinthian columns of the Ellis County Courthouse, pagan dissents from the ubiquitous steeples representing the solid median of the Protestant Reformation. The bronze statue of Hugh Renfro directing traffic blended naturally into this architectural hymn to mediocrity. Sally steered the car past her store, the Book Nook, and turned down the broad treelined avenue that they had grown up on. Carter noted with relief that the historic residential neighborhood looked much as it always had: turn-of-the-century Victorians and English Tudors surrounded by azaleas, rhododendron, English ivy, crepe myrtle, and jasmine, the worn brick streets canopied by live oaks.

Sally honked the horn twice as they pulled into the driveway of the Ransoms' whitewashed brick colonial. A large golden retriever came loping around the wisteria bush on the far side of the house. Willie, Sally's freckle-faced, red-haired six-year-old, trailed along behind.

"Riley!" Willie shouted. The dog jumped up to greet Carter as he got out of the car. Carter froze. Riley had been Emily's dog. She had bought him for Josh when the dog was a pup. Being a city girl, Emily hadn't realized how huge a golden retriever would grow, or how rambunctious Riley's personality would become; nor had she anticipated how little she would be at home to take care of him once her business took off. Carter had suggested taking Riley to Mississippi. His sister had been looking for a dog for Willie. Lots of ominous references to the ASPCA and a promise of a replacement beagle for Josh sealed the transfer, which had also allowed Carter to take Emily and Josh south to meet his family.

Willie tugged on Riley's collar to keep him from jumping on their new houseguest. "You want to go fishing with me and Grandpa, Uncle Carter?"

"Sure," Carter said.

"Your uncle's not doing anything but resting for a while, Willie. Why don't you take his luggage up to his room? Where's Grandpa?"

"Inside." Willie wrestled Carter's suitcase, which was bigger than he was.

Sally led the way into the house. "He's waiting for us. I called from the service station to let them know we were close." She shouted toward the back of the house. "Daddy!" No answer. "He must be in the basement." She led Carter downstairs, whispering, "He'll be so excited to see you." When they reached the bottom of the steps, Sally said, "Pop, look who's here."

———

THE FIRST TIME Carter had returned unexpectedly to Mississippi was in May of 1964, at the end of his first year of law school. Troy—located in the lower-right-hand corner of the state, about ninety miles from the state capital of Jackson and the same distance from the Gulf Coast town of Mobile, Alabama—was not the kind of place anybody was desperate to get to back then.

Carter had dozed sporadically on the long bus ride from Nashville, and he woke to the squeal of brakes as the Greyhound pulled up in front of the Troy post office, which also served as the depot.

Carter was an open-faced young man with close-cropped brown hair, dressed neatly in the khakis, Windbreaker, button-down Gant shirt, white socks, and brown penny loafers popular among the fraternity men and law students on the university campuses of the Deep South. Carrying a guitar case in one hand and a duffel bag over his shoulder, he stepped down off the bus into the heat and diesel fumes.

The bus driver pulled Carter's suitcase from the luggage bin in the belly of the bus and set it down in front of him. "This all of it?"

"Yessir," Carter replied. "Thank you."

"You got home just in time," said the driver, tipping his hat and climbing back up the steps onto the bus. "They say there's going to be trouble again on these buses."

"What do you mean?" Carter asked.

"Trouble all around," said the driver. "You'll hear about it soon enough. So long!"

The engine revved, and the bus pulled away. Carter stood surveying downtown Troy. He had been away only a few months, but it seemed like light-years, and he regarded Troy with the pleasurable existential alienation of the recent college grad.

Carter picked up his bag and guitar case, crossed the street to the pay phone, and called home. His mother answered on the second ring.

"Mama, it's me. I'm home. It's a long story. I'll tell you when I get there."

"Do you want me to pick you up somewhere?"

"No, I'll walk. Is Daddy home?"

He was still at work but would be home for supper. "Nettie's rolling biscuits and fixing peach cobbler," Katharine Ransom said, and then there was the first flicker of concern in her voice. "Son, did your father know you were coming? I'll wring his neck if he did and didn't tell me!"

"No, ma'am, he didn't know."

"Well, good—we'll surprise him then." For some reason his mother's insistent good cheer irritated Carter more than usual. "Your sister's going to be thrilled," she said. "Hurry home now."

An hour later, as Carter was trotting downstairs, he caught sight of his father coming in the front door, and he paused on the landing. The judge was a tall, commanding presence even when viewed from above. His slicked-back dark brown hair, streaked with gray at the temples, framed a tanned, handsome face lined with the burden of too many years deciding the fates of strangers. He turned right into the dining room, tie loosened, sleeves rolled up, coat over his arm, thumbing through his mail. "Nettie, where's Katharine?" he asked. "I'm starving."

The Hepplewhite table in the Ransom dining room was set for dinner. Nettie Knight, the family housekeeper, buzzed around the table, putting finishing touches on a flower arrangement on the sideboard, humming to herself. "Miz Katharine be down directly, Mr. Mitchell. She got a surprise for you."

"I hate surprises," he said without looking up from the mail. "I get enough surprises in the courtroom. When I come home, I want utter predictability. What's for supper, Nettie? Smells good."

"Country ham, Your Honor. You know that. It's Friday night, ain't it?"

"Ah . . . predictability. I can count on you, Nettie."

Carter had waited on the landing until his mother descended, and then he followed her into the dining room. "Oh, Mitchell, honey, I didn't expect you so soon," she said, kissing him. "Look who's home."

Carter entered behind her. "Hey, Daddy."

"Son! Well, this is a surprise." They shook hands, and Carter sat down at his usual place at the table, to the right of his father. "Where's Lonnie and Stephen and Jimbo? I thought y'all were heading to the beach for a few days?"

"I didn't come with them, Daddy. I took the bus."

"What happened to your car?"

"I lent it to Lonnie for the trip. His is in the shop. I'll join them later."

"Finished your finals? Aced 'em, I trust. Katharine, where's Sally? I'm starving."

Katharine called upstairs to Sally, then said to Carter, "That girl is driving me crazy. All she does is primp before the mirror."

Nettie entered with a platter of steaming ham.

"Sally!" Mitchell called.

"I'll go get her, Daddy," Carter said, but before he could stand, he heard his sister clamoring down the stairs.

Sally entered the dining room. She was dressed in a bright blue checked dress, her hair in pigtails. She twirled for all to admire. "How do you like it, Carter? I'm playing Ado Annie in *Oklahoma* at school."

"You look great, Sal," Carter said.

"Your little sister beat out all the older girls for the role," said their mother.

"Why not?" said Carter. "She's got some pipes on her."

"I just wish you were the accompanist, Pross," Sally said, sliding into the chair across from her brother. "Ol' Miz Greeley can't keep time. She's going deaf, I swear."

"Don't you say swear, young lady," her mother said.

Sally burst into song. *"'I'm just a girl who cain't say no.'"*

Her father frowned. "Katharine . . ."

Nettie entered with another serving dish. "Y'all gonna sing or eat? Boy don't look like he eatin' right," she said as she spooned mashed potatoes onto Carter's plate. "Lige was the same way. He'd a-wasted away to nothin' if I didn't stay after him."

"How's Lige doing, Nettie?" Carter asked. "Is he home from seminary?"

Nettie's face clouded, and she set the bowl down. "You know my boy. He don't tell his mama nothin' neither. 'Scuse me, now—don't wont the biscuits burnin'." She hurried to the kitchen.

Mitchell and Katharine exchanged glances. Mitchell bowed his head and held out his hands to join with the others before saying grace.

"What's the matter?" asked Carter. "What did I say?"

"Nettie's worried sick," his mother said.

"Is Lige in trouble?"

"He's going to be," his father said. "Damned fool's gotten mixed up with the outsiders. Troublemakers coming down here to stir things up between the races."

"Civil rights," Sally whispered.

"Hush," said her mother.

Sally looked at Carter and mouthed, "What are civil rights?"

"Lord, bless this food to the nourishment of our bodies," Mitchell intoned, "and thank You for reuniting our family today as we break bread again in Your name. Amen."

Nettie, who had paused at the door during the blessing, reentered with biscuits.

"So, Carter," said Mitchell, dishing mashed potatoes onto his plate, "how were exams? And why didn't you drop by the courthouse today when you got into town?"

"He came straight home like he should have," said Katharine, pouring the iced tea. "There's time enough for him to lollygag down there when he's clerking in the office this summer."

"Mason and the others at the firm keep asking me when you're going to start, Carter, so they can plan their vacation schedules."

"That's why I came home, Daddy." Carter cleared his throat. "I'm not going back to law school."

His parents stared at him. Nettie quickly exited to the kitchen. Sally held her glass of tea in mid-gulp, her eyes darting back and forth between both parents. Carter looked down at his plate. He could feel his father's temper and his struggle against unleashing it. Mitchell began cutting his meat. "We've already discussed this, son," he said in a restrained voice. "I thought it was settled."

"No, I mean it this time."

"Son, are you sure?" said his mother.

The judge raised his hand for silence. "Look, son . . . this is first-year-law nerves. Everybody has trouble their first year, and you went through college in three years. You'll mature and get over it."

"I don't want to get over it. I'm not happy."

"You're not supposed to be happy. You're in law school."

"Your courses will get easier, son."

"It's not that, Mama," he said. "Look, I was studying for my final in legal writing. What they teach you, it goes against everything I've ever learned about writing. How to make words flow with rhythm and feeling and meaning beyond their definition. Legal writing is the opposite of that. It's all about minutiae, rules, exceptions to the rules, exceptions to the exceptions. Even talking about it sounds constipated."

They had plowed this ground before—his father making the case for law school, conformity, delayed gratification; Carter having none of it; Katharine caught in the middle. "I skipped finals," he said, mooting the discussion. "They don't give them again."

"I'll call Dean Stanton," said Mitchell. "We were at Harvard together. I'm sure he can—"

"Carter, listen to your father—"

"Dammit, Mama, tell him to listen to me."

"Don't you curse at your mother." Mitchell braced his hand on the table, as if preparing to stand.

"Stop it!" Sally shrieked. "Leave him alone. Let Carter alone!"

"You keep out of this, young lady," Mitchell said.

"He's over eighteen. Why can't he decide for himself?"

Mitchell Ransom's face flushed red, and he ordered Sally to her room.

As Sally burst into tears and ran for the stairs, Carter saw Nettie peering into the dining room.

"Listen to me, young man," said Mitchell. "My family had it all, then lost it all in the Depression, and I damn well know what's best, because I had to find out the hard way. Everything I got I had to work for. I had to earn the privileges that you take for granted."

"That's just it, Daddy. And you taught me that privilege implies responsibility. I'm taking responsibility for myself and my decisions. I have a right to my own life. To choose my own destiny. I'm not one of the cases you decide."

"You're barely out of your teens."

"I'm old enough to die for my country."

"And you will die for your country if you're not careful! Haven't you paid attention to the news? Johnson's expanding the war in Vietnam. Three local boys were called up last week. They're drafting anybody who's not in school. What are you going to do when you lose your deferment?"

"I'd rather go into the army than the law. I'll take my chances."

"There you go again, talking foolishness. You don't know what you're saying."

"Save it for the jury, Daddy."

"I am the jury. And the judge in this matter."

Katharine was looking down at the napkin on her lap. "Please don't argue," she said, barely audible.

"Hell, I taught him how to argue. I taught him how to tie his shoes, how to walk."

"I'm walking." Carter pushed back from the table and tossed his napkin down beside his plate.

"Don't you dare walk out on me, young man," said the judge, but Carter was already out the dining-room door.

In the Ransom backyard, fireflies rose from the freshly mown grass like tiny spirits. The scarlets, oranges, and pinks in the twilight cloud-scape were dissolving into the blues and purples of darkness. Deep in the yard, across from a white gazebo, Carter sat in a rope swing hanging from the branch of an ancient white oak. He was strumming his guitar, cooling off. He could hear the clack of Nettie clearing the dinner dishes through the open window.

Sally came out and plopped down at his feet. To her amazement, Carter could play any of the Top 40 songs she listened to every night on the fifty-thousand-watt Little Rock station KAAY or on WLS in Chicago. He could replicate the guitar chords and arrangements note by note of almost any record he heard. His ear was a gift he took for granted, and his ability to find the root chords and re-create the sounds of others was a talent he hoped to transmute into something more nearly his own. Humoring his sister with the songs she and her friends heard on the radio was like performing magic tricks.

"Play it again, Carter," Sally said after a rendition of "I Saw Her Standing There." "You sound just like them."

Carter cranked up the opening chords of "I Wanna Hold Your Hand" and laughed as Sally went into a swoon. He had been drawn to folk music all through college—Peter, Paul and Mary; Bob Dylan; Joan Baez— but what caught his attention about the new sound out of Liverpool was the incorporation of folk changes and chord progressions into rock and roll. Like the rest of America, he and his classmates in law school had been glued to their television sets for *The Ed Sullivan Show* that Sunday night in February. The next day, they were all buying Beatles music.

"Sally, you've got homework," their mother called from the kitchen door.

"Just one more, Mama."

"Get going, sister," Carter said, shutting down his accompaniment. He offered his hand and pulled her up.

"I'm glad you're home, Pross," she said, giving him a charley horse to the shoulder. "Don't worry about Daddy. He's been really annoying lately. He'll get over this."

Across the yard, the screen door opened and slammed shut. Nettie approached, bearing a plate of ham biscuits left over from supper. Sally took that as her cue to disappear into the house.

"You didn't finish your supper," said Nettie.

Carter waved off her ham biscuits but took a glass of tea. "I'm not hungry, Nettie. Thanks anyway."

"Your daddy didn't finish his neither. Don't hurt my feelings none." She began nibbling on a biscuit.

"That's just a courtroom tactic, Nettie. A legal stratagem he uses to win sympathy from the jury."

"What jury?"

"You . . . Mama . . . the one in his head . . . Whoever. Every move my father makes is calculated to win his case: I leave the table. He leaves the table. I won't eat. He won't eat. Tit for tat. It's all about competition. Nobody gets the upper hand on Mitchell Ransom, no sir!"

"You took him by surprise. He's embarrassed he lost his temper."

"Oh, yeah. Surprise! Spontaneity! Impulse! Those words aren't even in his vocabulary. I'm surprised he doesn't ask you to iron his underwear!"

Nettie smiled. "You hard on your daddy."

"He's hard on me."

"The judge's got his heart set on you following in his footsteps, is all. Taking over his business. Ain't no sin in that. Parents want what's best for their children."

Carter set his glass of tea down on the grass. "Nettie, where's Lige?"

"I don't know," she said. "I know he's back in the area, but he ain't come to see me."

Carter couldn't believe what he was hearing. "Why won't he see you?"

Nettie looked away.

"Where is he?"

Nettie began fidgeting with her apron.

"Nettie," he said, "is everything okay?"

She looked back toward the house and then at Carter. Her voice broke when she finally said, "He won't tell me, but I hear he's registering voters out in the county."

"Registering voters?"

The dam burst, and the words tumbled out. "They way out off Shiloh Church Road. Nobody 'posed to know where. But they staying out there." Lige had not told her, but her cousin Daisy had seen them. "Some white folks from up North. Lige right in the middle. I don't know what got into him." Lige had gotten arrested with some classmates in Nashville, she explained. "Went to jail!" Nettie pressed her hands against her temples. "I started hearin' about it from folks at church. 'Y'all hear about Nettie and Wesley Knight's boy gittin' in all that trouble up in Tennessee? Got hisself arrested and throwed in jail.'"

Lige had written Nettie after that, trying to explain why he was doing it. "I wrote him back and I told him he won't raised like that. Jail won't no place for any boy of mine." Since then, Lige had stopped writing or calling. He had told his brother and sisters that he didn't want to be a preacher anymore. "All I know is he gonna git hisself killed. He growed up around decent white folks, like Judge Ransom, Miz Katharine. He don't know they's mean white folks too around here. Will you go to him, Carter? He'll listen to you. Tell him the danger."

The directness of Nettie's request threw Carter. She had never asked anything of him before, beyond that he make up his bed or wash his hands before supper. Carter agreed to look into it. She told him Lige was working out of an old juke joint off Highway 17 called Magic Time. Carter knew the place. It was an old colored nightclub he and his friends used to run off to in high school to listen to the blues. That's where he learned all he knew about blues chord progressions. He thought Magic Time would have ceded to the kudzu by now.

He put his guitar down and stood up. "What is it, Nettie?"

"Some of the white men upset about what they doing. Kluxers. They already burned a cross out there."

"Where did you get this?"

Nettie had overheard the judge talking to Pete Callahan, editor of the local newspaper, on the porch after dinner the week before. "Don't you tell him I was snooping," she said. "They don't know Lige is out there."

"Of course I won't tell, Nettie," Carter said. But clearly his parents already knew something.

"That ain't the worst. Your daddy don't know what all's been done." Nettie's expression was haunted. "They picked up a colored man on the highway up near Meridian. Thought he was one of the outsiders. Took him out to the woods and beat him. He didn't know nothin'. But it don't matter to them. They took a knife to his . . . to his—" She couldn't go on.

Carter had never seen her like this before. He put a hand on her shoulder to calm her. "What, Nettie? What did they do?"

"They cut off his privates. He pass out, and the highway patrol found him wandering dazed on the highway. Sent him away."

"My God! How did you learn this, Nettie?" Carter did not know whether to believe her.

"Church. It was our choir director's brother. He in the hospital in Nashville. Everything, it don't get in the papers. I don't want 'em doing nothing to my Lige. Go to him, Carter. Elijah look up to you. Bring him home to me."

Carter stood there helplessly as Nettie wept. He was uncertain what he was supposed to do. What would he say to Lige? He hadn't seen him since high school. He himself had changed a lot in those years. He had read about civil rights workers. Violence seemed to follow everywhere they went. It sounded like Lige had gone off to school and gotten ideas put in his head. But wasn't that what happened? Who was Carter to judge? "We'll see," he said finally. "I'll look into it."

Nettie reached into her apron pocket and pulled out a silver chain with some sort of medallion on it. She handed it to Carter. It was a Saint Christopher medal. "Give this to Lige when you see him," Nettie said, her eyes shining. "It'll keep him safe." She glanced at the plate of untouched food and frowned. "You sure you not hungry?"

Carter smiled and shook his head. Nettie turned back toward the house. "Be sweet," she said, and he stared after her, not at all sure he deserved her trust.

––––––––––

JUDGE MITCHELL RANSOM WAS at his worktable, regarding with relish the dozens of gears spread out before him—some as small as a dime, others the size of a silver dollar. Rebuilding grandfather clocks had been the judge's hobby for as long as Carter could remember. Since he had last been home, the walls in the basement workroom had been painted eggshell white and were lined with a luminous molding of fluorescent lights. Propped against a wall were several antique clocks in various states of repair.

Mitchell clutched a small screwdriver in his left hand like a scalpel. Through a magnifying glass mounted on a wire stand, he peered at the metal entrails spread out before him. Then, spotting his son, his eyes registered a look of measured satisfaction that Carter had seen a thousand times before.

"Carter, son, you're home." Hunched over the table, the judge's six-foot-plus frame looked frail and unexpectedly diminished. His snow-white hair was thin. He had been fighting a decades-long battle with baldness, his hairline retreating but never surrendering.

"How you doing, Judge?" Carter bent down and hugged his father in the chair.

Mitchell embraced Carter for what seemed like a long time. When finally he let go, he took Carter's hands. He looked him in the eyes, his expression serious. "How are you, son?"

"I've been better."

"I heard about your time in the hospital. I wish I could have driven up with Sally."

"I know you do, Daddy."

"Your sister and the doctors treat me like I'm an invalid." He motioned dismissively at the prescription bottles cluttering the tabletop and the blanket covering his lap.

"Hush, Daddy." Sally rolled her eyes and started Carter toward the stairs. "Carter needs to rest before supper."

"He just got here. Let the boy alone before you drive us both crazy."

Carter, feeling guilty for not staying to visit, said, "You still going down to the office, Judge?"

"Every day. They let me have a part-time secretary to handle correspondence." He gave Carter a long look. "Now do what your sister tells you. Rest up. It's quiet around here during the day."

"Until school lets out," Sally said, taking Carter's elbow.

"I won't be here that long," Carter said. "Or the paper might think they can publish without me."

"You don't worry about that, son. They can get along without you at that newspaper. Sometimes the mind doesn't know what the body knows."

Carter felt himself bristle. It wasn't what his father said; it was how he said it, or what Carter heard in it. Mitchell Ransom had never considered journalism a real profession. Carter was surprised that his sensitivity to his father's opinion could transcend the antidepressants. The arrogance rankled him, the judge's presumption that the law was so pure and sacred and superior to the journeyman rites of the free press.

"I'll be getting back to work as soon as I can," Carter said. "I appreciate your letting me rest up here." He offered his hand to his father, feeling, and not for the first time, as if they were shaking on a dare.

5

C ARTER STARED OUT the bathroom window and blew the smoke from his cigarette into the ceiling fan above the toilet. Outside, under the massive oak tree, Judge Ransom was sitting in a lawn chair sipping iced tea. Willie and Riley were playing Frisbee on the lawn. He should be outside with them, Carter thought, but the long drive and his new medicine had worn him down.

There was a knock. "You decent?" Sally called. She had served him his first home meal in bed—Campbell's chicken noodle soup and a grilled cheese sandwich—and was probably coming for the dishes. Carter stubbed out the cigarette, flushed it down the toilet, and stepped back into the bedroom. "I ironed your shirts just like Mama used to." Sally stood in the doorway waving the hangers like a matador's cape. She took them to the closet. "If you need anything else to eat, let me know."

Sally's softheartedness was legendary in the family. At sixteen, she worked over the Christmas break at McCorkle's, a downtown department store, to help out with the holiday rush. When an elderly colored lady came up and asked the price of an expensive crinoline dress for her granddaughter, Sally had replied, "How much do you have?"

"Seven dollars and fifty cents."

"What a coincidence," his sister said. "That's exactly how much it costs." The customer told her friends about the bargain she had come by and the nice young lady who had helped her, and before long Sally was helping all the woman's friends. Soon Mr. McCorkle confronted Sally, who explained that she thought she was acting in the true spirit of Christmas. After she was fired, Judge Ransom had to write Mr. Mc-Corkle a check for two hundred dollars.

Carter sat on the bed and stared at the photographs on the wall. The so-called guest room still retained much of the character of its earlier incarnation as his father's study. The room was a shrine of sorts to a distinguished career in jurisprudence. The photographs, mostly black-and-white, all mounted in simple black frames, showed his father with Presidents Kennedy, Johnson, and Carter. There were other, more personal photographs of the judge and his wife, Carter, and Sally—in front of St. Louis Cathedral on Jackson Square during Mardi Gras in New Orleans, sunning on the beach at Gulf Shores, fishing on the Chickasaw River. A world map papered one wall. On the opposite hung his father's undergraduate diploma from the University of North Carolina, his law degree from Harvard, citations from the Mississippi State Bar Association and various local fraternal organizations. On top of the judge's antique mahogany rolltop desk were bronze and marble busts of his guardian angels: Lincoln, Jefferson, and Cicero.

"Seems like yesterday we were in high school and had our whole lives before us." Sally moved to the window and looked out at her son and her father on the lawn. "Then you blink and twenty years have slipped by. By the time we know anything worth knowing, it's too late. We should all live life backward."

"What are you thinking about?" Carter asked.

"Look at them out there having a big time together. Daddy's been great for Willie. He's been there for him in ways he never was for us. For you."

"Is Robert helping out with Willie?"

"He pays the court-ordered child support, if that's what you mean," Sally said. "And he wouldn't do anything to consciously hurt Willie." She gave an ironic little laugh. "Amazing what we can find to be grateful for at our age."

After a moment she turned and looked at her brother with an urgency that made him uncomfortable. "I had misgivings about bringing you home, you know that."

Carter walked over to the picture of Mitchell with Robert Kennedy as attorney general and Burke Marshall, the head of his Civil Rights Division, and lifted it off the wall. "I don't know how this is going to work, Sal." He sat down on the bed and examined the picture. "Too much water under the bridge."

Sally sat down next to him. "I had an ulterior motive, Carter. I wanted Daddy to feel he was helping you by bringing you home, but actually I wanted you here for him."

"How so?"

Sally left and came back with a copy of *The Troy Times*. The headline read CHURCH BOMBER PAROLED. She said, "Sorry to spring this on you your first night home, but I figure you'd see it sooner or later. It's the big news around here. Lacey Hullender's getting out of prison."

"How did that happen?" Carter said as he skimmed the story.

Sally thought that the attorney general's office had pulled some strings. "Presumably, the reason they've reopened the Shiloh Church bombing case is that Hullender agreed to testify against Sam Bohannon."

"Yeah, I had heard that it was being reopened. But how could anyone consider Hullender fit for society?"

"Lonnie told me he was a model prisoner—leads Bible-study groups in his cellblock. He's had twenty years to think about what he did."

"That's not long enough." Disgust was building up against the drug-ensured flatness. "What does the old man say?"

"Daddy won't talk about these things with me. Anyway, he's so forgetful lately."

"Has he forgotten Hullender's death threats after the first Shiloh Church trial?" His father had ignored the crude postcards mailed from Parchman prison after he had presided over the convictions as a state court judge, but if he had been serving on the federal bench at the time, the threats would have been a felony.

"The sheriff offered a security detail," said Sally, "but Daddy won't hear of it. He thinks we're overreacting."

"Let's hope," Carter said. He felt himself submitting again to the medication. He opened the newspaper to the jump inside. He would put nothing past Lacey Hullender. There were things wrong with Hullender that no amount of time in prison could correct.

The article recounted the history of the Shiloh Church bombing, which occurred outside Troy in rural Ellis County in March of 1965 and left three civil rights workers and the daughter of the church's minister dead. Two men had been convicted of the murders in 1970, and the state was now reopening the case against Sam Bohannon, the defendant who got away when the jury could not reach a verdict. As the Imperial Wizard of the White Knights of the Ku Klux Klan, he had been the architect of a four-year campaign of terrorism in Mississippi. Between 1963 and 1967 he was believed to have personally ordered at least nine murders, seventy-five firebombings of black churches, and more than three hundred assaults, bombings, and beatings. After a second state trial ended in a hung jury, Bohannon had been convicted in 1972 on federal civil rights violations and, after losing all his appeals, had served six years of his ten-year sentence before being released in 1979. He still owned his popular catfish restaurant in downtown Troy but now spent most of his time at his fish camp, a few miles outside the city limits on the Little Chickasaw River. At the age of seventy-four, more than twenty-five years after the Shiloh Church bombing, Bohannon would stand trial once again for the murders of Randall Peek, Daniel Johnston, Celia Bunt, and Sarah Solomon.

Lacey Hullender, one of the two men convicted in Judge Mitchell Ransom's court, was now turning state's evidence against his former guru in the anti–civil rights movement.

"If Hullender's ratting on Bohannon," Carter finally said, "he may be the one who needs bodyguards. If I don't kill him first."

"Carter," Sally said. She had composed her face into an "expression." "Have you ever stopped thinking about Sarah over the years?"

Carter took a moment before he answered. "There were times when I could go for long periods, by which I mean weeks, without . . . But she shadowed my relationships. I couldn't help but compare. It's like these kids getting killed in the Gulf. To their war brides they'll always be that age. No one who comes after can compete with a war hero. It's never in the clear."

"I heard her father came to see you in the newsroom when you collapsed."

"Yes."

"What did he want?"

"I never found out. I was in no shape to ask that day, and the next thing I know, I'm on 'hiatus.' Isn't it great how many euphemisms we can come up with for *mental institution*? Hell, even that's a euphemism."

"I wish this trial would just go away, for Daddy's sake. And, God, for yours. The timing is atrocious."

She stood and smiled at him. "Anyway, I'm glad you're home, Carter." She tousled his hair. "Oh, and thanks for smoking in the bathroom." With a wink she disappeared down the hallway. Carter had climbed back into bed, and he lay awake in the guest bedroom of the house he had grown up in, alone in a way he hadn't felt since he was a teenager, thinking now once again of Sarah. It was then that he realized that his stealth cigarette had violated his bargain with God for having spared Emily.

———

CARTER RANSOM PULLED UP into the parking lot of Magic Time. It was nine in the morning when he stepped out of his air-conditioned '62 Ford Fairlane, and already the June heat and humidity felt like a sodden fur coat. The fragrance of honeysuckle and pine resin sweetened the heavy air. This was the first time Carter had visited Magic Time in broad daylight. On Saturday nights during high school, he and his friends Lonnie, Stephen, and Jimbo had snuck out late to go hear blues players who were making the rounds on the chitlin' circuit on their way to becoming legends—Howlin' Wolf, Big Joe Williams, Junior Kimbrough, and Memphis Minnie. Even then, Magic Time had been in need of repair. And now, in the bright light of morning, the joint had no glamour at all. It looked vulnerable and foreboding at the same time.

Set back in a stand of pines, the squat cinder-block building was barely visible from the highway. The place looked deserted, a road-scarred pickup in the rutted gravel lot the only sign of human presence. Beside the boarded-up window hung a Jax beer sign, its smashed neon lettering glinting in the dust below. A string of dead Christmas-tree lights encircled the weather-warped plywood. Flies moved in a lazy cloud above an oil drum that might have doubled as a garbage can. Carter thought he heard a radio playing inside. He knocked on the screen door. "Anybody home?"

He knocked again, then jimmied open the screen and banged on the wooden door behind it. It creaked open. He poked his head inside and called again. "Anybody here? Lige?"

Before his eyes could adjust to the dim interior, something cold and metallic jabbed his temple. A split second later a click, the sound of a pistol being cocked, and then a female voice. "One more step, cracker, and you're going to go see Jesus!"

"Please. Don't shoot. I'm a friend of Elijah Knight. I'm here to see Lige."

The girl holding the gun took a couple of steps back, glanced at the parking lot to make sure Carter was alone, and, keeping the gun leveled at his forehead, waved him inside. Now out of the shadows, he could see that his captor was pretty, slender, and white, dressed in faded jeans, a blue work shirt, and dusty tennis shoes. Her dark hair was pulled back in a ponytail that ended just below her shoulder blades. Carter, hesitating, stepped inside, his hands raised and his eyes locked on the gun.

"Who are you?" said the girl, gripping the gun handle now with both hands, as if she was afraid she would drop it.

"Carter Ransom. I'm here to see Elijah Knight."

"Who sent you?"

"Nobody. I mean Nettie. His mama! Please. It's hard to think with a gun pointed at my head."

"How do you know Mr. Knight?" she persisted.

"He's a friend."

"How do I know you're not one of those thugs who's been calling here and hanging up? Or who firebombed the house in Hattiesburg last week?"

"Because I'm wearing Weejuns?"

Despite the gun, she did not look dangerous. A smile threatened her face. She motioned Carter toward a chair. After he sat down, she pulled over a metal folding chair and sat facing him.

Carter allowed himself to take in the surroundings. Two ceiling fans suspended from the ductwork overhead churned the dank air. The pool table in the middle of the room was serving as a desk, from the looks of the papers covering its surface. A manual typewriter overhung the edge of a chipped and dented filing cabinet. The walls were papered with posters advertising blues acts and placards emblazoned with the words FREEDOM NOW and REGISTER TO VOTE and NO POLL TAX. Posters of Mahatma Gandhi and Frederick Douglass completed the gallery.

The girl had uncocked the pistol and rested it on her lap. "Welcome to the Ellis County headquarters of the Student Nonviolent Coordinating Committee."

"Thank you," Carter said. "Okay if I lower my hands now? And do you mind if I ask, where does the nonviolence come in?"

"That's becoming a figure of speech," she said, removing the bullets from the cylinder of the Smith & Wesson. Then she stood up, snapped off the radio, and pulled a large handbag from the filing cabinet. "Did I scare you?" she asked hopefully.

Carter said, "I'm still shaking."

She slipped the pistol in the handbag and locked the bundle in the cabinet drawer. "Lige is out with the others getting supplies. He should be back soon."

"Can I wait?"

"Suit yourself." She took a swig from a Dr Pepper, sat down at the pool-table desk, and picked up a dog-eared copy of *Anna Karenina*.

Carter scooted forward and offered her his hand. "I'm Carter Ransom."

She looked up from her book. "So thou sayest."

He withdrew his hand. "You're not from around here, are you?"

"Per*cep*tive. New York City."

"That would explain the rudeness."

Her expression was blank. "Rudeness: what a quaint concept. You obviously *are* a local."

"No."

"Where then?"

"Troy."

"I got news for you, *bubbeleh*—that is local."

"No, it's not. Troy's a good three miles from here."

"Ah, the South's legendary Sense of Place!"

"Oh, you're down here to get a good grade—anthropology class, I bet."

Ignoring him, she walked to the front door, scanned the parking lot, and stepped outside. She appeared to be checking the thermometer affixed to the doorjamb, the one with the fading Dr Pepper logo that Carter had noted was registering a hundred-plus when he came in. A moment later she returned, fanning herself, the screen door slamming behind her. "How can you stand living here? It's hotter'n hell."

"You could always go home," Carter answered.

She smiled for the first time. "So could you, white boy."

"My name is Carter. I live here. What are *you* doing here?"

"Registering voters." She waved a hand, indicating the flyers, forms, and envelopes on the pool table.

"Colored voters."

"That's right." She raised her eyebrows, as if challenging him. "Colored. Like your friend Lige."

The girl started at the sound of an automobile pulling up outside. She went back to the file drawer, took out the bag holding the pistol, darted to the boarded-up window, and looked through a gap between the boards. Carter, too, felt anxiety. He had to remind himself that he was in his own hometown, or at least three miles out. After a moment the tension left her, and she returned the pistol to the file cabinet. Behind them the screen door squeaked. Then the front door opened, and three men walked in, their arms full of grocery bags. Two were Negroes, one in overalls, wearing horn-rimmed glasses, and the other in khakis, a madras shirt, and sunglasses. The white man had short dark hair and was dressed in blue jeans, shirtsleeves, and a clerical collar. The men— Lige was not among them—were laughing and joking, but they fell silent when they saw Carter. The Negro in the madras shirt took off his sunglasses and said, "Sarah, who the hell is this?"

"He says he's a friend of Lige's," she answered. All three men eyed Carter as they set the groceries down on the pool table.

Carter stood and introduced himself.

The white man shook Carter's hand. "You here to help?"

"No, I—uh—"

"Where are you from?" the Negro with glasses asked.

"Troy."

"He's spying on us," the third one said.

"I'm no spy," Carter said. "I just wanted to see Lige."

"Why?"

"That your car out there?" asked the bespectacled one. "Mississippi tags. Vanderbilt sticker. You go there?"

"I was in law school there."

"Then you should know what 'you're trespassing' means," said the stocky one in madras as he unloaded the groceries.

The Negro wearing the horn-rims extended his hand. "I'm Randall Peek."

The phone on the file cabinet rang. For a moment they all stared at it. As Randall reached for the receiver, the front door swung open. A tall, lanky Negro entered, saying, "I told y'all to park in back. Whose Fairlane is that?" He spotted Carter and stopped in his tracks. Then a smile broke like a sunrise across his face. "Carter Ransom," he said, and cackled in disbelief. "Lord have mercy if it ain't Brother Man!" He dropped his bag of groceries on the pool table and wrapped Carter in a bear hug.

"Lige," Carter said when he could breathe again, "thank God."

Lige swept his arms wide. "Welcome to the Ellis County headquarters of the Student Nonviolent Coordinating Committee voter registration drive!" Noticing the girl's amused expression, Lige said, "I take it you two have been introduced."

"Oh, yeah," Carter said, and managed a small, dry laugh, now that Lige was there. "She's the finest hostess south of the Smith & Wesson line."

"Dadgummit, Sarah," Lige said. "I told you to get rid of that thing. You're going to hurt somebody." He turned to Carter. "Some of us are divided on the philosophy of nonviolence, but Sarah's heart's in the right place—for a Yankee white girl."

"From New York, no less," Carter said.

"Sarah Solomon," Lige said, "officially meet Carter Ransom—my oldest friend in Troy. Sarah's down here from Barnard College."

"We got another death threat this morning," she said. "I thought he might've come to carry it out."

Carter was stunned.

"Local sport," Lige explained when he saw the look on Carter's face. "It's the ones who don't call you got to worry about." Lige motioned the others toward him. "This is Dexter Washington from Deetroit," indicating the short, stocky Negro in madras, "and Daniel Johnston from Boston"—the white one in the clerical collar. The bespectacled Negro in overalls, Randall Peek, was from Atlanta. They all gave perfunctory nods and returned to storing their groceries.

"So how you doin', man?" Lige asked, pulling up two folding chairs. "How's law school?"

That Carter had dropped out came as no surprise to Lige, who was curious, though, as to how the judge was taking it. He asked how Carter was spending the summer.

"Helping out part-time with general assignments at *The Troy Times* till I figure out what I'm going to do when I grow up."

"Come work with us," Sarah said without looking up from *Anna Karenina*. "We could use a lawyer to spring us when we get thrown in jail for believing in the Constitution."

"I'm not a lawyer."

"We got some catchin' up to do," Lige said.

Behind Carter, a deep voice asked, "Who's this?" Carter turned to see a newcomer, a wiry, angular black man standing in a doorway at the back of the room. Smoke from a newly lit cigarette shrouded his face, then broke apart in the downdraft from the ceiling fan. Taut and muscular in a white T-shirt, he looked harder than the others, and his skin was lighter. He was wearing sunglasses, so Carter couldn't see his eyes, but sensed his disapproval nonetheless.

Lige said, "Carter Ransom, Charlie Lloyd from Brooklyn. Carter's a friend."

Charlie raised his shades to stare hard at Carter. "Ain't no friend of mine. I don't trust the white man."

Sarah said in a mock sulk, "Hey, I'm white."

"And who says I trust you?"

Lige, softly but with authority, said, "I said he's family."

But Charlie wasn't backing down. "And what does that make you— three-fifths family? Where I come from, a drawl like that means he'd as soon kill you as look at you."

"Well, down here," Carter heard himself saying, "and we're the experts, we call that prejudice." This insolence toward their comrade brought astonished looks from the others.

"Lige, it's Yolanda at COFO in Meridian," Randall said, cupping the phone. "The three boys who went up to Neshoba County yesterday haven't come back."

"Shit," Lige said. He dispensed with Charlie, saying with finality, "Carter's o-kay." Then he turned to Randall. "What happened?"

J.E., Mickey, and "the new college kid from New York" had been arrested for speeding late the previous afternoon and were put in jail in the Neshoba County seat, Philadelphia. That night they were released and told to leave town. Nobody had heard from them since. "Sheriff's saying it's just a hoax," Randall said. "That they're hiding out to get the publicity."

"Maybe they followed orders and left," Carter said.

The group gave him a disdainful look. "Who is this?" said Charlie.

"Lige," Randall said again, holding up the receiver, "Yolanda wants to talk to you."

"Just a minute." Elijah escorted Carter to the door, whispering as they went. "I'm sorry, man, but we got an emergency situation."

"Come by the house," Carter said.

"Can't, Pross. Mama'd have a fit."

"Lige, your mama sent me. She's worried about you."

Lige called back to Randall, "Tell Yolanda hold on." After a quick look at the lot, he hurried Carter out to his car, all the while watching the highway for passing vehicles. "Carter, I don't imagine you understand this, and I sure don't expect Mama to. But this"—he indicated the cinder-block building behind him—"this is my life now." Lige's pronouncement left Carter speechless. Worse, his opportunity to talk to Lige was now gone. Lige seemed to see the confusion and fear in Carter's face. "Listen, meet me Tuesday morning at Naked Tail. Nine or so. Okay? You remember how to get there, right?"

"Sure, but—"

"We can talk then. By the way, congratulations. You're blazing your own trail now, Brother Man." Lige jogged back toward Magic Time.

Carter climbed into his Ford Fairlane. The air within was hotter. He looked back toward Magic Time. Lige had disappeared inside. Sarah Solomon stood behind the screen door and peered out at him.

Carter cranked the ignition and threw the Ford into gear. As he passed the doorway, he rolled down his window and called out, "Nice meeting you, Miss Solomon."

Sarah stepped out, smiled sweetly, and said in a dead-on Scarlett O'Hara drawl, "Y'all come back and see us now, y'hear?"

Carter hit the gas pedal a bit too hard, spraying the building with dust and gravel before he could bring the car back under control. When he pulled onto the highway, he glanced in his rearview mirror. He thought he saw Sarah Solomon still standing there behind the silvery sheen of the screen door, watching him.

6

R ise and shine, boy. Breakfast time."
    Carter opened his eyes to a face he hadn't seen for years. He thought he was still dreaming. "Nettie?"

For a moment he was disoriented by the sight of Nettie Knight's round, smiling face, backlit by the morning sun shafting through the blinds. But the cold front off the air-conditioning vent and the lemon-scented bed linens convinced him he was back home. How he had gotten here was slower coming into focus.

"Hope you hungry, Pross," Nettie said as she placed the aromatic tray of bacon on the bedside table. Carter was amazed at how little she had changed. Her deep, dark eyes still shone with vitality despite the trials life had brought her. The furrows in her brow were more evident now when she frowned, and her once pitch-black hair had turned mostly gray, but her skin was as smooth as when Carter was a boy. She leaned down and hugged his neck. "I made them scrambled soft just the way you like them, son. And hot biscuits to boot."

Carter propped himself up on the stack of pillows.

Sally stuck her head through the doorway. "Doesn't Nettie look tip-top, Carter?"

The old woman shushed her. "You know I'm just the same Nettie I always been," she said.

"Daddy had a meeting at the courthouse," Sally said. "He was up and away at the crack of dawn." After Nettie left, Sally continued in a whisper. "When she heard you were home, she wanted to be here to serve you breakfast." Nettie helped Sally out during the day with her father and Willie, although she no longer needed to work. She was living with her daughter. "I don't know how she does it," Sally said. "Almost as old as Daddy and strong as a bull. And the only one who can make him eat right."

"What day is it?" Carter asked.

"Thursday."

Nettie returned with coffee. "Best not let them eggs get cold, or I'll take a switch to you like I did when you was a youngun."

With a mime's precision, Carter dutifully lifted his fork.

Sally pulled up a chair next to Carter and examined the label of the prescription bottle on the bedside table. "After you eat, I'll give you another pill."

Carter surveyed his surroundings as he chewed his wheat toast. His beat-up guitar case was leaning against the wall in the corner.

"That's your old Gibson," Sally said. "I brought it down from the attic. I thought you could maybe show Willie some chords while you're here." Carter had not played regularly since he was a teenager and had dreamed of making music for a living. When Sally went off to college, he had given the guitar to her.

"I brought you some books," she said, indicating a stack on the floor next to his bed. "You just take it easy. I'm heading over to the store. Here's my number if you need me."

"Going to teach you to cook your own meals," Nettie said, bringing in a tumbler of fresh-squeezed orange juice. "High time you learned. Your sister told me you had nothin' in your Frigidaire up there in New York City but hot sauce and Co'-Colas. No wonder you got sick." She went back downstairs.

"Clean your plate, Pross, and I'll see you later," Sally said. "Nettie'll be back up to get your tray."

"Sally," Carter said, "thanks." She gave him a "What are sisters for?" look and disappeared down the hallway.

Sally had left *The Troy Times* on the nightstand. Carter read more about the release of Lacey Hullender. On the front page was a photograph of Mitchell Ransom as a superior court judge twenty years earlier, when he had sentenced Hullender to life in prison. There was a second photo—of the young woman from the state attorney general's office who had reopened the Shiloh Church case. The piece again told how Hullender and another Klan hit man named Peyton Posey had been sent up for the crime. There hadn't been enough evidence to convict Sam Bohannon in the same trial. Posey had died in prison. When Hullender came up for parole, the state hadn't opposed his release, simply deferring to the parole board. The ruling in Hullender's favor was rumored to be part of a deal struck with the attorney general's office that would make him a star witness in the state's new case against Bohannon.

The phone rang on the nightstand next to Carter's bed. "Carter, is that you?" He recognized the voice of his editor, Ed Dennehy. "Your sister said it was okay to call. How you doing, big guy?"

"Okay."

"Listen, we miss you up here. But we'll survive. So just take it easy, okay? As long as you need."

Dennehy filled him in on the *Examiner*'s investigation into the museum bombing. The press was still feeling its way on the specific political motive of the incident. It didn't bear the familiar markers of the Israeli-Palestinian conflict. "By the way," Dennehy said, "I saw on the wire that they're reopening that old church bomber case down there." He paused to let his columnist weigh in, assuming that even in his weakened state Carter's instinct would be to write about it. When he didn't bite, Dennehy continued, "So if you pick up any leads, don't hesitate to pass them on to the national desk."

"Ed, you're fishing."

"Well, let's just say I hate to spring for somebody like Flynn to fly down there—or worse, to run wire copy on a story when we've got our star columnist on the scene, is all. There's going to be a slew of those cases reopened, and that trial's going to be big news. Meanwhile, buddy, if there's anything I can do for you, just let me know."

When Carter got off the phone, he glanced back at the old file photo of his father just above the fold of the newspaper in his lap. He lifted the section to his nose and inhaled deeply to take in the smell of printer's ink. Then he examined his fingers for any smear of newsprint and saw none. For the first time in his adult life, work seemed alien, like a foreign country he might visit at some future time.

Carter sank back into his pillows. Gospel music was playing faintly on the radio in the kitchen downstairs. Nettie must have been going about her chores. He hadn't had a chance to catch up with her and get a report on Lige. The sound of Nettie's "sacred music" had accompanied her kitchen duties each morning when he was growing up, just as the babble of TV soap operas—her "stories"—provided the backdrop for her afternoon ironing. Sometimes when Carter foraged in the refrigerator for snacks, he would find bundles of wet laundry stored there to keep until Nettie could iron them later. Her rhythms and routines had soothed and intrigued him, as did her secret addictions—the kick she would get from an afternoon BC Powder chased with a "Co'-Cola," a home remedy for the midday blahs. She shared this ritual of relief with the other "help" in the neighborhood—women with names like Sook and Ethel—along with gossip and complaints. Carter sensed that these women were proud of the prosperous white families they cared for, and that they derived social status from their employers' positions, but sometimes he overheard them telling tales about the white folks' foibles— from the misbehavior of their children to their personal parsimony or inability to enjoy their privilege, how they were so tight they would buy a pot roast too small or cook one chicken for eight people. Some, like Nettie, had grown up on the plantation tenant farms, still in the shadow of slavery, and they took pride in bettering themselves. Carter had often thought it ironic that their children's involvement in the civil rights "mess" caused the elders so much anxiety and alarm, even though it was partly the same upwardly mobile impulse that had brought Nettie into Carter's household.

CARTER FELT ILL AT EASE driving out to meet with Lige at their old swimming hole. The disappearance of the three civil rights workers had dominated the news for days since he first heard about it at Magic Time. The Yankee press had turned its attention on the college students pouring into Mississippi from up North and the risks they took coming down to his home state. For the rest of the world, the story was about the latest calamity to befall a great social movement, but for Carter it was a nagging reminder that he hadn't told Nettie about his visit to Magic Time, and until he had something more to report to her, he didn't want to increase the chances of his mission getting back to his father. The two were barely on speaking terms as it stood, without Mitchell Ransom knowing that his son had visited civil rights workers at their headquarters.

Steam lifted off the highway in vaporous wisps. Overhead, the sky was cloudless. Beyond the bridge spanning the Little Chickasaw River, Carter spotted an abandoned logging road veering off into the trees a few yards to the right of the highway. He would have missed it, the road to Naked Tail, if it had not been for a rusty chain strung between a set of rotting posts at the entrance. Weeds had grown waist-high, making the road nearly invisible from the highway. He turned off the blacktop and bumped down the embankment along the tire tracks to the chained posts. He pulled the Ford over and proceeded on foot. The logging road had reverted into little more than an extra-wide weed-strangled game trail. After a quarter mile or so, the road forked, and Carter bore right toward the river. The path plunged deeper into wilderness. Flies hovered in pestering clouds. Stickers snagged his dungarees. Just when the underbrush was beginning to seem impassable, the overgrown trail opened onto a shaded clearing blanketed with pine needles. The path became loamy as it wound through the trees. Then, finally, the trail ended at a sandy white beach that sloped down to a teal-green lagoon. Steep banks rose up on two sides to promontories that overlooked the Little Chickasaw beyond.

The glade had been a secret Shangri-la for Carter and his most

trusted friends. Lige had shown it to him. The swimming pool in town
was segregated (meaning "white only"), so the river had served generations of colored kids. Lige had named it Naked Tail because bathing
suits were not required. Black and white boys swam together and dried
themselves on the sun-warmed rocks, surreptitiously assessing proportional endowment. A wistful melancholy swept over Carter as he spied
what remained of the old rope swing dangling above the water from
the limb of the giant water oak atop the promontory. Carter slipped off
his loafers and walked barefoot across the beach to the embankment
that led up to the oak. Beneath the tree's umbrella of branches, the water from the Little Chickasaw River pooled into the perfect swimming
hole.

As usual, Lige was late. But he always showed up.

Carter had been six years old when he first met Elijah Knight. A green
weather-beaten flatbed truck had pulled up in front of his father's law
office across the square from the courthouse, on the steps of which
Carter was sitting, eating a cherry sno-cone. A tall, thin Negro man
climbed out of the cab, carrying two sacks of tomatoes and corn. Four
children sat in the back of the truck with the rest of the produce. Wesley Knight, a country farmer, had sought the services of Carter's father
when the bank tried to foreclose on his property, Carter later learned.
Mitchell had helped him stop the action. Lacking cash, Knight paid off
his legal fees with fresh vegetables from his farm.

When Wesley Knight was inside, Elijah herded his younger brother
and sisters to the rear of the flatbed and began preaching to them.
Carter watched the skinny boy—a bit older than he was—exhort his
congregation in the cadences of a seasoned preacher to change their
wicked candy-stealing ways before it was too late. The children grew
fidgety and eventually turned their attention to Carter, who had finished his sno-cone and was doing tricks with his brand-new Duncan yo-
yo. They fled their big brother's solemnities to watch him demonstrate
"walk the dog" and "around the world" and "rock the cradle."

Soon Lige, too, lost interest in the sermon and wandered over to join
them. "Where you get that?" he asked.

"My daddy gave it to me," Carter said, his eyes locked on the spinning orb. "Got it at Kress's."

"Never seen nobody do that before," the boy said.

Glancing up, Carter saw four sets of dark brown eyes staring at his shiny red yo-yo. "What's your name?" Carter asked.

"Elijah."

Carter nodded toward the flatbed. "What were you doin' with them over there?"

"Preachin'. My mama say I'm going to be a preacher when I grow up."

"At home he preach to the chickens," said the younger brother. Lige's siblings snickered behind their hands.

"Chickens pay better attention than my brother and sisters," Lige said, stern.

Carter held out the Duncan and asked him if he wanted to try it.

Lige's brother and sisters began to beg, but Carter slipped off the string and handed the yo-yo to their older brother. Lige's face beamed as he drew it tight around his finger and wound the string on the spool. His brother and sisters stepped back. With many false starts and much rewinding of string, Lige tried to make the yo-yo do what Carter had done, but to no avail. He kept at it, ignoring the hoots from his siblings, until finally he made the yo-yo "hesitate." A few minutes later he sent the Duncan spinning around the world. It had taken Carter much longer to achieve what Lige accomplished in only a few attempts. It was his first experience of competition with a Negro.

Nettie had come to clean for the Ransoms in order to work off more of the legal fees, and she ended up staying. That first summer, Elijah showed up with his mother on days when she needed him to clean the windows or clear the gutters. After Lige finished his chores with Carter's help, the two boys would race out into the backyard and play catch with whatever ball was lying about. They built forts with lawn furniture and devised schemes to torture Sally and her friends. "Let's 'ten-like we're firemen and the garage is on fire," Lige would say. Or "Let's 'ten-like you're Superman and I'm Batman!" He would yank a towel off the clothesline and secure it around his neck with a clothespin, and they'd climb the tree and leap to the ground, capes flying.

"That's 'pretend,' boys," Mrs. Ransom, the former English teacher, would offer when she heard his directives. "Not ''ten-like.'"

One day when they were ten years old, Carter and Lige went wading in Sugar Creek after a heavy rain. The creek was a small tributary of the Chickasaw River, and it cut a serpentine path through the country-club golf course on the edge of town, then meandered through the north side neighborhoods and the woods behind Carter's house. Under normal conditions the creek moved at little more than a trickle, but after a downpour it would overflow its banks, and the boys would wade into the swollen waters searching for golf balls washed downstream from the flooded water hazards and sand traps of the golf course. They would move with the current like minesweepers, their short pants rolled up, scouring the milky brown waters and massaging the muddy bottom with their bare feet until they felt the unmistakable roundness of a golf ball. If the Wilson or Titleist they hoisted with their toes was salvageable, not too disfigured with cracks and nicks, they would deposit it in the plastic bucket Lige carried and sell it to the country-club pro shop for a nickel.

On that day, they emerged from the creek bank near the road that bisected the golf course, and they spotted a noisy group of boys huddled around a shelf of rock under the overpass that crossed Sugar Creek. Carter recognized them as a rough crowd from the south end of town. They were smoking cigarettes and laughing and pointing at something on the creek bank below. Lige and Carter joined the neighborhood children who had gathered on the bridge to watch. The raucous boys below had captured a large turtle and dragged it up onto a rock. They were poking it with sticks to force the animal from its shell. Carter recognized the ringleader, Lacey Hullender, the biggest of the boys and oldest by a couple of years. Lacey was blind in one eye, having lost half his sight to a BB gun. Rumor had it that his drunken daddy shot it out. The eyelid was sewn shut. His handicap gave him an unsettling but oddly endearing way of cocking his head in order to see with his good eye. He was constantly surveying the peripheries, nervous about dangers unseen. Lacey had rigged up a gallows from an uprooted tree stump and was trying to wrap a length of clothesline around the turtle's neck. Lacey's comrades grew louder and more excited, shouting for the execution of the turtle.

Watching from the bridge, Carter felt his stomach clench. Then, without warning, something crashed into the water below with a loud splash, drenching the revelers. The startled boys snapped their heads toward the railing above. "Stop that!" The voice came from right beside Carter, and he was horrified to discover it belonged to Lige, who was hoisting a second cinder block over his head. "I said stop it!" The boys stood frozen on the creek bank. The one holding the turtle panicked at the sight of another cinder block aimed in his direction, and he lost his balance and his grip on the creature. As the boy staggered back over the rocks, the turtle slipped from the noose into the creek with a splash. When Hullender and the others lunged for the animal, Lige, like Zeus hurling thunderbolts from the heavens, launched the second cinder block, crashing it into the swift-moving stream between the boys and their prey. As the turtle disappeared downstream, the lynch mob shouted epithets at Lige. They tried to scramble up the steep banks after him, but the slippery red clay caused them to tumble back upon one another.

Carter sensed that Lige was going to stand his ground and face them down. "They got knives," he yelled at Lige. Carter could see the glint of steel flash from the pants pocket of Lacey Hullender, who bounded up the bank past his clumsy colleagues, cursing them for losing the turtle and now the nigger. Lige hesitated another second; then, ditching his bucket of golf balls, he broke out in a sprint across the road and disappeared into the woods. Carter followed.

"Hey, Car-turd," a red-faced and panting Lacey Hullender shouted, his good eye cocked toward him, "you better tell that little nigger his black ass is mine." As Carter disappeared into the trees, Lacey gave up the chase, calling out, "I'm gonna git him if it's the last thing I do!"

By the time Carter reached home, Lige was hiding out in the backyard tree house. Carter joined him and tried to coax him down, but Lige's red-rimmed eyes were fixed on a Red Ryder comic book, and he would not respond. Nettie tried to bribe him down with cookies and chocolate milk. He remained there all afternoon. Carter had given up, climbed down, and gone inside. "I don't know what's the matter with that boy," Nettie told Carter's mother. "He's so tetchy."

At the end of the day, Carter was sent to fetch Lige.

"Carter," he said, finally breaking his silence as his feet touched the ground. "I'm sorry."

"About what?"

"I left the bucket of golf balls back at the bridge."

"Pross!" The voice came from the trees lining the sandy beach. Carter turned and saw Lige lope down the embankment. He looked lean and muscular, and his face glistened with perspiration.

He and Carter hurled themselves at each other like linebackers and ricocheted in playful wrestling feints and grapplings until they clasped each other's forearms. "You made it," Carter said, checking his watch.

Lige looked at a nonexistent watch on his wrist. "CPT," he said. "Colored People's Time."

Lige was dressed as he had been at Magic Time, in overalls and T-shirt, and today he wore a red bandanna tied around his head. He removed the bandanna and dabbed at his forehead, taking in the surroundings. "Couldn't get away. Lots of activity at headquarters. The disappearance of the guys in Philadelphia has got everybody worked up. There's eight hundred volunteers up in Oxford, Ohio, ready to bus south for their assignments, and already we got three missing." Carter saw in Lige's dark eyes something he hadn't noticed before: maturity.

"Did you know them?" he said.

Lige's face was somber. "I know two of them. Mickey was pretty visible. He had a beatnik beard we used to tease him about. Some of the Klan had talked about getting him. Andy's a newcomer. Just got here from New York for the summer. I met him last week in Oxford. Chaney I didn't know, but he's from Meridian—a Negro hooked in with CORE."

Carter looked at his old friend as if at a stranger. He could not fathom Lige's enthusiasm for such a hazardous undertaking. He had read all about the Mississippi Summer Project—or Freedom Summer, as the organizers were calling it—in *Time*. Local newspapers were full of headlines like MISSISSIPPI MARKED FOR NEW INVASION and NEGROES ARMING FOR REVOLUTION: ARE YOU GOING TO SIT IDLY BY? His father simply shook his head at editorials that warned of student groups, biracial commissions, intellectuals and academics, organizations with acronyms like SNCC, NAACP, COFO, CORE, SCLC, radical idealists like the American Friends Service Committee and the American Civil Liberties Union, Communist-inspired anarchists and world savers, all of whom shared but a single goal: to bring Mississippi to its knees. Though not a defender of segregation per se, Judge Ransom considered them interlopers, "outside agitators" who were "looking for trouble."

"How did you get mixed up in all this?" Carter asked Lige. "I mean, I don't know what to say, and I don't presume to tell you what to do, but I've got to be honest, man—I understand your mother's concern for your safety."

Lige gave Carter a look of infinite patience.

"And I can't condone breaking the law," Carter continued. "I don't know—you weren't talking this way the last time I saw you. What's happened?"

"I went to seminary and studied the Bible just like Mama wanted," Lige said. "The Hebrew prophets, the Sermon on the Mount. But the only thing was, they also taught us about something called the social gospel. About how these things apply to real life. Not just the sweet by-and-by but the nasty now and now. You ever read Tolstoy on the Sermon on the Mount? I did. And Gandhi. And Thoreau on civil disobedience. I met some folks like me who realized those ideas we'd been reading about weren't just Sunday school memory verses but real-life, down-to-earth blueprints for social change."

Carter felt the blaze of commitment behind Lige's words, but he had no means of engaging with them. They didn't provide any traction for the rule-of-law arguments he had brought home from law school.

"Pross," Lige said, "remember that Halloween when Mama dressed us both up as ghosts and we went out trick-or-treating. Remember when old man Calvander saw my black skin under my costume and snatched back my candy—reached right into my bag and grabbed the Tootsie Roll he'd just given me."

"Calvander's a moron. Everybody knows that."

"Remember when you threw a tantrum back when we were real little because we couldn't drink from the same water fountain in Kress's?"

"I do."

"And how we played ball together all them years growing up—till Little League, and we had to be in different leagues? How y'all had uniforms and we didn't?"

"It's just the way things are" was all Carter could muster.

"It shouldn't be that way," Lige replied evenly, "and it doesn't have to be." He stood up and slipped off the straps of his overalls. By the time he made it down the promontory and onto the sandy beach, he was removing his T-shirt and underwear. He plunged into the clear waters of Naked Tail, disappeared for a few moments, and surfaced in the middle of the pool. "Come on in, Pross! I'll race you across the river." Carter had taught Lige to swim, but he remembered how it had stung after Elijah had a growth spurt in high school and began beating him.

Carter stripped down and dived from the mammoth roots of the oak into the darkest part of the pool. The cold hit him like a migraine, but he wasn't about to show it. He surfaced briefly when he was nearly beside Lige, then continued stroking toward the sandbar separating Naked Tail's still waters from the swift current of the river. The boyhood race had resumed. They reached the sandbar in a dead heat.

Standing in waist-deep water, Carter noticed scars on Lige's shoulders and back. There was an opening gouged into his scalp like a chalk mark, a shaved indentation that had recently been stitched.

"What happened to you, man?" Carter said.

"Battle scars, souvenirs." Pointing to the top of his head, Lige said, "Birmingham." Then, fingering a discolored scar in the shape of a check mark on his forehead, he said, "Montgomery." He craned his neck to glimpse the scar on his shoulder and back. "Parchman."

"Parchman prison?" Carter could not believe his friend had spent time in the notorious Mississippi state pen.

Elijah toppled backward into the water, floating on his back. "It's been a long road," he said, gazing up at the clouds.

Carter shoved off the sandbar and drifted toward Elijah.

"Believe it or not," Lige said, "it all began with you." Carter turned his head toward him, and Lige returned Carter's perplexed look with a taunting smile. "When we went with your daddy up to North Carolina to pick up that old grandfather clock." Carter's grandmother Ransom had passed away in Delaney, a small town in the eastern piedmont part of the state, and Judge Ransom's siblings had divided the estate. Mitchell Ransom arrived in a truck with Carter and Elijah, both strapping teenagers, and loaded the truck with a sideboard and a rolltop desk bequeathed to Mitchell along with a prized antique grandfather clock he had grown up with on the rural Ransom family estate. They spent all day Sunday and half of Monday packing up and clearing out the things that could not be sold, then headed home. Somewhere close to High Point, they decided they needed more rope to secure the tarp over the furniture, and they drove into town to search for a hardware store. "Woolworth's may have something," Carter's father said. He parked the truck and told the boys he would be back in a minute.

"Bring us a Coke, please," Carter called to his father. Standing on the sidewalk, stretching their legs, he and Lige saw a crowd gathering outside Woolworth's. Customers entered the store and came out whispering, but the boys couldn't hear what was being said. Soon Carter's father returned, carrying a reel of clothesline. He glanced back at the crowd as a police cruiser arrived and officers raced into the store.

Mitchell started up the truck and pulled into traffic, his expression troubled.

"Was it a holdup?" Carter asked.

"Those people look mad," Elijah said.

"The damndest thing," said Mitchell. "Some kind of protest. Students from a local Negro college."

"What were they protesting?" asked Carter.

"They were sitting at the whites-only lunch counter big as you please, ordering Cokes and sandwiches same as white folks. Since they were breaking the law, the manager closed the counter and I guess he called the police. The coloreds were sitting in the dark by the time I paid and left. I have to buy your Cokes at a service station."

They pulled into an Esso station, and while the attendant filled up the car, Mitchell went inside to get the boys their Cokes.

"Judge Ransom?" Lige said when he returned.

"Yes, Elijah."

"When you bought the Co'-Cola, did they know you were going to give it to a Negro?"

"They didn't ask me."

"Would you have been breaking the law buying me one?"

"No, son."

"Why not?"

"The crime is for white and colored to sit down together."

Lige looked at Carter, and Carter looked at Lige, squeezed in beside each other in the cabin of the truck. Then they both stared at the broken white line of the pavement dividing the road before them. The incident was not mentioned again.

Lige and Carter were now paddling toward the shallows. "That was fate reaching out to me, Carter," Lige said. "A year later I was in Nashville taking part in protests myself."

Carter remembered the North Carolina trip, but it wasn't the sit-in that remained most vivid. It was the two cute white girls who had walked by the truck while he and Lige were standing on the sidewalk waiting for the judge to return. Lige had whistled softly, just short of earshot, and nudged Carter. Carter was as hormone-addled as anyone else his age, but he found Lige's behavior unsettling, brazen. He had convinced himself that his irritation was not discomfort with the breaking of a racial taboo, but concern for Lige's safety.

Carter had read about the troubles in Nashville while he was a student there at Vanderbilt, but by then he and Lige had lost contact. It had not occurred to him that a relationship between them might exist outside the demilitarized zone of the Ransom household. Mitchell Ransom had paid Lige's tuition to seminary, but Carter had no idea his friend was being arrested in the same town where he was attending fraternity mixers and tailgating at football games. By then they had been swallowed up in the baroque machinery of separate-but-equal, and their estrangement was taken for granted by both of them.

"The first time I felt there was something I could do about the illogic and injustice of segregation was sitting in that truck with you, but when I got to Fisk, I discovered there was a lot of Negroes like me. A whole group of us there began talking about nonviolence as a means of social change." Lige saw Carter's troubled expression and said, "And those sit-ins led directly to the Freedom Rides."

"You were part of that, too?"

"Yes. I got involved my first year at school in Nashville. Now, that was scary, although I was late to the party. By the time I came on board, there'd already been trouble in Rock Hill, and then Anniston was the worst. They burned the bus. Mob set it on fire and blocked the exits. They were going to fry them all. If an undercover cop hadn't been on board and pulled his gun on the mob, they'd have been cooked." Carter remembered seeing the photograph of the incinerated bus outside Anniston, Alabama, in the Nashville newspaper. "Some of the CORE organizers got cold feet after that. That's when my group, Snick, got involved. I was part of the replacements." Lige pointed to his forehead. "Got this in Montgomery on the Freedom Rides."

Carter felt a humility that flirted with shame over the chasm between their college experiences. His crisis over dropping out of law school now seemed so insipid. "Look," he finally said, "it's your life. Your mama asked me to talk to you. You can't blame her for being protective, espcially since your dad passed."

Lige searched Carter's eyes. "I can understand my mama's disapproval. She brought me up to stay *out* of jail. She makes no distinction between being jailed for civil disobedience and being jailed for drunkenness or robbing a bank." His face clouded, and he looked away. "But I don't feel ashamed. The Movement's my family now."

"I'm family," said Carter.

Lige looked at him with something close to pity. "I can say that, Carter, but you can't." He dived under the water and came up smiling. "But you should have been there anyway, Brother Man."

The sound of a splash in the water nearby caused them to jerk their heads in the direction of the shore. "Just another bass," said Lige. All morning they'd watched the fish surge heroically into the air. A breeze loosened leaves from the oak and fluttered them to the surface of the water. Off in the distance a squirrel chattered. Then, in response to another splash, Carter and Lige turned toward shore. A girl was squatting on the water's edge, clasping her knees, pointing at them and laughing.

"Sarah," Lige shouted, and the dark-haired girl Carter had met at Magic Time picked up another rock from the riverbank, hurled it into the water. This time it landed a few yards from Carter.

"I was wondering when you'd notice me," she said with her hands on her hips. She wore a cream-colored sundress with a subtle floral print. Her hair was pulled up off her face. Carter thought she looked magnificent.

Lige was less enchanted with her sudden appearance. "What on earth are you doing here?" he shouted. "How'd you find us?"

"That wasn't hard. You left a trail plain as day, Tonto. Once I spotted the Fairlane, I just followed the bread crumbs."

Lige swam to shore and, signaling Sarah to turn around, scrambled up the bank, grabbed his clothes, and pulled on his underwear and his overalls.

"You know the rule is nobody goes out alone," she said.

Sarah had taken off her sandals and now edged forward into the sand of the beach. She picked up a stray tree branch lying in the sand, broke off a stick, and knelt down and began marking the sand with the point.

After a sufficient interval signaling his displeasure, Lige said, "Why did you really follow me here?"

Sarah exhaled and stopped stirring the sand with her stick. "The call came right after you left. They found their car," she said. "Blue Ford station wagon. It was pulled from a swamp just outside Philadelphia up in Neshoba County. No bodies were found. Just the car—charred, gutted. No sign of Mickey, J.E., or Andy. It'll be all over the news tonight."

"Damn!" Lige said. "I better get back."

"I thought you'd want to know."

"How'd you get here?"

"Same way you did. I drove."

"I didn't drive. I walked."

"Are you crazy?"

Lige explained that he had not walked down the highway, but had taken a shortcut from Magic Time along the river. He declined her offer to drive him back. "A black man and a white woman. Too risky."

She tossed her keys to Lige.

"How will you get back to Magic Time?" he said.

"I'll take her," said Carter, standing waist-deep in the water.

Sarah reported that Mickey Schwerner's wife was flying in. Lots of Movement folks from all over the country were assembling in Philadelphia.

Carter was already wondering what his father would say. He considered himself lucky to have gotten away unscathed with one visit to Magic Time. What if his car was seen there? And him, the son of a judge.

"Thanks, Brother Man," Lige said, slipping on his T-shirt. Then he scrambled up the bank and disappeared into the woods.

Carter had forgotten that he was stark-naked under the water, but when Sarah turned to appraise him, he suddenly became self-conscious.

"What is this place?" She indicated the lagoon before her.

"Naked Tail," Carter said.

"It certainly is." Sarah laughed and pointed at Carter's clothes lying on the ground at her feet.

"Lige and I used to come here when we were kids. Back then we didn't bring bathing suits or towels. Too much of a hike to pack a bag."

"It's pretty unusual down here for whites and Negroes to mix like that, right?"

"I don't know. I guess." Carter felt his hackles rise despite the absence of attitude in her voice. "His mother worked for my family, and we were around each other growing up." He checked himself from saying "almost family" and continued. "It was no big deal. Not like now when everything is so—so *political*."

"Sounds pretty natural to me." Sarah dipped her toe into the water. "Like Schwerner, Goodman, and Chaney."

"That's different. That's forced. They were looking for trouble."

"Like we are," Sarah said, wading in up to her ankles. "Lige and the rest of us."

"Hey, you said it."

Sarah sat down in the sand with both feet in the water. "I think we may have found it. Carter, have you ever heard of a man named Sam Bohannon?"

"Everybody knows Mr. Bohannon. He owns a catfish joint in town. Sambo's." Carter pointed out beyond the sandbar. "He also has a fish camp on the river a few miles north of here that's just open in the summer. We used to canoe up there when we were kids. I delivered his paper in town when I was a boy."

"Now that you're a reporter, why don't you investigate Sam Bohannon? Did you know he's the Imperial Wizard of the White Knights of the Ku Klux Klan?"

"Mr. Bohannon?" Carter laughed. He had always thought of the Ku Klux Klan as a joke until Lonnie had brought to school a pamphlet called *The Klan Ledger* he said had been tossed on his lawn. It was filled with racial and anti-Semitic propaganda and was printed, or so it claimed, by the local klavern. He and Lonnie had been out cruising the countryside late one night and had come upon a cross-burning in the middle of a field. But the small ragtag crowd of Kluxers looked like some Halloween dress-up, or one of those pitiful men's fraternal organizations like the one Ralph Kramden and Ed Norton belonged to on *The Honeymooners*.

"We think Bohannon is behind the death threats we've been getting," Sarah said. "And I wouldn't be surprised if he was mixed up in the disappearance of Goodman, Schwerner, and Chaney."

"Then why don't you go to the police?"

Sarah looked at him as if he were a cretin. "Sheriff Mizell in Troy? Yeah, right."

"He's a good guy."

"He was probably in on it."

Carter searched her face for signs she was joking.

"Mizell's Bohannon's lackey," she explained. "Probably a card-carrying Kluxer himself."

"I've known Mr. Bohannon my whole life," Carter said. "My family eats at his restaurants. My father would have nothing to do with him if he was a murderer. And Sheriff Mizell may be a Neanderthal, but he's no Kluxer." Mitchell dealt with Mizell all the time. They weren't close, but Judge Ransom respected him. Carter stared off into the trees along the path where Lige had disappeared minutes earlier. "Lige was telling me about his—uh . . . political activities."

"You know, Lige is the bravest person I've ever known. And the most modest. Unlike a lot of these Movement people." Carter noticed she pronounced "Movement" the way he'd heard Lige say it: *Move-mint*.

"Who's this Lloyd guy?"

"Charlie Lloyd? Oh, did he intimidate you?"

"Hell, yeah." Carter flashed what he hoped was an insincere smile.

"Oh, he has that effect on everybody."

"How long have you known him?"

"I knew him back in New York."

"Oh."

"Since I know you're wondering,' she said, punching each word lightly, "we didn't go out or anything. Although the standard greeting for the white female workers is, 'Have you put your body in the Movement?' " She looked at Carter's face and said, "Don't be shocked. Anyway, I met Charlie at a CORE function in New York. He's a pain, all right. He's hostile to me and competitive with Lige. You know, the Northern Negroes are always shocked when the Southern guys stand up to them."

She swiped her brow with her hand, then stood up and began flouncing her skirt to cool off. "I'm not like Lige. He and some of the others have already written out their wills. I'm a coward. That's why I carry a gun. I just wanted to help register voters. Damn, it's hot standing up here lecturing. Mind if I come in?"

The request took Carter by surprise. "No—not at all. Did you bring your suit?"

She widened her eyes briefly to register the point. "Just turn around." He did as she ordered, moving back out to the deeper water. Then he heard her shriek, splashing past him until, waist-deep, she could run no more. She dived beneath the surface and came up a few yards away, sputtering and laughing and shuddering. "Why didn't you tell me it was so cold?"

"You'll get used to it," Carter said. "I'm surprised a girl like you can swim."

"A girl like me? What would that mean? Would that mean a girl who was on the Fieldston swim team?" She splashed Carter. "Actually I was more a diver. You need a diving board out here."

"We used that tree," Carter said, pointing to the oak on the promontory. He and his friends used to dive from the branch with the rope dangling from it.

"I shall demonstrate," she announced. Sarah swam ashore and scrambled up the banks, revealing both to Carter's relief and disappointment that she had worn her bra and underpants in the water. She was slender, but Carter had not been able to appreciate how well-proportioned until now. Her legs were long and shapely, her waist narrow and her breasts full. Carter couldn't believe he was alone with this girl in this situation. After backing out onto the wide branch, she turned gracefully and without hesitation pushed out into a perfectly executed swan dive, knifing into the water at a 90-degree angle. Carter was so mesmerized by her confident performance that he couldn't take his eyes off the concentric circles rippling outward from her point of entry. She stayed under for an unusually long time. Then, just when he was beginning to worry, she surfaced a few yards away, looking back as if a fish had bitten her. "Uh-oh," she gasped.

"What's wrong?"

"My top came off. She rotated in the water 360 degrees, her eyes searching the lagoon.

Carter remained where he was, shoulder-deep, paralyzed as to what the proper role of a gentleman was in this situation.

"Well," she said, looking him straight in the eye, "are you going to help me or what?"

Carter dived in and swam underwater in her direction, surveying the murky bottom for the renegade bra. The water was reasonably clear, and he caught a glimpse of her slender white legs churning as she moved into his view, but her back was turned, and he caught no glimpse of her naked breasts. When he surfaced again a few yards away, Sarah said, "I think I saw it over there," pointing at a spot between them. He dived again and glided along the haze of sand and silt until he saw a hint of white. He went down to retrieve the undergarment and surfaced triumphantly, extending it like a speared trout.

"Thank you," Sarah said primly, but with a smile, as she effected the transfer, then turned her back, slipped it on, and fastened it into place.

"So," Carter said, careful to look the other way, "what do you do when you're not losing your underwear or saving the world?"

"I read," Sarah answered.

"*Anna Karenina.*"

"How observant." Sarah sounded impressed.

"You like the Russians?" he asked.

"I like Tolstoy."

"How about Dostoevsky? If I had to have one book with me on a desert island, it would be *The Brothers Karamazov.*"

She pitched her head back and spit a stream of water into the air. "Too cranky, too religious."

Carter flared. "And Tolstoy wasn't? Is there anything you don't have an opinion on?" He began backstroking away toward the sandbar.

Sarah considered his question, then answered matter-of-factly, "No."

"Boy, you're something else—coming down here from New York City to straighten us out. Oh, and it's a Garden of Eden up there."

"Ever been there?"

"No."

"You're an expert, then!"

The truth was, Carter spent a lot of time daydreaming about getting out of Troy and moving to New York. His hometown had always felt to him like spiritual Thorazine. Only years later would he realize that he had been a literary cliché, lying in bed at night listening to the train whistles in the distance and dreaming of far-off places—anywhere but Troy, but especially New York City. He had learned that *Mad* magazine's offices were on Lexington Avenue (where they made fun of the ad-men on Madison Avenue) and that Holden Caulfield and the Glass children in J. D. Salinger's novels had grown up on the Upper East Side.

Sarah lowered her chin until her mouth just cleared the surface. "Look," she said, "are you going to ask me out on a date or what?"

"Good God," he said. "You're presumptuous."

"Well, I mean, that's what this is all about, isn't it?"

"Are all Yankee girls this . . . bold?"

She laughed. "Only in the South would a Jewish girl from New York be called a Yankee. Have you ever been out with a Jew before?"

Carter stalled, feeling perhaps there was something wrong with him that he hadn't.

"You haven't. What religion are you, anyway?"

"Baptist."

"Well, are Baptists not allowed to date Jews?" Sarah seemed to be enjoying herself, but then she lowered her voice to signal the end of the joust. "Lige says you're talented at writing and music," she said. "I wanted to be a folksinger and move to the Village. But my father's a professor. My mother's in analysis. I grew up privileged, culchahed, overeducated."

"Greenwich Village? That's where I want to go someday. To the Café Wha? and Gerde's Folk City. I want to hear Bob Dylan and Joan Baez; Phil Ochs; Peter, Paul and Mary."

"You like folk?" She sounded incredulous. "Who would have thought a Mississippi boy like you would get our music."

He fell back into the water, laughing at the absurdity of their conversation. "It's folk music. People's music. I may be from Mississippi, but since when am I not people?"

His taste in music seemed to have made Sarah reappraise him. "Why don't you come with us to register voters?"

"You're crazy. Are you kidding?" He tried to look as aghast as he felt.

"We could use a clean-shaven white boy with a Southern accent. All we've got are Jew boys with goatees and Brooklyn accents."

"No, uh-uh." He laughed again in disbelief. "My father would kill me. He's already practically disowned me."

"Cover it for your newspaper."

"I don't think so."

"You should see what it's like, talking to these people," she said. "If I were a writer, I'd want to leave behind a record of this. Old people in their sixties and seventies who've never voted before, learning how to write their names in order to register. Their hands tremble. And the ones who come up after church or a meeting and press a dollar in my hand—and you know they have no money—and say, 'I've waited eighty years for you to come, and I just have to give you this little bit to let you know how much we appreciate you coming.'"

For the first time, Carter could sense the heart beating underneath the bravado.

"Come with us next time, Carter. Lige'll look after you." Sarah had drawn nearer as she made her case, and they were standing face-to-face. Carter had forgotten his self-consciousness about being naked. Their bodies were inches apart. "Mississippi's the middle of the iceberg," she said. "This is the turning point. If we can crack Mississippi—"

She stopped in mid-sentence, as if she suddenly remembered whom she was talking to. "Well, I guess it's time we got back to Magic Time, *Mistah* Ransom," she said, Scarlett O'Hara again. She turned her back to him and headed toward the shore. "Now, look away while I get out and get dressed."

Carter again did as he was told and stood gazing out at the river beyond the sandbar and watching the swifter-moving currents of the Little Chickasaw. He thought about her suggestion that he cover their activities for the newspaper. After first dismissing it, he found himself intrigued by the outrageousness of the idea. But he wasn't sure he could justify it to Mr. Callahan or to himself, or define his emerging ardor, whether it was for her or for a story bound to end up on the front page, sooner or later, even in Troy.

7

U NDER NETTIE'S AGGRESSIVE DIETARY REGIMEN, Carter began putting the pounds back on, and the color returned to his face. If his physical progress was steady, the interior path to recovery consisted of dead ends and collisions with reality, tricked by occasional mirages of normalcy. One day, he would feel better, energetic enough to play catch with Willie in the backyard; the next day, depressed, morose, withdrawn.

Carter's feelings of hopelessness were aggravated by his guilt that the hopelessness was self-inflicted. The reason he was not with Emily— the reason he was, in fact, with no one—was his inability to claim her. His depression had hardened into paralysis. It stopped him from being a mensch and simply calling Emily to let her know he was in good hands. Sally had told him that Emily had visited him several times in the hospital, but the only contact he could recall after his collapse was a phone conversation in which she said she still cared about him, but "if I could help you, I already would have." Essentially, she was telling him that it was his battle, not theirs. She was agnostic about how it would turn out. It was just out of her hands.

Sally had clued Carter in, with a minimum of guilt-tripping, that she and Emily were in touch by phone. Apparently, the museum scare had

had one beneficial effect: opening up Emily's ex-husband to the responsibilities of fatherhood. She had told Sally that Josh would be spending more time with his dad when school let out. If Carter was feeling up to it in a few weeks, Josh would welcome a phone call.

Sally urged Carter to contact Dr. Abernathy, the Atlanta psychiatrist he had once seen, but he resisted. The shrink-accessible part of what he was going through seemed almost too obvious, the recapitulation of the traumas too exact. He felt the need to experience the blackness for a time before talking about it. He had stopped taking the medication.

"Somebody here to see you," Nettie announced, rapping gently on the guest-room door.

"Are visiting hours over?" said a mischievous male voice.

Nestled in a backrest of pillows, Carter looked up from his dog-eared copy of James Thurber's *The Years with Ross.* "Stephen! What are you doing in Troy?"

"Testing Thomas Wolfe's theory—same as you. Sorry about the circumstances that brought you back, though, Pross."

Stephen Musgrove, slender and ethereal, with a shaggy mop of brown hair, wide green eyes, and a lopsided grin, had changed little since high school. He wore a stylish herringbone sports jacket over a black T-shirt that matched the penny loafers he wore sockless. "I brought you some of my world-famous chocolate chip cookies, Carter." He presented a green Tupperware container topped with tinfoil, and leaned over to hug Carter. Pulling up an ottoman to sit on, he said, "Sally told me you were home."

"I thought you were in Hollywood," said Carter, removing the foil from the cookies. Stephen was one of his very few Mississippi friends who, like him, had managed to escape to the big city. He had studied piano and composition at Juilliard and remained in New York to make his mark in musical theater. Having struggled for years writing scores for shows that sometimes made it out of workshop into regional theaters, he finally had a hit in the early eighties, a musical comedy called *Cut 'n' Curl*, about murder in a beauty parlor, set in a small, Troy-like Mississippi town. It had run for a year off-Broadway before moving to Broadway. The two Mississippi refugees had caught up with each other when

Carter moved to the city, but soon after, Stephen had left for Hollywood to write scores for Disney animated films.

"I took an early retirement from show business," Stephen said. "Moved back a few months ago. Didn't Sally tell you? Mother's getting on, and there's nobody else to take care of her." He spoke in a honey-dipped baritone that seemed larger somehow than Stephen himself. "I'd been touring nonstop in the stage band with a friend's show for the last year and figured I could use a break."

"How's Miz Nell doing?" Carter asked, sinking his teeth into a still-warm cookie.

"Not good." Stephen sighed. "Alzheimer's. She's deteriorated since I've been home. Can't remember her name, where she is."

"Your mama deserved better," said Carter. Nell Marie Musgrove had been the town's much-revered music teacher, the organist at First Baptist Church for as long as Carter could remember, and a force of nature known widely as Miz Nell, the Southern Belle from Hell.

Stephen never knew his father, who had been killed in World War II and had received posthumous Bronze and Silver Stars. The town had embraced the young widow and her aspiration to bring music to the children of Troy, whether they had any talent or not.

"Well, Mother remains the eternal debutante," Stephen said. "The one thing she always remembers is not to leave the house without putting on heels and makeup." He checked his watch. "I can't stay long. A neighbor's keeping an eye on her while I'm gone." Stephen looked into Carter's eyes. "I'm so sorry I haven't gotten over sooner, Pross. Sally told me you aren't doing so well."

"I'll be okay."

"She told me you'd say that, too."

Seeing his boyhood friend lifted Carter's spirits more than the drugs had been able to, but he felt uncomfortable in his new role as a focus of concern. Uncertain how to handle it, he did the only thing he knew to do: play reporter. "You're the last person I would have thought would come back to Troy," said Carter.

"Same here," Stephen said. "I doubt I would have if it wasn't for Mother's condition. Being here for her is so poignant. Every day, she insists that I do her makeup, and she keeps asking me, 'Stephen, when are you going to get married?' I say, 'Mama, you know I'm gay.' I came out to her years ago, even introduced Jimmy to her when we found out he had AIDS, but she keeps forgetting. She gasps and starts hyperventilating and fanning herself. And we have to go through it all over again. I came out to her every day for a month, till finally I said, 'Mama, I'm not getting married, because you're the only girl for me.' "

When they were growing up, Carter didn't know his friend was homosexual. People didn't speak of such things. Stephen was popular and athletic as well as musically gifted. They had met in Sunday school at First Baptist Church. As a kindergartner, Carter had noticed that the church organist's son—the shy little boy wearing short pants, kneesocks, and a bow tie in his Sunbeams class—stammered excessively when called on to recite a Bible verse but sang the class theme song with louder confidence than all the others. *"A sunbeam, a sunbeam, Jesus wants me for a sunbeam . . ."* Stephen had learned to deal with his speech impediment by playing it up, beating would-be tormenters to the punch. In high school, as the student council member delegated to read the morning announcements over the intercom, he would turn routine recitations of club meeting notices and special chapel events into Porky Pig shtick, intentionally getting stuck on certain words: "The school cafeteria manager doesn't want to be a dick . . . dick . . . dick . . . dictator about this, but she asks you to please replace your condom . . . condom . . . condiments."

At Troy High, as the first male in the school's history to get chosen (on a dare) for the all-girl cheerleading squad, Stephen would hoist the bright green megaphone to his lips to spell out TROJANS and cheerfully shout to the stands: "Give me a Tuh-Tuh-Tuh-Tuh-TEE!" And in unison, the crowd would answer, "Tuh-Tuh-Tuh-Tuh-TEE!" Within a year or two of leaving home, Stephen had begun to talk with the silky resonance of an NPR commentator.

"Mama's a handful all right," he said. "But when she turns in at night, I get some work done. I've been composing. First time I've felt inspired since Jimmy died."

"So has there been anyone else?" Carter asked. James Hertz had been Stephen's creative as well as life partner. He had written the book and lyrics for *Cut 'n' Curl.*

"I've resigned myself to a life of celibacy. Just like when I was growing up. I associate Mississippi with sexual abstinence. It's practically Pavlovian now. But I swear, Troy's become one big floating cocktail party. There's always some celebrity coming through, either for the college or to read at your sister's bookstore. It's changed since we were kids, Carter." Stephen got up and moved to the window. "And not all for the better. Crime's up. Drugs in the junior high schools. You can't leave your doors unlocked at night like you used to. That's why I'm going to be armed."

"Armed?"

"Believe it or not, I've been spending time on the firing range."

"You're kidding."

"I'm serious. Target practice. I mean, things have changed some for the better, but it's still Mississippi for a gay man who'll be living alone soon. Lonnie introduced me to a retired cop who teaches women self-defense techniques and handgun safety."

Carter felt a smile coming on for the first time in weeks. "There's so much wrong with this picture."

"I know," Stephen said, grinning. "When I go to class, I tell Mama I'm taking a course in advanced macramé at Troy U. continuing ed."

"THEN SINGS MY SOOOOUL, . . ." A raucous crooning rang out from the hallway. *"My Savior God, to Theeeeeeee!"* The door flew open. *"How great Thou arrrrt . . . How great Thou arrrrt!"*

A short, stocky bearded man stepped into the room, bellowing at the top of his brassy tenor, one arm lifted heavenward, head tilted back. *"Then sings my soooooullll,"* he started in again. *"My Savior God, to Theeeeeeee . . ."* Carter and Stephen covered their ears as the singer approached the foot of the bed and stood before them, arms and legs spread triumphantly, to conclude his rendition of the Billy Graham Crusade hymn made famous by the legendary baritone George Beverly Shea. *"HOW GREAAAAT THOU AAARRRRRRRT!"*

"Jimbo Stein, you sorry son of a bitch!" Stephen said, his face contorted in pain. "You ruined a perfectly good song and nearly punctured my eardrum!"

"Are you done?" asked Carter.

"Why the hell didn't y'all join in?" Jimbo said. "That's a friggin' sacred standard!"

"Jesus, Jimbo," Stephen said, "not here, for God's sake. Not now." He raised his forefinger to his lips and nodded in Carter's direction. "Our friend is trying to rest."

Carter winked dutifully at Jimbo.

"How the hell are you, big guy?" Jimbo said, approaching Carter and pinching his cheek like a little boy's long-lost uncle. "Pross." He held Carter's chin up for inspection. "You never write. You never call. I have to learn this from your sister."

"Thanks for dropping by, Jimbo," said Carter. "Always a pleasure to play your straight man. How's it going?"

"How does it look like it's going?" Jimbo asked, stepping back and twirling on his heels, showing off his light gray Italian-cut suit, which hung on his stubby frame like a pup tent. "It's just off-the-rack Armani," he said. "I'm slumming today." He shot the cuffs of his peach shirt.

"Sally says you're in computers now," said Carter. "But there's got to be some other reason why you're dressing like a pimp."

"It's the future, Pross. Jimbo Stein is always on the cutting edge."

"Like that Nehru jacket outlet he got into right out of college," Stephen said.

Jimbo raised his hand in contrition.

"And it seems I recall a chain of discos you wanted to open in towns across the state in the seventies?" Carter added. "Towns that barely had Coke machines."

"You were always ahead of your time, Jimbo," said Stephen. "Did I ever tell you that?"

"Yeah, but you were ahead of your time when you told me, so I didn't listen."

"Actually, Jimbo's really done well," Stephen said to Carter. "He opened a campers' outfitting shop in the late seventies in Hattiesburg before it was hip."

Stein dug his toe in the carpet. "Now hush," he said.

"And now this computer gig of his is really going gangbusters."

Jimbo tousled Stephen's hair, then grabbed him in a hammerlock as he explained. "I got in on the ground floor. Read all those prophecies about the electronic revolution. The information highway. The third wave of technology. And I decided I was gonna surf that wave. Cowabunga!"

"Isn't selling computers in Mississippi like opening a barbecue joint in the Catskills?" said Carter.

"PCs, laptops, VCRs, satellite dishes, whatever you need. Hey, you've got to come by the store. Daddy's retired from selling Christmas-tree ornaments to the goyim, and he's bored shitless, so he and Mama're working for me at the shop. By the way, she sent along this card." Jimbo handed Carter an envelope from his breast pocket, a get-well note from his mother. Evelyn Stein's neat, cursive concern over Carter's health was also an expression of the gratitude that mothers of misfits and outsiders had for boys like Carter who befriended their sons during their belea-guered childhoods. Carter and Jimbo's friendship had been sealed on the playground in sixth grade when Carter was choosing sides as cap-tain of one of the softball teams and picked Jimbo early enough in the selection process to elicit groans from his teammates. "He's a Jew," Carter overheard someone whisper as they moved onto the field. "They crucified our Lord."

"Tell your mom I said thanks for this note, Jimbo," Carter said.

"Hey, we've all been thinking about you, buddy." Jimbo reached over and squeezed Carter's shoulder. "When you feel up to it, I'm going to take you dove hunting up the Little Chickasaw and into the Bogue Homa." Jimbo Stein had grown up to become an enthusiastic out-doorsman and hunter, with a gallery of glassy-eyed bucks mounted over his fireplace. "I want to take y'all out in my new all-terrain vehicle," he said. "You, too, Stephen. You can come along with us now that you're armed and dangerous."

Carter smiled at the thought of what his Upper West Side cronies would make of his friends, this tableau of "diversity" according to Ten-nessee Williams.

Another voice called up from the stairwell. "Carter, are you decent?"

Stephen got up and moved to the door. "Carter's naked as a jay-bird," he called down. "Who wants to know?"

"It's me, Lonnie," the voice replied. "We're coming up."

"We who?" Stephen said.

Nettie opened the door, and Lonnie Culpepper leaned into the door-way, holding a large white paper cup with a red straw. "One Wad's cherry Coke, with extra ice, for Mr. Carter Ransom." Lonnie, with a golfer's tan and thinning auburn hair, was dressed in a conservative dark blue business suit that slenderized his athletic bulk without quite civilizing the piney woods residue of his tough upbringing. Lonnie was now a partner in the law firm founded by Carter's father: Ransom, Davis and Culpepper. "Hey, buddy, can we come in?" he asked with a sympathetic smile that conveyed a subtle territoriality. "I got somebody here wants to meet you."

Lonnie held the door, and Carter was startled to see an attractive woman enter behind him. She wore a tailored celery-green suit over a pink silk blouse, her blond hair pulled back in a French braid. "This is Sydney Rushton, from the attorney general's office," said Lonnie. "I brought her by to meet you, Carter, maybe help us cheer you up."

Carter nodded to the visitor, whom he recognized from her picture in the newspaper, and averted an involuntary glance at her above-the-knee skirt. He was wondering how Lonnie thought his spirits might be improved by someone who had a role in setting Lacey Hullender free.

"It's my solemn duty," Lonnie explained, "to escort Ms. Rushton around town and help her meet whoever might be of help to her. She's spearheading the state's new prosecution of the Shiloh Church bomber case."

"I read about you in *The Troy Times*," said Carter, taking her ex-tended hand.

"And I've read about you. Or should I say 'read you,'" Sydney said. "I was a summer associate in Atlanta at King and Spaulding when you were writing your column for the *Atlanta Constitution*. I'm a fan."

Lonnie leaned down and hugged Carter. "How you feeling, Pross? I've been worried about you."

"I'll be all right. How's Loretta and the kids, Lonnie?"

"Fine. You won't believe the girls. Tall as their mama." He walked over to a corner of the room, picked up the Gibson, and handed it to Stephen, who strummed a G chord. On one of his better days Carter had tuned it.

Jimbo leaned into Stephen insistently until he joined him on the last few bars of "How Great Thou Art," and together they coaxed Lonnie into adding his resonant bass to the harmonies they had long ago perfected as young gospel singers. *"Then sings my soooooullll . . . My Savior God, to Thee . . ."* As their voices rose triumphantly, they encouraged Carter to join in, but he shook his head, settling back against the pillows to listen.

Jimbo dropped to one knee before Sydney Rushton. *"How great Thou arrrt, How greaaat Thouuu arrrrrt!"* He then stood and declared, "Madame, you have just heard the twenty-fifth reunion of three-quarters of the Goyim Brothers Gospel Quartet. The Goys of Troy."

"Boys of Troy," said Stephen.

"Whatever," Jimbo continued. "Mississippi state champions of the 1961 Gospel Jubilee Quartet Competition held at First Baptist Church, Jackson. If ol' Carter here had held up his vocal end of the deal, you'd have gotten the full and glorious effect. But he's been under the weather of late, and it may have been too much for you to endure anyway. Best you didn't hear us all, or you would have been ripping off our clothes and ravaging our bodies."

Sydney Rushton was laughing with her mouth closed.

"Hey, this is like the scene from *The Wizard of Oz!*" said Jimbo. "Carter's Dorothy; and Lonnie, Stephen, and me, we're the farmhands." Then he climbed into bed beside Carter and, in a high-pitched voice, said to the assembled gathering, "And you were there, Lonnie . . . and you, too, Stephen. And Toto and Nettie, and the beautiful prosecutor from the attorney general's office, and . . . and . . . Oh, Auntie Em! Auntie Em!"

Carter shoved Jimbo off the bed as the laughter died down.

Lonnie said to Carter, "I hope you're here for the big shindig. You know, the firm's fortieth and the judge's seventieth birthday. You, too, Sydney."

"Oh, I expect I'll be around," she said. "The trial is scheduled for soon after Labor Day."

"Did you see that Hullender's getting out this Friday?" Lonnie asked, taking the newspaper off the night table and handing it to Carter.

"Speaking of homecomings," said Jimbo.

"I saw," Carter said.

"Just the kind of person we all want to see walking around on the streets," said Stephen. "Your father should be canonized for sending him to prison."

"They say he's a new man," said Carter somewhat sourly, for Sydney Rushton's benefit.

Jimbo snorted. "Oh yeah, a new man. I heard he had a penis transplant, but the penis rejected him."

"He used to call me faggot and homo," said Stephen. "I'd never even heard those words—and didn't know I was one."

"World-class prick," said Jimbo.

Stephen said, "He sure hated your guts, Carter. And then your father sends him to prison."

Carter glanced at Lonnie's guest, who had been listening quietly to the discussion. "I suspect Ms. Rushton here may have had something to do with his release," he said.

"Call me Sydney," the assistant attorney general said to Carter. "I can't comment on that officially to a journalist, you know that. But off the record, we expect Hullender will be helpful for the case we're putting together against Bohannon."

"Well, Sam Bohannon's a worthy target," said Stephen, "but Hullender's a piece of work, too. I just hope the attorney general knows what he's doing letting him out."

"It was my case and my call," Sydney said. "We wouldn't be releasing him if we thought there was any danger."

"And how well do you know Lacey Hullender, Sydney?" Carter replied.

Lonnie interrupted. "The sheriff's been alerted, Carter, but honestly, your dad doesn't seem too concerned."

"He may not be the best judge of the danger," said Carter. "My father took away twenty years of this man's life. What if Hullender wants my father to pay for that?" Carter was surprised at the energy he was able to summon on the topic.

"I understand your concern, Carter," Sydney replied, "but we and the parole board gave every consideration to Hullender's history. As you pointed out, he's been locked up for twenty years. He hasn't exactly walked away from his crimes unscathed. And he met all the criteria for release."

"What criteria?" asked Jimbo.

"He's gone through all the stations of the cross as far as rehabilitation is concerned. For the last seven years he has had no infractions for violence. He worked in the prison library, got his GED high school equivalency, and has taken college-level courses. He's been a model prisoner, not just for a few months, but for years. Hullender has qualified for parole on every count."

"Because he claims to have found religion?" asked Jimbo.

Sydney's eyebrows lifted in skepticism. "I'm sure the fact that he led services on Sundays had some influence on the board. After all, this is the Bible Belt. But it wouldn't have cut any ice with me. I formed my decision purely on the merits."

"Well, I hope he's helpful to you, Sydney," said Jimbo, "because he's as worthless a human being as I've ever known."

"What about Sam Bohannon?" she asked with a slight edge. "May I assume all of you would like to see the mastermind responsible for the Shiloh Church bombing—and dozens of other crimes—behind bars?"

"They tried to get Bohannon before, remember?" Carter said. "But he walked."

"He did some time," said Jimbo.

"For federal civil rights violations," Carter said, and then turned to Sydney. "Two sets of prosecutors before you haven't been able to make murder charges stick. What makes you think you'll be any different?"

Sydney looked at him for a few moments before giving her answer. "Because I don't like to lose," she said. "He's a murderer, and he's never been held accountable for his crimes. And time's running out." There was a studied, youthful, hard-assed quality about her that both impressed and challenged Carter. Just as he was beginning to feel some of his reporter's metabolism kick in, his sister appeared at the door.

"What is this—a class reunion?" Sally said, with Nettie peering over her shoulder. "Okay, everybody, thanks for dropping by, but shoo, shoo, shoo." She moved into the room waving her hands like feather dusters. "I hate to be the big, bad spoilsport, but Carter needs to rest."

Stephen and Jimbo leaped to their feet as if they had been caught smoking in the boys' room, even though they had come at Sally's urging.

"And so do we," said Lonnie, rising deliberately and kissing Sally on both cheeks, continental-style, then gallantly offering Sydney his arm. "After that command performance of the Boys of Troy, we all need a rest."

The visitors filed past Sally while Nettie checked the thermostat and fluffed Carter's pillows. Bringing up the rear, Lonnie said, "Sal, have you met my colleague, Sydney Rushton, with the state attorney general's office?"

"No," said Sally, smiling and offering her hand, "but I've read about her."

"Lonnie was nice enough to bring me by to meet your brother," Sydney said. "I hope, when he's feeling better, to get a chance to talk with him about the Shiloh case."

Carter heard his sister say to Sydney in a lowered voice, "I really don't think he'll be in any shape to talk about that for a good long while."

Lonnie interceded. "Sydney just wants to discuss some background on the case with Carter at some point down the road, since he knew the—uh—principals."

Nettie closed the door behind them, but Carter could hear them talking in the hallway. He closed his eyes and sank into the softness of the pillows, listening to their hushed voices grow fainter, knowing that the subject was, once again, Sarah.

8

S INCE INFORMING his father that he was dropping out of law
school, Carter had been working at *The Troy Times*, just as he had
every summer since high school, writing obituaries and covering city
hall, the county commission, the school board, local sports—until he
could come up with a plan for what to do with his life. Pete Callahan
had taken Carter under his wing, assuming the boy was destined to become a lawyer but grateful for his resourcefulness in a profession that
didn't always attract the sharpest tacks on the bulletin board.

Spring had turned to summer, and Carter had still not told Nettie or
his parents that he had been in touch with Lige. Instead, he approached
Callahan about doing a story on the civil rights workers in Ellis County.

When Carter appeared in his office, Callahan leaned back in his
swivel chair behind an antique mahogany desk stacked with newspapers. He lowered his smudged glasses and peered at Carter
with pterodactyl eyes. Callahan was like something out of *The Front
Page*, with his ill-fitting suits, coffee-stained ties, salt-and-pepper
buzz cut, and matching day-old stubble. He spoke in a steady stream of
U.S. Marine Corps–honed profanity and the jaundiced aphorisms of
the fourth estate. "I was born in the middle of the night," he would
mutter in disgust over some politician's lie, "but not *last* night." His

brutal candor was legendary. He once described a recently elected Miss Ellis County as "so ugly she could haunt a nine-room house from across the street," unaware that she was the niece of the society editor who was proudly showing him the photo running in her section. Carter had thus far dodged Callahan's standard retort to bad copy: "He couldn't write shit with a turd in both hands."

Callahan bounced his right knee up and down like a jackhammer as Carter stood in the office, making his case. When listening to a story pitch, Callahan would always take a deep drag on his cigarette. The cigarette was like an egg timer. You had only as long as he could hold the smoke in his lungs to spit out whatever you had to say. In the event of an unnecessarily long verbal drumroll for a story idea, Callahan would shoot smoke through his nose and, alluding to the loquacious circus ringmaster who oversells his star attraction, say, "Bring on the dancing bear, son, bring on the bear."

The Troy Times, a small-town daily dedicated to "Covering Dixie Like the Dew," had reported on what was being called Freedom Summer with wire copy, under headlines like STATE FACES RACE AGITATION. Pete Callahan was no crusading liberal, and he viewed the influx of "outside agitators" as the last thing the state needed—disruptive elements in an already volatile mix of street demonstrations, NAACP lawsuits, and a civil rights bill rammed through Congress by LBJ. He had recently published an editorial titled "With Dignity and Restraint," criticizing the idea of Freedom Summer but admonishing his white readers that "while there is much to resent in this summerlong program, there is nothing to fear and, most certainly, nothing to justify intemperate action or reaction on the part of any citizen of Troy, Ellis County, or Mississippi."

Appealing to his boss's professionalism, Carter argued that because the disappearance of the three civil rights workers had thrust Mississippi into the glare of the national spotlight, the *Times* would simply look bush-league if it didn't cover at least the search for the bodies in Neshoba County—the FBI dragging rivers, and teams of military personnel combing the swamps of east Mississippi. Readers were also going to be curious about the white college students who had swarmed into the state. As he took a sip from his cup of diesel-grade coffee, Callahan's first response to Carter's proposal was, "I don't mind readers throwing rocks at me, Ransom, but I don't believe in handing them the rocks." He wouldn't promise anything until he saw what Carter came up with. "If it's any good, I'll run it," he said through a cloud of smoke from the Camel dangling off his lower lip. "But probably not on the front page."

"How much space will you give me?" Carter pressed.

"Four Troy cops."

Carter grinned, pleased that a story he covered a couple of summers earlier had entered newsroom lore. When a local policeman was charged with the statutory rape of a fourteen-year-old girl, his lawyer had offered a novel defense: his client could not have committed the crime in the backseat of the squad car as charged, because, given the position and angle from which the girl claimed to have been assaulted, his client's penis was too small to have completed the act. The judge ordered the officer's privates measured, and a court-appointed physician testified that the alleged assault weapon, even fully tumescent, was indeed only three inches long. Ever since, the *Times* editor measured copy length by that unique standard—a Troy cop. Four Troy cops was a twelve-inch story. An extended feature or series was the entire Troy police force.

Callahan's parting injunction to Carter was, "Remember, you're writing for the average Mississippian. And the average Mississippian is below average."

Early one morning the following week, Carter drove back out to Magic Time. He, Lige, and Sarah crowded into a white '54 Ford station wagon with the quiet, bespectacled Randall Peek, the sullen Charlie Lloyd, and the white boy in the clerical collar, Daniel Johnston. They were headed out into the county to register voters.

"You here to help?" Randall asked as Carter joined him in the backseat, with Sarah sandwiched between.

"Carter's going to do a write-up for the local paper," said Lige from behind the wheel. "He's here as an observer."

Carter nodded and tried to appear suavely professional, but he was nearly undone by the pressure of Sarah's knee against his in the tight legroom of the backseat.

"It'll be a breakthrough if we can get the local press to lift its black-out on the Movement," said Randall.

"I don't trust the white media," Charlie Lloyd said from the front seat.

"I can't promise the story will run," Carter said, addressing the back of Charlie's head.

"Can you promise it'll get written?" Charlie replied, not turning around.

"I can promise that."

Charlie gave an elaborate sigh. "I just don't know why we need another white face in this car. We're vulnerable enough with Johnston and the Princess."

"Hey, Dexter chose not to come along," Sarah said. "Carter took his place. Don't hold that against him."

Charlie Lloyd turned for the first time and looked at Carter. "Dex don't work with white people if he don't have to," he enunciated. Carter got the impression that the "don'ts" were an affectation.

"I invited my friend to join us today to take a look at what we're doing," said Lige evenly, "if that's all right with you, Charlie."

"Your friend? You mean your mama cooks and cleans for his mama, don't you?"

Lige let the remark drop. Carter noticed that Lige seemed worried and distracted. He and Dexter had just returned from Neshoba County, where they had taken part in the search for the missing civil rights workers. Lige eased the wagon out onto the highway. "People are afraid of what they don't understand," he said. "And Carter can help tell our story to the readers of The Troy Times. Besides, I kinda like traveling with white folks. I got used to it on the Freedom Rides. In my opinion it increases our chances of survival."

"It makes us even more of a target," Charlie Lloyd said, looking out the window.

It was sunny but breezy, cool for that time of day. Early morning showers had taken the edge off the July heat. Their first stop was Shiloh

Baptist Church, a white clapboard building with a squat, square cupola and a puny steeple rising not much higher than the roofline. It was set back off the road in a stand of sweet gum and scrub pine. The Little Chickasaw and the turnoff to Naked Tail were less than half a mile away. They got out of the car, and Lige introduced Carter to the Reverend Curtis Bunt, who awaited them in the dusty gravel parking lot. "Reverend Bunt has agreed to let us hold voter drive meetings here at his church on Monday nights."

"Freedom Mondays," said Bunt as he looked over the mimeographed form Lige handed him.

"And we are mighty grateful," said Lige. "First and third Tuesdays of the month, the registrar's office is open in Troy, and we want to get people ready the night before. We're going to have them lined up around the block at the courthouse."

Bunt was a large, barrel-chested black man with short-cropped gray hair and small, soot-black eyes set close together over a broad slab of a nose. Perspiration darkened the armpits of his short-sleeved white dress shirt and matted it at the small of his back.

"Reverend Bunt was a marine in the Pacific during the war," Lige said. Carter had noticed a red and blue tattoo of the Marine Corps motto SEMPER FI glistening on the veined muscles of his forearm.

Bunt raised his pant leg and pointed to a jagged white scar on his calf. "I caught shrapnel at Iwo Jima fighting for freedom. I reckon I can keep fighting in Ellis County." He glanced toward the modest parsonage next door. "Of course, my wife's a little nervous about all this, but she'll come around." Carter saw a figure at the window curtain draw back into the shadows when they looked in her direction.

Lige handed Bunt a stack of registration forms to pass out. The SNCC volunteers would come back at seven Monday evening to help folks fill them out. "We'd appreciate you mentioning it in your sermon Sunday, too, if you don't mind," Lige said.

"Mention it? I'm preaching my whole sermon Sunday on 'Render unto Caesar.'"

As they returned to the car where the others were waiting, Lige tapped Carter's notebook and explained that the number of voting-age

Negroes who had actually registered to vote in the state was five percent. "One percent in Ellis County," he said. "Imagine that. And Mississippi with the largest Negro population in America."

"Reverend Bunt lets us use his fellowship hall for our Freedom School," Sarah said. "I've been teaching kids remedial reading there on weekends."

Their next stop was a dilapidated old farmhouse about a mile or so from the church. An elderly black couple waved from the porch when the car pulled into the yard, scattering chickens and dogs and dust. The old man, dressed in overalls, stood and steadied himself by the rickety railing, beckoning them out of the car. The woman remained seated in her rocker, shelling peas, a toothless smile on her face. "Harold and Wanda Isley have worked this farm for forty years," Lige said. "Raised a family of seven children, paid their taxes, sent their sons off to war. They've been responsible, law-abiding churchgoing citizens and have never once in all that time voted. Their children are now all grown up and married and moved north to Chicago or Detroit. They've been among the biggest supporters of what we're doing in the area. They helped me and Charlie with the Freedom ticket last fall."

Gathering that Carter didn't know what that was, Lige explained that SNCC had held a mock vote alongside the gubernatorial primary to test black strength and gauge interest. They set up hundreds of ballot boxes around the state—in churches, beauty parlors, grocery stores, on street-side tables. Reverend Bunt and the Isleys helped in Ellis County, and once word spread about what was going on in the Negro communities to get out the vote, there were assaults and harassment.

"Crosses were burned. Late-night phone calls were made. The Isleys got a nine-thousand-dollar water bill," said Randall.

"They don't even use county water," said Daniel Johnston. "They're on well water."

"Somebody poisoned one of their dogs," Charlie said.

Carter grimaced. He knew rednecks could be vicious, but he had always assumed without really articulating it to himself that those who "asked for trouble" could somehow handle it. The Isleys were not the sort of "agitators" he had in mind.

The "Freedom vote" was a huge success, according to Lige. More than ninety thousand Negroes across the state "voted." The point was to demonstrate the impact they could have on the real election.

Everybody got out of the car and joined the Isleys in the shade of their front porch. They talked about the weather, the crops, their chickens, their children. Even Charlie Lloyd seemed more relaxed, offering to help shell peas while they talked. After telling them about the Monday night meeting at Shiloh Church, Lige left the couple some registration forms to fill out, and they all said their farewells.

"Those are our success stories," Lige said. "Now we'll show you more of our day-to-day reality."

They pulled up to a tar-paper shack set back in a stand of scraggly scrub pine on a dirt road intersecting the highway. A thin brown woman was bent over a washboard doing laundry, surrounded by children dressed in rags. A rusty bucket improvised a step to the front porch, itself nothing more than a few rotten planks nailed together over mud. Some missing windowpanes were covered with cardboard. The vague, dank smell of feces and pig slop explained the colony of flies. Carter had never seen poverty this raw, even in Troy's "niggertown," whose sorry condition he somehow blamed on the residents.

"Hey," Lige shouted as he got out of the car. The woman said nothing, but bent down and picked up a baby and retreated into the shadows of the porch.

"We're here about voter registration and wondered if you're a voter."

The woman stood there in the shade, looking panicked and suspicious. Finally she said, "My husband be back soon."

"If we could just have a moment of your time."

She raised her voice. "Get on away from here."

"Are you going to vote for president this year?"

"They'll see you," she replied ominously, her eyes darting toward the road and trees beyond.

"Who?"

She didn't answer, but instead disappeared back inside the screen door. Her children remained on the porch, waiting to see what their mother would do. She stood motionless in the shadows inside the door and watched through the screen as Lige remained rooted in her yard. He signaled the others to stay in the car; then slowly, deliberately, he approached the porch and left some leaflets on the steps, turned around, and calmly returned to the vehicle. He waved to the woman before driving away. Carter turned to watch her through the rear window as she emerged and gathered all her children back inside the house with her.

Lige, Randall, and Charlie got out at the next farmhouse, leaving the three whites, Sarah, Carter, and Daniel, in the car. "We usually let Lige break the ice," Daniel explained.

Daniel Johnston had an open face, a GI haircut, and a polite, easy manner. Carter asked him if he was a student. He turned in his seat up front to face Carter and pointed to the clerical collar under his light Windbreaker. "Does divinity school count?"

"Are you a priest?" When Carter first noticed the collar at Magic Time, he had been surprised that it was on someone so close to his age.

"Not yet. I'm at the Episcopal seminary in Cambridge. The organizers suggested I wear the collar, though. I guess they figure the locals will be slower to beat up a minister."

"Daniel's another one of us damn Yankees," said Sarah. "Oh, sorry, Reverend. Darn Yankees."

He hastened to say he had gone to college in the South. "Virginia Military Institute. And you went to Vanderbilt, right?" Daniel said. "Good school."

Outside, Lige and his comrades were having no luck. They knocked on the door again. There was no answer, though music could be heard from a radio playing inside.

"It happens a lot," Sarah said. "Intimidated."

After giving up and leaving leaflets on the porch, the three got back in the car. "Can't force folks to be brave," Lige said.

"Is it a problem having whites with you?" Carter asked when they were driving away.

Charlie Lloyd snorted.

Lige answered, "It's controversial. Believe me, we debated inviting the white students down." Some SNCC members, like Dexter and

Charlie, had been against white involvement, he explained. Lige glanced over at Charlie for affirmation, but he just stared out the window. "I wouldn't presume to speak for anybody else," Lige continued, "but I think it's fair to say they believe whites should go to work in their own communities." A lot of Movement folks were sensitive—with reason— to whites taking over and were beginning to insist on a black leadership. "Me, I won't be involved in a segregated Movement," said Lige. "I'm still holding out for the Beloved Community."

"Thank you, Lige," said Sarah, playfully popping the back of Charlie's head with a rolled-up leaflet.

"Yeah, that's mighty white of you," said Charlie.

"I think even Charlie would admit that there's one compelling argument about letting white folks participate," Lige said.

"What's that?" said Sarah.

"The danger. If white America won't respond to the slaughter of innocent Negroes," Lige said, "maybe they'll respond to the death of their own children."

"I agree," said Daniel. "It is strategically sound. When we sons and daughters of white privilege risk our lives, maybe things will change."

"Some would say you're being used," said Carter.

Randall turned to face Carter. His eyes flashed behind his thick horn-rims, his serenity suddenly alive to argument. "Why shouldn't whites face the kind of terror Negroes face every day?"

"Even if it is just 'How I Spent My Summer Vacation,'" Charlie Lloyd said.

"Ain't nobody being used," said Lige evenly, glancing at Carter in the rearview. "No one who came down has any illusions about what we're facing. No one is being led to slaughter. We made sure when we held our recruiting and training sessions at Berkeley, Columbia, Harvard, Swarthmore, that the white kids knew what they were getting into. I'd tell them, 'You're going to be classified into two groups in Mississippi: niggers and nigger lovers. And they're tougher on nigger lovers.'"

Daniel Johnston said, "Lige recruited me, and he said, 'Don't come to Mississippi to save the Negro. Only come if you understand, really understand, that his freedom and yours are one thing.'"

Sarah nudged Carter with her elbow and said, "You taking this down?"

At the next farmhouse they came to, a man in overalls met them with a double-barreled shotgun. Before Lige could shift into park and turn off the engine, the man shouted, "Get on outa here!"

As Lige opened the door, the man said, "I know who you are. You're staying over at Magic Time. You just causing trouble for us."

The shotgun went off, the muzzle pointed in the air. Hundreds of sparrows lifted out of a tree and moved across the sky, holding the shape of the tree. A baby started crying in the house.

Once they were back on the road, Randall said, "It's gotten worse since the disappearance of the workers in Neshoba."

"Shit, it's been like this," Charlie Lloyd said. "They ain't the first ones to disappear without a trace. Remember Charles Moore and Henry Dee from Meadville? Nobody knows what happened to them either. Of course, they're Negroes, so who cares?"

"There was another church burned down in Petal last weekend," Randall said.

"Folks are scared," said Lige. "And they got a right to be."

They rode the rest of the way in silence. That morning's itinerary took them to another half dozen farmhouses and crossroad settlement homes. Some belonged to families whose children Sarah had helped learn to read at the Shiloh Church Freedom School. After several less-than-enthusiastic, if not armed, encounters, the mood in the station wagon turned morose, and everyone was ready to call it a day. Lige proposed that they make one last cold call.

An old lady sitting in a rocking chair on the porch of a tiny shotgun shack at the end of a dirt road greeted them happily when they pulled up. "Mornin'," she called from the porch before they even got out of the car.

"Mornin'," said Lige. "You mind if we come up and visit?"

"I don't mind. Your friends can come set, too."

They got out of the car and warily approached the woman. "This is unusual," Sarah whispered to Carter.

"I noticed," he said.

The old woman invited everyone, including the whites, onto the porch. "There's a whole mess of you, ain't there?" she said, grinning down at them when they had gathered in the yard. "Now don't be shy. Come on up here so I can speak atcha without hollering." They looked at one another, and Lige led the way up onto the porch. Only when Carter stood a couple of feet in front of her did he realize, by the tilt of her head and the rolling of her eyes, that the woman was stone-blind.

"I don't get many visitors out here." She grinned toothlessly. "Are y'all here from the social service?"

It was almost lunchtime, and the sun had risen high in the sky by the time they said goodbye to the blind woman. They left her some canned goods they had brought along just in case. Carter was relieved when Lige asked if anyone could use some refreshment. They pulled into the gravel lot of an antique gas station and country store called Scarborough's. The owner, a Negro named Thad Scarborough, had allowed his store to be used as a polling place for the mock election the previous fall and had been selling supplies to Lige and the SNCC workers that summer, allowing them to run a tab. He also owned the Magic Time property.

The filling station looked no different from the countless rural white-owned stations that dotted the back roads of the Deep South. A rusted tin RC Cola sign adorned the cross-slat on the rusty screen door. The air inside Scarborough's was cool and damp, like the interior of a refrigerator. The shelves were lined with staples like bread, peanut butter, and crackers, but there was also row upon row of hardware, engine oil, windshield-wiper replacements, and fishing gear. The old-timers in overalls sitting on stools and in rockers around the cold woodstove by the cash register were all Negro. Their laughter had subsided with the creak of the screen door and the jingle of bells announcing the new customers, and the old men had glanced furtively at Carter and Sarah and Daniel, staring at the empty checkerboard set up on a barrel before them. Charlie Lloyd and Randall took RC Colas from the icebox and beelined to a pinball machine in the back. Sarah challenged Daniel Johnston to a game of darts at a target hung precariously on the wall next to the pinball machine.

Lige signaled Carter to join him outside. "Have you got your story?" he asked, taking a swig of his Nehi Grape.

"Maybe," Carter answered. "Just wondering, though: What are you going to do with all these folks we visited when you get them registered to vote? Who are they going to vote for?"

"Good question," Lige said. "This is off the record, Brother Man, but the mock election we held last fall was a test run for the presidential election this year. Our target is the Democratic National Convention in Atlantic City in August." The plan was to challenge the regular state Democratic Party—its segregated, whites-only delegates—for Mississippi's seats at that national convention. "We're calling ourselves the Mississippi Freedom Democratic Party."

"Good luck," said Carter, emptying his bag of Tom's salted peanuts into his Dr Pepper.

Lige seemed undeterred by Carter's skepticism. "We'll participate in the precinct, county, and state conventions coming up this month, where we'll be barred, of course. But we have to go through all the proper procedures, so the Freedom Democratic Party will have legal grounds to challenge the regular party at the national convention. Right, Counselor?"

Carter was impressed with the audacity of Lige's campaign. And he could imagine the reaction of the local Democratic Party. "Sounds like a plan to me," he said with a noncommittal shrug.

"What's the matter, Pross? You look worried."

"I was just thinking about talking to your mama at some point. I don't know what I'm going to tell her. She wanted me to persuade you to come home."

"It's not your job to bring me home. Besides, she'll find out soon enough what I'm doing with Snick and the Movement."

"What do you mean?"

"You saw that Johnson signed the Civil Rights Act last week. It says public accommodations must be desegregated."

"Seems to me like that would mean your work is done."

"That's just what we're afraid of. That folks will think our work is done, when it's only just begun. So we're going to test it."

"How?"

"That's none of your business." The voice belonged to Charlie Lloyd, standing at the screen door behind them.

"Come on," said Lige, unperturbed. "Carter's covering the Movement. What are protests for if not to get publicity? 'Demonstrations'—get it?"

"Knight," Charlie said, opening the squeaking door and stepping out into the sun, "what makes you think he won't tip off the police?"

"I already tipped off the police. I sent them notice of everything we're doing. Just like Gandhi did. There's nothing Carter can say that they don't already know from me."

"Gandhi." Charlie snorted. "If Gandhi was in Mississippi, he'd be just another dead nigger."

"What's going on?" asked Sarah, standing at the door behind Charlie, chewing on a Snickers bar.

"I'm telling Carter about the future impact of the Civil Rights Act of 1964 on his hometown," Lige replied. "We were just discussing tactics."

"Great. I love tactics. I'm better at tactics than darts."

Lige continued explaining to Carter. "I'm going to have my first lunch at Kress's. I always wanted a grilled cheese and a Coke. And to sit on them twirly stools." He hesitated for a beat before saying, "Cover it for the paper, Pross."

"You've got your own personal public relations man?" Charlie said, eyeing Carter suspiciously. "I bet your buddy here's got his own ideas about the Movement."

"Hey, I've got no agenda," said Carter. He was suddenly uncomfortable with the perception that he was doing a favor for a friend. "I don't want anybody *expecting* anything but the facts from what I write." He looked at Lige and then at Sarah. "Besides," he warned, "who says I get this in the paper?"

"There could be a story there," said Lige. "If we're lucky, we'll get arrested."

Carter still couldn't wrap his mind around the concept of volunteer jail time. "You want to get arrested?"

"It's the only way to focus attention. Gandhi said, 'Fill the jails.' 'Course, the only time that's ever been done in this country was a year ago in Birmingham."

A loud challenge from Daniel and Randall at the dartboard inside summoned Sarah and Charlie away from tactics. Carter watched Sarah disappear back through the screen door, and he turned back to Lige, who was observing him. Lige took a final pull on his Nehi Grape and, with the faintest smile, said, "In the end, Brother Man, it's all about sex." A look passed between them like a secret handshake, transcending the calculus of race and power, that Carter found both liberating and unsettling.

Having had their fill of dusty snacks, they piled into the white Ford station wagon and headed back to Magic Time. After a mile or so, they rounded a curve before crossing the river. Lige glanced in the rearview mirror and said, "Uh-oh." He slowed the car. "Po-lice."

Before Carter could swivel to look, he heard the wail of a siren. Lige pulled off the highway onto the gravel shoulder near the bridge over the Little Chickasaw.

Carter froze. He had to remind himself that he was on assignment for *The Troy Times* and had a legitimate excuse for being with the civil rights workers. Glancing back at the car, he could see two men in the front seat. The officer emerging from the driver's side was wearing a hat and shades. When he got out and removed his sunglasses, Carter recognized him. It was Sheriff Mizell. Carter felt a mixture of concern and relief. In the minus column, Sheriff Lawrence Mizell knew Carter and would tattle to his father. But he was also a decent man who would treat the others fairly. Still, Carter would prefer not to be spotted. He lowered his head when the sheriff's swollen gray-uniformed abdomen passed by the rear window and stopped at the driver's window. Mizell tapped a nightstick in the palm of his hand. As he leaned down to survey the interior of the car, Carter cocked his head away.

"Where you going in such a hurry, boy?" Mizell asked Lige.

"What's the problem, Officer?" Lige replied quietly.

"You was speeding." Mizell spoke in a deep, guttural drawl. He bent down and again surveyed the backseat. Carter looked out the window. The sheriff still did not appear to have recognized him and turned back to Lige. "What do you got to say for yourself?"

Lige said nothing.

"Get out of the car. All y'all." Mizell twirled the nightstick as he waited for them to comply. "Get out of the car," he ordered again, louder. Lige opened the door, got out, and stood in front of the sheriff.

"What's the charge, Sheriff?" The others remained in the car.

"Don't you smart-mouth me, boy. Did y'all hear me?" he demanded, squinting into the car again. "I said to get out."

Charlie Lloyd and Daniel Johnston emerged from the wagon. Carter, Sarah, and Randall stayed where they were, hoping the sheriff would be satisfied with the front-seat half. His attention was focused on Lige. "Where you fum, boy? Let me see your driver's license."

"Troy, Mississippi." The sheriff looked at him, then turned his head to the side and spit his wad of gum onto the highway.

He looked across the hood of the station wagon at Charlie Lloyd, standing next to Daniel Johnston. "How about you, nigger?"

Charlie said nothing. Carter was stunned with shame that a public official would use the ugly word in the line of duty.

"I'm talking to you, boy." Mizell slapped his baton into the palm of his hand with a loud pop. "Cain't you talk? Ever' time I turn on the television, I see one of you Snick nigras talking about how bad us white Mississippians are. Whatchew got to say now?"

"Brooklyn," Charlie mumbled.

"Where's that?"

"Brooklyn, New York," Charlie said louder.

"Well, what business does a New York nigra have doing down here in Mississippi?" asked the sheriff. He turned and called back toward the cruiser. "Hey, Posey, come look a-here what I got."

Carter turned and watched the stocky man in civilian clothes put down his walkie-talkie and get out of the police car's passenger side. He was hatless, with short reddish-brown hair. He stooped to look into the backseat, where the others remained. His eyes settled on Sarah.

"Which one of them coons is you screwin'?" he demanded.

No answer. Carter felt light-headed. He waited for Mizell to admonish the deputy.

"Did you hear me?" Posey continued to look at Sarah.

"Get out of the car," Mizell ordered. "I ain't going to tell you again."

Randall opened his door and got out. Sarah waited for Carter to open his door. Slowly, Carter emerged from the backseat on the far side of the car, followed by Sarah. The sheriff's eyes were on Lige. "Mr. Posey asked y'all a question."

"Which one of you is fuckin' the white girl?" Posey said. He glanced toward Sarah. Her jaw was set, and there was fire in her eyes.

The sheriff said, "I vote for this buck here," and shoved Lige up against the car door.

Randall said quietly, almost soothingly, "That's not necessary, Officer."

Posey backhanded him across the mouth, drawing blood.

Daniel Johnston was circling the car, his fists clenched, glaring at the sheriff, who now had Lige flattened, spread-eagled, against the car, with his arm twisted up behind him.

"No, Daniel," said Lige.

Posey let loose a swift blow with his billy club to Daniel Johnston's abdomen. He crumpled to the pavement. Sarah screamed. Lige dropped to his knees beside Daniel and prayed over his supine body.

Carter scrambled around the car to the spot where Daniel was lying. He dropped to his knees beside Lige. Then he looked up at Mizell, full in the face.

"Carter Ransom!" the sheriff said. The others stared at Carter as if they were being introduced to him for the first time. He felt exposed, embarrassed almost, to be suddenly exempted from this living nightmare by layers of heritage and generations of pedigree. Mizell's expression was a montage of confusion, irritation, and finally a dim panic. His voice lowered to a hush. "What the hell are you doing here, son?"

9

D EPLETED BY the morning session with his old friends, Carter slept through lunchtime, waking in early afternoon with a gnawing at his midsection that felt remarkably like hunger. A note from Nettie was on the nightstand. She had left some chicken salad for him in the refrigerator.

When Carter went downstairs, he found his father sitting in the breakfast nook staring out the kitchen window, an uneaten bowl of soup, a glass of milk, and a folded newspaper on the table in front of him. "Dad," Carter said, sitting down next to him, "I didn't know you were home."

Judge Ransom was looking at the row of bird feeders on stilts along the ivy-covered brick wall enclosing the patio. "Just watching the blue jays," he said. Katharine Ransom had set up an elaborate system of feeders in the backyard so she could pursue her bird-watching hobby from her kitchen window while cooking or washing dishes. Sometimes she would gasp or shriek so loud that everyone would rush in, only to be both relieved and slightly irritated that it was just the sighting of some unprecedented titmouse or hummingbird. Since Katharine's death ten years earlier, her husband, who had shown little interest in her hobby when she was alive, had taken it up like a fallen battle flag.

The day before Katharine Ransom died of cancer, Mitchell had been sitting next to her wheelchair in front of the window, watching the birds with her for what turned out to be her last time. An eastern grosbeak flitted down to dine on some millet. The grosbeak was unusual for that part of the world, Katharine explained, and she had never seen one in the yard before. Mitchell would later describe how he had witnessed the light flare down deep in her exhausted, hollowed-out eyes, and he cherished her delight in her fine new bird species. At five o'clock the next morning she died in her bed, with him lying awake beside her in the dark, holding her hand. An hour later, hospice arrived. Carter, who had flown down from Washington that weekend, sat with his father at the kitchen table, drinking coffee and staring out the window. As the sun came up and the first light illuminated the backyard, the two of them beckoned Sally to come see an entire flock of eastern grosbeaks flurry down upon the feeders, as if on cue. It was six o'clock in the morning, exactly one hour after she died. Mitchell, who was not an especially religious man, would see these rare, wayfaring birds as conveyors of his wife's spirit. Staring out the window, he shed tears for the first time since she had been diagnosed with leukemia less than a year earlier.

Now Mitchell Ransom broke away from the spectacle of the blue jays sparring over some crumbs and looked over at Carter. "How you feeling, son?" he asked. "You were sleeping when I got home."

Carter saw that the newspaper on the table was the one he had been reading that morning. His father must have slipped in and taken it from the nightstand. Lacey Hullender glowered up at him from the front page.

"Have you eaten?" Carter asked, indicating the untouched bowl of soup on the table.

"I wasn't hungry. Nettie made me eat a big breakfast."

Carter found the plate of chicken salad in the refrigerator and poured himself a glass of milk. "You seem troubled, Pop. Is it Hullender's release?"

His father shifted in his chair and grunted, looking out the window. "It was all so long ago. I just wonder what good can come from opening this case again."

"I thought you'd been frustrated by the way the trial turned out—that Bohannon walked."

"Back then was a different time. We were lucky to get the jury to reach the verdict they reached. Sometimes you have to take what you can get."

"It wasn't enough to me."

"It's never enough. But now what can come of it?"

"Justice, maybe?" Carter sometimes wondered if his father was mindful of his son's connection to the case.

"Justice." His father said the word as if he were recalling an old friend from law school he had lost track of. "It's not going to bring anybody back. This young prosecutor's got the idea she can—"

"Who is this prosecutor?" Carter asked.

"Alabama girl—from Birmingham. She became obsessed with some of these old unsolved civil rights cases in law school, from what I hear. Now she's gotten herself in a position to do something about them."

"She came by this morning."

Mitchell Ransom seemed to perk up. "What did she want?"

"I don't know. Nothing. She was with Lonnie—he stopped in to say hello. He was showing her around."

"Lonnie should watch himself."

His father's directness surprised Carter. "Why?"

"I think he's got a crush on her."

"She's attractive."

"He's got a wife and two kids. He's a partner in the firm now."

Carter had never known his father to be other than circumspect about the private lives of those around him. It was a quality appealing in a judge. "You don't like this woman?"

"I don't know her. I don't like crusaders."

Carter nodded noncommittally. He couldn't count the times he had been called that by his father.

"Son, I want you to listen to your sister now. You take care of yourself."

"Sounds to me like she's worried about you, too, Pop."

"Me. Why?"

"Hullender. She remembers his threats."

Mitchell waved his son off and stared out the window. "I've gotten threats all my life. Besides, there's a lot of water over the dam since then. Twenty years behind bars sometimes has a way of taking the starch out of you. That's why they call it a correctional facility."

"They call it a penitentiary, too, but do you think he's penitent?"

"Believe me, son, at my age, Hullender's the least of my worries." Mitchell reached over and squeezed the top of Carter's hand. "Now eat your lunch." Carter studied Nettie's latest variation on the theme of mayonnaise. "And let the dead bury the dead."

———

THE STORY Carter had written on the voter registration outing had not run, and he doubted if it ever would. There was still no word on the whereabouts of Schwerner, Goodman, and Chaney in Neshoba County, and the recent passage of the Civil Rights Act of 1964 had set loose a volatile paranoia in the state. It was rumored among the *Troy Times* staff that Pete Callahan had received an anonymous threat for his editorial urging moderation in response to civil rights activities in Mississippi. Carter hadn't pushed his editor on printing his piece. He still wasn't sure what he would say to Nettie about her son when she found out he had gone to Magic Time.

On the Tuesday that SNCC was to test the public accommodations section of the Civil Rights Act, Carter spent all morning writing obits. Nobody in the lightly staffed newsroom seemed to know about any planned sit-ins at Kress's, and he had spoken to no one at Magic Time, so he didn't know for sure if the demonstration was still on. He had considered it pointless to ask Callahan's permission to cover the Kress's sit-in, but as he left the newsroom early for lunch, he borrowed a staff photographer's camera, just in case.

A little before noon, he drove from the *Times* building on the edge of the commercial district to the post office on the square. On a sultry July day like this one, the town of Troy usually moved at a slug's pace. But today was different. Carter could feel it the minute he got out of his car. The streets were quieter than usual, with minimal traffic, as before a Fourth of July or homecoming parade. He sensed that word had gotten out about the sit-in and the news had spread on the street. He wondered if Sarah Solomon would be there. The thought of seeing her in that public context made him nervous.

When he turned the corner onto Main, he saw a smattering of people in front of Kress's a block away. They seemed skittish, like cattle before a thunderstorm. Just then Lacey Hullender sprinted past him, a blur in a T-shirt and a Cat hat. Lacey paused and turned to flash Carter a nicotine-toothed grin. "Hey, Ransom," he shouted, "the niggers are in there."

Carter broke into a run toward Kress's. The gathering on the sidewalk had grown thicker. Hullender disappeared into the store. By the time Carter got there, he had to push through to get inside.

Shoppers and onlookers filled the aisles, craning to see what the commotion at the lunch counter was about. Carter circled the swelling throng to the far side of the counter, where he could survey the entire serving area from behind a pillar. The sight he beheld, of black citizens seeking service at Kress's five-and-dime, his childhood friend among them, took Carter's breath away, as if he were seeing the Grand Canyon or Niagara Falls for the first time.

A row of young Negroes, the males dressed in unseasonable suits and ties, sat stock-still on the stools, staring straight ahead. Some Carter assumed were students from Jackson State. They had spread themselves along the length of the L-shaped counter, leaving seats between them, presumably in case any white people got hungry. Lige Knight and Randall Peek sat tall at the outer corner of the L that angled toward the crowd. "Oh, my Lawd!" Carter heard one of the Negro waitresses shriek when she emerged from the kitchen.

Jeers and catcalls from the crowd were escalating along with the heat inside the store. Carter fumbled for his camera to take a picture before the spectators closed in, and he found himself wishing he had gotten there in time to check his flash. The protesters remained motionless on their stools, like carved mahogany chess figures. A young waitress looked stricken as the white store manager whispered at her animatedly. She approached Lige, apparently sensing he was the leader. "I'm afraid we're closed," she said in a shaky child's voice. "Y'all are going to have to leave."

Lige replied calmly, "One grilled cheese sandwich and a Coca-Cola, please."

The crowd let out a collective gasp. From his position by the pillar, Carter spotted Hullender and his friends shouldering their way to the lunch counter. "Niggers!" they yelled. "Jungle bunnies!" "Go home, black bastids!" Carter searched the white faces in the crowd for any sign of Sarah or Daniel. An overweight middle-aged white woman in a flower-print dress pushed her way to the counter and let out a scream. Carter thought there might be some medical emergency, but she began to shout, "What in Sam Hill are y'all doing here? Get on back to Africa!" Some of Lacey's buddies tried to force the confrontation onto terms they were comfortable with. They jabbed the protesters with fingers and silverware, then taunted them for not fighting back. The muscles in his neck straining, Hullender zeroed in on his old nemesis Elijah Knight. Spittle flew with the profanities, but Lige would not respond. Carter's heart pounded. He wanted to tackle Lacey, yet he could not move. And then he realized, with both relief and shame: for all Lige was forced to endure, this was a war of his choosing. Hullender, unable to get a rise out of Lige, finally smashed a ketchup bottle into his temple, then grabbed him around the neck from behind and threw him off the swivel seat to the floor. He kicked him up against the counter and started punching him. Lige curled up into a fetal position, covering his head with his arms. At last the crowd recoiled.

Carter raised his camera and snapped a picture. As the shutter clicked, he felt someone grab the camera by the lens and jerk it out of his hands. One of Hullender's running buddies, known to Carter only as Skeebo, stood before him, grinning in triumph. Then he swung the camera and smashed it against the column.

"What the hell are you doing?" Carter yelled. "That doesn't belong to me."

Skeebo handed the mangled Nikon back to Carter and said, "It does now." Then he dissolved back into the mayhem around the lunch counter. Carter looked around for police. There was no security in sight. Lige was still curled on the floor, covering his face and head. Hullender continued to whale away at him. Like everyone else around him, Carter remained frozen.

Then he became aware of a hand on his shoulder. "Son, what are you doing here?"

"Dad?" Carter said, turning tentatively. He was confused to see his father away from the courthouse.

"I was out with my bailiffs for lunch, and we heard there was trouble." His father had an expression of apprehension that Carter had never seen before. "Somebody told me they saw you running in here."

"I'm covering this for the paper," Carter said unconvincingly.

"Get out, son," the judge said, his anxious eyes surveying the mob scene. "This is a job for law enforcement."

"You are the law, and you are here." Carter had raised his voice.

His father watched helplessly as one of Hullender's buddies stubbed out his cigarette on Randall Peek's neck and snapped his glasses in two. Then someone else squeezed mustard onto his head. The crowd, which had withheld judgment during Hullender's battering of Lige, began to laugh and egg them on again.

Mitchell Ransom grabbed Carter by the wrist and pulled him back up the aisles of the store toward the entrance. Spotting a police officer at the door, the judge demanded, "Where's Sheriff Mizell? Does Mizell know what's going on here?" The taunts of the mob in back of the store were so loud that Carter couldn't make out what his father was saying. The policeman pointed to two more officers standing outside. Carter followed his father out onto the sidewalk. Those cops, too, seemed indifferent to the ruckus inside until Judge Ransom began jotting down their badge numbers. After he said something to them about vigilante justice and the rule of law, the officers looked at each other and sauntered inside. Carter and his father stood across the street and waited.

The concerned citizens of Troy filed out of Kress's. Lawbreakers were arrested: the students who had been sitting at the counter were marched out of the store and into the waiting police wagon. Lige was holding his head with a bloody hand.

• • •

Carter showed up at the courthouse with bail money for Lige, which he had drawn from his personal childhood bank account. But Sheriff Mizell had apparently thought better of having his prisoner die on his watch and, after booking Lige for trespassing and disorderly conduct, had sent him to the emergency room instead of jail. Carter went back to the paper and wrote his story. By the time he checked the hospital, Lige had been released. When Carter walked through the front door of the Ransom home shortly after eight, Lige, his head wrapped in bloody bandages, was sitting on the sofa in the living room, comforting his sobbing mother.

"It looks worse than it is," he said. "It's just a mild concussion. You know how hardheaded you always say I am."

Nettie smiled through tears. "That's the truth."

Mitchell Ransom entered from the kitchen, saying, "Sheriff's sending somebody out to Magic Time—" He stopped when he saw that Carter had arrived. He seemed agitated, and he moved to the fireplace in front of the sofa, massaging the back of his neck. "You realize you've both had your mothers worried sick," he began.

Katharine moved to her husband's side, hoping to soften his words with her look of concern.

Carter saved her the trouble by going on the offensive. "Sheriff Mizell?" He summoned his best derisive laugh. "The same Sheriff Mizell who sics his deputies on 'the niggers'?"

"I'll not have that word spoken in this house."

"I saw it with my own eyes."

Mitchell blinked in furious disbelief.

"I was working on a story about voter registration. Mizell pulled us over, and he and Posey roughed up Lige and the others. Until he saw me."

Facing the cold fireplace, his profile to Carter, Mitchell digested this revelation, then addressed Lige. "This may be none of my business, Elijah," he said, "and I have no idea as to who you've been influenced by, but I will say, in all candor"—he turned to them as he finished his statement—"you have no right to involve my son in this."

"Daddy, don't insult Lige, and don't insult me," Carter said.

"I'm sorry, but he has no idea what he's setting loose with this sit-in nonsense!" Judge Ransom said. He was shaking with the effort to restrain himself.

Lige gathered himself, inhaling deeply, as if preparing to dive underwater. "All due respect, Judge Ransom, segregation don't feel like nonsense to those of us who suffer under it—"

"Listen to me, son," Mitchell interrupted. "Nobody understands the inequities of our system of justice more than I. I see it every day in the courtroom, but change must come slowly through reason and the rule of law. Not lawlessness. Not through taking to the streets and flouting the law—even laws that you may not consider fair."

"What about the hoodlums who beat us up, sir?" said Lige. "What about their lawlessness?"

"That was inexcusable."

"They weren't arrested. Not one of them was down at the jailhouse."

"You provoked a bunch of hooligans," said the judge. "What can you expect from people like that?"

Carter was sure his father was about to launch into his "poor devils" speech and remind them of the Christmas when the church had collected toys for Lacey and his siblings after their father died. Carter felt the logic rising in him like a temper.

"Oh, so if white trash like Hullender suffer, then they get a bye, but colored people have to do their Stepin Fetchit routines and bear it."

"Elijah was breaking the law, son," he said, and turned to Lige. "You may disagree with certain statutes, and you have a right to try to change them, but it still is the law of the land."

"Not anymore. The U.S. Congress passed—"

"Congress," Mitchell said, shaking his head dismissively. "We cannot legislate morality. Besides, you were charged with disorderly conduct and trespassing and disturbing the peace. You were just as culpable as those—that riffraff who beat you up!"

"The peace you talk about *should* be disturbed," Lige answered. "It's a corrupt peace, a hypocritical and false peace based on the lies and falsehoods of segregation, on inequality and injustice."

Sally had slipped downstairs and was peeking around the corner from the hallway. The siblings exchanged a look. Carter sensed that Lige was embarked on a sermon he had preached often. Nevertheless, he was shocked at Lige's audacity.

Lige continued to address the judge. "We believe a positive peace can come out of conflict when those lies are exposed to the light of day. All the dirt and filth and trouble has to be brought to the surface so it can be expelled. We are performing surgery, removing the cancer of injustice. It may be painful, but if done nonviolently, in the spirit of love—"

Mitchell interrupted. "That's anarchy! You don't know what you're unleashing. The human heart is darker than you suppose, young man. You're just twenty-one. You're young and naive. You're making decisions now that could ruin your life."

Carter spoke up. "Don't condescend to him, Daddy."

"He's headstrong just like Wesley was," Nettie said. "But your daddy would be boiling mad at what you done, Lige. He was tickled when you went off to seminary. I don't know what it'll all lead to. Prison, like your cousin Deac more than likely."

Lige looked down at his feet. Carter had seen that downward gaze before. It meant that Lige was trying to control his temper, collecting his thoughts. Lige began speaking slowly. "My daddy struggled all his life to scrape out a living from cotton and peanuts and corn, Mama. He didn't get past the sixth grade in schools that were poorer than the white schools, riding there in broke-down school buses on unpaved roads. Those were hardships put on him because of his black skin. And he died because he couldn't afford no decent doctor. He died too young, Mama."

Katharine tried to intercede again. "Lige, we understand you feel strongly about these things. Stay here tonight if you want to, son."

"No, thank you, ma'am. I'm needed at Magic Time."

Nettie cried, "Baby, don't go."

Carter thought his friend was being foolhardy. "Stay here just for the night, Lige," he said.

Mitchell raised his voice. "Good God, son, can't you see what you're doing to your mother?"

And then something in Lige seemed to snap. "Can't I see," he repeated, as if mulling over the words. "The question, Your Honor, is, can't you see?"

"Elijah," Nettie said, "don't talk to Judge like that!"

Lige headed for the door. Then he pivoted and addressed the room. "Yes sir, as you can see, my mother is devoted to you and your family, and you have been good to us, no question. But in all the years she has worked for you, cooked for you, cleaned for you, cared for your children when we were at home by ourselfs, not once has she been asked to sit down with you at the same table that she sets every blessed day!"

Katharine gasped.

"Elijah," Nettie said quietly.

To his mother: "Mama, I've got to go."

Carter turned and, looking directly at his father, said, "I'll drive you."

Mitchell moved past his son and blocked the doorway. "You'll have to get past me."

Sally bolted into the room from the hallway and hurled herself at her father. "Leave him alone," she screamed, tears streaming down her face.

Caught off-balance, Mitchell sent Sally sprawling. "Get ahold of yourself, young lady!"

Mitchell Ransom gently helped her up, but Sally, sobbing, squirmed until she could escape into her mother's embrace.

"Now stop it!" Katharine cried. "All of you. Sally, go upstairs this minute."

For a long moment, the scene froze. Carter looked at the pain on Nettie's face and realized she had never seen "her white family" fall apart like this. Then he turned to Lige. After the briefest eye contact, they disappeared together out the door and into the Mississippi night.

Y OU SURE you feel up to this?" Lonnie Culpepper asked Carter, who was strapping himself into his friend's navy blue Lincoln Town Car.

It was Saturday morning, and neighbors were doing yard work—watering lawns, clipping hedges. As the aroma of freshly mown grass hit his nostrils, Carter was reminded that nothing seemed as fresh and redolent of promise as a spring day in Troy, Mississippi.

"You won't believe the transformation," Lonnie said while they cruised down Magnolia. It was Carter's first venture out of the house since coming home. "Most towns in the state are worse off than they were twenty years ago," Lonnie said. "But Troy . . . you'll see."

Carter thought he detected a note of chamber-of-commerce pride. When they were young, Lonnie had seemed even more restless, dissatisfied, and itching to get out of Troy than Carter had. Lonnie grew up in a three-room house on the highway outside of town, sharing a bedroom with two brothers and the washing machine. His father, who had grown up outside Troy, in Shady Grove, worked construction and made ends meet by selling fireworks. Lonnie's beloved grandfather had spent two yearlong stretches in the federal pen for moonshining. PawPaw had lived one hundred percent off the land until the day he died, hunting squirrel and rabbit and deer, rounding up hogs from the swamps, and growing everything else. Lonnie's mother, a moody, petite woman who had fought life-threatening illnesses all through his childhood, had been valedictorian of her class of twelve at Petal High School and had instilled in her son a love of learning. But it was Lonnie's athletic ability that had gotten him the college scholarship offers in track (triple jump and javelin), baseball (pitcher), and basketball (forward). He accepted a track scholarship to Ole Miss but quit the team after his coach died in a plane crash. He changed his major from physical education to prelaw and entered law school at Vanderbilt a year after Carter.

Lonnie was the most driven kid Carter knew. He would make a contest out of whose sno-cone melted faster. His father's drinking and his mother's illness had consigned his siblings to his care, and his maturity made him a natural leader—the president of the student council, National Honor Society, and Key Club. He subscribed to *Time* in junior high and watched the *Huntley-Brinkley Report*. It was Lonnie who first made fun of the highway billboards touting products that were "Made in Mississippi by Mississippians." Though "Thank God for Mississippi" was an unofficial state motto for other Southern bottom-feeders like Alabama and Arkansas, Mississippi seemed perversely proud of its humble status. The state had self-esteem issues that no amount of football worship or Miss Americas per capita could offset.

Carter studied his friend, tanned and fit, slick in his shades and Izod shirt, his thinning auburn hair neatly coiffed, looking the part of the Sunbelt burgher. "I must confess," Carter said, "I never would have expected you to end up here."

Lonnie smiled. "You'd be surprised how many stayed. Or have come back. This place just has a hold on people. It's like there's some giant electromagnet under the state that draws us all back."

"Yeah, the same magnet that crashes to earth any creative impulse, brilliant insight, or leap of the synapses whatsoever."

Lonnie's smile tightened. "Okay, okay. It's true," he relented. "Troy's like an abusive parent. We hate it and can't leave it. But don't let anybody else bad-mouth Mississippi. It may be a bastard, but it's our bastard."

"Well, you're certainly doing all right here," Carter said. "For a rapidly aging boy wonder."

Lonnie shrugged. "I thought being one-third of Ransom, Davis and Culpepper would change my life. I guess nothing does."

"What's that mean?"

"Things could be better at home." Lonnie glanced over at Carter. "Loretta had an affair." He let the revelation hang for a moment between them. "Can you believe a stud muffin like me would wind up a cuckold?"

Carter took a second to adjust to the abruptly intimate turn of the conversation. "I'm sorry, Lonnie. I thought you and Loretta were solid."

"I guess I'd been working too hard, not paying enough attention to her. Her tennis instructor at the club, if you can believe that. She broke it off when I found out. We got counseling, the whole thing. We're staying together for the kids. But the truth is, I didn't blame her. I'm not a good husband. I haven't been faithful either. Nothing serious, but the women in the office like me a whole lot better than Loretta does."

Carter was less surprised by what Lonnie was telling him than by the swiftness with which he had been pulled back into his teenage role of father confessor.

"I don't mean to unload on you," said Lonnie. "When I heard you were drifting toward getting married, I wanted to scream, 'Don't do it!' I was so jealous of your ability to stay single all these years." They rode awhile in silence as the remark sank in. "Sorry," he said.

They pulled up in front of an old gray Victorian house with green shutters and trim and a wraparound porch. Stephen was waiting by the giant magnolia tree in the front yard, just as he did when they were teenagers, looking abandoned and forlorn in his blue T-shirt and baggy jeans. His hands were in his pockets, and his hair was in his eyes.

As soon as Stephen slid into the backseat, he announced that he couldn't stay too long. He had imposed on Aunt Peatsy to watch his mother until he got back. Carter thought of how irritated Miz Nell had been at him and Lonnie for encouraging Stephen to go out for basketball in the ninth grade. Although, at the time, Stephen shrugged off his musical gifts and practiced his piano sporadically, his mother was nervous about him hurting his fingers playing sports. After riding the bench for the first part of the season, Stephen had been tapped in January to start against the crosstown rivals from Maddox Junior High, when his mother announced a catastrophic scheduling conflict. The night of the game was Stephen's birthday, and Miz Nell had bought two tickets to see Van Cliburn, world-famous pianist, in concert in New Orleans. The ensuing battle of wills was fierce and apocalyptic, but in the end Stephen's attendance at the concert became a formative example of the connection between art and sacrifice, all the more so because Miz Nell had been right: Stephen would always cite Van Cliburn's thrilling performance of Rachmaninoff's Piano Concerto no. 2 that night as the turning point that made him dedicate his life to music.

Lonnie drove Carter and Stephen past Troy High School on the north end of town, the all-brick football stadium built by the WPA during the Depression, and the looming water tower that Lonnie had once climbed and spray-painted over the Jaycees' WELCOME TO TROY sign with the words GATEWAY TO NOWHERE. Then they retraced the route they used to cruise in their souped-up Mustangs, T-Birds, and family Ford Fairlanes. They went down to the Dairy Queen and the icehouse at the south end of town, where they had bought beer without an ID. Finally, they pulled up into one of the diagonal parking spaces along Main Street, whose once abandoned storefronts were now occupied by attractive shops and boutiques, including Sally's store, the Book Nook.

"Schmucks! You made it. I thought you'd stood me up." Jimbo Stein, in tan khakis, white sneakers, and a green Troy High football jersey, stood checking his watch outside the entrance to their favorite high school hangout. Wad's lunch counter, tucked away inside a drugstore that sold everything from greeting cards to socket wrenches, had been the official gathering place for countless after-school gripe sessions and senior prom postmortems. Back then it had been identified by a peeling hand-painted sign over the door: WAD'S in large red letters, with the words LUNCHEONETTE AND SUNDRIES stenciled in blue underneath. Now above the entrance a sign flashed a strip of pink and purple neon in Miami Beach art deco script: WAD'S AT SAWMILL SQUARE.

Carter turned to Stephen. "Sawmill Square?"

Stephen looked at him with tragedy in his eyes. "You're not going to believe it, Pross."

Inside, the former pharmacy had been gutted and remodeled with wall-to-wall mirrors. Gone was the greasy old lunch counter with its open grill and red stools patched with duct tape. Wad's was now a fifties-style diner, with bright red countertops, checkerboard floor tiles, a gigantic jukebox, and life-size cutouts of Elvis and Marilyn, James Dean, William Faulkner, and Eudora Welty.

Carter and his buddies slid onto shiny red vinyl seats and were handed laminated menus by a ponytailed waitress in a poodle skirt. Wad's classic chili cheese dog was now "the James Deanee Weenie." There was "Miss Eudora's Egg Salad," and the fried bologna sandwich was called "Death by Grease."

"They've really spruced the old place up, huh?" Lonnie said.

Carter felt he was in a time warp, but it wasn't the one that the folks behind the new, improved Wad's had in mind. Instead he was transported back to Atlanta or Nashville ca. 1978, the heyday of fern bars, Tiffany lamps, and genuine brass foot railings. The lower South always seemed to be playing catch-up, and even Mississippi's nostalgia was anachronistic.

"They've replaced an authentic nineteen-fifties soda shop with a nineteen-nineties impression of a nineteen-fifties soda shop," Carter said.

Stephen agreed. "A real thing with a false thing."

"That's right," Jimbo said, cackling at their dismay. "They've turned a genuine, authentic cultural artifact into an inauthentic, completely false, and phony idea of a cultural artifact. I love this country."

"I think the new owners wanted to make Wad's a franchise and set them up all over the South," said Lonnie.

Stephen groaned. Carter sighed.

"Come on, you two are such Calvinist prudes," said Jimbo, who enjoyed working all sides of an argument. "This place has a lot of advantages over the old Wad's. You're not going to catch any diseases eating here, for starters. Remember the roaches you'd see crawling across the Formica right next to your cheeseburger?"

Lonnie laughed. "Hell, that was part of the Wad's charm."

"I'm surprised they haven't installed little Disney audio-animatronic roaches," said Stephen.

Jimbo laughed. "When those Nissan executives agreed to move here, they wanted authentic small-town Southern charm, and by God, the town fathers are going to give it to them."

The waitress returned. Lonnie, Jimbo, and Stephen ordered hot dogs, but Carter decided to stick to cherry Coke. Though he wasn't hungry anyway, he preferred to think of it as a strike.

The conversation turned to the other new industry locating in Troy: WunderCorp, a German conglomerate. All that was needed before construction began was for the referendum to pass in November, and that was looking like a fait accompli.

"They plan to put their headquarters out on the Little Chickasaw," said Stephen.

"Unless we can stop them," said Jimbo.

Lonnie said parentally, "Nobody's going to stop them. It's going to mean a lot to this town—growth, development, improved schools."

"It's going to take out that whole area," said Jimbo. "Magic Time. Maybe even Shiloh Church. The entire river."

"Surely they won't tear down Shiloh Church," said Stephen. "It took forever to get it rebuilt after the bombing."

"That's a lot of acreage," said Carter, hoping to avert further discussion of the church bombing.

"It's a humongous deal," said Lonnie, "expected to bring two thousand employees here. One of those modern companies with day care, shopping, and recreational facilities for their employees. The president's supposed to be some kind of visionary. Chamber of commerce is salivating. There's not much resistance."

"Except yours truly," said Jimbo. Everyone turned to wait for the punch line. Jimbo remained nonchalant. "Sierra Club, Nature Conservancy, all us local tree huggers have some concerns. Magic Time's slated to become a parking deck or something." Jimbo launched his straw's paper wrapper in Lonnie's direction. "If our boy here would just do some pro bono work for us."

Lonnie said, "What do you think, Carter?"

"I've been away too long to have an opinion. But I do have a question."

They all looked at Carter expectantly. He took a pull on his straw and said, "When did Jimbo become such a grown-up?"

Stephen said, "It is pretty disturbing."

Jimbo looked wounded. "Hey, I got married and had kids. So sue me." He held up his hand and sighed patiently. "Of course, goyim like you can't appreciate my Personal Journey. I wasn't the quarterback like you, Carter. Or the president of student council like Lonnie. Or Mr. Musical Prodigy like Stevie here. I didn't date cheerleaders and homecoming queens."

Lonnie began playing the air violin.

"You laugh, but you don't know what it's like to be short and fat and ugly and smarter than everybody else in high school."

"Come on, Jimbo," said Stephen. "You weren't that smart. Besides, Carter's the one who skipped a grade."

"You guys were the first to be nice to me. But I kept waiting for the other shoe to drop."

"Here comes the story about 'the pitch,'" Stephen said indulgently.

Jimbo was undeterred. "Kids would invite me over to their house to play. I'd get there, and they'd sit me down in the parlor and offer me milk and cookies and get out their Bibles. Sometimes their preacher would be there, and they'd start witnessing to me. Telling me about their Lord and Savior and how, because I was a Jew, I was going to hell. Asking me if I wanted to pray and ask Jesus Christ into my heart."

"Singing tenor with the Boys of Troy gospel group must have been sweet payback," said Lonnie.

Jimbo grinned. "About killed my father. He practically disowned me. Daddy didn't want to do anything to piss off the Baptists. They were his best customers."

"I'm impressed," said Carter. "You are definitely the most deraci-nated Jew in history."

"Yep. I'm the last Jewish man in America married to a Jew. Hell, Carter, you're more Jewish than I am. All your girlfriends are Jewish."

Carter adjusted his straw.

"Hey, sorry, man," Jimbo said, and rampaged on. "But now's the time to reclaim your rightful destiny. Grayson's moved back to town, you know. And she's looking goo-ood."

Carter had heard from Sally that his high school sweetheart was in Troy. Everyone had assumed that he and Grayson Boutwell would marry, but they had broken up definitively the summer after he dropped out of law school. Carter had not seen her since and had not expected to see her again.

"Jimbo's wife is with child again, Carter," said Stephen, tactfully shifting topics.

"Yeah, we just saw the sonogram. Another boy."

"Mazel tov," said Carter. "What are you going to name him?"

Jimbo's eyes lit up. "The most revered name in the American South." He paused. "Coach. Coach Stein." Jimbo began his tutorial. "See, in the South, once you've been a coach, football, basketball, T-ball, girls' soccer, no matter what else you do in your life—you can be a school superintendent, president of the university, or president of the United States—everybody still calls you Coach. So we figure, why not just cut to the chase? So we're naming him Coach Stein."

"Jimbo," said Carter, "nobody in New York would believe you exist. You're more of a good ol' boy than Lonnie is."

"Talk about assimilation. Lonnie's a faux Bubba if I ever saw one. He's Vanderbilt-educated, on the *Law Review*, upscale all the way. But to hear him down at the courthouse, you'd think he just stepped out of *Hee-Haw*."

"What about our president," said Carter. "Texas by way of Kennebunkport and Andover."

Jimbo said, "The faux Bubba gets all the perks and bennies of the true Bubba, like chewing tobacco, pork rinds, and Pabst Blue Ribbon, with none of the downside, like getting laid off your job or cut in a knife fight."

"Speaking of sorry Southern stereotypes," said Lonnie, staring out the front window, "look who's crossing the street right now."

"Holy shit," said Jimbo.

Carter and Stephen turned to see a burly black man in a white coat and a tie pushing a wheelchair with someone hunched over in it. His features obscured by an old-fashioned brown fedora pulled down low over the face, the figure in the wheelchair looked frail and mysterious. Wisps of white hair splayed out over the collar of a light gray sweater. Dark pants rode up on legs too spindly to support the man's white socks, which flopped over his black patent leather shoes.

"Samuel H. Bohannon," said Lonnie.

Jimbo whistled. "The Inferior Lizard himself."

"What is he doing in town?" Stephen said. "The trial won't start for another few weeks."

"Probably wants to be seen," said Jimbo. "In all his wounded glory."

Bohannon had been a recluse for years, spending most of his time at his fish camp out on the Little Chickasaw. But lately he had been making appearances in town. "Prosecution hints it's all for public consumption," said Lonnie. "To contaminate the jury pool."

Carter said, "You got to admit, if this is a sympathy ploy"—he took a sip of his cherry Coke—"it's effective."

"Yeah," said Lonnie. "Who'd ever believe that puny little old man in the wheelchair attended by that gentle giant of a black male nurse is a serial killer?"

They watched as the large African-American man helped Bohannon out of his collapsible wheelchair and into the backseat of a silver late-model Chevrolet Impala.

"A genocidal maniac," Carter added, his voice catching slightly as he stared at Bohannon's face dissolving in the glare of the car's back window. The scene was so cinematic, the stuff of a lede, that Carter felt the impulse to reach for his reporter's notebook, which he had not carried since leaving New York. Then, just as powerfully, a feeling hit him that he knew wasn't the faux nostalgia prompted by Wad's cherry Cokes. Something in the slant of the afternoon light outside reminded him of the pleasant aquatic ache of sinuses after a day showing off his dives.

———

PETE CALLAHAN HAD no choice but to run Carter's story on the sit-in at Kress's, even though he had sat on the voter registration piece. After the story appeared in *The Troy Times*, Sarah had sent a note to him at the newspaper thanking him. He wrote back to her in care of Scarborough's, where the SNCC workers received their mail, suggesting that they meet. She called him at the newspaper office from the pay phone at Scarborough's, accepting his offer and telling him not to call her at Magic Time. She explained that the phones were probably tapped and not to communicate anything important on the telephone. Carter would have loved to buy Sarah a cherry slush at Wad's, but he knew that would be asking for trouble, and he wondered where else to meet in town without drawing attention. Sarah suggested Naked Tail. "Bring along a bathing suit this time," she said, laughing, and hung up.

Sarah was waiting for him in the parking lot when he pulled up to Magic Time. She seemed shy when he got out to open the door for her. The last time he had gone to Magic Time with Lige after the sit-in, Sarah had rushed to him and clasped him tightly. Her warmth and physicality surprised him, but he later decided it was related to that day of the voter education excursion, when Carter's presence had inhibited the casual brutality of Sheriff Mizell and his deputy and prevented something worse from happening. He wondered how his immunity must have made Sarah feel about the security and privilege she had left behind in New York.

By the time they reached Naked Tail, the afternoon light was shimmering off the water in flecks of pink and gold, and the oppressive heat of midday had begun to shift into the subtropical languor of evening. While Sarah waded into the water from the beach, Carter stood on the promontory under the giant oak's twisted branches, soaking up the dazzle of the end of a perfect summer day. He reached for the knotted rope dangling from the gnarled limb overhead and pulled it back as far as it could go. Then, clutching with both hands, keeping the rope taut and his elbows bent, he began running fast and hard until the ground gave way as he launched himself into space off the oak's serpentine root. At the apex of the arc, Carter tucked in his knees and executed a full gainer into the pool below. His body adjusted abruptly to the cold as he sank straight down until his feet felt the squishy suction of the muddy bottom, and he recoiled instantaneously into his upward kick. When he broke the surface into sunlight, the first thing he heard was Sarah Solomon's laughter, the sound of male addiction. He swam in her direction. Sarah treaded water in the shallows near the sandbar, watching his progress toward her, her mouth opened slightly in a half smile.

"Nice swing, Tarzan," she said. "I'd give it an eight-point-five." Though he had enjoyed their jousting the last time they were at Naked Tail, he was relieved by how friendly and accessible she now seemed. "Lige told me you and he used to compete on who could swing the farthest."

"How is Lige?" Carter asked.

"Much improved since you saw him last. And busy. You know Lige. After the thing at Kress's, it was right back to work as if he'd never been hurt."

Carter said, "I wish he'd take some time off."

"That was nice of you to bring him out to Magic Time that night," said Sarah. "Sorry Dexter and Charlie were so hostile, but you can understand."

"Where were they that day?" Carter asked. "I didn't see them at Kress's."

"At Magic Time, like me," said Sarah. "Holding down the fort."

"I see," he said. He felt a flicker of jealousy at the thought of Sarah with the other field-workers. Young black males had not been a type he had ever considered romantic rivals. "Lige and Randall wouldn't let me sit in with them," Sarah said. "They say I'm too valuable typing up leaflets." She gave a little snort.

"What about Charlie and Dexter? What are they too valuable for?"

"Oh, Charlie and Dex talk a good game, but they're essentially chickens, too. Though to be fair, Dexter has his talents. He's older and has executive skills. He worked in community relations for A&P in Chicago."

"The grocery chain?"

"I know. Hard to figure," Sarah said. "Anyway, he's willing to take on mundane administrative chores that the others avoid. He'd make a good manager in corporate America, if he wasn't a revolutionary."

"What about Lloyd?"

"Charlie Lloyd is just a glorified street thug, though brilliant. He went to Stuyvesant, one of the really hard public high schools in New York. When it comes to putting his body on the line, though, he's always got some excuse. He wants the authority Lige has, without the risk. I don't blame him. I don't know how Lige and Randall do it. They've got brass balls."

Sarah explained that everybody else begged off when they heard there would be a contingent from Jackson State at Kress's. "Lige doesn't insist," she said. "He says Gandhi taught that people must make their own moral decisions. He dresses it all up as strategy, but he's just letting the rest of us save face."

Sarah said that Dr. King had sent SNCC a telegram congratulating them on the sit-in, and Lige wrote back asking him to come to Ellis County for the registration drive, which irritated some of the others. "They don't trust King," she said. "They call him De Lawd. He's 'old.' But Lige knows that a visit from King would help rally the troops for the voter registration drive, a big morale boost. But of course, that's not going to happen."

"Why not?"

"Sending King into Ellis County, Mississippi, might get him killed."

Carter's reflex was to be offended on behalf of his hometown, but he quickly realized that he had no standing. For the first time, he felt fear on Sarah's behalf. "Then how chicken can you be—to be here at all?"

Sarah acknowledged the compliment with a slight smile. "A lot of Movement folks think none of us should've come here, that we're tempting fate. Some Snick leadership thinks we're crazy, foolhardy. Coming to Ellis County was Lige's idea. They call it the Heart of Darkness."

Carter was undergoing a phenomenon he had learned about his freshman year in Psych 101: cognitive dissonance.

"It's known in Movement circles as the deadliest area in the state because it's Sam Bohannon's home base," Sarah explained. "Headquarters of the White Knights. Lige had to lobby to set up at Magic Time. He felt an obligation to take it to the heart of the beast, to show that Snick wouldn't be intimidated."

"I had no idea about Bohannon until you told me the other day," said Carter.

"I know. You thought he was just your friendly neighborhood purveyor of catfish. Everybody's on edge since the guys disappeared in Philadelphia."

She revealed that the bodies of two young Negroes who had vanished a couple of months earlier were found by a fisherman in the Mississippi River a few days before. One had been decapitated. The FBI rushed to the scene to see if either was one of the three missing, but they were locals named Charles Moore and Henry Dee. "Believe me, the guys at Magic Time interrogated me before I left with you." She tilted her head back to dip it underwater, then shook it into a wet veil behind her ears. "We're all watching out for each other," she said, "and Dexter's driving everybody crazy slipping out on MoonPie runs to Scarborough's."

Carter laughed at the thought of Dexter's transition from A&P headquarters to Scarborough's. "He's going native."

"Can't beat the 'Marshmallow Treat,'" she said. "He probably thinks they'll make him blacker. There are rumors of a white wife in his past. Anyway, he goes to Scarborough's without telling anybody—worries Lige to death." Sarah's expression turned more serious. "And my parents write now all the time, begging me to come home. The search for the three missing guys is all over the papers up North."

"What do you tell them?"

"I say not to worry, that I'm just a glorified secretary, which of course drives them crazy in a different way."

Carter inhaled deeply and spread his arms, leaning backward and letting the water lift him up to float on his back. "Do you like your work?" he asked, his eyes on the cloudless sky.

"Yeah, because the challenge is not in the stenography, but in the human relations."

Carter stood up again in the water. She could see the puzzled look on his face.

"The white volunteers aren't always appreciated." She explained how a skilled, college-educated white girl like her shows up, types like the wind, cranks out newsletters, speaks at meetings—everything they could want in terms of organizational skills, but at the expense of the pride of the Negro girl working in that same office who hasn't had the privilege of going to a place like Barnard or Smith or Wellesley, who in fact had to drop out of school in the ninth grade to help her family at home. "She's never been outside the town she was born in. My parents can fly me around the country. You get the picture."

Carter said, "And to make matters worse, the white girl's easy on the eyes, too."

Sarah said, "You're smart," drawing out the vowel. "The Negro girls don't like the Caucasians poaching on their territory, tempting their men."

"Is that what you do out there?"

She shook her head wearily. "The guys leave me alone. Truth is, I think they're scared of me."

Carter splashed her. "Do you think it might be the gun?"

"We're not all nonviolent," she said, splashing him back. "And we're not all heroes like Lige."

Carter felt a competitive pang over her unabashed admiration for his friend. "How well do you know Lige?" he asked, hoping he sounded casual.

Apparently he did not. "Don't worry," Sarah said, looking at him askance. "Lige already had a white girlfriend."

She savored his expression of shock for a moment. "Oh, now I'm beginning to understand the terms of your friendship: Lige has to be a eunuch."

Carter considered what she said, and rather than address her comment on the merits, he went to the political. "But isn't it sort of an insult to his cause to go with a white girl?"

Sarah paused for a second, trailing her fingers in the water. "Well, I have a couple of thoughts about that. One of the things that surprised me when I got down here was that there's a color line among Negroes—

the lighter ones look down on the dark ones. They have this saying, 'If you're white, you're all right. If you're brown, stick around. But if you're black, get back.' Lige is ambitious. And if you grew up in a society where whites were the be-all, end-all, then why wouldn't you want a white girl? I mean, with the guys it's almost a *rite de passage*." She pointed her toe out of the water as Carter absorbed what she was telling him. "That's French for rite of passage."

Carter felt vaguely queasy.

Sarah disappeared underwater and after a few seconds shot back up like a porpoise. "This is so nice just to get out like this," she said. "Next time I'm bringing a picnic and you bring your guitar."

"Next time?"

"Where else are we going to meet?"

"You know, my high school coach always said, 'When we *assume*, we make an *ass* out of *u* and *me*.'"

Sarah splashed him again. "I've always wanted to be serenaded. I bet you serenade all your girlfriends."

"What girlfriends?"

She replied with a sly smirk. "Don't tell me you don't have any."

Carter didn't answer.

"Well? Do you?"

"Sort of."

"Sort. Of."

"There's this girl I've been seeing on and off since high school."

"Does she have a name?"

"Grayson. Grayson Boutwell."

"A name fit for a shiksa goddess." There was a little edge in her voice.

"Huh?"

"Never mind—is it love?"

Carter glanced up at the sky. "I don't know."

"Oy, men," she said, shuddering, though facetiously. "What are you doing here with me?"

Carter felt his face flush, and he looked away. "She's not too happy with me quitting law school."

"If you were my boyfriend, I wouldn't be happy if you weren't happy."

Carter gave Sarah a tolerant smile; she would have to read entire libraries of Faulkner to begin to grasp the dynamics of families like those he had grown up among. "You don't understand," he said. "Her family is very big in this town. She could have anybody she wants. Her father's ambitious for her." He looked off across the river. "Sometimes I feel like I was drafted."

He pushed off backward again into his floating position. "What about you?" he asked the sky. "Do you have a boyfriend?"

"Show me how you do that," she said, "and I'll tell you."

"Come on," Carter teased. "A champion diver doesn't know how to do the back float?" He righted himself.

"Well, swimming was never a fun thing for me. It was more of a duty. My father's sister drowned when they were kids," she said. The family was from Odessa and had escaped the pogroms to come to America. They had had to cross a river carrying all their belongings. The bridge had been washed away by heavy rains. "It was at night," Sarah said. "Dad's job was to hold on to his sister's hand. He couldn't. I guess that's why I'm a very good swimmer."

Herbert Solomon now taught social psychology at Columbia. "Typical immigrant story," said Sarah. "My grandfather worked selling *schmattes.*"

"*Schmattes?*" Carter injected a syllable between the *sch* and the *m*.

"Garments, rags, cheap clothes. He just worked to make a living so that his son, my father, got the finest education. He wouldn't be happy unless my father got his master's degree."

"And I guess he did."

"He got his Ph.D. Although he still has a slight accent. He spoke Yiddish until age six, then had it beaten out of him at school. He still speaks it at home, at least when he and my mother want to keep secrets from my brother and me. You'd like my father. He's not religious, although we observe the High Holidays—you know, Yom Kippur, Rosh Hashanah—down to the dietary restrictions. I can tell you all the foods we can and can't eat for each holiday. We're not Orthodox, Conservative, or Reform. We're Food Jews."

Sarah suddenly threw her head back and stretched out, stiff as an ironing board. Her feet broke the water only for a moment before she lost her buoyancy, her squeal turning to gurgles as her head sank beneath the surface.

"Come over here," Carter said when she reemerged. "Let me see if I can teach Anna Karenina how to float." She placed one arm on his shoulder and lifted up into his tensed forearm. "Now relax," he said as she allowed him to hold her like a bride. "Breathe normally. Stretch out flat and become weightless. Arch your back slightly so your belly breaks the surface." He felt her thigh against his chest and forearms. She was wearing a simple black bathing suit. He moved his arms under the small of her back and felt the roundness of her bottom where it narrowed into her waist. The cleavage of her full breasts rose and fell before him as she breathed steadily.

"Can you feel the water lift you?" he asked. He supported her until her feet stopped sinking and remained near the surface. When he removed his arms, she began to sink again until he took her back in his arms. They repeated the process until finally she found the right lift in the small of her back. "Good," Carter said.

"I can float," she announced.

"Now you have to answer my question."

"Okay," she said, standing on the sandbar. "I've been known to have gentleman callers."

"Please. What are you, trying to speak my language?"

"Nobody I go swimming with. In Mississippi."

"Nobody your parents selected for you?" he said.

She smiled at his self-mockery. "Lige told me your father was not happy about your visits to Magic Time. You really should be careful."

Carter had become distracted by a drumming sound from the stand of pine trees beyond the promontory. "Hey, listen," he said. She turned and faced the pines. He came up behind her and pointed over her shoulder toward a small black-and-white speckled bird pecking the bark high on the trunk of a pine. "Look."

"What is it?" she whispered.

"It's a species of woodpecker. But that's impossible. They're not found in this area anymore."

"How do you know that?"

"My mother's a bird-watcher. She won't believe this when I tell her. It's a species that's supposed to be dying out."

When Carter was nearly touching Sarah, she turned and looked up into his eyes.

"Are you close to your mother?" she asked.

Carter felt her thigh graze his underwater. "I'm very close to you," he said. Her hand slipped into his, and their fingers entwined. His eyes fixed on hers, Carter turned Sarah squarely toward him. The water lapped at their chests as they stood facing each other on the sandbar. Still holding on to her hands, he clasped his around her waist and pulled her to him until their mouths melded like liquid fire.

II

I FEEL LIKE Tom Sawyer going to his own funeral," Mitchell Ransom said morosely. His daughter straightened his bow tie, the way her mother had done whenever the Ransoms attended formal functions.

"Quit your bellyaching, Daddy, and hold still, or I'll have to start all over," Sally said. "It's not every day you celebrate the fortieth anniversary of a law firm."

"There better not be any speeches, that's all I can say." The judge would have preferred to spend the evening sitting in the breakfast nook playing checkers with his grandson.

Sally, who was already dressed and looking stylish in her aquamarine sheath, hadn't mentioned that the mayor was going to announce a major highway to be named after Mitchell Ransom.

"Whoever organized a black-tie affair in August in Mississippi must have been a sadist or a Yankee or just plumb crazy."

"I'm sure they have air-conditioning, Daddy." Sally sighed with infinite forbearance. "It won't kill you to look nice."

Carter listened to them squabble as he struggled with the cuff links on his rented tux. He empathized with his father's resistance. His recuperation, which he at first assumed would be only a matter of days, had turned into weeks, and the weeks had begun to accumulate. That he had shed his column-writing regimen so effortlessly alarmed him. He seemed to suffer no deadline addiction withdrawal, no compulsion to weigh every event according to its potential as a story idea. That, Carter thought, was the surest sign he had undergone a nervous breakdown.

He had not talked to Emily since coming back to Troy. When she, reciprocally, made no attempt to reach him, his guilt at abandoning her acquired a dimension of hurt at her abandoning him. The hardest nugget of regret was over his failure to have stayed in touch with Josh, but even that he rationalized by convincing himself that courting the boy and not the mother might upset the tenuous equilibrium they had all achieved. Mostly it all just seemed weird. The more time passed, the more impossible it became to just pick up the phone. Sally, with only a hint of disapproval, had told him that she had stopped giving Emily any encouragement.

Although his social encounters were kept to a minimum those first weeks at home, when he finally did venture out into the community, he was surprised by how naturally he eased back into the familiar template. For a big-city convert and devout urbanite, becoming reacquainted with the rhythms and grooves of small-town living—the heat and turgid pace of summertime in Troy—was not as stifling as he had expected. For the first time in his life he seemed to enjoy the lack of event, the lowered expectations, the uncaffeinated passage of time.

The celebration of Judge Mitchell Ransom was being held at the home of Sheppard Boutwell, granddaughter of the sawmill baron Hobart Grayson, who had founded the Graysonite Manufacturing Company. She had christened her only daughter with the proud family name. Since her husband's death, Sheppy had lived alone in the turn-of-the-century mansion that Mr. Grayson had built on the north side of town, where some of the finest houses in Troy were clustered in an enclave called Stonehaven, along an oak-lined, brick-paved cul-de-sac with a stone-pillared entrance. The Grayson manse—Grayburn—was the only Stonehaven house designed in the antebellum Tara style, a Greek revival set among a row of Victorians. The house had white Doric columns and verandas, terraced gardens, and a gazebo and swimming pool positioned discreetly under the magnolias and live oaks.

The Graysonite Manufacturing Company had been headquartered in Oak Park, Illinois, outside of Chicago, and many of the early local lumber barons were midwestern transplants, bringing their wealth and a sense of noblesse oblige to the company outpost in Mississippi. Hobart Grayson, a Catholic, supported the local schools and the arts, establishing a museum surprisingly fine for a town Troy's size. His granddaughter Sheppy inherited not only her family's faith, money, and refinement but also its sense of civic responsibility. Her marriage to Glen Boutwell had been something of a scandal at the time. Boutwell was the son of a timber cutter, up from the turpentine camps, but what he lacked in social cachet, he made up for in ambition and industry. In his own right, as well as through his marriage to Elizabeth Sheppard Grayson, Glen Boutwell had become one of Troy's leading citizens, a successful businessman and respected civic leader who spearheaded March of Dimes drives, was active in the Boy Scouts, and had coached Carter's Little League baseball team. He died in the seventies, when his daughter, Grayson, was in graduate school, and his widow never remarried.

Sheppy Boutwell greeted the Ransoms in the high-ceilinged entrance hall. "Mitchell, you came," she said drily. "I wasn't sure you'd make it." She was still attractive, with immaculate silver hair, high cheekbones, and intelligent, luminous eyes.

Judge Ransom, suddenly beaming in her presence, replied, "Why, I'm delighted to be here, Sheppy. I'd never miss one of your soirées, you know that." Sally lifted her eyes at her father's mood swing and shrugged at Carter.

"Well, look who's here." Bradley Crawford, one of the cohosts of the event, greeted the Ransoms. As Sheppy led Mitchell toward the garden in the back, Bradley announced over her shoulder in a high-pitched squeal, "Y'all! Y'all! Look who's here! The guest of honor! Judge Mitchell Ransom!"

Bradley was the local celebrity writer, a blowsy faded debutante with bottle-blond hair piled like cotton candy atop her head, her breasts on display in a flowing apple-green silk tunic, with matching palazzo pants. Her bestseller, *Sweet Tea Afternoons*, was a coming-of-age tale set in a small Mississippi town; in it, a young bipolar girl from the wrong side of the tracks falls in love with the sawmill baron's son. Sally called the genre "sugar-tit lit."

Bradley air-kissed Sally and opened her arms to Carter as if he were the Prodigal Son. Multiple bracelets jangled from her wrists, and neck-laces rappelled down her cavernous décolletage. "Oh, Cah-tuh, Cah-tuh, Cah-tuh," she tsked, shaking her head. "Oh, my God, Cah-tuh Ransom! What hath befallen you, my poor sweet, sweet pea?" Carter realized his sister must have conveyed the news of his breakup with Emily, since no mere mental collapse would have unleashed so extrava-gantly his host's muse. "We all go through a dark valley on our journey to the mountaintop of connubial bliss that is but all our destinies."

"Hello, Bradley," Carter replied, hoping his brevity might be returned.

Sally hastened her brother onward, but Bradley was not done with her mission of mercy. "Oh, Cah-tuh, honey," she gushed, "I loved your column they reprinted in *The Troy Times*—the one that compared the awful museum bombing to our late troubles. I just wept when I read it. So fiendish."

"Thank you, Bradley," Carter said.

"It wasn't *that* good," said a voice over Carter's shoulder. A bearded man wearing rimless glasses and a curdled expression walked up beside them.

"Have you met my husband, Harold Bernhardt?" Bradley asked. "Harold's a Yankee carpetbagger from Schenectady, New York, if you can believe it. He's a columnist, too, like you, Carter."

Carter had seen Harold's work in *The Barricade*, a weekly given away in a rack at the grocery store. Now, twenty years after the counter-culture ended, Troy finally boasted an alternative newspaper, consisting mainly of groovy anarchy and agitprop for a variety of guilty white lib-eral causes, and ads for pizza parlors.

Bradley pulled Carter toward her one last time and whispered, "Grayson's home. We must talk."

"Just saw your father at the bar," said Bernhardt, watching his wife move on to greet another couple, her breasts preceding her like two bul-bous footmen before a royal sedan. "Doesn't sound like he's too keen on all this attention." Carter knew Bernhardt's columns on "The Good

Judge" had made his father's skin crawl. Mitchell referred to them as "donkey flatulence."

"He's shy," Carter replied.

"How's the judge feel about them reopening the Shiloh Church bombing case?"

"Why don't you ask him?"

"I will. I'm writing a column about it. When my friend the attorney general was here last week, he assured me they would win this time. Send Bohannon to the slammer for keeps." Chewing on a canapé, Harold Bernhardt blanched, as if it contained a bad oyster.

"Are you okay?" asked Carter.

"Just my arthritis acting up again." Harold arched his back, then bent his knee several times, as if trying to get rid of cramps. "I've tried everything, including gold shots."

"Have you ever considered intensive psychotherapy?" Jimbo Stein, wearing a red plaid tie and matching cummerbund, approached Bernhardt with a grin. "Or a lobotomy?"

"Jimbo Stein?" Carter was delighted to be rescued. "How the hell are you?" he asked, pretending he hadn't seen his old buddy in years.

"Can't complain," Jimbo said, pulling Carter into a bear hug. "Unlike Blowhard here. Look in a medical dictionary under hypochondria and there's Harold's picture."

Bernhardt attempted a comeback. "Oh, Stein, were you talking to me? Hey, that VCR you sold me. It's broken."

"It's all that porn you play on it. It's slime-proofed. Shuts down when perverts use it."

Bernhardt decided on a strategic retreat. "Is that Governor Wheaton on the terrace? I think I'll try to corner him on the WunderCorp deal." Then, to Carter, "Come on out, I'll introduce you. Wheaton's a buddy."

"Too bad name-dropping ain't an Olympic sport," Jimbo yelled as Bernhardt made his exit.

"Stein, that laptop I bought from you has been a lifesaver." A thin, balding man approached. He had a crooked yellow smile and an ostentatious British accent. What remained of his hair was long and a wispy reddish brown, and there was a drooping mustache to match. He was wearing Birkenstocks with his tux. Jimbo introduced him to Carter as Simon Lester—"all the way from California." He was the producer of the movie of Bradley's novel, which had provided the town a free makeover.

"You're Judge Ransom's son," said the Brit. "Yet another writer, like Bradley."

Carter smiled.

"What brings you back to Troy, Lester?" asked Jimbo. "Don't tell me there's a sequel to the movie."

"No. Actually, it's the church bombing trial. There might be a documentary in that." He turned to Carter. "I'd love to talk to you about it, Mr. Ransom. Bradley tells me you were close to one of the victims."

Carter didn't answer. He stopped a passing server and snagged a drink.

"You know, Simon," Jimbo said, draping his arm around Lester's shoulder, "Carter might not be interested in reliving that particular episode of his life story."

"Oh," said Simon, "I'm sorry." He seemed genuinely mortified. "I guess I was caught up in the presence of all these distinguished Southern writers."

"That's what we do in the South," said Carter, hoisting his glass to put Lester at ease. "Write and drink."

"Why yay-us," Jimbo drawled. "We go out on the front porch on those warm Mississippi evenin's at the end of a swelterin' summer day and just sit and rock and listen to the crickets chirpin', and the pickup truck idlin', and the coon dogs bayin' off in the distance, and we sip sweet tea and chew tobacco and dip snuff and eat MoonPies and shuck corn and shell peas. And we make biscuits and corn bread and sing hymns and strum banjos and catch fireflies as the sun sets behind the wisteria, and we drink moonshine and tell lies and speak in tongues and handle snakes, and we bury Mama and hide from Daddy and integrate the schools and look after the idiot man-child next door, and just do all the things we Southerners do whenever two or more are gathered—you know, contemplate the hold of the land over us and our abiding sense of place and the awful responsibility of Time."

"You're spoofing me," Simon Lester said with an uncertain smile.

"No, I'm not," Jimbo said. "I'm spoofing Bernhardt's wife."

"What is it about the American South that produces so many writers?" asked Simon.

"It's complicated down here, Simon," said Jimbo. "For one thing, here I am, a Jew, explaining the South to you. But that's a whole 'nother story. Just look around you. See that guy over there talking to Carter's father right now?" He pointed to a barrel-chested, red-faced man wearing a white short-sleeved shirt and a tan Stetson hat. "Former Mayor Ishee, biggest jug-eared racist you ever saw when he first got elected in the sixties. Now he's on the governor's Human Rights Commission."

"What happened?" asked Simon.

"He had a change of heart," said Harold Bernhardt. He had beelined back to Carter and Jimbo when he spied them chatting up his wife's producer.

"Learned to count, more likely," said Carter. "More blacks registered to vote, so bold visionaries like Mayor Ishee and ol' Strom over in South Carolina plunged their index fingers in their mouths, held them up to the breeze, and, lo and behold, figured out which way it was blowing."

"It's a little more complicated than that, Ransom, don't you think?" said Bernhardt.

"No," Carter lied.

Bernhardt seemed on the verge of another pronunciamento when something caught his eye from across the terrace. Carter turned to see Bernhardt's wife, Bradley, casually lift her empty glass aloft, à la the Statue of Liberty, and, without looking up from her coterie, rattle her ice cubes in her husband's direction. As Bernhardt vanished to accommodate his thirsty wife, Jimbo, Carter, and Simon made their way through the dining room to the bar on the terrace, heading toward the trills of Gershwin rising above the murmur of the crowd. Seated at the keyboard of a baby grand was Stephen Musgrove. "What are you doing here, Stevie?" asked Jimbo as Stephen segued to Cole Porter. "Lobbying for NAMBLA?"

"I'm here to keep an eye on you, Jimbo," Stephen replied, "to make sure you don't throw a rucksack over your shoulder and start peddling merchandise."

Draped over the other side of the piano was a husky black man in his mid-twenties. He wore wire-rimmed glasses and a crisp baby-blue shirt with white cuffs and collar, a red silk tie, and matching red suspenders. He looked untested yet world-weary, in the manner of precocious youth. He seemed to be listening seriously to Stephen's music. "Oh, excuse me, gentlemen," said Stephen. "This is—I'm sorry, I didn't get your name."

The young man took a long draw on his cigarette and exhaled out of the side of his mouth. "Rasheed Lovelace." After stirring his drink with his finger, he indicated Stephen at the keyboard. "Just listening to this man wail. Dude's got some chops."

Stephen looked pleased with the tribute as he shifted into Ellington. " 'Sheed's a reporter for the *New York Tribune*, Carter. You two know each other?"

Carter extended his hand. "Carter Ransom."

Rasheed eyed Carter. "Not *the* Carter Ransom." He took Carter's hand and twisted it up into a "bro" shake. "I'm a fan, sir," he said elaborately, but without affect. "Since I was in J-school, I wanted to be Carter Ransom when I grew up."

Carter knew Rasheed Lovelace's byline and his reputation as one of Haynes Wentworth's pets, a rising *Tribune* star with an uncanny front-page track record for a rookie in his twenties. As a stylist, he was not without talent, or at least facility. But he also had a reputation for making stuff up, piping quotes, though Carter had written off such accusations to jealousy.

"You work out of the *Trib*'s New Orleans bureau, right?" asked Jimbo.

Rasheed was vague. "I'm kind of a roving correspondent," he said, lighting another Kool. "They let me do my own thing." He punctuated each sentence with a sniffing sound that Carter did not think was the result of a summer cold.

"You didn't say what brings you to our scenic little community, Rasheed," said Jimbo. "Judge Ransom's fortieth anniversary?"

"Maybe. A town like Troy is just brimming with stories. Like a great big pussy. Just waiting to get nailed. Got the church bombing trial coming up. Maybe something on the blues. I'm talking to a professor at Troy

U., a Yale folklorist who teaches American studies. Guy wants to restore an old blues joint around here."

"Magic Time," said Stephen to Simon. "A local juke joint. All the blues legends used to play there."

"Yeah, that's it," said Rasheed. "He got some foundation money to create a place where some of these old blues musicians who are getting on in years and have no place to go can retire. Kind of assisted living for musicians, where they can maybe record their music." He continued his tutorial. "The only problem is, the property is now owned by that German chemical company that's moving here. WunderCorp wants to put their headquarters out there on the river. They're planning to tear Magic Time down. I'm going to talk to their CEO—see if we can't save it."

"We?" said Carter.

"The *Trib*," said Rasheed, taking a drag off his cigarette and flicking it to the ground.

"I hear Schlank's here tonight," said Stephen. "The WunderCorp honcho."

"I'm not against his company moving here," said Rasheed. "I just want them to leave that juke joint alone. It's part of our national heritage."

Carter was riveted by the casualness with which Lovelace had made a cause of a story he was covering. This was not your father's *New York Tribune*.

Lovelace continued. "Not only for its history as a blues club, but you know, for a while during the sixties it was a civil rights meeting place of some kind—something about voting."

"Snick," Carter said, and then regretted taking the bait with even that elementary a show of one-upmanship.

"Stokely," said Rasheed, smiling. He lifted his fist in the black power salute, sniffed, and moved off toward the bar.

"Well, well, the Three Musketeers!" said a female voice from across the patio.

"Curly, Larry, and Moe," said Lonnie, approaching the baby grand with his wife by his side. Loretta Niles-Culpepper was a small, attractive redhead with watchful eyes. Lonnie had met and married her while they were both in law school at Vanderbilt.

"Looking fine as always, Loretta," Carter said as he embraced her. "How are you?" Loretta had worked as a lawyer in Memphis until the couple moved to Troy so that Lonnie could join the Ransom law firm. Once there, she gave up her career for full-time parenthood, a job to which she brought the same determination and organizational skills that she had to intellectual property rights.

"I'm sorry I haven't gotten by to see you, Carter," Loretta said. "Just so busy with the kids and all."

"Hey, Lonnie, that lady lawyer is here—the one you brought to Carter's house," said Jimbo. "Quite a cupcake."

"You mean Sydney Rushton," said Lonnie. "I don't know if the assistant attorney general has ever been called a cupcake before. I doubt she'd even appreciate lady lawyer."

"When do I get to meet this cupcake?" asked Loretta.

"Hey, Stephen," Jimbo intervened, in a rare spasm of diplomacy, "give us a few bars of that old sacred standard, 'The Fourth Man.'"

Stephen began bouncing and slapping the bass-driven boogie-woogie piano style of white gospel, and Lonnie led off with the first verse in his rich bass-baritone: *"Now the prophet Daniel tells about three men who walked with God . . . Shadrach, Meshach, and Abednego, before the wicked king they stood . . ."*

He was joined by the others on the chorus.

"They wouldn't bend," Jimbo sang in his rich tenor, and the rest of them—Lonnie, Stephen, and Carter—followed with the refrain. *"They held on to the will of God so we are told."*

Sally moved into the circle that was forming around the Boys of Troy and had a gratified look on her face: the old Carter Ransom had come out to play. The party had abated for the spontaneous reunion of the Goys of Troy Quartet, as Jimbo Stein introduced them at the close of the song. "Thank you very much." The guests applauded. Carter glimpsed Grayson Boutwell on the edge of the terrace, looking at him with a skeptical, albeit dazzling, smile. More time had passed since their last encounter than the number of years either of them had been alive up to that point, but the feeling that overcame Carter as he took in Grayson's benign glamour was as true and predictable as the tides: resignation, the burden of inevitability.

As the other Boys of Troy headed for the bar, Carter slipped away for a smoke, making his way toward the gate opening onto the garden. Under tall pines, a giant white oak, and magnolias at the back of the Boutwell estate were the pool and cabana that had been a prime party venue during his teenage years, when he and Grayson were dating.

He had taken a seat at the canopied wrought-iron table and was about to strike a match to light up when he heard someone talking beyond the pool house. Sydney Rushton rounded the corner of the cabana, her head down as she spoke intently into a cordless telephone. She wore a short black cap-sleeved cocktail dress and high-heeled sandals, her blond hair piled precariously in a French twist. In profile she looked like a Gibson girl, a vision from another century. Strolling out to the pool diving board, talking animatedly, she was unaware that Carter was watching her. "Send the files down on Monday. I don't care if they're not in order. I can't believe these are just now turning up. Just get them here." Carter detected a bit of agitation underneath the easy authority with which she spoke. Feeling awkward about eavesdropping, he decided to let her know he was there by striking his match. The phosphorus pop made her look up. He turned away as he lit his cigarette. She said, "I'll call you back," and clicked off the phone.

"Smoke?" asked Carter.

"No, thank you. I quit."

"So did I."

"Quite a performance back there," she said, taking a seat at the table. "How are you doing?"

"I'm doing okay."

"Looking better," she said. In her playful tone, Carter couldn't read whether she was commenting on his health or flirting. "I realize we had no business barging in on you that day—"

"No, it was fine."

Her gaze was direct and candid, and a bit troubled. "Lonnie tells me you're on hiatus."

"That's what I like to call it," he said. "What are you doing back here?"

"Fielding phone calls from the office in Jackson."

"On a Saturday?"

"I had staff looking up some things for me." She straightened her spine and said, " 'Hello, my name is Sydney and I'm a workaholic.' A prosecutor's work is never done. The trial's starting pretty soon."

"I hear."

"My offer still stands, you know. I'd love to take you to lunch and talk with you about what you remember."

Carter exhaled and pulled the ashtray on the table toward him. He flicked ashes into it and replied, "I'm sure you've already read the transcripts of what I remember. That was a long time ago. Besides, it sounds like you've got more reliable witnesses than me."

"Was that a dig?"

Her tone was not challenging, so he reciprocated. "I'm not aware that it was."

"Oh, I just know you don't approve of Hullender's release. But if he's the only way to put Bohannon away, it would be worth it, don't you think? The mastermind?"

"Bohannon's already done time," said Carter, reciting a fact without conviction. "Just like Hullender."

"Bohannon was slapped on the wrist for a federal civil rights violation. That does not let the state off the hook." Now she was sounding peevish. "Why can't we Southerners chew our own tough meat—because it's bad for the Sunbelt?"

"More power to you. You sound pretty zealous—"

She cut him off with a little mock jolt, as if she had been hit by a slingshot. "Zealous prosecutor? That's like calling a woman 'feisty,' isn't it? But more to the point, why am I being put on the defensive? Why do you sound so defeated?"

Now Carter felt irritated, because he could think of no good reason. "It's just that nobody's been able to prove— Have you got new evidence?"

Sydney inhaled. "I can't talk about that with a reporter."

"Yeah, yeah," Carter said. In his experience, some of the most voluble sources were prosecutors who publicly professed not to want to "try their cases in the media." But Sydney seemed a bit snappishly close-mouthed, so he changed the subject. "What's in it for you? How did you get so interested?"

"What's my motive?" She paused. "I don't like to see killers living in my community as ordinary citizens."

"Okay. What else?" Smart-ass, he barely refrained from saying.

"Oh—you want my Freudian reasons."

"Well, it usually comes down to either Freud or Marx, doesn't it?" he said.

"I'm not sure which this is. Maybe both." She thought for a moment. "Okay, I grew up in Birmingham, a smug, rich daddy's girl."

"A Mountain Brook girl," Carter said with an "I'm impressed" inflection.

"God," she groaned in mock agony. "You can't escape the 'Tiny Kingdom' even down here in Troy."

"The snottiest brothers in my fraternity at Vanderbilt were from Mountain Brook."

"Well, I probably know their families, though I'm a little younger than you. I was eight years old when the Sixteenth Street Baptist Church was bombed in 'sixty-three."

Carter said, "So that's what got to you—the four girls killed in the bombing?"

"Well, in the sense that at the time, their deaths affected me not one bit. Nobody I knew—and that would include the adults—had the moral imagination to think, Hey, that could have been me, that could have been my daughter, if I had been born with the wrong skin color."

"So what turned you into the Blond Avenger?"

She gave him a slow double take and pursed her lips, as if she weren't sure whether he was teasing her or diagnosing her. Carter maintained a pleasant, noncommittal silence. He noticed her profile again. It was vaguely soft, as if it had not yet arrived at its adult contours, and seemed at odds with her sleek professionalism.

She turned back to stare at him for another few seconds before responding. "I don't know the answer to that. I went off to college in the Northeast—Smith—and became part of the anti–Vietnam War generation, I guess you'd say. I just missed the whole civil rights thing. After I finished at Yale Law, I considered working for Legal Aid, but then I thought, Let me deal with people I *know*: rich white men. So I worked as a white-collar-crime prosecutor in the U.S. Attorney's Office for the Southern District of New York for five years before coming back to the South."

"What brought you back?"

"The North just didn't have enough bodies of water with stumps in them."

Carter laughed. "I never thought of that, but you're right. Okay, so why Mississippi, although it's true we have the best bogues. Why not go back to Alabama?"

"Ambition. I want to grow up to be a federal judge." She paused for a second and said, "I can't believe I'm saying this! Anyway, I figure I can get there faster here than any other place, even Alabama, which, God knows, has its quota of 'unsolved' "—she made digital quote marks—"civil rights crimes."

"Thank God for Mississippi." Carter stubbed his cigarette out in the ashtray. "So, quite the young woman in a hurry. This is your career-making case."

She sighed. "You know, I'll bet it took you years of living up North to learn how to be that condescending. Fortunately, I got all that out of my system early." Her tone was sardonic but sweet. It was hard to say whether she was flirting with him. Carter had a feeling she didn't know either.

"Folks around here may think you're just harassing an old man," he said, repeating one of the instant clichés he had always pulled from the man on the street.

"Well, you know, old age would be a luxury and a privilege to Randall Peek. Or Celia Bunt. Or Daniel Johnston." She paused before she said, "Or Sarah Solomon."

Carter showed no reaction.

Sydney looked down respectfully.

Carter reached for another cigarette and lit it. Then he quietly asked, "Are you in contact with her family?"

"Her father may be flying in for the trial. Her mother passed away a couple of years ago. Have you stayed in touch with him?"

"I just saw him a couple of months ago. He came to the memorial service for the museum bombing victims. We met up in the newsroom later that day."

"Will you be at the trial?"

"I wouldn't miss it."

Sydney seemed surprised. "I thought you wanted this just to go away."

"I'll be writing about it for the *Examiner*. My editor called me yesterday afternoon and asked me, and I didn't have a good excuse."

"Carter!" It was Sally moving purposefully through the garden toward them. "Carter, the ceremony's about to start. They want the family up front."

"Sally, you've met Sydney Rushton."

"Hi, Sally. I love your bookstore." Sydney had begun rummaging in her purse.

"Thank you, ma'am," said Sally. "Sounds like you've been busy lately. Trial opens in September, right?"

Carter noticed Sydney's mounting frustration as she continued foraging in her purse. "Lose something?" he asked.

"My keys," she said, and without looking up at him, she added, "Why are you smiling?" She dumped the contents onto the tabletop and turned to face him. "It always happens when a case is coming together." Carter continued to smile rather than say he suspected that wasn't the only time it happened.

"Carter," Sally said, "one of our hosts wants to see you before the ceremony."

At last Sydney held up her car keys triumphantly. "I may not be able to stay for the remarks," she said to Carter, and began to punch up a number on the phone.

Once Carter and his sister were back on the terrace, a rouged dowager, the wife of Mitchell's longtime law partner Mason Davis, stopped

Sally and said, "Did you get the message I left on your machine? I wanted to invite you to a dinner party, but you didn't call me back."

Sally looked confused. "I got a message saying you had a great maid for me, but I don't need a maid."

"Oh, silly, I know that," the woman said, leaning toward her conspiratorially. "But in Stonehaven, that's what you say to get somebody to call you right back." Mrs. Davis, as Carter recalled, washed her phone receiver after her maid left each day.

A deep voice greeted them. "Sally Ransom, you must be so proud of your father." Mayor Otis Jameson, Troy's Republican mayor, was a dark-skinned black man with white hair and mustache. "He was a positive force around here, sure was," said the mayor. "A voice of moderation and sanity can make all the difference in a place where the clay is still soft."

"Yes," said Harold Bernhardt, joining the conversation. "Judge Ransom is one of those who seemed to grow even more progressive over the years. His rulings on civil liberties, nuclear power, environmental laws, made him one of the most liberal Southern jurists." Carter suppressed the urge to point out that at the time, his father had been vilified for the very actions now being celebrated. Bernhardt was subtly repositioning himself to intercept a passing guest. "And speaking of making a difference," he said, "have you all met Helmut Schlank, CEO of WunderCorp, American division?"

Schlank was tall, blond, gray-eyed, and handsome, with slicked-back hair and fashionable designer eyeglasses. His "How are you?" revealed a faint German accent. He reminded Carter of one of his heroes from the 1960s, the rocket scientist Wernher von Braun.

"I understand you're locating here," said Sally.

"We certainly hope to, with your support."

"If we're lucky," said the mayor. "There's still some resistance."

"Oh?" said Sally.

"Your congressman," said the mayor, widening his eyes disapprovingly.

"No kidding," Carter said. He was surprised that any local politician would have the temerity to reject the blessings of progress.

"He's been working with a local group trying to drum up support for having that old juke joint and Shiloh Church declared historic sites," said Mayor Jameson.

"Elijah Knight may have cost himself reelection come November," Bernhardt announced knowingly. He took the mention of the congressman as an opening to join the conversation.

"Where is Congressman Knight?" said the mayor. "I'm surprised he'd miss this occasion."

"He had to be in Washington for a big vote," Sally said.

Carter was sorry Lige couldn't be there for Judge Ransom's celebration. They had not seen each other all summer, though Lige had called to check on him a couple of times. Their paths had crossed frequently during the years in the early 1980s, when Carter was the *Atlanta Constitution*'s Washington bureau. When Lige had announced for the Mississippi congressional seat, held by an unreconstructed racist octogenarian who was finally forced to retire because of Alzheimer's, the media made a great deal of his return, after years working in Atlanta City Hall, to the place where he had been beaten up as a young man seeking the right to vote. His opponent happened to be the former mayor Ishee, who had once gone on TV and set fire to a petition Lige sent him. Lige's landslide victory, making him the first black congressman from that district since Reconstruction, made national headlines. Carter wrote a piece on Lige's swearing-in: the House Speaker, who administered the oath, had commanded the Mississippi National Guard in 1961 when they met Lige and the Freedom Riders' Trailways bus at the Alabama state line and escorted them into Jackson.

"Congressman Knight is no problem," said Schlank pleasantly. "We've had opposition everywhere we've gone in."

"Just like the Third Reich." It was Jimbo. "Well, I guess they didn't have opposition in Austria and Finland—okay, and France." He and Stephen had now joined the expanding group.

Jimbo introduced himself to Schlank. "I'm on the board of the Nature Conservancy," he said.

Schlank enthusiastically offered his hand to Jimbo, as if he could absorb any opposition by sheer force of charm. "I welcome the opportunity to acquaint you, Mr. Stein, with our company's proud tradition of community enrichment."

Carter winked at Jimbo, who rather indiscreetly mimed the motion of autoerotic activity.

Sally nudged Carter. "Somebody's waving to you, Pross."

From the look of her, Grayson Boutwell seemed to have moved in an unbroken continuum from homecoming queen to the cusp of middle age. She still had the glow, her dark brown hair sun-streaked—from the hours on the tennis court, Carter assumed. She appeared more fashion-forward than anyone he had seen in Troy, wearing a simple short silver-gray sleeveless top, buttoned down in the back, over matching pants that tapered tightly to her ankles.

"Hello, Grayson," Carter said when he reached her and leaned down to kiss her cheek. "Beautiful as ever."

"You clean up nice, too, Carter," she said. "I hope you're bearing up okay under the social onslaught."

"Sally thinks of this as a form of therapy."

Grayson looked at Carter, holding his gaze for a moment. He was relieved to see some not unattractive dullness in her eyes, the only outward sign that all her days had not been sunny.

"So what brings you back to the wood-paneling capital of the world?" said Carter.

"I was living in Dallas until last year. I came back home to raise the kids around family and go back to school at Troy U. to try to finish that degree so I can teach."

"I heard you were divorced," said Carter. "I'm sorry." As an heiress to the Graysonite fortune, Grayson Boutwell was in no need of a paycheck, and he admired her desire to get her degree.

"No need to be. I got two beautiful children out of it. Two girls, seven and nine." She reached for her wallet photos. "I've followed your career, Carter," she said as he looked at the pictures. "I'm so proud of you." Then her face clouded with concern. "And I was sorry to hear you've not been a hundred percent. Are you okay?"

Carter nodded.

Grayson took a sip from her wine spritzer while continuing to appraise him. "I saw you talking to someone at the pool house. I thought she might be your date."

Carter felt himself flush. "No. I'm unfettered these days," he said. He glanced back toward the garden where he had left Sydney Rushton and saw her in intense conversation with Lonnie. He wondered where Loretta was. Carter felt strangely defensive, as if Grayson were making some moral judgment.

A man appeared at her side. "Oh, Tom, have you met Carter Ransom? Governor Wheaton is my escort tonight." Grayson gave a reflexive little coquettish shimmy.

They shook hands, and Tom Wheaton said, "Carter, I met you at the Democratic convention in Atlanta in 'eighty-eight. You were with a New York newspaper, as I recall."

"The *Examiner*. Still am."

"But you used to be in Atlanta, right? I read you when I was working at the Presidential Library there in the early eighties."

"Oh, yeah, I remember," said Carter. "You were one of Jimmy's boys. Thanks for coming tonight."

"Grayson, may I sweeten your drink?" the governor asked.

"He seems likable," said Carter as the governor headed for the bar. He had read about Tom Wheaton's bachelor exploits even in the New York tabloids. His single-man status had made him fodder for the gossip columns as well as cause for concern among Democratic power brokers.

"Just a friend. I'm not ready."

"I understand," Carter said.

"Good. Maybe we can be friends. You know, Carter, seeing you here at the house is so strange. And now this trial—it's so eerie. It's like she's bringing all of us back together again."

Carter stalled uncomfortably for her to continue.

"You know. My rival. The woman who stole you from me. Well, let's be real, she was still a girl."

Carter was contemplating the mixed benefits of aging—like the instant cut-to-the-chase in reunions between old friends—when the screech of feedback from a sound system set up on the terrace brought all conversation to a halt. The crowd of more than two hundred pressed onto the terrace. Sheppy Boutwell introduced Mayor Otis Jameson, who would serve as master of ceremonies. Standing beside him at the microphone was Judge Ransom, looking ill at ease. Next to him was Sally, who summoned Carter to join her. Governor Wheaton, Dr. Raymond Renfro, Mason Davis, and Lonnie Culpepper all stood close by, waiting for their turns to speak.

Carter scanned the crowd and spotted Nettie Knight for the first time that evening, looking prosperous in a topaz knit suit. She stood next to the mayor's wife and watched the judge from the doorway. Catching Carter's eye, she protruded her chin and gave a little proprietary nod—meaning, Carter inferred, that he seemed to be coming along nicely.

"Friends, we're here tonight to celebrate the fortieth anniversary of Troy's most distinguished law firm, Ransom, Davis and Culpepper, and the birthday of its founder, Judge Mitchell Ransom." The mayor ran through the boilerplate of the judge's résumé: he came to Troy from eastern North Carolina as a young man out of Harvard Law School; served distinguished terms as president of the Mississippi State Bar Association; was a superior court judge; was appointed to the federal bench by President Jimmy Carter.

Governor Tom Wheaton read a congratulatory telegram from the former president and spoke with slightly official-sounding eloquence of the impact of Mitchell Ransom's rulings during his long career on the bench and of the importance of men like him in transforming the South during the crucible of the civil rights revolution—how he had inspired Wheaton himself to go into law. Next, Dr. Renfro told how he and Mitchell Ransom had been shot down in the Mediterranean during World War II and got to know each other in a German POW camp. Doc joked that he had convinced Mitchell to settle in Troy after the war and practice law so he could handle his malpractice suits. The judge's law partner Mason Davis weighed in with forgettable reminiscences about the burden of Mitchell's long absence from the firm during his time on the bench. Lonnie Culpepper ended the official remarks after reading a telegram from Congressman Elijah Knight. Lonnie spoke with feeling about what it had been like to grow up playing in the Ransom household and later to clerk for his best friend's father, of whom he had been terrified as a boy. As articulate as Lonnie was, Carter noticed that he seemed subdued and distracted, not quite himself.

Over and over the literary model invoked in the speeches had been Atticus Finch. Carter had heard his father compared to the hero of Harper Lee's *To Kill a Mockingbird* when he was younger, but he had never taken it seriously. He didn't feel at all like Jem. Street angels can be home devils. Not that Mitchell was a bad father, by any stretch. It just hadn't been easy living with Mount Rushmore.

The mayor announced the naming of the new highway. Pete Callahan presented Judge Ransom with a souvenir copy of the next day's front page of *The Troy Times*: a story and a four-column color picture of the judge, with the banner headline declaring JUDGE MITCHELL T. RANSOM EXPRESSWAY OPENS.

The judge took the microphone and thanked everyone. His comments were brief, but Carter had never seen his father so overwhelmed. He seemed genuinely surprised, if not a bit amused, to have a namesake highway. Then Nettie and Sally brought out a gigantic birthday cake, and Stephen played an up-tempo "Happy Birthday." The waitstaff—all black, the reporter in Carter observed—moved through the crowd with flutes of champagne.

Carter saw Sally standing off to the side, tears streaking her face. He glanced around to see if Sydney Rushton was still there, but she seemed to have made good on her word and left.

As Carter watched the crowd envelop his father to congratulate him, Lonnie sidled up and said, "Can I speak to you for a moment?" He looked worried.

"Sure. Hey, thanks for your comments. I know Dad appreciated them. What's up?"

"We'd better go somewhere else."

They threaded through the guests toward the back of the garden and walked down to the pool. Lonnie checked the cabana to see if they were alone. Carter wondered if what he was going to say had something to do with his marriage.

"I was just talking to Sydney Rushton about the case," he said. "Apparently, some new documents have turned up in the old Mississippi Sovereignty Commission files, and they corroborated Hullender's testimony."

"And—"

"She seemed pretty shocked herself and swore me to secrecy, but I thought you should know. It's about the judge."

Carter looked at Lonnie. He had never seen him so troubled.

"Of all the times to talk about this," Lonnie said, glancing nervously toward the noise of the reignited party. "I think she's got the goods on Bohannon. Hullender's testimony can put him away. But . . ." Again Lonnie looked over his shoulder. "Hullender's also going to testify"—he lowered his voice—"that your father covered up evidence against Bohannon."

"What? That's ridiculous. Does she think anybody's going to believe a murderer?"

Lonnie looked away. "I'm sorry, Carter. I hate being the one to tell you this. She says the judge was protecting a friend, another Klan hit man."

Carter stared in disbelief.

Lonnie's eyes locked in on his friend. "Apparently, there's proof."

12

W HEN CARTER ARRIVED at the old Pinehurst Hotel, Sydney
Rushton was already waiting in the lounge off the lobby.

"You're on time," he said, sliding into the booth across from her.
The bar was cool, dark, and as sparsely populated as Carter had hoped
it would be in late afternoon.

"Is that surprising?" she asked.

"No. I'm just impressed. I find that the schedules of lawyers do not
always accommodate us mortals."

Sydney was dressed in skinny black pants and a sleeveless white top.
She pawed through her briefcase with one hand and with the other adjusted the lime silk jacket draped over her shoulders in deference to the
Pinehurst's notoriously frigid air-conditioning. "I wouldn't be late," she
said, retrieving eyedrops from the briefcase. "I'm much obliged that you
agreed to an interview. What changed your mind?"

"Just want to be helpful."

"Or nosy?" she said, her eyes lifted ceilingward as she put drops in
her eyes. When she recovered her vision, she gave him a bright grin.

Carter stifled a smile and ordered a Heineken from the bartender.
Then he leaned back and took in the mahogany-paneled elegance of
Troy's finest hotel. "How do you like your accommodations?" he asked.

"Room service closes down a bit early, but otherwise it's peachy," she said, blinking as she dabbed a cocktail napkin at the saline solution tearing at the corner of her eye.

"Well, it's not the Tutwiler," Carter said, dropping the name of the only hotel he knew in Birmingham, "but this place holds a lot of memories for me. Every senior prom, sock hop, and graduation party in Troy was held here. Whenever I see these old hardwood floors, I get an uncontrollable urge to get down and Gator."

Sydney's glistening green eyes registered the image appreciatively as she sipped her gin and tonic. "How does it feel to be back at work?" she asked.

"I don't know yet. I haven't written anything."

"It must be strange covering something you had such a personal stake in," she said, looking at her drink as she stirred it with a swizzle stick.

"The ethics of it are a little dicey, even for a columnist," he said. "Especially if you subpoena me to testify." He eyed her for a reaction. "I suggested the *Examiner* send another reporter to cover the trial for our news pages."

"I don't mean ethically." She speared the lime wedge on the lip of her glass with her swizzle and squeezed it into her drink. "I mean emotionally."

"I always try to write about things I feel something about."

Sydney sipped her drink and gave the slightest sigh of defeat. "You and Congressman Knight are friends."

"Since we were kids. His mother worked for my family. Still does."

"Did your relationship change when he got involved with the Movement?"

Carter smiled at her pronunciation—Move-mint, as if she had been there. "Yes, Oriana Fallaci," he said, looking at her quizzically.

She put her drink down with a hint of fatigue. "I'm just making conversation here, Carter," she said. "The congressman's already agreed to testify. I'm hoping I can get you to do the same."

Carter studied her face, trying to read her. Could she be so tough that she would ask him to testify in a trial that, if what Lonnie said was true, she knew would hurt his father? As a journalist, he was used to sources leveraging him for information, and maybe this was Sydney's way of trying to get something out of him about the judge. "So let's make conversation about you," Carter said. "What's your story?"

"Could you be more specific?"

"Married? Single? You were at the party alone, right?"

Carter thought he detected the beginning of a grimace, and he wondered if he had made a sexist faux pas. But her answer was surprisingly straightforward. "I've been in a serious relationship for several years. We haven't set a date." She speared her lime again and added, "Yet."

"What does he do?" Carter asked.

"He's a litigator," she said. "We met when I was in Birmingham, clerking for a federal judge after law school, before I went to work for the U.S. Attorney's office in New York. His firm had a lot of business up there, so we got to be together quite a bit. Since I got this case, we haven't seen much of each other. I drive over from Jackson on weekends once a month."

"Will he come to the trial?"

She laughed. "Are you kidding? I wouldn't allow it. I'm nervous enough as it is."

"Does he second-guess your game plan?"

Sydney shifted in her seat. "Why do I feel like I'm being cross-examined?" She answered anyway. "He just wants me to do well. Sometimes he's a little meddlesome, that's all."

"A control freak?"

She paused to consider, as if she had never thought of him in those terms. "I wouldn't say that. He's older. More experienced. This trial's big. He wants to help."

Sydney seemed flustered. Carter was surprised she had allowed him to pry so casually.

"Want another drink?" he asked, signaling the bartender.

She demurred. "You still haven't said whether you'll help me out."

"Make your case," he said.

"I have to call witnesses early in the trial to establish the crime and introduce the victims." She cleared her throat. "What happened was horrific, but you know, the sixties were a long time ago. People forget the context."

"There are other graduates of the Movement." He pronounced it the way she had.

"As 'outside agitators,' they're not as jury-proof as you."

Again Carter was amused by her fluency with the period vernacular. "You must be talking about Charles Lloyd, reverend and New York mayoral candidate."

"I've spoken to him. And I may call on him—his current troubles notwithstanding."

Carter tried to keep his expression neutral.

"I've read your columns, Carter. I know how you feel about Charles Lloyd." She smiled patiently and excused herself to go to the ladies' room.

As the bartender set down a fresh Heineken, Carter watched Sydney exit. She was principled, perhaps to a fault. He could tell that. She saw things clear-eyed, up and down, right or wrong, but she had a supple intelligence for a prosecutor. He stared at her as she walked with a little swagger toward the lobby. It was hard to believe that a quarter of a century had slipped away since he stood in that lobby waiting for Grayson Boutwell to emerge from the same restroom Sydney disappeared into, back in the waning days when youth still seemed like a series of dances and cotillions gliding seamlessly into adulthood.

———

IT WAS LATE MORNING on a Saturday in July, and the sun was blazing in a cloudless sky when Carter, Lonnie, and Stephen pulled off the highway in Carter's Ford Fairlane and parked along the logging path next to the white station wagon from Magic Time. Jimbo's beat-up blue Corvair was also there, and he was sprawled across the hood, dressed in black lace-up boots and camouflage fatigue trousers. "What took y'all so long?" he asked, squinting out at them from the shade of his forearm draped across his face. "I've been up since five this morning."

Jimbo had been out with Doc Renfro, his hunting companion since junior high, when he had been "blooded" by Doc—the ritual of having his face smeared with the blood of the first deer he killed.

Lonnie said, "Bag anything?"

"A sunburn," said Jimbo. "No raccoon dicks this time."

"Raccoon what?" said Stephen.

"Doc collects coon dicks," said Jimbo. "They're supposed to bring good luck. He's got them strung across a beam in his shed like scalps. Little skeleton bones of all the raccoon peckers he's cut off."

"Lucky he don't hunt bear," said Lonnie. He lifted a cooler of beer from the trunk of the Fairlane.

"My old man's going to be thrilled if his customers find out I'm hanging around with civil rights workers," Jimbo said. "He'd prefer I was fraternizing with brownshirts from the American Nazi Party."

"It's just a picnic," Carter said. "You don't have to march with them or anything."

"Do they all have beards?" Lonnie asked Carter.

"Just the women," said Carter.

"I haven't been to Naked Tail in years," said Stephen. He had taken a picnic basket from the car. "I wonder if the rope swing is still there."

"Oh, yeah," said Carter. "And the water's just as cold."

"My poor weenie's shriveling in anticipation," said Jimbo. He was stepping into a pair of baggy bright yellow swim trunks.

"How could you tell?" said Lonnie.

"It looks like a raccoon dick," said Carter. "Only smaller."

Jimbo snapped his towel at Carter's butt as they started down the winding trail. Carter led the way, carrying towels in one hand and his guitar case in the other. Lonnie toted the Jax beer and a football. They paused from their laughing and joking and cussing as they drew near the river and heard music, the dum-diddy-dum of banjo picking, claw-hammer style. Emerging from the trees, they saw picnickers arrayed in the bright sunlit glade of Naked Tail. The white seminarian, Daniel Johnston, was leaning against a poplar; he was playing a five-string banjo and singing the Cuban folk song "Guantanamera."

Carter searched for Sarah. She was sitting on a log next to a picnic basket, wearing tan Bermuda shorts over her black bathing suit, her hair pulled back in a ponytail. She leaned forward with legs crossed, singing along on the chorus. Next to her was Randall Peek, in his overalls and taped-up horn-rims. He was singing as well, while Dexter Washington, shirtless in cutoff dungarees, sat cross-legged on a blanket, reading a paperback. Next to Dexter on the blanket lay Charlie Lloyd, dressed in khakis and a white T-shirt, holding a cigarette and a beer in one hand while trying to find a station on a transistor radio with the other. A Negro girl with large, liquid eyes and skin the color of creamed coffee—Carter recognized her as Celia Bunt, the oldest daughter of Reverend Bunt—sat opposite them on a red cooler, barefoot in a pink skirt and white cotton top, smiling shyly but not singing along.

Daniel Johnston paused to greet Carter. "You play that thing?" he called, indicating the guitar case. Everyone turned to see who had arrived.

"A little bit," Carter answered. "Stephen here's the real musician."

"N-n-not really," said Stephen, who was carrying his mandolin. The new situation had set off his stutter, dormant since he had gone off to Juilliard.

Carter looked around. He had expected a bigger crowd. "Where's Lige?" he asked.

"He had business in Jackson," said Sarah, who had gotten up to greet him. "He may make it back in time to join us." Carter felt his heart rate pick up at Sarah's approach. The two still felt a bit of town-gown awkwardness at expressing their fondness in public. The Magic Time crew had acknowledged their relationship only by failing to object on the occasions when Sarah took off with Carter, who had not mentioned his new love interest to anyone in his "real life." Carter had grown so used to Sarah's SNCC bosses that even Charlie's hostility had come to seem automatic and routine, like a tic that has ceased to be noticed. Their impression of white Southerners was limited to two stereotypes—the redneck racist and the bleeding-heart do-gooder, and Sarah's boyfriend was neither.

"You made it," she whispered as she leaned into him ambiguously.

After Carter made the introductions, Jimbo Stein grinned and said, "So y'all are the Commanists Carter's been telling me about."

Sarah laughed, though the joke did not go over with the others. There was a billboard on the highway north of Troy showing Dr. King at the Highlander Folk School—MARTIN LUTHER KING AT COMMUNIST TRAINING SCHOOL. It had been posted by the United Klans of America.

"And now you're a fellow traveler," said Daniel, continuing to tune his D string.

Jimbo said, "You call this a party? I swear I thought you had a battalion of reds and pinkos out there at Magic Time." He removed a can from one of the six-packs of Jax in Lonnie's cooler, offering one to the others, with no takers except for Lonnie himself. Jimbo popped his open with the can opener on his Swiss Army knife and took a long pull.

"Are any of y'all still in school?" Lonnie addressed Sarah and Daniel, the friendliest and whitest people there, plying the skills he had developed at countless frat parties.

"I'm from Barnard," Sarah said, "and Charlie is from Howard."

"Brooklyn," Charlie corrected her.

"College?" asked Lonnie.

"No, it's a borough."

The others laughed, and Lonnie flushed.

"Jock, huh?" Randall indicated the jersey Lonnie was wearing. "You play football at Vanderbilt?"

"No," said Lonnie, now seeming anxious to shed the spotlight. "I'm going to law school there. How about you? Where did you go?"

"Randall dropped out of grad school at Harvard to come down here," Sarah said. "That's why he wears those glasses and has a pointy head, even though he's just a bougie from Atlanta."

"Hey, Clark Kent," Charlie said to Carter, "where's your notebook?"

"Good job on that article, by the way," said Daniel.

"In the *Troy Behind-the-Times*," said Dexter.

"Lige was amazed it ran at all," said Sarah.

"Oh, the one Carter wrote on you guys registering voters out in the county," said Jimbo. "It raised a stink in town all right." After the Kress's sit-in, Callahan had relented and printed Carter's first article.

"Where did you get that stuff about the tensions in the Movement?" Dexter asked, sounding impressed more than annoyed. Carter had included a paragraph in the story about the split between the Movement's tactical nonviolent people, who saw nonviolence simply as a useful strategy, and those who embraced nonviolence as a way of life. He had also noted the related conflict between the fast-talking Yankees and the religious "natives." Carter was pleased that the piece had been read so closely.

"I'll bet the local yokels loved learning about divisions in the Movement," said Charlie.

"Yeah, divide and conquer," said Dexter. "Same old same old."

"Was I wrong?" Carter demanded. He thought he saw the first sign of a smile on Charlie's face. He didn't know whether that meant "touché" or that Charlie enjoyed having his role as provocateur acknowledged in print.

Daniel began frailing the chords to "Guantanamera" again. Before he reached the chorus, Stephen had his mandolin out and had picked up the melody. Lonnie took the football and sent Jimbo out for a pass on the sandy beach, and when he overthrew the ball, Jimbo kept running up the promontory to the oak tree and the rope swing. Snaring the knotted rope, he ran off the embankment, swinging out over the lagoon and descending in a cannonball to the cry of the ape-man. "Aaaaaaah-ah-ah-ah-aaaaaah!"

Jimbo surfaced, screaming "Hotamighty!" and shaking dark bangs out of his face. "Come on in, you pussies."

"That white boy's crazy," said Dexter.

"I know," said Carter.

"You ain't getting me out there," said Charlie Lloyd, still fiddling with the radio. "Freeze my ass off."

Randall said to Celia Bunt, "I'll go if you will."

"I can't swim," she said.

"I'll show you how," said Randall. He removed his glasses, dropping his overall straps and taking off his T-shirt. Carter noticed scars on his shoulders and back.

Dexter announced to no one in particular that he would stay on the shore with Charlie and play lifeguard. It occurred to Carter that they might not know how to swim. As a boy, he had been surprised at how colored folks did not take to the water as readily as white people, and when he taught Lige how to swim, Lige told him he was the first in his family to learn.

While Randall gave Celia swimming lessons, the others tried to outdo each other jumping, diving, or swinging creatively from the oak tree. Watching Sarah's perfect jackknife, Jimbo whispered to Carter, "Pross, you didn't tell me about the delectable femme working with the *schvartzes*. One of my people no less. And mozzarellas."

"Must you, Stein?" Carter said.

Jimbo turned sharply to look at Carter and then looked back at Sarah. "Don't tell me she's been tasting the flesh of the uncircumcised! Jeez, Pross, you been holding out on me!"

Carter tried to affect a noncommittal look.

"Oh, man, you're a goner. Ay, caramba! You're gonna have some serious 'splainin' to do to Troy's favorite debutante."

Carter shushed Jimbo and said, "Listen."

"Trying to change the subject?"

"Look there," Carter said. "On that tree." He pointed to a stand of pines behind them. "It's the red-cockaded woodpecker. The one I told you about."

Jimbo stood there watching the small black-and-white-speckled bird jackhammer the pine. Jimbo knew more about wildlife than any of his friends, and almost as much about birds as Carter's mother. "Listen to that little sucker," Jimbo said. "The red-cockaded pecks all around the nesting hole so the sap runs out around it and keeps predators out. I've never seen one of those around here."

"Race you to the lightning tree," Sarah called up to Carter from the water as he prepared to dive. She began her butterfly stroke toward the fallen remains of a water oak on the sandbar. Carter dived long in her direction, almost catching up with her underwater before surfacing, and they swam freestyle the final few yards to the tree. Their hands simultaneously slapped the submerged trunk. Laughing, they faced each other, water spewing off their faces.

"No fair diving so far," Sarah gasped. "You cheated."

"I beat you," he said.

Catching their breath, they turned to face the shore. In the shallows, Randall was showing Celia how to lift her head out of the water with each stroke. "I think Randall has a crush," Sarah said. "Celia's so smart, Carter. She should be going to college, but that's just not in the cards. You should have seen her at my Freedom School classes. She just devoured the books I gave her." She turned and looked at him. "I like your friends."

"They like you."

"Lonnie's competitive with you."

"He always has been."

"And Stephen's a sweetheart. And so talented. Is he homosexual?"

Carter had never had anyone ask him such a thing about his friend directly before. "I don't know," he answered, feeling slightly disloyal. "I've never asked him."

"There are a lot of boys like him in the city."

"How about Jimbo?"

"Jimbo Stein," she said, and laughed. "Underneath all that wiseass bravado, I sense there's a mensch."

"A mensch?"

"It's Yiddish. The Jewish equivalent of a good ol' boy. But a lot gets lost in translation."

Carter stood behind Sarah and put his hands on her waist, keeping his eyes on Charlie and Dexter playing cards under the trees. "Why won't they swim?" he asked.

Sarah cocked her hip, but so discreetly, into his touch. "Oh, that's just their sullen pose. Charlie wouldn't know what to be if he wasn't being a pain in the ass."

"It's nice to have an identity."

"Actually, I worry more about Dexter. The guy is so driven. He's trying to inject a little Chicago efficiency in Mississippi, and it's not going to happen. Today's the first time I've seen him relax since I got here."

"You call that relaxed?"

She turned toward Carter. "Hey, I liked your guitar playing, Señor Hombre Sincero." She pushed back and held her foot up to him. He took it in his hands. "I dare you to kiss it," she said. Carter slipped his head under the water and kissed her instep, rotating her ankle so that he could gnaw on her arch. When he came up out of the water, she was giggling maniacally. "You still owe me a serenade, you know."

"After lunch," he said. "One should never serenade on an empty stomach."

"I'm starving." She turned and began to kick toward shore.

Carter grabbed her ankle. "Sarah, hold on," he said. "We may not get another chance to talk."

"Yeah?"

Carter felt moved to do something he had contemplated only vaguely. "There's going to be a dance at the Troy Country Club next week."

"Really."

"You can think about this if you like, but"—he could feel the blood rushing to his face—"would you want to go with me?"

Sarah smiled. "A dance? At your country club?"

"Yes. Black tie." He could tell that she was intrigued by the idea.

"You're asking me to a dance?"

"I'm asking you to go with me."

She looked at him skeptically. "Are you sure they let Jews in?"

Carter had not thought of that.

"Will Mr. Stein be there?" Sarah asked.

Carter felt awful. Of course the Steins weren't members.

"You really are naive, aren't you?" she said sympathetically. "I think you'd better check." She turned again toward shore. Then, looking back over her shoulder flirtatiously before swimming away, she said in the perfect pitch of an Ole Miss coed, "But it's darling of you to ask."

Carter had overlooked the Jewish problem because his own misgivings had been focused on another concern: Troy's favorite debutante and his on-and-off girlfriend, Grayson Boutwell. Watching Sarah's shapely form emerge from the shallows, the long thighs and broad shoulders of a swimmer's physique, Carter suppressed a shiver of remorse.

In the shade of the trees on the shore, the picnic basket that Celia's mother had stocked was being unpacked. Carter approached to inspect the contents—fried chicken, potato salad, bologna sandwiches. "Wasn't that thoughtful," Sarah said. "Mrs. Bunt packed a box of MoonPies for dessert. She must have known Dexter was coming."

Carter sat silent and ate while Lonnie engaged Sarah in a conversation about what it was like living in New York City. When she got up to get more potato salad, Lonnie sauntered to the cooler to get another beer and joined Carter on the hollow log. "Man, I wish I'd brought a date along."

Daniel began frailing his banjo and intoned in an AM deejay voice, "I'm sending this song out with hugs to Charles Lloyd, from Brooklyn, New York."

"Let me tell you the story of a man named Charlie, on a tragic and fateful day." Stephen had picked up his mandolin. Carter reached for his guitar. *"He put ten cents in his pocket, kissed his wife and family, went to ride on the MTA."*

By the chorus—*"Did he ever return, no he never returned"*—the Boys of Troy had transformed themselves into the Kingston Trio. After the song ran its course, with Charlie's fate still unlearned, Lonnie told of one of the Boys' exploits at a gospel sing at First Baptist, Jackson. While practicing outside in the alley, a hobo wandered over off the street to listen, and he began shouting and moving and singing along. Before they were through, he had thrown away his bottle and rededicated his life to Christ right there in the alley.

"Jimbo couldn't resist giving an altar call," said Stephen.

With that, Jimbo stood up and faced his congregation. "Brothers and sisters," he declared in an unctuous stained-glass voice, "friends and neighbors, my sermon this glorious Sunday morning is on the First Three Words in the Bible. That's right—" He worked his lips with emotion. "The First . . . Three Words . . . in . . . the Bible." Dramatic pause. "Genuine morocco leather." Everyone burst out laughing, and Jimbo barreled on in a rapid-fire staccato punctuated with index finger jabs. "Now take that word 'Genuine'—'Genuine' means 'real.' My faith is real to me. And Morocco—Morocco is a place. Jesus said, 'I go to prepare a place for you.'" Finally, after some free association on leather from the hide of the donkey Jesus rode into Jerusalem, Jimbo bent over, his hands on his knees, and gasped, "I ran out of stupidity."

Carter persuaded Stephen to spell Jimbo with his Elvis impression, a sequence of swiveling hips, rolling shoulders, tossed forelock, twitching upper lip, and a seditious growl. *"Well, since my baby left me . . ."*

After Stephen reached down for napkins from the picnic basket to mop his brow and tossed them to Sarah and Celia, Charlie Lloyd started in again. "Yeah, Elvis stole our music, all right."

Sarah groaned. "Oh, come on, Charlie," she said. "Could it be appreciation instead of larceny?"

"You got to admit the white boy has soul," said Dexter.

"Probably stole that, too," said Charlie, lighting a cigarette.

Carter got the feeling that the remark was directed toward him, which somehow emboldened him to pick up his guitar, capo up to his key, and let rip with Bob Dylan's "The Lonesome Death of Hattie Carroll."

"How in the world did a cracker like you learn music like that?" Dexter asked.

"They didn't figure out a way to segregate the airwaves," Carter said. "Besides, Dylan's white."

"Yeah," said Charlie. "He's a Jew pretending to be a peasant. Why can't white people be satisfied with who they are? What more do they want?" Charlie, again on the verge of a smile, seemed to be burlesquing himself.

"That does it," said Jimbo, standing up with Lonnie's football in one hand held high over his head. "The only way to settle this is on the gridiron."

Carter looked at Lonnie, thinking Jimbo had lost his mind.

"Me and my lily-white friends, the Boys of Troy, issue a challenge to the Magic Time Purity of Negro Music Society to a game of touch football on the beach."

A spark of interest flared in Dexter's eyes, and he looked at Charlie and Randall and Daniel. "I'm in," he announced.

The game was raucous, even in the afternoon heat, and for the first time that day, Charlie did not pretend he was not having fun. They started out loose and lighthearted, but the competition intensified as they traded touchdowns. Sarah and Celia, on opposite teams, acquitted themselves nicely, catching passes and harassing opposing quarterbacks. Tension arose when Charlie tagged Jimbo a little too hard, shoving him into the sand on a touchdown reception. But Jimbo defused the situation by rolling over backward multiple times, lying on his back, and churning his feet while holding up the football.

The game reached a conclusion only when Lonnie turned his ankle and had to sit down. The Boys of Troy commanded a two-touchdown lead. The teams retired to the sidelines to cool off and listen to the transistor radio that Charlie had finally gotten to work. After time in the shade to dehumidify, Randall took some photographs with Magic Time's communal camera. Finally, Charlie stood up and said, "This heat's getting the best of me. I'm heading back."

Celia had promised to bring some blackberries home to her mother, and Randall said he would help her pick them. Jimbo offered to show them where the bushes grew, off the river trail that Charlie and Dexter were taking back to Magic Time. Jimbo slipped on his camouflage trousers and boots and led Charlie and Dexter and Randall and Celia across the beach and over the promontory. Lonnie, Daniel, Carter, Stephen, and Sarah remained in the shade, drinking beer and soft drinks. Sarah announced that she was going for one last swim. Carter and the others got out their instruments again.

As they were finishing the last verse of Dylan's "When the Ship Comes In," they heard the swush-swush sound of feet trudging through the pine straw coming toward them down the trail. Carter assumed it was the return of the blackberry pickers, but he turned to see two white men approaching. One was tall and gangly, with a red-haired flattop. He wore a T-shirt and blue jeans and had a large crescent-shaped birthmark on his cheek, the color of grape Kool-Aid. The other man was short and stocky, with a pug nose and greasy black hair swooped back on his head. He wore an unseasonably long waistcoat, and when they drew near enough for Carter to see the beer in the lanky stranger's hand, he knew they were in for trouble.

"What can we do for y'all?" Daniel asked.

The men didn't answer but kept walking toward them.

Carter could see Sarah standing on the sandbar out beyond the lagoon, rubbing water out of her eyes, trying to see who had arrived.

"Where's the niggers?" the tall red-headed one asked.

No one answered. Carter now recognized the short dark-haired one as Skeebo, who had been a member of Lacey Hullender's posse at Kress's. He didn't know his last name. Skeebo walked up to Daniel, who was still leaning against the tree with his banjo, and asked him, "Do you know 'Dixie'?"

"I'm not sure," said Daniel, smiling faintly.

"Well, you better be sure, and quick."

Daniel said, "Why don't you sit down and join us and we'll see if we can work it out together?"

Daniel looked at the others and began strumming. Carter thought Skeebo's companion also looked familiar—another representative of Troy's rough trade from Graysonite who hung around the Dairy Queen on Friday nights, starting fights with the high school boys. He was called Strawberry, after his birthmark and bright red hair.

"Play it," Strawberry ordered Daniel. Skeebo pulled a .22 pistol from his overcoat.

"Hey, there's no need for that, fellas," said Lonnie, starting to stand up. Skeebo turned to face him, cocking the gun. "Whoa, now," said Lonnie, raising his hands and sitting back down.

"That y'all's station wagon out by the highway?" Strawberry asked as Daniel carefully began picking out the melody to "Dixie."

"Yes," said Daniel. "Why?"

"You got a flat," said Skeebo.

"In all four tires," Strawberry added, snickering breathlessly. Although he was physically more imposing, the role of bully did not come to him as naturally as it did to Skeebo.

"And the winder's busted out," said Skeebo. "Y'all must've had a accident." Both of them guffawed.

The new arrivals had not yet noticed Sarah swimming, and Carter's pulse raced as he saw her paddling toward shore. From where he sat with the sun in his eyes, the intruders appeared as two sun-dazzled silhouettes.

Lonnie, trying to divert their attention from Sarah's approach, slowly stood up, his hands still skyward. Summoning his patented fraternity-boy warmth, he said, "Hey, Strawberry, don't you remember me? Lonnie Culpepper. How y'all doin'? I used to play softball with you at the Graysonite company picnics, remember? My daddy runs the fireworks stand out on the Soso highway every Christmas holiday season. I sold y'all some cherry bombs and silver salutes one year. This is Carter Ransom from Troy, Stephen Musgrove, and—"

"Who's that?" said Strawberry. Sarah had emerged from the water and grabbed her towel on the beach. She was drying off as she crossed the beach.

"Whooeee," said Skeebo, turning toward her. "What we gotcheer?"

"Howdy," said Sarah. "How y'all doing?" At first she seemed unsure of the dynamics, whether perhaps these were arriving acquaintances of Lonnie and Carter, but then she saw the gun pointing at Lonnie.

"This here's my cousin down from Greenville," said Lonnie, gesturing toward Daniel. "And that's his sister, Sarah."

Daniel smiled. "Hey. We're down visiting for the weekend."

"Y'all want some potato salad?" Lonnie continued. "We got some chicken left over, I think."

"We know that wagon up there belongs to the niggers," Strawberry said, foraging in the cooler for a beer. He opened the bottle with his teeth. "So where are they?"

"We don't know what you're talking about," said Lonnie.

"They lying, Skee," said Strawberry.

"It's their car, all right," said Skeebo. "The license belongs to the niggers." Carter wondered how he was so sure about the plates.

"These people have done you no harm," said Stephen, stepping into the conversation.

"Well now, little man, who asked you?" said Skeebo, shoving Stephen backward, then kicking over his mandolin case with the heel of his boot.

Carter looked past Strawberry, and his heart sank. Randall and Celia had just crested the promontory, back from their blackberry hunt. Jimbo was nowhere to be seen. Randall carried a jar full of berries under one arm and was shooing gnats with his other. Deep in conversation, he and Celia were already past the rope swing down the path to the beach before they looked up.

"So here's the niggers," Strawberry said. "They friends of yours?" he asked Sarah.

Before she could answer, another voice said, "That's right, the niggers are here, and so are the nigger lovers." Lacey Hullender stepped forth from the trees along the same path Strawberry and Skeebo had taken. He was being pulled along by a large yellow black-mouth cur on a chain leash. "You boys got ahead of me and Samson here." The dog began growling and barking at the picnickers. "Shut your trap!" Hullender commanded, reeling the hog-hunting dog in and smacking it across the nose. The dog howled, then quieted to a whimper. "Samson don't like niggers." Lacey trudged up the promontory with his dog and chained him to a tree near the great oak. His stagger told Carter he'd been drinking. Lacey pulled the rope swing back and made a run off the cliff, swinging out over the water. "Yeee-hawww!" he shouted, cutting a wide arc over the water before the rope brought him back to the ledge.

"That was fun," he said. "But I don't reckon I can go swimming after niggers done stunk up my river." He unzipped his fly and urinated off the ridge into the water below. Then he turned and angled his good eye at Carter, apparently noticing him for the first time. "Well, what do you know," he said, ambling down the promontory to face them. "Carturd Ransom. Picnicking with the niggers." He surveyed the others. "And his little homo friend, Stevie Musgrove." Lacey's eyes narrowed. "And who else we got here? Lonnie Culpepper. College boy, fancy fuck. I bet old man Culpepper won't like it one bit hearing that his son is mixing with niggers and nigger lovers. Any better than Judge Ransom."

Carter sensed that the recognition of him, Lonnie, and Stephen had subtly altered the class dynamics in their favor now. Like feudal wardships, the civil rights workers were now under their protectorate. Carter felt a twinge of superiority at Lacey's presumption to speak for his father.

Lacey strolled toward the beach. "Me and Skeebo and Strawberry was just taking Mr. Bohannon's hog dog out for a ride in the country, and Skeebo wanted to do some target practice with his new gun, when we saw that civil rights veehickle parked up by the highway. Lo and behold," he said, spying the musical instrument. "Y'all been playing music and having a big ol' time. When does the fornication begin?"

Strawberry reached for Daniel's banjo, took it, and walked away, fingering the strings and pretending to examine it. When he reached Lacey on the beach, he handed him the instrument. Lacey plucked the strings roughly, turned and smiled at Daniel, and then broke the banjo over his knee and flung it far out into the water.

"Jesus," said Sarah. "Why in the hell did you do that?"

Daniel shushed her.

"Whooeee," Strawberry said, walking back toward the shade. "Your sister's got quite a mouth on her, banjo man."

"That ain't all she's got on her," said Skeebo. He was eyeballing Sarah.

"You ain't from Miss'ippi, that's for sure," Lacey said. "And you been swimming in my river."

"I don't see a sign that says it's your river," said Sarah.

Lacey gave her a look that briefly resembled respect. "You like mixing so much, Jew bitch, I'm going to let you and the nigger gal here go swimming together." Lacey turned to Celia and said, "Both of you get on up there where I took a piss." When neither of them moved, he screamed, "Now, godammit!"

As the others watched in silence, Sarah joined Celia on the beach, and they walked up the promontory to the top of the ridge and the rope swing. The yellow cur sitting on his haunches in the shade of the oak began growling, then barking. Celia started crying. Sarah put her arm around her trembling shoulders.

"Now take your clothes off, or I'll come up there and do it for you!" Lacey shouted.

Strawberry and Skeebo snickered.

Stephen called out, "Leave them alone!"

Lacey looked him over. "Okay, you little queer. You're going with them. You ever been with a naked woman before?"

When Skeebo turned his pistol on him, Stephen threw his shoulders back and crossed the beach.

"Strip," Lacey ordered.

Celia struggled with the buttons on her blouse, her hands shaking so much she couldn't undo them.

"Come on, Jew girl. Never mind the nigger. What's taking you so long?"

Sarah directed a look of fury at Hullender and began lowering the straps on her suit.

Carter's mind raced with schemes. He looked at Skeebo standing in front of him, the gun held casually by his side. Carter caught Lonnie's eye and nodded subtly toward Strawberry, who was absorbed by the strip show on the promontory. The old telepathy that had served them so well on the basketball court and football field still worked.

Lonnie was poised to hurl himself at Strawberry, and Carter tensed to do the same with the distracted Skeebo. But Lacey turned and shouted, "Hey, Ransom, where's your backyard buddy now? Elijah Knight. He's the one who started up this race-mixing mess in Ellis County. Why ain't he here innergrating the river?"

"I'm right here, Hullender." Elijah Knight stepped out from behind the giant white oak on the promontory.

"Lige!" shouted Sarah.

Samson was barking insanely, straining at his chain as Lige walked onto the ridge inches from the dog's jaws.

Carter's relief at Lige's unscheduled appearance evaporated when he saw that his friend wasn't armed. Skeebo pointed the .22 in Lige's direction, but Lige sustained his air of quiet confidence. "Tell your buddy to drop his gun," Lige said to Lacey over the hog dog's barking.

Hullender laughed. "Now, why should I do that?"

"Because I asked you nicely."

"Don't sound like a good enough reason to me," said Skeebo.

"I'll give you a reason, then," said Lige.

"What's that?" said Lacey. "That you're Judge Ransom's nigger son? No wonder you think you can screw Jew girls."

Lige nodded toward the growling dog. "Because if you don't drop your gun, I'll kill that dog."

Hullender and the others burst out laughing again, but this time with a hint of uncertainty. Lacey pulled a knife from his back pocket. With a flick of his wrist, its blade was glinting in the sun. Lige looked out over the river as if he were gathering his thoughts. The dog had quieted to a growl.

Lige took a pistol from a pocket of his overalls. It was the gun Sarah had pulled on Carter at Magic Time.

"This is a nonviolent thirty-eight," Lige said, pointing it at Lacey's dog, "but it works the same as a regular one."

"Lacey?" Skeebo said nervously, still aiming his .22 at Lige.

Hullender said, "He's bluffing."

"Try me," said Lige.

Hullender began walking toward Lige across the sand, shifting his knife to his right hand. Lige cocked the pistol.

"Come on, let's get out of here, Lacey," said Strawberry.

"Elijah Knight won't shoot," Hullender said. "It's against his religion."

"Yes," said Lige, "but Augustine said if you're going to sin, sin boldly."

Lacey had reached the oak and was standing next to the animal, a few feet from Lige.

"One more step and you'll find out what a sinner I am, Lacey," said Lige. He steadied his aim at the dog. Samson strained at the chain, his eyes bulging, and emitted a low rumble from deep within his throat.

"Move out the way, Lacey, and let me shoot him," Skeebo shouted.

But before Lacey could answer, Skeebo was hit from behind with the full force of Carter Ransom's six-foot-two-inch frame. Carter's head plowed into his shoulder blades in a fierce clipping action that sent the two of them sprawling. Carter had clasped Skeebo's arms to his sides, pinning his shooting hand to his hip. As the two wrestled for the gun, Lonnie hurled the beer cooler at Strawberry, drenching him with melted ice. Then Lonnie rushed over to disarm Skeebo, who had still not let go of the gun. Skeebo elbowed Carter in the ribs and broke away long enough to struggle to his feet. Then he took aim, alternating between Carter and Lonnie. Carter's thought as he stared down the barrel of the pistol was of Sarah. He felt ashamed, responsible for the behavior of his fellow Mississippians, and full of regret that his chivalry had been thwarted by such a low form of human being. When he heard the report of gunfire, Carter flinched. Splinters sprayed from the bark inches from Skeebo's head. Skeebo yelped and staggered backward, his gun dropping to the pine straw.

Lonnie scrambled to pick up the pistol. Carter was still trying to figure out what had happened, when a voice resounded in the pines behind them. "Schmuck, the next time, I shoot to kill."

The smoking barrel of Jimbo Stein's Enfield 30.06 was still trained on Skeebo, who was rubbing specks of bark from his eyes.

"Me—," said Jimbo philosophically, "I'm not nonviolent."

Across the beach on the promontory, Charlie and Dexter stepped up behind Lige, holding a shattered beer bottle in each hand.

Lacey let his knife fall to the ground.

"I forgot to mention," Lige continued. "On my way down here I took the river trail and ran into my reinforcements here. The pickup truck I saw on the highway made me think I might need them."

Hullender was trembling with fury. "You won't get away with this, you black bastard."

Lige turned to Charlie and Dexter, and motioned them toward Sarah, Celia, and Stephen. "Y'all go get the others," he said. The two of them made their way down the hill past him, giving the dog a wide berth but moving with fierce intent toward Lacey. The jagged glass in their hands flashed in the afternoon sun. "Drop the beer bottles, boys," Lige called after them. "Somebody might get hurt."

Charlie and Dexter looked over their shoulders at Lige, then at each other. Reluctantly, Charlie hurled his bottle into the high weeds beyond the promontory. Before following suit, Dexter turned and thrust the broken glass under Lacey's nose and whispered, "Now who's bluffing, you one-eyed motherfucker?" Then he turned to Lige with mock sincerity. "Sorry, man, I lost my nonviolence there for a minute."

Lige ordered Skeebo and Strawberry to join Lacey on the promontory. Jimbo walked toward them and said, "Good. Now take off your clothes. You wanted a strip show."

"You Jew son of a bitch," Hullender hissed through gritted teeth.

"Drop trou, Lacey," said Jimbo. "Or I'll drop them for you."

The three followed instructions. They stood there stark-naked in the late afternoon sun, as Carter and Lige had when they were little boys, waiting their turn on the swing. Jimbo circled around the three and with a big grin on his face said, "Now let's see each one of you dog turds swing off that rope butt-naked."

The prisoners glumly launched themselves off the ridge one by one. Cursing the cold as they treaded water, they looked up at Jimbo for further instructions. It was Lige who pointed toward the river beyond and ordered them to swim out to the sandbar.

Then Lige called to the others on the beach, "Picnic's over."

Lige bent down and picked up the bathers' clothes. "You can fetch these from Sheriff Mizell's office once you've figured out how to get the air back in your tires," he called. "Carter here, being the judge's white son, is going to tell the sheriff all about your little hunting trip today. I think even in Mississippi you still need a license to hunt coon."

Jimbo remained on the beach, standing watch until the others had made it to the trail. Lige, Carter, Lonnie, and Stephen, their arms loaded with ice chests and musical instruments, paused to look out over the river at the other boys of Troy.

Lige turned to Carter with a wry smile. "Naked Tail."

———

BY THE TIME Sydney returned from the restroom, Carter had ordered her another gin and tonic.

"Sorry I took so long," she said. "I had to use the pay phone."

"Work-related?"

"Isn't everything? Just got word on the independent psychiatric evaluations. Bohannon's competent to stand trial."

"Bravo," Carter said drily.

"It's kind of absurd, really. A racist murderer and religious fanatic, a criminal psychopath responsible for some of the worst crimes of that era. And I'm praying he's found sane."

"But have you tasted his catfish combo platter?"

Sydney laughed with such genuine pleasure that Carter laughed, too. "Oh, I've eaten at Sambo's. Lonnie took me my first week in town."

"And?"

"I had a salad, if that's what you call the white part of the iceberg lettuce."

"Orange French dressing?" Carter said. "Well, what did you expect from a catfish joint?"

"Sorry. I had to be perverse. I just didn't want to end up admiring the frying technique of a sociopathic killer."

"So can you convince a jury?"

"He's slippery. Bohannon had a genius for getting others to do his dirty work. He always had deniability, always made sure nothing was traceable to him. He's protected by layers and layers of alibi. That's why he walked the first time."

"Because the jury didn't have enough evidence to convict?"

"Weren't you there?"

Carter explained that even years after the bombing, when Bohannon was tried with Hullender and Peyton Posey, Sarah's death was still too raw for him. He was a young reporter working in Nashville, and he seldom returned home. "I probably would have strangled Bohannon," he said. "I definitely would have strangled Hullender. Pleaded not guilty, as I recall. What's he giving you now?"

"Confession."

"Oh, I forgot. He's found Jesus."

"He's also got new information."

"Something he forgot he knew twenty years ago?"

"Something he didn't know twenty years ago."

"And how does my father figure into all this?"

She looked at him to see if he was going to elaborate. "What do you mean?" she asked.

"Come on, Sydney, cut the crap. Hullender's playing out his revenge fantasy on the judge who sent him up, you know that."

"He's got information that seems to taint your father. But I can't discuss it."

"You discussed it with Lonnie."

"I told him we had new evidence that seemed to incriminate the judge, but I didn't tell him what it was. That'll come out in the trial. I did talk to your father about it."

"You told him?"

"Of course. I wanted to hear what he had to say. Believe it or not, your father has been a hero of mine. We studied his opinions in law school."

"What did he say?"

"Not much. Thanked me for sharing, basically. It was a couple of days after the party. I'm surprised he hasn't mentioned it to you."

"I'm not," Carter said. "Lonnie said you have some sort of proof."

"I've got something that makes it difficult to draw any other conclusion."

Carter stared into the remnants of beer foam in his glass. He was on unfamiliar terrain, uncertain what to ask, unclear as to his obligations as reporter, as witness, and in the hardest role of all, as son. "Can you let me in on it?"

"Will you help me establish for the jury who Sarah Solomon was?"

"If I say yes?"

Sydney looked up at him with a dubious squint. "I'm usually the one browbeating witnesses, not vice versa." She paused, as if trying to assess the source of his resistance. "I understand your reluctance to revisit this," she said. "But I wonder if it really has to do with your father. I get the sense that you don't want to see yourself as one of Bohannon's victims. But you were. And if you can't feel pity for yourself, the state will do it for you."

"I've always preferred sorrow to self-pity," Carter said. "There are fewer expectations."

"I know you don't have any expectations about this case, but I swear it's different this time. If you work with us, I'll show you what I've got. Another possible Klan witness has also shown up."

"And if I say no?"

"I'll subpoena you anyway," she said with a pleased little snort. Then she turned serious again. "In order for me to win this case, I need to have someone testify who knew Sarah Solomon."

"You mean someone of the same race."

"Much as you and I wish it weren't still an issue in Mississippi, it would be helpful. Although at least the jury won't be all white this time."

"Progress," he said. "What about her father?"

"Even attending the trial may be too much for him. Plus . . ."

"You need an Anglo-Saxon."

Sydney exhaled, as if trying to keep her patience. "Congressman Knight told me that Sarah broke up your relationship with another girl and also caused strain within your family. Is that because she was Jewish?"

Carter looked away. He didn't know how to answer.

"Hey," Sydney said, "we're off the record, okay?"

Carter nodded.

"We've hired a trial consultant to help us with jury selection. We try to determine what moves people. In this case, my team narrowed it down to two possibilities: disgust with the Klan and sympathy for the victims. After testing our focus group, we discovered nobody cares about the Klan. It's an abstraction to most folks—maybe because of that little collective amnesia problem we have down here in the Southland. No one wants to admit how bad it was back then, how blasé the whole community was about it. But people will allow themselves to feel for the loss of innocent lives. We need to make sure the jury has an emotional stake in the outcome of the trial." She looked suddenly self-conscious. "I apologize for being so 'market-oriented.'"

"You do what you have to do to win." Carter wondered whether the judge would be a pawn in Sydney's game plan—and whether he deserved to be.

Sydney opened the leather binder on the table and began to charge the check to her room. Carter reached over to stay her pen. "Can't be indebted to the state of Mississippi for a Heineken," he said, picking up the bill. "I'm writing about it, remember?"

She stood up while ransacking her briefcase for her room key. "Come see me in my office Friday," she said, and looked up into his face. "I'll show you what I've got on your father." Then she turned her head away, avoiding his eyes as she said, "And next time, you can tell me about your relationships."

Carter was pretty sure she wasn't flirting. He examined her profile, trying to read her, and realized to his surprise that he had not recoiled from the invitation. Whatever it meant.

13

ARRIVING JUST BEFORE NOON at the Troy Country Club, Carter requested a seat in the Grille near the bay window in back. The more casual 19th Hole Terrace Room—overlooking the velour grass of the fairways and the tastefully sub-Olympic-sized pool—was already beginning to fill up with boisterous golf foursomes, businessmen in seersucker, trophy wives in tennis whites, and helmet-haired middle-aged ladies who lunch. Carter hadn't been back to the Grille since college, but little had changed—the crystal chandelier, the Oriental rugs, the high-backed leather-upholstered chairs, the white linen tablecloths, the balletic black waitstaff.

That morning at the Troy Public Library, while reading the old clips on the first Shiloh Church bombing trial, Carter had run into Grayson Boutwell, who was checking out books with her girls, and she had invited him to join her for lunch after her tennis match. He sank into the massive wine-red chair, avoiding eye contact with the parade of regulars waving to one another across the room as they were seated for the popular weekday luncheon buffet. The club members' masks of studied complacency reminded Carter of the predatory edge that underscored the parent meetings he had attended with Emily at Josh's private school in New York.

Even as a boy, when his parents brought him and his sister to the Grille for Sunday lunch after church, Carter had felt out of sorts. During the seventies and eighties, on his visits home, he had refused to patronize the club because of its ban against Jews and blacks. Then in the mid-eighties the Chicago-based Graysonite Corporation sent a Jewish CEO to Ellis County, and the club couldn't very well blackball the town's largest employer. Carter had heard that Elijah Knight, after he was elected to Congress, was encouraged to join by one of the younger club members. Carter savored the thought of Lige's police mug shots from the sixties showing up in the monthly newsletter in the New Members Showcase column.

Grayson was late—as usual, Carter thought, checking his watch. Her chronic tardiness had always been a point of tension between them. Punctuality had been drilled into Carter from birth. ("When you're late," his father said, "you're saying that your time is more important than others'.") Now he found something comforting about his high school sweetheart's consistency.

"Sorry, the last set ran long," Grayson said as she bustled in. She wore the uniform of the wealthy young matrons of north Troy—tennis whites, with a colorful silk scarf, a straw tote, and sunglasses perched on her head.

"No problem," Carter said. He stood to get her chair, but a waiter beat him to it. "I just arrived myself."

Grayson looked tanned and fetching, her long brown hair tied back with a yellow scarf into a ponytail. After giving their drink orders, they skimmed the menu and wrote down their selections. "Sally told me you've been great with Willie this summer since school let out," Grayson said. "And you're expecting company."

Carter stared blankly for a second before figuring out what she meant: Apparently Sally, the Mouth of the South, had told Grayson about the call he had received a couple of evenings before. He had just loaded the dishwasher, and his sister's deadpan expression as she handed him the phone didn't prepare him for the voice on the other end. It had been many weeks since Carter had spoken to Emily, and his initial reflex at hearing from her was a jolt of joy, which dissolved into ambivalence.

They exchanged heartfelt niceties, in which Carter admitted for the first time to anyone, "I'm better." Then he promptly had an urge for a smoke.

Emily caught him up on the essentials—her firm had gotten the Houston account, Marcy and Boz were pregnant—and after an awkward silence she said, "Carter, the reason I called, I've got a favor to ask."

"Sure," he said, trying to show enthusiasm.

"I talked to Sally, and I hope we wouldn't be imposing, but—could Josh come visit you?"

Carter was a little taken aback and had a rush of guilt, realizing that other than the gift he had sent the boy for his birthday—an illustrated version of *Huckleberry Finn* from Sally's store—he had not made contact with him since coming back to Mississippi. Although Carter got a pass from everyone else for his emotional condition, he felt that he had let Josh down.

"He asks about you," Emily said.

Carter had said of course, and they agreed that Josh would visit at the end of August. He was grateful for the opportunity to make it up to the boy and had found Emily's maturity and generosity liberating.

Carter said to Grayson, "Yeah, I guess I'm playing the role of, uh, stepdad—"

"Bring the boys over to Mother's and let them swim with my girls," she said. "They're out there in the pool every day."

In the daylight dazzling through the bay windows Carter could see Grayson's face clearly for the first time. Delicate laugh lines at the corners of her eyes were the only indication of a woman in her forties. She could have passed for ten years younger.

After ordering, they discussed the strangeness of being home again and having a Proustian moment courtesy of the Grille's famous cheese biscuits.

"You're still biting your nails," Grayson observed as he passed her the butter.

He glanced down at his hands as if he had never noticed before. "I still smoke, too," he said, "if you're keeping a tally. I hear your tennis game hasn't slipped any since high school. Sally says you're the club's female champ." He da-da-dummed the opening of the *Rocky* theme.

Across the dining room, Lonnie was being seated for a power lunch with three other men. "That's the CFO from Graysonite and his flack," Grayson said. "And of course, your former brother-in-law. He's the company's tax attorney." Carter recognized the rangy gray-templed guy in the tailored tan suit as Sally's ex-husband, whom he hadn't seen since the harrowing divorce.

Lonnie caught sight of Grayson and Carter and gave him a thumbs-up sign, with the index finger extended like a gun. Grayson flashed him a smile, then rolled her eyes ever so subtly at Carter. "He came on to me recently," she said. "At a party, with his wife in the other room. Midlife, I guess."

"Lonnie's always liked you."

"That's because you liked me. Anyway, I don't date married men, especially not Lonnie." Her lips pursed in a way he remembered from high school when she was irritated.

"How are you and the governor?" Carter asked.

"I told you I'm not ready for anything serious. I've had enough of marriage for one lifetime." She filled Carter in on the bare details of the divorce from her philandering husband—final straw, the masseuse.

"Men end up wanting less, not more," she said. "But I'm well rid of him. If it weren't for the girls having to see him, I'd never look back. I'm just grateful Daddy is gone and didn't have to see his daughter divorced. He probably would have killed Keith."

"Your father was your biggest fan."

Grayson smiled. "He always wanted a son. I think he was jealous of Judge Ransom for having a son like you."

"Your dad was good with boys. A great coach."

"I was so mad that I couldn't play Little League with the boys."

"I don't know why you weren't allowed to. He let everybody else play." Carter needled her affectionately. "Even Hugh Renfro got to wear the uniform and travel on the team bus."

Grayson smiled. "Both my girls were T-ball aces." She took a sip of her iced tea and gave him a sincere "end of small talk" look. "Carter," she said, "how are you doing?"

"I'm getting by," he said.

"Sally told me about your breakup," Grayson said. Carter wondered if she meant "crack-up" or the separation from Emily, but then she sighed. "It's hard to find the right mate, isn't it?"

Carter settled back in his chair. "I was in my forties when I met Emily, and you know, by that age, there is so much to 'deal with' that even the courtship isn't exactly a walk in the park. For starters—not being able to stay over at her apartment because the ex was looking for a reason to bust her."

"You always were something of a prude," she said with a trace of a smirk.

Carter smiled uncertainly. He stopped himself from telling her about how he had briefly become a legend in the matrimonial bar, a favorite example of the dangers of asking a witness questions to which you don't know the answer. The ex, Dr. Mark Lerner, had hastily remarried during their drawn-out custody battle, the better to establish his superiority as caregiver. At the custody hearing he sat with his new bride across the aisle from Emily and Carter, looking smug, as if he were in his own OR. On the witness stand, Carter was asked questions to establish the frequency of his contact with Emily. Moving in for the kill, Lerner's lawyer said, "Mr. Ransom, did you ever have sexual relations with Mrs. Lerner in her home while her child was under the same roof?"

Carter was ready for the question. "Which Mrs. Lerner?" he answered. The judge leaned forward. "I've had sexual relations with both Mrs. Lerners." The more recent Mrs. Lerner, who was now trying to disappear into her shearling coat, had failed to tell her new hubby that she had dated Carter Ransom a few times back in his wild New York bachelor days. Lerner's lawyer informed Carter that the court was not interested in his checkered personal history—only if he had had sex with Mrs. Lerner in her house. This time he pointed at Emily. But Carter kept his eyes focused on Dr. Lerner's wife. "Oh, yes. As I said, I had sex with Dawn, uh—Dr. Lerner's wife—and it was a long time ago, but as I recall, we had sex in the living room, the dining room, the den, the bedroom, the kitchen, the bathroom, hanging from the chandelier." The judge began to gavel at the mention of the chandelier, reminding Carter he was under oath. Afterward, Carter apologized to Emily, who was pretty stunned by this side of her boyfriend. The hearing ended with her retaining custody and Lerner having to pay her attorney's fees. "I always wondered why I kept that bastard's name," Emily said to Carter, "and now I know."

Grayson was staring at Carter contemplatively. "I guess we've ended up having more in common than we did in high school," she said, stirring Sweet'N Low into her iced tea. Carter looked back inquiringly. "Despite how easily things came to us back then, we now know better."

Carter couldn't tell where this was going, so he just listened.

"All the talk about the church bombing trial, and just being here at the club—it reminds me of something we've never discussed, and I wanted to straighten it out after all these years." She stopped for a beat before saying, "Sarah Solomon." It shocked Carter to hear Grayson say the name.

"Remember the night at the Pinehurst?" she said. "The night we broke up for keeps? The things I said have always plagued me."

"Don't be silly, Grayson. You were a kid, for God's sake."

"I was old enough to know better."

"You were hurt."

"I never forgave myself. After the church bombing, I wanted to contact you about it, but I was too ashamed." She glanced away. "Please. Let me apologize."

THE ELITE OF Troy's motley bourgeoisie had gathered in the lobby of the Pinehurst Hotel to honor the 1964 Jaycee Man of the Year: Grayson's father, Glen Boutwell. There was talk that Boutwell had a good shot at winning the title statewide. The annual Man of the Year ceremony was one of the biggest events on the town's social calendar, and the elegant Graysonite Room of the Pinehurst Hotel was the perfect setting, with its mahogany walls and ornamented panels and brass sconces. Stamey's Florist had prepared two hundred white carnation corsages for the ladies and red rose boutonnieres for the men.

Carter had been invited to sit with the honoree's family at the head table. Grayson looked radiant in a white chiffon dress. When she appeared so happy to see him, Carter knew that out of his own selfishness and cowardice he had let things go too far. They had broken up during his junior year in college, but when she came home from the Mississippi State College for Women this summer, they had picked up again because it was the path of least resistance—and he needed some continuity after dropping out of law school. It wasn't that Carter didn't find her attractive, but as they resumed their physical relationship, with its glacial evolution, he felt as if he were embracing not a woman but an entire species of genteel Southerners whose survival depended on him.

The night Carter came to get Grayson for their first date in high school, Glen Boutwell greeted him at the door as if he had been waiting for that day all his life. Carter felt that he had been chosen—as much by his girlfriend's father as by Grayson herself—to become the Boutwell heir apparent, the son Glen never had. Carter found Glen Boutwell liberating as a role model, the entrepreneur versus his father, the judge. Boutwell was respected in the community for maintaining his autonomy from Graysonite. He had managed to find in his own family's misfortune—a sawmill accident that took his brother's arm—the inspiration for a successful business, the Troy Artificial Limb Company. Boutwell was also a Civil War buff, full of legend and lore linking his ancestors to all of Mississippi's major battles in the "late unpleasantness," and he was fond of explaining to anyone who would listen, "Just after the Civil War, a fifth of the Mississippi state budget went to prosthetic devices."

A tall, handsome, broad-shouldered man with a powerful build, ink-black hair slicked back from a high forehead, thick eyebrows, a broken pug nose, and challenging wide-set blue eyes, he had been an athlete in his youth and kept in shape lifting weights and running two miles a day. He was proud of the way he could still fit into the suit he had worn when he and Sheppy got married. Carter had been devoted to Glen Boutwell—"Coach B"—throughout the intense summers of Little League, even before he fell for his daughter.

That evening at the Pinehurst, Glen Boutwell had accepted a bronze plaque from Dr. Ludlow Shoemaker, pastor of First Baptist Church and the evening's master of ceremonies, and thanked the Jaycees for their commitment to excellence. "I am deeply moved and humbled by this award and what it represents. It is a token and a symbol of the intentions of the good people of this community to reward citizenship and public virtue in a time of turmoil. Today the forces of anarchy and discontent threaten us from the outside. We seek shelter in our own strength and safety in our own values as we face the whirlwind around us."

Afterward, there was a private party at the Boutwells' house in Stonehaven. On the short ride there, Carter and Grayson said little. Carter could not help thinking about the picnic at Naked Tail and how Sarah and the civil rights workers from Magic Time were the anarchists Coach B had referred to. The exhilaration of novelty that Sarah evoked collided with the loyal familiarity of the Boutwells. He felt as if he were living the Russian novel he had read that summer, in which Dr. Zhivago's feelings for his childhood friend Tonia had been swamped by his passion for Lara.

When Grayson finally spoke, it was to note how distracted Carter had seemed at the Pinehurst. She then tried to engage him in conversation about his leaving law school. It degenerated quickly into an argument. "Lonnie said you had the worst professors there, that if you had the right teachers, you never would have quit."

"Grayson, I'm not going back to law school."

"I'm not talking about law. I know how much you like writing. I heard that the graduate faculty in English there is phenomenal, too. Some of the Fugitive Poets are still there."

"I'm not a poet, Grayson."

"You could be a novelist. Surely you're not thinking of wasting your talent in newspapers?"

"A lot of writers started out that way—Hemingway, Evelyn Waugh."

"You're a leader, Carter. You should be leading, not reporting about those who do."

Carter pulled up behind his parents' car in the Boutwells' circular driveway. He turned off the ignition and felt Grayson's hand on his sleeve. "Before we go inside," she said, "you should know something." Carter looked over at her face reflecting the porch light. She was staring out the windshield. "Daddy didn't like what you wrote about the outsiders in the paper," she blurted. "He said you sounded like you had been brainwashed by them."

"Because I was fair."

"I know you were trying not to hurt your maid's feelings. But I just wanted to warn you. He may bring it up. You know how he likes to tease."

"I'll stand by what I wrote." Hearing himself sounding so pompous made Carter cringe.

Grayson shifted in the seat to face him. "People are talking, Carter. Didn't you hear the conversation over dinner? The civil rights troubles. The outside agitators. That's all anybody talks about. And you gave them publicity. They know Nettie's son, Elijah, is out there. They say he's become a Communist."

Carter had to laugh. "Lige is not a Communist. He's just committed."

"You sound like you agree!"

"I don't agree. I'm just not stupid."

"Don't condescend to me, Carter. I'm just telling you what it looks like." Grayson sank back into her seat and stared straight ahead.

Carter made an attempt to finesse the evening. "You look nice tonight," he said, smiling bleakly.

"I bought this dress in New Orleans," she said. "Mama says I have to wear it to cotillion, too. The summer dance at the club is coming up, or have you put all that behind you?"

Carter found himself in the middle of the conversation he had hoped to avoid until the end of the evening. "Grayson," he said softly, "I can't take you to cotillion."

"So you *aren't* going," she said.

"I am going."

She looked as if she had been slapped. "Who, then?"

"Grayson, we haven't really dated since my junior year. This summer's been nice, but"—Carter felt himself floundering—"we agreed to go out with other people, remember?"

"Who is it?"

Silence.

"Where did you meet her?"

"This summer." He could not look at her. "Nobody from Troy."

"It's that girl, isn't it?"

"Who?"

"The one Jimbo mentioned."

Carter blinked. He wanted to strangle his loudmouthed friend.

"Does your father know?" she asked.

"Know what?"

"That you're dating one of them."

"One of who?"

"Oh, Carter, how could you?"

"One of who?" he insisted, feeling self-righteousness well up.

"What's her name?"

"Why do you want to know?"

"Tell me her last name, then. Or are you ashamed?" He knew Grayson was hurt, but for her to respond so viscerally was out of character. The thrust of her chin suggested that she could not accept that a rival from one of the lesser orders had won the contest on a level playing field. "It's because she's easy, isn't it?"

"Come on, Grayson. This doesn't sound like you."

"I knew it. I knew you'd hold it against me that I wanted to wait."

Carter retreated under the assault. "Stop, Grayson."

"She's probably sleeping with them, too."

"Grayson."

"You know it's true!" There was hysteria in her voice, and Carter looked over his shoulder, worried that the arriving guests approaching their car might hear her, that she might start hyperventilating. "My God, Carter, she's not . . . like us."

"Neither is Jimbo Stein—co-chair of the Pep Club, remember?"

"Daddy's right. They've brainwashed you. You're one of them. Have you thought about what you're doing to your family? To me?"

"What is that supposed to mean?"

Tears were streaming down her face. "Does your mother know? This is going to kill her, you know that."

Carter went silent.

"And your father. Does your daddy know you're dating a—a—" She couldn't bring herself to use the word, and with that, she pushed open her door and ran up the driveway.

———

"I'LL NEVER FORGIVE MYSELF for saying those things." Grayson's eyes were moist.

Carter reached over and patted her hand. "Come on, Grayson, we were all products of our place."

"But *you* had managed to see the light. I was horrible." She looked at Carter pleadingly. "I was such a little bigot."

"I hadn't seen any light. I was just a boy in love."

There was a gap of uncomfortable silence before Grayson resumed. "I swear it would make me ill when those country-clubbers in Dallas went on about how they needed to go hire a 'Jew lawyer' to take care of some piece of business. I despise anti-Semitism. My best friend in Dallas is Jewish." She laughed and raised her voice to an insincere falsetto. "*Some of my best friends* . . . But seriously, she's my daughter's god-mother. I'd die if Franny knew what I said to you that night." She got out a Kleenex and dabbed at her eyes. "I want to teach my girls to respect people of all races. I'm on the Interfaith Council. I have Afro-American friends and colleagues. God, we were so ignorant back then. I love this little town in so many ways, but I despise it, too, for its power to deform."

"You came out of it okay," said Carter, squeezing her hand. "More than okay." He was touched by the markings that Grayson retained of the Deep South, its defiant innocence and straightforward pieties, and faith in expiation.

"After the church bombing . . . I felt so guilty. And by then, we weren't in touch, and . . . it was devastating."

It was hard for Carter to fathom the weight of those lost emotions, how they could still burden the present even after so much time had passed. All he could say was, "I'm sorry, Grayson."

"Thanks for hearing me out," she said, smiling gratefully. "I've wanted to say that to you for years." She pressed the Kleenex to her nose and glanced at her watch. "Now I've got to pick up the girls before they drive Mother crazy. She feels obliged to babysit and doesn't want to admit what a drain two little girls can be."

"How is Sheppy?"

"A little run-down lately. She drives herself like a thirty-year-old. All the talk about this trial coming up disturbs her. 'Why can't they let the past alone?' The usual. She doesn't like this prosecutor—the woman."

"Why not?"

"I don't know. She talked to her at the party for your father. Maybe it's because she's blond, or from Alabama. But you know Mother. She thinks any gainfully employed female should be at home raising a family—largely because she's mad she missed out on having a career."

The two of them got up and made their way toward the exit through the broken field of white linen–topped tables. Carter could feel the eyes of polite Troy following him and Grayson, speculating on their couplehood.

Lonnie and his guests were seated on the terrace. Sally's ex nodded at Carter, who didn't stop. Mayor Otis Jameson was seated at a table near the door, the only black face in the room besides waitstaff. "Who was that with the mayor?" Carter asked as he and Grayson exited into the foyer. "I've met him before."

"That's the WunderCorp CEO to his left," she said, glancing back at the table. "He was at the party."

"Oh, yes. Schlank," said Carter.

"I don't know the two women," Grayson continued, "but one is a state senator and big Republican fund-raiser, and the other I think is the head of the Ellis County League of Women Voters."

"Looks like Herr WunderCorp is in DefCon One lobbying mode," Carter said.

"His only serious opposition on the WunderCorp referendum in the fall is Congressman Knight. I hope Elijah doesn't end up collateral damage."

Carter figured Lige could take care of himself. "So the mayor's a member here now, too?"

"Yes. All of that changed over the last few years. Jews, blacks—now everyone's allowed in. Except LSU fans."

Grayson excused herself to detour to the women's room. Waiting in the foyer, Carter observed two silhouettes enter through the front door. The sun backlighting them obscured their faces until they were nearly in front of him. One was white and the other black. Rasheed Lovelace spoke first. "Hello, Ransom, have you met Arthur Puckett?"

Carter offered his hand, which was gripped firmly.

"This is Sam Bohannon's defense lawyer," said Rasheed, enjoying the shock value of his introduction. "But I'm sure you knew that."

"No. We haven't met," said Carter, taking in the blue seersucker suit, red bow tie and matching suspenders, longish receding blond hair, rimless glasses, and slight stubble on the pockmarked defense attorney's face. He had heard how Bohannon had abandoned his longtime Klan lawyer for undisclosed reasons and had retained Puckett, a former prosecutor in New Orleans with a real legal reputation. Puckett was reputed to be very good.

"Have you met Bohannon?" Rasheed asked.

"We've met at his restaurant. But I don't know him," said Carter.

"But you knew some of his victims," said Lovelace. Puckett showed no reaction, and neither did Carter.

"Oh, yes, Carter Ransom," Arthur Puckett said, as if Lovelace hadn't spoken. "We were in the same class at Vanderbilt."

"Excuse me?"

"Law school. You dropped out, am I right?"

"Right."

"Good decision. But if you'd stayed, we'd have graduated the same year. I was in the class ahead of Lonnie Culpepper. You're friends, right?"

"Art's going to fill me in over lunch with our host from the local bar association on why he's defending this scumbag Bohannon," said Rasheed, winking at Puckett and snuffling, as if he just came down with a head cold. "So what are you doing here, Ransom? Does the *Examiner* expense country-club lunches?"

"Just catching up with an old friend."

"I'm going to let Puckett here try to spin the *Trib*, convince me that Bohannon's an Eagle Scout. Hey, my editor, Wentworth, may come down for the trial. Imagine that. I'll have to bring him out here for a round or two on the links." The editor of the *New York Tribune* once ran the Atlanta bureau, and as the voice of the reconstructed South, he considered the trial his story. "He sees it in terms of closing a chapter in American history—achieving closure, redemption, reconciliation, et cetera, et cetera," Lovelace said, adding a Yul Brynner *King and I* flourish.

Lovelace asked Carter if he was covering the trial.

"Thinking about it."

"Ha!" Lovelace laughed and punched Carter's arm. "Goddamn, that's rich. That's the *Examiner* for you. You're so lucky to work on a tabloid with no fucking standards. The *Tribune* would never let a reporter with such an obvious conflict of interest cover this story."

Carter went cold. "I'm not on the national desk, Lovelace."

"He's a columnist, Rasheed," said Puckett. "He can have an opinion about this."

Carter was surprised to hear Puckett leap to his defense, and slightly uncomfortable at his familiarity with his résumé.

"And your old man was the judge who blew this case twenty years ago, right?" said Lovelace. "They're still going to let you cover it. That's not kosher, is it?"

Carter felt his ears burn as the blood rushed to his face. He had assumed that the conflict Lovelace had in mind was Sarah, but now he wondered if the *Tribune* reporter had talked to Sydney. "What makes you say that, Rasheed?"

"Come on," said Lovelace, holding up both hands in resignation. "Why do you think we're back here? Hey, forgive me, fellas—and Art, I know you've got a job to do, and I mean, I was practically in diapers when this case was tried, but from all I can tell, it's a joke that Bohannon walked when his water boys did hard time in the big house."

Carter stared at Rasheed Lovelace, wondering if his wanton in-your-face style was part of his reportorial arsenal, a ploy to keep his subjects off-balance, or simply drug-induced bad manners. He spotted Grayson emerging from the restroom. He offered his hand to Puckett. "See you round the courthouse, 'Sheed!" He moved toward Grayson, took her arm, and ushered her out the front entrance, skipping the introductions.

14

WITHOUT KNOCKING, Carter charged into Sydney Rushton's cramped quarters in the rear of the district attorney's suite at the courthouse and tossed a copy of the *New York Tribune* onto her cluttered desk. "Did Lovelace get this from you?"

Hunched over her computer keyboard, cradling the phone between ear and shoulder, she muttered into the receiver, "Let me call you back." She swiveled her chair and, sweeping strands of blond hair out of her eyes, reached for the newspaper. "Who's Lovelace?" she said without looking up.

"Rasheed Lovelace. Did you talk to him?"

She began reading the front-page story. PAINFUL PAST SHADOWS MISSISSIPPI PROGRESS. Carter looked around for a place to sit. Cardboard boxes filled with file folders cluttered the floor around her desk and were stacked high on the copier as well as on the seat of the only other chair besides hers. He removed the file folders and sat down.

"I haven't talked to any journalists except you," she said.

"Well, where did he get that bullshit about my father?"

"Not from me." She looked irked as she skimmed the piece. "I heard there was a story coming, but I thought it would focus on Troy's economic turnaround."

"That's what reporters always tell the city fathers."

Carter reached over and turned the page to the jump and pointed to the paragraph that dealt with the judge. Sydney massaged her lower lip with her thumb as she read it.

While the Troy business community welcomes this long-awaited economic upturn, they're not so keen on reliving past embarrassments like the Shiloh Church bombing. In this latest Southern expiation drama, the Troy town fathers may be especially reluctant to face what might be revealed about past collusion of local leadership with rougher elements in the community in an unholy alliance to keep integration at bay. The 1970 exoneration of notorious racist Sam Bohannon in the courtroom of Judge Mitchell Ransom, later appointed to the federal bench but a Superior Court judge at the time, may turn out to be the most egregious example of an old-boy network gone awry. Sources familiar with the reopening of the case indicate that new testimony will show that the revered Judge Ransom may have turned a blind eye to evidence that would have convicted Bohannon. Considering that one of the four victims in the church bombing was the intimate companion of his son, Carter Ransom, this information raises questions about why Mitchell Ransom did not recuse himself from the case. The judge could not be reached for comment.

"So if you're not the source, who's Lovelace talking to? I saw him with Bohannon's lawyer at lunch yesterday."

Sydney waved her hand. "Puckett may be out of control sometimes, but he's not stupid. It's not in his interest to suggest that there was foul play in a trial that got his client off."

"What about Hullender? Is he talking to Lovelace?"

Sydney hesitated. Carter could tell she didn't even want to consider it. "Not possible. Look, I know this must be upsetting—"

"You think I'm upset? You should see my sister. She went to every newsstand in town this morning grabbing up the few copies of the *Tribune* available so my father doesn't see it. Lovelace has a reputation for playing fast and loose with the facts, but this is libel." Carter wasn't sure how much of what he was feeling was competitiveness. Dennehy had called early that morning to tip him that the Lovelace piece was in the paper. For the first time in months, Carter thought about his New York reputation and couldn't believe he had been scooped in both his hometowns. "So what's this evidence everybody seems to know about but me?"

"Have you thought any more about what we discussed?" Sydney asked.

"I'm here, aren't I?" Carter said sulkily.

Sydney shot him a look that said "Spare me" and got up and closed the office door. She unlocked a drawer in the file cabinet next to Carter and removed several folders. After relocking the cabinet, she sat back down at the desk and began flipping through them.

"What do you know about the White Knights of the Ku Klux Klan?" she asked.

"Other than that they murdered my girlfriend?" he said.

"Carter, I realize this is hard," she said. "Just let me tell you what you need to know to understand my case." She described the hierarchy in the White Knights. As Imperial Wizard, Bohannon, like a dictator, oversaw a network of Klan groups throughout the state. He was smart enough not to divulge any information to anybody else around him unless absolutely necessary. He was clever, and he was no redneck—educated, the grandson of a congressman, a successful restaurateur and dog breeder.

"He's one of those marginally respectable paranoid personalities we run into who are attracted to the intrigue of the intelligence world," Sydney said. "If he hadn't been such a racist lunatic, he might have worked for the FBI."

"It didn't stop J. Edgar Hoover."

Sydney did not acknowledge Carter's joke. She continued her lesson on the Mississippi Klan. Under Bohannon, the White Knights considered themselves the last bulwark against the international Communist conspiracy, which they saw as a Jewish cabal that was using the civil rights movement to bring down Christian civilization through the mongrelization of the races. The White Knights were the violent enforcers. Bohannon was a stickler for hierarchy and chain of command, and he was fascinated with spying and secrecy and codes. Because he was paranoid about being bugged and wiretapped, he had a coded system for ordering his mayhem. A cross-burning was called a Code One. A beating was a Code Two. A Code Three was a firebombing, and Code Four meant annihilation. Under Bohannon's system, only he, as Imperial Wizard, could authorize a Code Three bombing or a Code Four murder. Subordinates could order lesser actions, such as a cross-burning or whipping. In the first trial, Hullender testified that he and Peyton Posey, the resident Klan hit man on Sheriff Mizell's staff, had gone out to Shiloh Church on a Code One, a cross-burning that could have been ordered by one of Bohannon's lieutenants.

Carter sat and absorbed what she said. "So how did a Code One turn into a church bombing?"

"I think Bohannon had always intended that this was going to be more than a cross-burning," said Sydney. "But I also believe something went wrong that night, and it didn't go according to plan. All hell broke loose."

When the smoke cleared, four people were dead, two injured, and the church was burned to the ground. Hullender's gun had fallen out of his quick-draw holster when he was escaping from the scene. It was found by the police and traced to him.

"Hullender and Posey blamed your father for letting Bohannon beat the rap." Sydney drummed her pencil on the desk.

"But why hold my father responsible? It wasn't his fault that the jury couldn't reach a verdict."

Sydney paused, as if trying to decide how much to say. "Did you know about the witness who didn't get to testify, the one your father wouldn't allow?"

Carter had read the transcript of the first trial, but there was nothing in it to suggest that a witness had been dropped.

"The prosecution tried to call a witness Judge Ransom disqualified on the grounds that he was incompetent to testify: Hugh Renfro."

Carter blinked. "Baby Huey?"

"Yeah," Sydney said, watching his reaction. "Tell me about Hugh Renfro."

"What's to tell? Doc Renfro's mentally challenged son. He was the town mascot, the village idiot. He directed traffic up on the square. I doubt he'd have been much help as a witness."

"Every Southern town has a Baby Huey, though Troy is the first one I know of that put up a statue of theirs. Did you know him well?"

"As well as anybody could. Why?"

She looked at her papers. "He was about your age, right?"

"A little younger."

"And still with the mind of a child?"

"That sort of thing doesn't improve with age."

"Any involvement with the civil rights movement, pro or con?" she asked. "Any trafficking with the local racists that you know of—people like Hullender and Peyton Posey?"

"Speaking of the mentally challenged," Carter said. "No, of course not. His mama and daddy may have kept him on a loose leash, but not that loose. The Renfros certainly weren't among the 'outspoken' segs." Carter patted his pocket for his pack of cigarettes, and as he did, a memory registered. "If anything, he was a pain in the ass to the Hullenders and Poseys."

"How so?"

"Baby Huey Renfro," Carter said, tapping out a cigarette into his palm as he thought back to a summer day in 1964.

———

DOWNTOWN TROY was especially pungent that morning, the yellow factory smoke having rolled in like fog. Carter drove past the Pinehurst Hotel to the courthouse and parked a few blocks away in front of Wad's Pharmacy. It was late July, and since the passage of the Civil Rights Act of 1964, the summer had been filled with what was known in Mississippi as "incidents": the sit-in at Kress's, the disappearance of the three civil rights workers, and now the demonstration Carter was about to cover, a march on the courthouse to attempt to register Negro voters. On the evening news the night before, the new mayor had condemned the organizers of the march—Lige's Student Nonviolent Coordinating Committee and Dr. King's Southern Christian Leadership Conference—

as "outside agitators," coyly mispronouncing King's name for the benefit of the barbershop racists. "Martin Luther Coon—I mean, King,"
said the young, recently elected Mayor Braxton Ishee, smiling slyly on
camera.

The streets had emptied. Trucks displaying network logos and call
letters of television stations from Laurel, Meridian, and Jackson were
parked in the post office lot across from the Ellis County Courthouse.
Journalists paced the sidewalk, smoking cigarettes and palming reporter's notebooks. Carter had convinced Pete Callahan that *The Troy
Times* could not allow itself to be scooped by out-of-town competitors,
even though his feature on the SNCC workers had cost the paper some
advertising.

From the sidewalk, Carter could see the marchers forming a line
down the block, perhaps a hundred or more. The voter registrar's office
was open just two days a month, and the authorities would arrive late,
leave early, and take long lunch hours. And if a Negro managed to catch
them at just the right time, they could disqualify him for not giving the
correct answer to "How many bubbles are there on a bar of soap?" This
was the second time in the last two months that SNCC had led regis-
trants to the courthouse, and the numbers had swelled to include minis-
ters, undertakers, beauticians, and even teachers, who were under peril
of being reported to the white board of education.

Carter squinted into the sunlight to see who among the demonstrators was there from Magic Time, half hoping and half dreading he
might see Sarah. The marchers, dressed as if for church, included a
sprinkling of white faces he didn't recognize, but the incongruous figure
of a white man moving among the demonstrators caught his eye. He
wore a yellow raincoat and a green Troy High baseball cap: Hugh Renfro had abandoned his traffic post in front of the Starlite Cafe to join in
the action. The hulking, stoop-shouldered Hugh was blowing a whistle
and shouting commands in all directions, his arms flapping in the yellow rubber slicker like a giant Easter chick. Hugh was six feet tall, two
hundred and fifty pounds, with a perpetual goofy grin on his face, and
he walked with a strange, skittish sideways gait, as if he might suddenly

bolt in the opposite direction. He flitted around the arriving demonstrators, rhyming his delight over the parade forming close to his traffic jurisdiction. The marchers dealt with the presence of this overgrown child either by ignoring him or by folding him into their preparations.

Carter watched Lige, formal in a white shirt and tie, contend with Hugh's constant interruptions. Lige was conferring with Randall and Dexter, who was wearing a denim jacket and some sort of African skullcap. Charlie Lloyd was absent, Carter noted. When the impatience began to show on his colleagues' faces, Lige took Hugh aside for a word. Carter wondered how Lige would explain to him that he couldn't be part of the parade today. Since they were kids, Lige had always treated the retarded boy with deference. Teasing, taunting, and playing tricks on Baby Huey had been a favorite pastime for most of the white boys in town, an impulse that passed as they matured, or once it finally dawned on them that Hugh was oblivious to their ridicule and even enjoyed their cruel whims. Lige would never have joined in. Handicapped or no, Hugh Renfro was white.

Lige pointed Hugh toward the entrance of the magistrate's office across the street from the courthouse and watched him hustle off to man his post there on the doorstep. Hugh shouted directions at the marchers in his cheerful singsong, blasting shrill punctuation with his traffic cop's whistle.

From the top of the courthouse steps Sheriff Lawrence Mizell surveyed the square like some ancient potentate casting a wary eye over his beloved but troubled realm. He was dressed for combat, wearing a helmet like Patton's, an Eisenhower military-style jacket, and dark shades. He fingered his swagger stick as he moved in and out of the shadows of the vestibule, consulting with the deputies who lined the top steps of the courthouse, motionless. A noisy crowd of whites had gathered behind a police barricade in front of the courthouse. Carter didn't know whom to fear mayhem from more, the hecklers or Sheriff Mizell and his men. Mizell had not been happy about the run-in between Hullender's crew and the civil rights workers at Naked Tail. After hearing out Carter, Jimbo, Lonnie, and Stephen about the incident, he warned them that he could not be held accountable for retaliation from Hullender and the Graysonite toughs. Carter wondered if today was payback time.

Mizell's mumbling drawl rose above the murmur of the crowd. "Get on back! Move on back, now! Move back! You're blocking the sidewalk traffic!"

"Go back to Africa, niggers!" Carter recognized the voice of Lacey Hullender. The whites burst into laughter. Hullender stood just behind a police barricade, smoking a cigarette. Those behind him jostled and slapped him on the back. Hugh Renfro left his post at the magistrate's office to join them.

"Go back to Africa, niggers!" Hugh shouted in joyous mimicry of the laugh line that had gotten the crowd's approval. He scrambled down the block and was absorbed into Hullender's group.

Mizell advanced down the courthouse steps and into the throng of marchers. A cheer rose from the white onlookers. The phalanx of dark-skinned protesters retreated before him. Deputies and highway patrolmen spilled out from the shadows of the courthouse portico, jaws set, billy clubs drawn. Peyton Posey, the deputy who had been with the sheriff when they pulled over Lige's station wagon, stood off to one side. Dressed in civilian clothes, a dark suit and a narrow black tie, Posey watched from behind the shiny opacity of his sunglasses.

Carter searched the crowd again and spotted Sarah with Daniel Johnston toward the rear of the march. Most of the people were older Negroes, among them the Isleys, whom Carter had met on his assignment. Reverend Curtis Bunt from Shiloh Church was there with his daughter Celia and the store owner, Thad Scarborough, who wore a brown pin-striped suit.

Sheriff Mizell was lecturing at Lige, Randall, and Dexter, pointing down with his swagger stick. "You're blocking the sidewalk. Now move on."

"Move! Move! Moooooove!" shouted Hullender.

"Moo! Moo! Mooooo!" Hugh Renfro bellowed, grinning proudly from the center of the crowd. Some guffawed and slapped him on the back, and others tried to swipe his baseball cap.

Carter couldn't hear what Lige said to the sheriff in response, but he saw Dexter and Randall shaking their heads. Mizell turned his back on them with an air of finality and climbed back up the stairs, to the applause of Hullender's mob. Instead of dispersing, the demonstrators closed in again on the steps.

The sheriff had disappeared from view. Suddenly the protesters began shifting and scattering as Mizell charged back down the steps, jabbing his nightstick into stomachs, backs, and sides. The elderly Wanda Isley wasn't moving quickly enough for Mizell, so he grabbed her by the arm, spun her around, and shoved her backward down the sidewalk. Then he and his deputies poked her with their nightsticks as she tried to pick up her pace, until finally she lost her balance and went sprawling to the pavement. Hullender let out a whoop from the sidelines, and his band of hecklers cheered as marchers rushed to the old woman's aid.

Sheriff Mizell and his deputies returned to their stations on the courthouse steps. Reverend Bunt, standing on the sidewalk down the block, raised his hand for the marchers to regroup and form their line. Carter stared in disbelief as they solemnly fell into formation, two by two. As the protesters began marching, the lyrics to a freedom song rang out over the square. *"Ain't gonna let nobody turn me around, turn me around, turn me around."*

With Lige, Randall, and Dexter leading the way, backed by Reverend Bunt and Thad Scarborough, the line of marchers stretched down the block like a gigantic centipede. Mrs. Isley was claiming her place near the front, leaning on her husband for support. The marchers began to ascend the courthouse stairs for a second time. Sheriff Mizell, his back to the demonstrators, shouted instructions to his men from the vestibule. The verse the marchers were singing changed. *"Ain't gonna let Mizell turn me around."* Mizell swiveled his head slowly, then wheeled the rest of his body around and strode out to meet the protesters on the stairs. The crowd tensed. So did the reporters out front recording the scene. The white hecklers behind the barricades fell silent. A camera crew from one of the networks pushed forward onto the steps.

"The courthouse is a serious place of business," the sheriff lectured the crowd. "Do you have business in the courthouse?"

"The only business we have is to register to vote," answered a voice directly in front of him. It was Lige, who spoke evenly but loud enough for the microphones to record every word. Clearly, the demonstration today was aimed not just at the powers that be but at the media that had been notified to cover it.

"Didn't you hear me, boy?" the sheriff demanded. "The office is closed."

"It's always closed when we come to register."

Mizell, too, began to play to the cameras, drawing himself up into the full dignity of his office. "The board of registrars is not in session this afternoon, as you have been adequately informed. You come down here to make a mockery out of this courthouse, and we're not going to tolerate it. Now move or I'm going to move you."

"Sheriff, by refusing to allow these American citizens the right to exercise one of their most precious freedoms, you make a mockery of the words carved on the front of this building. 'Equal Justice Under the Law.' "

"Shut the nigger up, Sheriff," Lacey Hullender shouted.

"Shut up!" Hugh Renfro echoed. "Shut up!"

Mizell made another grand display of indifference, turning his back on Lige, then slowly moved into the shadows. The crowd of whites hooted and cheered.

Lige's voice rose above the din. "You can turn your back on me, Sheriff Mizell, you can turn your back on these people here today, but you can't turn your back on the United States Constitution." His voice built. "You can turn your back on me, but you can't turn your back on the Bill of Rights. You can turn your back on me, but you can't turn your back on the Fo'teenth Amendment."

The marchers began picking up the rhythm and called out "Nawsir!" and "Tell it" and "Amen!"

Baby Huey's childish yelps could be heard from across the plaza. "Amen!" he hollered, with a big smile on his face. "Amen!" he called to Lacey Hullender.

Lige hit a register that could be heard above all the other voices, his baritone taking on the eloquent authority of his "preacher's voice." Turning to the deputies lining the courthouse steps behind Mizell, Lige opened up his oratory to all of them. "We want you to know, gentlemen, that every one of you is capable of much better. There were those who followed the Pharaoh in their day and those who followed Pontius Pilate and those who followed Hitler. You are not bad, but you are racists in the same way that Hitler was, and you are blindly following a man who is going to lead you down the path of destruction."

The sheriff stepped toward Lige and said, "Why, you're just an outside agitator."

"No sir. I'm from right here in Troy, Mississippi, just like you, Sheriff Mizell. And I think you know that."

"Shut him up, Sheriff!" shouted Lacey Hullender. "Shut him up, and you'll shut them all up."

"Shut up!" Hugh echoed, grinning at Hullender. "Shut up!" Hullender elbowed him, but Hugh turned his enthusiasm exclusively on Lacey. "Shut up!" he shouted. "Amen! Shut up!" Hullender swung a fist this time and buried it in Hugh's stomach. Hugh doubled over. "Owee! Owee!" he cried. Hullender's cronies spun Hugh around and shoved him toward the rear of the crowd.

On the courthouse steps, Mizell addressed Lige and said, "You got people from other parts of the country coming here to stir up trouble."

"This is not a local problem," Lige replied. "This is a national problem. Democracy is built on the right to vote."

The sheriff was standing partially in shadow when the CBS affiliate's cameraman turned on his lights. "Get that light out of my face," Mizell erupted. "I can't enforce the law with you blinding me." He withdrew toward the courthouse entrance.

Lige followed Mizell. "You're not a bad man, Sheriff. You're a better man than this."

Suddenly Mizell whirled and lashed out, planting the butt of his baton across Lige's skull.

Lige dropped to his knees on the steps, holding his head. The crowd gasped. The cameras rolled. Blood streamed in rivulets down his face. He staggered to get up and dropped to his knees again. The others rushed to help him, but he shrugged them off and struggled to his feet. Then he stood holding his head and wiping his nose with a handkerchief.

"You don't have to beat us," he said. "You don't have to beat us. Arrest us if you want to, but don't beat us." Lige's voice was hoarse and strangled. The television cameras closed in on his blood-streaked face. "If we're wrong, why don't you arrest us?" he asked Mizell.

"Get out from in front of that camera and go on," Mizell shouted.

Lacey Hullender leaped over the barricade, sprinted across the open sidewalk, bounded up the courthouse steps two and three at a time, and plowed into Lige from behind, sending him splayed onto the concrete. He began kicking Lige, who curled into a fetal position and covered his head with his arms.

Carter was astonished that none of the police acted to stop Hullender. Carter was about to cross the press barricade himself when he saw Hugh loping up the steps, his raincoat flapping behind him, shouting, "No hitting! No hitting!"

The 250-pound Baby Huey was on Hullender in a yellow fury, leaping on his back and riding him like a pony. Lacey whirled and lurched under the weight of Hugh, who pounded his face, then scratched his eyes. "No fair! No hitting! No hitting Lijah!"

"Get him off!" shouted Hullender, cupping his hand over his good eye. "Get the dummy off me!"

"Hugh, no!" Peyton Posey shouted. He removed his shades and rushed to Hullender's rescue. "You crazy fucker. Let go right now and get on home!"

It took Posey and two other cops to pull Hugh off Hullender. Lacey then dropped to his knees, flailing at anyone who tried to help him.

Posey and another cop clasped Hugh in a bear hug from behind, pinning his arms by his side. They led him away down the steps beyond the police barricades. Hugh looked back at Hullender and the sheriff, his eyes bulging, crying out, "No fair! No hitting! No hitting Lijah!"

Carter watched Randall and Dexter hovering over Lige, trying to help him to his feet. He felt he should be there, but some prehistoric inhibition had overpowered him. The reporters around Carter were pale and stricken, jotting notes furiously. Only the television camera crews had been jolted into action, jostling and scrambling for advantage.

Carter finally saw Sarah among the demonstrators spilling down the steps. She was on the sidewalk, her arms around Mrs. Isley, facing now in his direction. She looked up, and their eyes met. The recognition that passed between them made him go cold in the July sun: she was a participant, and he was not. The expression he caught on her face just before she turned to hustle Mrs. Isley on down the sidewalk was one not of fear or anger, but of infinite sadness.

Carter fought off a stirring of shame and resumed writing in his notebook.

———

"SO HULLENDER AND POSEY WERE acquainted with Hugh Renfro," said Sydney. She had been jotting down notes.

"Oh, yeah. Everybody knew Hugh," Carter said, rubbing his temple. "As the statue suggests, Hugh represented something for this town, something damaged yet sweet and innocent and sad. But to me it was something else he stood for, something wild and unhinged. He was out of control, a reminder of the perversity of creation, the lack of symmetry. God's unreliability." He looked up at Sydney. She had a half smile on her face. "What?" he said.

"Oh," Sydney said. "I'm not used to hearing poetry when I interview my witnesses."

Carter again noted her odd combination of sardonic and sincere and felt a bit insulted at being called her witness. "Well, I still don't understand what Hugh could have to do with this case."

"Did you know he was there the night of the bombing?"

"There?"

"At the church."

"No way."

"The prosecution in the first trial wanted to call him. Apparently, the day of the bombing, Hugh overheard Posey talking to Hullender at the Starlite Cafe about 'fireworks' planned for that night out in the county. Hugh thought it was a party, and he stowed away on a lumber truck Hullender drove in the caravan of Kluxers heading out to Shiloh Church."

Carter smiled humorlessly. "Hugh loved his fireworks. He used to hang around the stand Lonnie's daddy ran. What did he see?"

"That's what I'm piecing together. He never testified. Your father decided that Hugh was unreliable, that the defense would humiliate him on the stand, and he didn't want to put him through the stress—and possible danger of Klan retribution."

"Makes sense."

"But Hugh was interviewed by the FBI. They made a tape that the prosecutors in the first trial didn't know existed. It's got a lot of crazy things on it, as you can imagine. He named one of Troy's leading citizens as being at the church that night."

"What?" Carter said sharply.

"He mentioned a prominent local businessman among the Klan vigilantes."

"Who was it?"

"I'd rather not say until I nail it all down. It'll come out in the trial this time. Suffice it to say, nobody would have believed it at the time. He's dead now."

"So how does it fit into your case?"

"We now know the man Hugh named was Bohannon's second-in-command," said Sydney. "Even Hullender didn't know his identity at the time—he was always hooded—but Posey told him who it was in prison."

"So he's the missing link."

"Yeah. We think he's the one who relayed the order from Bohannon to bomb the church that night. And Hullender believes that's the real reason your father didn't want Hugh to testify. He was protecting this man."

"Why would he do that?"

"Because he was a friend . . . Because he owed him a favor . . . Because he was protecting somebody else—"

"My father's too much of a hard-ass to ever do that."

"Or because the man had something on the judge." She sighed and reached for another folder. "You've heard of the Mississippi Sovereignty Commission?"

"God, yes. The state gestapo from the civil rights period. They kept records on 'subversive activities' around the state—civil rights workers, outside agitators, white liberals, anyone to the left of Strom Thurmond."

"Yeah, it was sort of the official arm of the White Citizens' Councils," said Sydney. "I was interested to find out that—unlike in my state, for example—the Klan didn't have much of a role in Mississippi until 1964: Freedom Summer. Until then, the Citizens' Councils, the Sovereignty Commission, and law enforcement had been able to handle things without any vigilante help."

"Hell, there was no such thing as a vigilante in Mississippi," Carter said. "You could just blow 'agitators' away in broad daylight."

"That started to change when Goodman, Schwerner, and Chaney were murdered," Sydney said. "Up until then, Posey had been moonlighting for the Sovereignty Commission as an investigator. But beginning in 1964, he also became the intermediary between the state—and I include the Ellis County Sheriff's Department in that—and Bohannon's up-and-coming Klan."

"My father hated the Sovereignty Commission."

"The feeling was mutual."

Sydney got quiet. He looked at her to go on. She wagged the folder she was holding. It held copies, she said, of some of the commission records about to be made public under the Freedom of Information Act. She had persuaded the FOIA office to hold up on their release until after the trial.

"There's something in here that suggests that the Sovereignty Commission may have been trying to muscle Judge Ransom to back off Bohannon," she said. "They had something on your father."

"And what was that?" Carter said with all the nonchalance he could summon.

Sydney hesitated for a moment, as if to let Carter get his bearings. "That the judge had an affair with a woman from a prominent Troy family."

Carter sat stock-still. "That's ridiculous."

"And if the man who linked the crime to Bohannon was fingered, the affair might have come out in the trial."

"Why?"

"Because the woman he supposedly had an affair with was married to Bohannon's second-in-command."

"Good God. Who is it?"

"I can't say."

Carter's mouth was dry, and his hands had gone clammy. "I have a right to know what's behind this bullshit about my father! What's Hullender's role in all this?"

"Hullender didn't find out about any of this till he was in prison," Sydney said. Posey was by then bitter that the Sovereignty Commission had sacrificed him to protect the big boys, and he told Hullender the whole story.

"It's payback and you know it," Carter said.

Sydney speared her pencil into the ceramic penholder on her desk. "I think he's beyond that now, Carter. I believe it's Bohannon Lacey wants to get." She knitted her brow. "Obviously, this is very sensitive. Some of the parties who would be affected are still alive."

"You bet your ass we're still alive."

"I mean the principals, besides your father—the ones implicated by the allegations. We have to be careful how we handle this. There's no need to name names unless and until it's necessary. I'm working on some physical evidence that ties Bohannon to Shiloh Church. But if that doesn't pan out, I'll have to use this information."

"You don't *have* to do anything, Sydney. That's your ambition talking."

Sydney gave him a look of disappointment. "Ah, you're playing the old 'opportunism' card. That's how white Southerners used to taint their own for doing the right thing. Look, your father's got every chance to defend himself. But I will do whatever I have to do to make sure that evil fuck Bohannon never deep-fries another hush puppy again."

Carter stood to leave. *"La belle dame sans merci."*

Sydney came around and leaned against the front of her desk. "You should know, Carter, that when I asked your dad about the Sovereignty Commission allegations, he didn't deny them."

"And you should know, Sydney, that my father wouldn't dignify charges from those quasi-fascist bozos—the great state of Mississippi's officially sanctioned lynch mob."

As he turned to exit, Sydney said, "Carter." He pivoted back around to face her. "Sometimes the people who are closest to us are the very ones we can never really know."

"Is that the professional opinion of someone who contends with the criminal mind all day, Counselor, or some friendly personal advice?"

"I know it professionally, and I know it personally." She tucked her lower lip into her teeth for a second and then turned back to unlock the file drawer.

15

O N A LATE AFTERNOON in August, Carter picked up Sarah at Magic Time for what would be the last time that summer. She was waiting for him in the parking lot, dressed in a gathered cotton skirt and a sleeveless white blouse buttoned up the back. The kiss she gave him as she slid into the passenger seat could not cover the anxiety on her face.

Schwerner, Goodman, and Chaney, as the lead story of Freedom Summer had been abbreviated, had taken a toll on the mood at Magic Time. Fights broke out regularly over nothing. There was renewed grumbling about her going out "unaccompanied," a mark of Carter's limbo in the minds of her colleagues. Sarah and Carter rode in silence for a short distance until he pulled off the highway onto a dirt road and then into a cluster of trees behind a kudzu bower.

"Where are we going?" she asked as he put the car in park.

"Naked Tail," he said.

Sarah hesitated. "You're joking, right?"

"Where else can we go?" he asked. "Don't worry. Lacey and them would never expect us to return after the last time." Lige had told Carter to park near the entrance to the river trail to keep from being spotted from the highway.

Carter took Sarah's hand and led her down the path that opened up through the trees. The trail traced one of the tributaries of the Little Chickasaw, past blackberry thickets and honeysuckle vines along an old hunting path pocked by an occasional cigarette package or crushed beer can. After a short distance, Sarah said, "I wanted to run to you that day at the courthouse."

"Me, too," Carter said. He stopped and turned to her, taking both her hands in his.

Sarah had always seemed so vivacious and carefree, but today she looked peaked and less self-assured. Carter brought her head to his chest with the crook of his arm, but she pulled back and looked up at him, her eyes as trusting and hurt as a child's. "Why didn't you?" she asked.

"I couldn't," he said, and looked down the hill at the river glistening through the foliage like diamonds. "I was working," he said, turning from her and continuing along the path.

"I've never been so scared in my life," said Sarah, following close behind. "More terrified of the police really than the crowd."

"Is Lige fully recovered?"

"I think so. You know Lige. He never complains."

"I know," Carter said. "And Mizell." A tone of disgust entered his voice. "Like some storm trooper. Lige wasn't the only one to catch it."

"What do you mean?"

"Jimbo's father runs the dry goods store in town, Stein's. Its windows were broken the other night, and swastikas were sprayed on the door."

"Because of Naked Tail?"

"I'm sure. Probably the only reason they haven't moved on Magic Time is they got the message that you're armed out there." Carter gave the back of her neck a little squeeze and said, "Annie Oakley."

The trail opened out onto the river, and they could see the bluff overlooking the lagoon and the presiding oak. They stood together, Carter's arm around Sarah, taking in the scene.

"You heard they found the bodies," Sarah said as they resumed their way down the path toward the sandy beach. "Mickey, Andrew, and James." She pronounced their names with the wonder reserved for martyrs.

"It came over the wire yesterday," he said. Schwerner, Goodman, and Chaney had been buried in an earthen dam on a farm outside Philadelphia.

"They'd been shot," she said. Her voice broke. They stopped walking, and Carter pressed her head to his chest again. "Isn't it strange," she said into his shirt, "how a term you've never heard can suddenly change the way you look at everything? 'Earthen dam.'"

"'School book depository.'"

She started to cry. "I knew Mickey. Not well, but we attended some of the same meetings in the city. He was from Brooklyn. He was so committed."

Carter pulled her tighter to him. She pushed him away and turned her back. "My parents are very upset. They want me to come home now. They sent a telegram last night. My father bought a plane ticket for me to come home." She was quietly sobbing.

Carter felt the breath go out of him. "When?" he asked.

"Tomorrow morning." She seemed to struggle for breath. "I may not see you again."

Carter turned her back toward him and drew her close. Her cheeks were streaked with tears. They kissed. This revelation had altered the molecules in the air. The heat seemed suddenly more oppressive. They stood there on the beach, holding on to each other.

Finally Carter said, "You can't leave."

"I'm coming back," Sarah said. "I just have to calm my parents down."

"What does Lige say?"

"He says I should go."

"I'll come see you."

She looked up at him. "In the city?" The anxiety on her face subsided. "You could drive up with Lige," she said. "He's going to Atlantic City in a couple of weeks for the Democratic convention. The Freedom Democratic Party's going to challenge the regular Mississippi delegation. That's not too far from the city."

His mind reeled with the logistics of such a trip and the questions he would face from his family. He had already braced himself for the controversy over his not taking Grayson to the dance, but now it looked as if that invitation stood moot. "My father would have a fit," he said.

"Tell him you're visiting friends in the city," Sarah said. "You're almost twenty-one. Do you have to explain your every move?"

Sarah didn't understand how volatile he and his father had been all summer. Soon after the incident at Naked Tail, Mitchell Ransom called Carter from his office and said his car had been seen out at Magic Time more than once and the sheriff had his license number. His father seemed as irritated with the way he had found out as he was with what he found out. The judge had gotten harassing phone calls at his office saying his son was a nigger lover. Sarah would never understand how constricting it felt to be responsible not only for himself but for his old man's reputation as well. "Because you are Mitchell Ransom's boy, you may be held to a higher standard," Carter had been instructed by his mother from the time he started school.

"I'll figure it out," Carter said to Sarah, and he meant it. "I'll come see you." He pulled her to him again. The last rays of afternoon sun warmed their faces and arms, its heat glistening off the sand.

"Listen," Sarah said, her head on his shoulder.

"What?"

"Shhh." The distinctive drumming sounded again, the vibrations of a woodpecker drilling into a tree. "Those pines beyond the bluff. Isn't that the bird we saw before?" She pointed past the oak on the promontory.

A tiny flash of red caught Carter's attention. "It's back," he said.

"Is it the same one?"

"It has to be. I told my mother I saw it. She didn't believe me. But when I described its coloring, she went to her books and found it."

"It's a sign. It's good luck." Suddenly the bird flittered off and circled out across the cove. Carter watched Sarah as she watched the bird disappear into the trees. "It's beautiful," she whispered.

"You're beautiful," said Carter. He took her hand and began leading her toward the water.

"Wait," she said. She reached behind her back and, arching it slightly, began unbuttoning her blouse. Carter kicked off his loafers and removed his shirt and trousers. "Can you help me?" she asked, with her back to him. He moved to her. His trembling fingers fumbled the buttons at first but then found their rhythm. He could feel the cinched blouse loosen as he reached the top button and she let the top fall from her shoulders. She stood there without turning around. "One more," she said. He undid the clasp on her bra. She let it drop onto her blouse in the sand.

With her back to him, she removed the rest of her clothes. Carter had never been completely naked with a girl before. All his sexual experience had been at the drive-in or parking up on the ridge with the lovely prick-teases the region was famous for, and they all seemed to have graduated from the same school for technical virgins—full nudity a strict prohibition. Even he and Grayson had never seen each other totally undressed. In the course of their incremental intimacies, Carter had felt the presence of the entire Troy Country Club as well as Grayson's formidable maternal pedigree. With Sarah, for the first time, his psyche was clear of everything except pure instinct.

She turned. "Oh, Carter, what does all this mean? Why did this happen? How did we find each other?" she whispered. It was the kind of line Sarah would ordinarily have put an ironic twist on, but Carter knew it was sincere. She gave out a little whimper as he pulled her close. The warmth of her skin poured into the contours of his own. Her hair had that clean, burnt smell of sunshine. She was sinking back onto the sand, pulling him with her. Carter cradled her into his left arm, using his right to execute a smooth tandem landing. They pressed their weight into each other. And in the seclusion of their fresh universe, all his hometown inhibition dissolved.

CARTER PUT OFF confronting Judge Ransom over Sydney's revelations for as long as he could, looking for the right time to bring it up. There was no right time.

On Saturday afternoon he descended the stairwell to the basement, listening over the thrum of the air conditioner for the familiar sounds of his father tinkering on one of his clocks in the workroom below—the whirr of his drill, the testing of gongs and chimes. He stopped to look at the groupings of photographs along the wall of the landing. Framed in the same thin black enamel as those in the guest bedroom, these pictures, arranged by his mother with a curator's eye, chronicled the earliest stages of Mitchell Ransom's life, before the family or his legal career.

Carter remembered staring at these old pictures when he was a child, looking for clues to the towering enigma of Mitchell Ransom—faded yellow images of his father as a young boy growing up on the Ransom family cotton and tobacco farm in eastern North Carolina, a gangly teenager driving a tractor. There were shots of a slender, haunted-looking student at Chapel Hill, looming awkwardly over his classmates and fraternity brothers. And then there were the pictures that entranced Carter the most, the ones hinting of the man his father would become, the man he had known growing up. They were the ones of his father going off to war.

Mitchell Ransom had finished at the University of North Carolina in 1942 and, as expected, returned home to the family farm upon graduation. But the war was raging, and shortly he enlisted in the Army Air Corps, entering preflight school in Bakersfield, California, for accelerated basic training. He moved on to Roswell, New Mexico, for advanced training and finally to Columbia, South Carolina, for tactical training in B-25 twin-engine bombers with the 310th Bomb Group. Just before shipping out to Cornwall, England, he came home on a weekend furlough and eloped with his college sweetheart, Katharine Cantrell, from the mill town of Eno, North Carolina. They were married by a justice of the peace in Chapel Hill. Nine months later, Carter Ransom was born.

The sepia tones of one of those antediluvian war photos foretold Mitchell's unlikely pilgrimage to Troy, Mississippi. The picture showed his father, at perhaps twenty-one or twenty-two, dressed in his aviator's cap and leather flight jacket with the wool collar, squinting into the camera, standing jauntily in front of his B-25. The picture next to it captured his crew before they took off in the doomed bomber, their faces tensed with adrenaline, testosterone, and fear, yet unaware that their plane would never touch down on that tarmac again. There were seven on board the B-25, including a Mississippi-born flight surgeon named Raymond Renfro, whom Mitchell met for the first time that day in

North Africa when the young medic asked to hitch a ride on his plane so he could better understand the stresses faced by the pilots and crewmen.

It was Mitchell Ransom's first combat mission and his last. The directive was to intercept an Axis convoy that was moving supplies from Italy to General Rommel's elite armored divisions in Tunisia, and the airmen were briefed by the fabled Jimmy Doolittle, who would lead the raid. They were shot down over the Mediterranean by a German Me-109 fighter in a turn after dropping their payload. Mitchell Ransom and Ray Renfro were thrown clear of the plane and were the only ones of the crew, including a *Life* photographer, to survive. The two of them spent the remainder of the war in POW camps, first in Italy, then in Germany, until they were liberated eighteen months later by General George Patton's tanks.

When they got home, Ray Renfro persuaded Mitchell, whose brothers by that time were running the farm, to come to Troy, Mississippi, and take a summer job clerking in the legal offices of the Graysonite Corporation before going off to Harvard Law that fall on the GI Bill. As it turned out, the Graysonite general counsel was a Harvard man, and the day Mitchell left for school, he was offered a job there in Troy when he finished.

Throughout his adulthood, Carter had kept in his desk drawer a letter his father wrote him from Stalag Luft 3, dated Christmas Eve, 1943, a month after he was born. He hadn't received it until the war was over and Mitchell delivered it personally to Eno, North Carolina, where Katharine was living with her sister while finishing her education at Duke to become a schoolteacher. This first missive from a new father to his firstborn was probably the single most direct, unmitigated outpouring of emotion Carter would ever experience from Mitchell Ransom:

Dear Son,

Welcome to the family. You weighed eight pounds and eleven ounces when you were born and were twenty-three inches long, so it looks like you are going to be quite a bruiser when you grow up. Your mother and I are so proud of you.

I want you to know that we both thought long and hard about what to name you and decided finally on Carter, a name that represents quite a legacy in this family. I'm sure there were probably some horse thieves and drunkards along the way among the Ransoms and Cantrells, but we've had our share of honest, upright citizens as well. And even a hero or two. Your great-great-grandfather on the Ransom side, Carter Teague Ransom, served with distinction at Gettysburg with the 26th North Carolina Regiment, Pettigrew's Brigade, Heth's Division, Hill's Corps, Army of Northern Virginia. He and those valiant Tar Heel boys almost took the stone wall during Pickett's charge on the afternoon of July 3, 1863. They got within 10 paces before they were forced to retreat with the brigade back to Seminary Ridge. One out of every four Confederate soldiers who fell at Gettysburg was a North Carolinian, mind you, including your great-great-granddaddy, who was wounded trying to help a fallen buddy. His company had gone into the fight that day with 33 men and came out with only 8 men. Carter Ransom recovered from his wounds to fight again until he was paroled two years later at Appomattox Courthouse and walked barefoot all the way back home to his little farm in Johnston County with nothing left to his name but his land and the clothes on his back. He carried a Yankee minié ball lodged there in his right shoulder for the rest of his life.

So hold your head high, Carter. You come from good stock. And I know when it's your turn you're going to do the Ransom family name proud, too.

Love,
Daddy

When Carter appeared at the bottom of the stairs, the judge was bent over his worktable like an elongated question mark, looking between the face of a grandfather clock and a small mountain of screws, gears, and washers. "Sally, is that you?" he said without looking up.

"No, it's me, Dad," said Carter. "Can we talk?"

"Come in, come in." His father removed his glasses, rubbing his eyes with knuckles swollen from arthritis.

The claustrophobic room's fluorescent lighting cast a stark blue luminescence over the off-white walls, providing the ambience of a morgue. In the unforgiving light of the workroom, Mitchell's face looked drawn, his eyes flat and limpid blue. His hair was unkempt, an unusual grooming lapse in the judge, who, though by no means a dandy, took pride in his appearance, especially his haircut.

"Don't let me disturb you," said Carter.

"You never disturb me, Pross, you know that."

Carter stepped around a Big Wheel that his nephew had outgrown. "I saw Willie's daddy at the Grille the other day," he said casually. "I didn't know Robert was with Graysonite now."

"He should do well there," his father replied. "He's a talented young lawyer."

Carter picked up a stray screwdriver and examined it as his father went back to his clock. "Sally says he's finally making his child support payments."

Mitchell shook his head but declined comment. As irritated as he was with his daughter's ex-husband, he could not bring himself to disparage a fellow lawyer, however protective he remained of Sally. Once, when she was three years old, she had veered too close on her tricycle to one of Mitchell's prize rosebushes that lined the driveway, and its thorns slashed her face and arms. She cried and cried while Katharine tended the injuries with Mercurochrome and Band-Aids. Later that morning, Carter and his mother stood at the window, watching, as Mitchell took a chain saw to his favorite rosebush and cleared it forever from the driveway where his little girl played.

Mitchell sighed. "I wish I'd been home more when you and your sister were growing up," he said out of nowhere. "But I guess I was just too much of a young man in a hurry. Like Sally's Robert." He began combing the pile of metal parts with his fingers, looking for something. "Sally says you're bringing the boy down before school starts. Willie will enjoy having somebody to play with besides his old granddad. Which reminds me, Pross, your editor called. I took a message for you."

"I called him."

"What did he want?"

"He had some questions about the *Tribune* piece on Troy and the Shiloh Church case," Carter said, watching his father's reaction. "I think he's concerned about me covering the story."

"Conflict of interest?"

Carter cleared his throat.

"Frankly," said Mitchell, "I'm surprised you're going back to work so soon."

Carter bristled. "It sure beats sitting around on my *tuchis*." He never dropped Yiddishisms into his conversation when he was in New York. "Besides, who better than me to cover that trial?"

"I suppose." His father let it go, returning to his washers and gears. "Just don't let your emotions get the better of you."

To Carter, the expressions of concern sounded tinged with condescension. "Dad, I saw the prosecutor on the case. She says she talked to you about Hullender's testimony."

"She did," said Mitchell without affect, reaching for the denuded clockface. Carter could feel the screen coming down between them, the bolts locking.

"Looks like he's giving her another angle, one that didn't come up in the first trial."

Mitchell sniffed. "Sounds to me like she's got her own angle."

"Well, she may be a bit ruthless at that," Carter said, and smiled inwardly at the thought. "But that doesn't make her wrong. Did you see the *Tribune* piece?"

"No, but I've been fielding calls all week."

"Lovelace is a sloppy reporter."

"I doubt there were any disclaimers to that effect under his byline."

It was an ancient argument between the two of them that they could slip into like an old shoe. His father's contempt for his son's profession was barely concealed. But Carter proceeded. "So how did you feel about the story?"

"I didn't read it." Mitchell reached for the screwdriver Carter was holding. "I learned a long time ago not to believe everything I read in the papers. And not to read anything with my name in it." He looked up at Carter over the rims of his glasses. "It would just piss me off."

"I know you hate having cases tried in the paper," said Carter. He turned his back to his father, strolled over to a swivel stool opposite the workbench, and straddled it.

"That's why we have trials and don't leave it to the mobs," said

Mitchell without looking up. "Including the press mob. So all the evidence can come out in an orderly fashion in a courtroom. Not in the headlines."

"Well, I like trying cases in the paper. Lucky for me, I guess, that the press isn't an arm of the government in this country." Carter wasn't sure whether it was he or his father who had risen to the bait. "The prosecutor tells me there are new Sovereignty Commission files and FBI testimony this time around. Dad, she says they were trying to blackmail you."

"I wouldn't have been the only one."

"Were you being blackmailed?"

"You're only blackmailed if you go along with it. It takes two."

"They're saying you were withholding evidence, protecting a friend."

"I see." Mitchell finally made eye contact with him. "So the prosecution didn't make the case against Bohannon in the first trial, the jury failed to convict, and now I'm the one who dropped the ball." He shook his head. "What I'd like to know is why this young prosecutor's so willing to air malicious gossip that those Sovereignty Commission peckerwoods couldn't get anybody to listen to twenty years ago. Now she's doing their dirty work for them."

"Will you tell me about it?"

"There's nothing to tell." His father seemed pained but oblique. "All I know is, if they take this nonsense seriously, a lot of people are going to be hurt for no reason."

"You know I'm covering this for the paper. I need to know what's coming and if there's anything to it."

"You're the reporter. Why don't you find out?"

"I'm trying to," Carter said peevishly. "Watch how I do it, Dad: Who was the businessman?"

"You've got to give me more than that, son."

"The one you were supposed to be protecting. The one they say was a Kluxer. Did you even know the guy?" Carter didn't let on that he knew about the alleged affair.

"I know everybody in a town this size. And a lot of folks have dealings with dubious characters they know very little about. Not that I'm saying he was a Kluxer. I have no proof of that. If he was, he would be the last person I would protect. Besides, it's all based on testimony from somebody with a double-digit IQ and the attention span of a hummingbird. It seemed unreliable to me at the time and still does."

Carter registered that his father had confirmed his awareness of Hugh Renfro's testimony. "Who was the businessman?" Carter leaned forward in the swivel chair, nearly losing his balance.

Mitchell hunkered over his worktable and lowered his voice until it was barely audible. "I guess they're talking about Glen Boutwell."

Carter felt his forearms tingle. When Sydney mentioned a Klan collaborator in the Troy business community, he had vaguely conjured a suspect or two from his dusty adolescent memories of questionable town leadership, but he certainly hadn't considered his coach. Glen Boutwell, who had died in the 1970s, was about the furthest thing from the profile of a violent racist Carter could imagine. He was remembered fondly in Troy as a pillar of the community, Jaycee Man of the Year. He worked with disadvantaged kids, the handicapped. He raised money for the United Way. Carter scanned his own history with the man he revered, searching for any hint of racism, or politics of any sort, for that matter. Coach Boutwell had always seemed apolitical. He may have mouthed the segregationist sentiments of the era, but that was standard fare among white civic leaders, even for Jews like Jimbo's father. Segregation was the official state religion at the time in Mississippi, like being Catholic in Italy.

"Grayson would die if she heard this," Carter said. "And her mother—"

"Sheppy would be devastated," Mitchell concurred. "There's no need whatsoever."

Carter wanted to call Sydney right away and warn her that she was way off base. He tried to imagine the ramifications if this became public, but his mind just shut down. It would not compute. As Carter stared at his father slipping a tiny washer over a tiny bolt with still-steady fingers, a sliver of a memory rose out of his mind's recesses, a thought that hadn't occurred to him in a quarter of a century. He wondered if he would have even recalled the incident had he not been discussing the night in question with Grayson so recently. At the time, it was something he had glossed over as nothing more than a curiosity—something absorbed, rationalized, and buried.

————————

SHEPPY BOUTWELL HANDED Carter a flashlight when he stepped into the foyer and said, "Carter, would you be a precious angel and run down to the basement to fetch our special champagne glasses. Glen, tell him where they are, and give Carter the key." Carter was glad for any opportunity to make himself scarce after his disastrous conversation with Grayson in the car about the upcoming cotillion. The temperature in her parents' house seemed to have dropped, even with guests still arriving and the party for the Jaycee Man of the Year in full swing.

"There's a set of twelve in a rosewood box with pearl inlay in a cabinet behind the furnace," said Glen Boutwell, handing over the basement key on a circular key ring. "Be careful now. They're heirlooms, Austrian cut glass. Don't dawdle, son. I know you'll be tempted to admire some of my Civil War collection." He winked conspiratorially. Then, to his wife in a stage whisper, "Better send Grayson with him, Sheppy. He'll get sidetracked." But Sheppard Boutwell seemed to sense something amiss with her daughter. "Carter can handle it," she said, smiling. "Grayson's helping me greet the guests."

"The furnace is along the wall to the right of the door," Glen shouted as Carter disappeared down the stairwell off the kitchen. "Beyond the wardrobe," he heard Boutwell calling down to him as he unlocked the door at the bottom of the steps. Fumbling in the shadows, Carter swept the area with the flashlight beam until his hand found the switch. The dim bulb suspended by a wire barely penetrated the darkness to the outer edges of the room. His eyes adjusted as he shone the flashlight beyond the furnace and moved slowly in that direction. The basement was walled entirely with Graysonite paneling, a remarkably well-appointed storage area even for a house in Stonehaven as nice as Grayburn. The smell of heating oil and mothballs assaulted his nostrils, and a roach skittered across the floor just beyond his flashlight's beam.

Along the wall he stumbled across a basket filled with baseball equipment—mitts, bats, balls, and a catcher's mask—and Carter wondered if any of his old Louisville Sluggers were among the relics of Little League seasons gone by. When he reached for one of the mitts, he realized that it was fitted over an artificial arm and that, along with bats and gloves, the basket contained various discarded prosthetic limbs and devices from Boutwell's business. The wall behind the basket was covered with a giant Confederate battle flag, and in front of it stood a lifelike department store mannequin dressed in a butternut-and-gray Confederate uniform. A typed three-by-five card clipped to the pocket read "11th Mississippi Infantry Regiment, Company A, University Grays (fought at First Man-assas, Sharpsburg, Gettysburg, Antietam, et al.)." Next to it was another mannequin with a similar Civil War–era uniform, but in dark blue, once belonging to a Yankee enlisted man.

Carter's flashlight caught a display case lining the far wall, gleaming with muskets, pistols, sabers, swords, and bayonets. Though feeling a tug of curiosity, Carter focused on finding the rosewood case of cham-pagne glasses. He spotted the carved box on the shelf of a cabinet just beyond a cedar wardrobe against the wall to his right. He reached past the wardrobe for the rosewood box, and as he lifted it, his belt buckle caught on the wardrobe door handle. The door swung open. When he turned to close it, something luminous and white caught his eye. He opened the door wide to shine his flashlight inside, and that's when he saw it: a white silk robe with a hood. The red insignia of a Maltese cross was stitched on the front of the robe, which was draped over the hanger, and two eyeholes in the cowl peered out from the darkness like empty sockets.

The prickling on the back of Carter's neck came even before he rec-ognized it as Ku Klux Klan regalia. Then he quickly figured out that it was part of Coach Boutwell's extensive collection from the Reconstruc-tion period. Given Coach's reputation for collecting only artifacts of the highest interest and value, Carter imagined that the robe might have once been worn by the Confederate cavalry general and Klan founder, Nathan Bedford Forrest. As he lifted it to inspect the patched red and gold insignia of the cross, the garment slipped off the hanger and onto the floor. He scrambled to pick it back up. As he bent down, his flash-light beam caught a faint smudge of orange on the hem. It crossed his mind that it might be the residue of some ancient bloodstain, but even as he realized that blood dried brown, he noticed a crushed blade of grass still clinging to what was in fact a remnant of red clay.

"Carter, where are those champagne glasses?" A voice shouted down from above. It was Coach Boutwell. "We're dying of thirst up here."

He closed the door to the wardrobe, hefted the hand-carved wooden box of champagne glasses, and made his way back toward the laughter and light.

———

AT THE TIME, the Klan attire in Glen Boutwell's basement had impressed him no more or less than the Confederate uniform and the collection of swords and sabers and muskets. It never crossed Carter's mind that his Little League coach might actually be wearing the robes and regalia. They were simply collector's items, a reenactor's dream.

"So, Dad," Carter asked, "why do you think they'd be going after Coach Boutwell?"

"Because they can," his father answered. He began putting away his tools. Carter knew their conversation was coming to a close. "He's not around to defend himself. And they're looking for a scapegoat and a way to get Bohannon."

"What does he have to do with Bohannon?"

"I don't know. Could be some business dealings we know nothing about. But it doesn't make him a Kluxer any more than eating Bohannon's catfish makes you or me one."

"And what does Boutwell have to do with you?" The directness with which Carter posed the question seemed to have a sobering effect on his father.

"I don't know. Glen Boutwell and I were never close. What he did in his private life was no concern of mine."

Carter seized the opportunity for moral outrage. "Are you saying that wearing a mask makes terrorizing black people a 'private matter,' or do you really mean your private life was no concern of his?"

The judge peered blankly at his son over the rims of his glasses. "If this prosecutor thinks Glen was mixed up with the bombing and I was protecting him, I'd like to see what proof she has. I've seen some of those Sovereignty Commission files, and it was a disgrace what they could get away with. This is the sorry result: posthumous character assassination."

His father replaced his tools in the chest and slowly stood up. It was time to go upstairs and wash for dinner, which was just as well. Carter couldn't bring himself to press the judge further about the affair, and he balked at the thought of his father having a sex life at all, let alone one with his girlfriend's mother. But Mitchell's inscrutability, which had always seemed judicial, now appeared to conceal something threatening to Carter's sense of origin. The anxiety that had fluttered in his chest when Sydney first mentioned his father's involvement settled in the pit of his stomach as fear.

"Dad, you mentioned my conflict of interest in writing about the trial," Carter said, following his father's slow progress up the stairs. "What about your conflict of interest? Why didn't you recuse yourself from presiding over the Shiloh trial?"

His father turned to face him near the top of the landing. "There was no one in the county or even in the state who would have had no connection with the case," he said. "A recusal would have done nothing to serve the cause of justice. Nothing whatsoever. I believed I could be as fair and impartial as the rest of them. Besides," he said as he continued up the stairs, "I wouldn't have trusted anyone else with it."

It wasn't completely clear whether the judge understood that the conflict Carter had in mind was the heartbreak of his own son.

16

THE DELTA DC-IO BANKED over the city, making its final descent into LaGuardia. Through the wisps of clouds, the honeycombed grid of Manhattan far below appeared to Carter like the motherboard of an antiquated computer. The morning sun glinted off the twin towers of the World Trade Center. If he leaned forward and pressed his cheek against the windowpane, he could see the Statue of Liberty, tiny and forlorn out in the harbor, with the wilds of New Jersey in the distance beyond. He closed the window shade to avoid catching sight of the midtown topography that had once been the Institute of Modern Art.

Summer was ending, and Carter hadn't written anything since the columns on the museum explosion a few months before. He was going to pick up Josh to take him back down to Mississippi for a couple of weeks before school started. Jury selection for the church bombing trial was to begin the week after he got back, and Carter would have a front-row seat as a prosecution witness, but not as a reporter. After weeks of weaning from his dependency on daily deadlines, he had finally been ready to get back to work. But the Lovelace piece in the *Tribune* had brought home to his editors how enmeshed in the story Carter was. He had just gotten the call from Dennehy informing him that he was being pulled from the assignment.

As the plane leveled its wings with the horizon over Flushing Bay, Carter settled back into his seat. He tried to imagine a worst-case scenario for the Shiloh Church trial. Bohannon gets off. Mitchell Ransom is disgraced for withholding evidence and having an affair with the wife of a Klansman whom he was protecting. Rasheed Lovelace wins a Pulitzer Prize covering Carter's own story. And Hullender gets a sandwich named after him at Wad's. Carter closed his eyes. As he listened to the high-pitched whir of the wing flaps adjusting, his thoughts drifted back to a lost summer day when the world was still new.

———

THE MANHATTAN SKYLINE APPEARED without warning from a rise and a curve on the New Jersey Turnpike. Carter, at the wheel of his family Ford Fairlane, let out a low whistle.

"Home, sweet, home." Stephen exhaled smoke from the last of his Luckies, affecting the jaded cosmopolitan, then returned to his mission of tuning to as many consecutive Beatles hits on the radio as possible. They were both bleary-eyed, running on nicotine and caffeine after the long trip up through the lower South, the Carolinas, and Virginia, and along the eastern seaboard. Carter had told his parents he was going to help Stephen move into his new apartment. He failed to mention that they were giving a ride to delegates from the Mississippi Freedom Democratic Party to Atlantic City—where a couple of hours earlier they had dropped off Elijah Knight and Dexter Washington at the Democratic convention. Or that he hoped to spend every minute of his week in New York with Sarah Solomon.

They had left Troy in the middle of the night, careful not to draw attention to an integrated automobile, with both pairs of young men taking turns slumping inconspicuously (and segregated) in the backseat. After depositing Lige and Dexter at a fleabag hotel in Atlantic City, Carter and Stephen were on their own and fast approaching the greatest city on the planet. Carter's adrenaline pumped as they locked in on the Lincoln Tunnel, with that diorama of teeming ambition and sheer possibility sculpted out of the rock and tidewaters just across the Hudson.

On the other side of the tunnel, the late morning traffic was rendered surprisingly manageable by the neat mathematical certainty of the street numbers, reassuring in a city so overwhelming and infinite. Stephen guided them expertly uptown to a cheap parking lot not far from his apartment near Juilliard, at Claremont Avenue and 122nd Street. Once there, in the cramped, dingy fourth-floor walk-up Stephen shared with an oboist from Seattle, Carter showered and shaved. Then Stephen walked him to the downtown subway on Broadway. "I don't need any help moving today," Stephen fibbed. "You can help me unpack tomorrow."

It was just past noon when Carter arrived at the magical address stenciled on the garnet awning of a limestone building on Eighty-fifth off Amsterdam. He had stopped at a market on the corner down the block from Sarah's building to buy a bouquet of daisies. The doorman called up to the apartment number Carter gave him and waved him into the elevator. A young man with a Schwinn bicycle entered behind him as the door was about to close. Carter wondered for a moment if the fellow, dressed in a dark suit with a skinny red tie, was a Mormon missionary, like the ones he had seen back home who traveled in pairs by bicycle. He was as tall as Carter and handsome, with aquiline features and a haircut in a modified ducktail that was a cross between Fabian and Frankie Avalon. The man watched Carter punch the elevator button and, as the interior wire-mesh gate accordioned shut, looked over at him with penetrating black eyes and said, "Nine. You going to the Solomons'?"

"Yes."

He stared at the daisies in Carter's hand. "Me, too." The elevator rose at a painfully slow rate, and Carter and his companion didn't make eye contact for a couple of floors. On four, an old man got on with a basket of laundry and got off on six. When the car lurched upward, the bicyclist spoke without looking at Carter. "You must be Beauregard."

"Excuse me?"

"Sarah's new boyfriend. I heard you were coming to visit. I'm the brother, Michael."

"Oh," Carter said, presenting his hand. "Nice to meet you." But Michael had affixed his eyes on the arrow above the door again and did not look over. Carter let his hand drop.

"First time in the city?" Michael asked without curiosity.

"Uh-huh."

Michael snorted. "Good luck."

The elevator door finally opened, and Michael wheeled his bicycle out and down the narrow corridor to the door at the end of the hall marked "A." While Michael fumbled with his keys, the door opened, and Sarah stood staring at her brother with a look of disappointment and confusion. "Michael, I thought—" Then she saw Carter behind him. She squeezed past her brother and the bike and hugged Carter. "You found us," she said without letting go.

Carter reached around and pressed the flowers to her nose.

"My favorite," she said. Then to her brother, "Michael, did you introduce yourself to Carter Ransom?"

"We met," he replied, leaning his bike against the back of a leather recliner in the living room.

"My brother," Sarah whispered, squeezing Carter's arm, "is a bit of a pill."

Carter had not yet kissed her. It was strange to see her so somehow filial. Waiting on the other side of the door was a short, handsome, dignified-looking man with a shock of black hair, graying sideburns, and kind blue eyes under charcoal eyebrows. Gold wire-rimmed reading glasses were balanced on the tip of his nose. He held a newspaper under his arm.

"Mr. Solomon," Carter said, clasping the extended hand.

Strange but agreeably pungent kitchen aromas hit Carter's nose as Sarah pulled him into the airy, high-ceilinged prewar apartment. A small, buxom woman in Capezio flats, a khaki dirndl skirt, and a crisp white sleeveless shirt arose from the couch to hug Carter. "Just in time for lunch." Sarah's mother wore her graying hair in a popular bouffant style, punctuated with gold earrings.

"So you already met Michael?" said her father.

"We met," said Michael. He then took a brown paper bag from the handlebar basket and removed a steam iron from it. "I brought back the iron."

"I was wondering where it was," said his mother.

"I thought a big shot talent agent had his shirts pressed professionally," said his father.

"No time to explain, Pop. I've got to get back to the office."

"We have a guest, Michael," said his father. "You can stay for lunch."

Sarah explained that Michael had just gotten a job with the William Morris Agency.

"In the mailroom," her father added, tossing his newspaper onto the sofa.

"With a Harvard degree he's sorting mail," his wife said, and disappeared into the kitchen.

"Got to start somewhere," Michael shouted, heading for the dining-room table.

Mrs. Solomon returned with a basket of toasted bagels and said in a loud whisper to Carter, "He wants to run a movie studio."

"I heard that, Roz!" her son shouted.

"Carter, come eat. What a lovely name. My husband's not teaching today, so we get to have a meal like a normal family. I hope you like lox and bagels and kugel."

Carter looked at Sarah. She gave him a smile that said, You have so much to learn.

"Has he ever had a bagel?" said Michael with disgust.

They all sat down, and Mr. Solomon began the interrogation while spreading cream cheese on his toasted bagel. "So Sarah tells me your father's a judge down there."

"Yes, sir."

After Carter's alma mater had been extracted, Mr. Solomon said, "Fine school. It's kind of the Harvard of the South, right?"

"Funny," said Carter, smiling, "we always said Harvard was the Vanderbilt of the North."

"So, Michael," Sarah said mischievously, "did you know that Carter played football?"

Michael was attacking his lunch with the single-minded focus of a noseguard. He paused from his smacking and looked up. "In college?"

"No. I had an injury and probably wasn't good enough anyway," Carter said. "Did you play?"

"I'm afraid not," he said.

"Michael's a big Packers fan," said Sarah. "More of a stat guy, though. I'm sure he's impressed to meet someone who's actually thrown a football."

"You were a quarterback?" said Michael, looking at him sharply.

"High school."

"Did you run the T or the I formation?"

"We were the first high school team in south Mississippi to run the wishbone," Carter said. "How's that for a stat? Our coach was a big Bear Bryant fan."

"Green Bay picked up a halfback from Vanderbilt last year."

"Lucas."

"Yeah, Lucas. Doesn't see much action."

Mr. Solomon seemed impatient to make better use of his rare lunch at home. "Did you know Andrew or Mickey?"

Sarah answered for Carter, explaining that he had only known the civil rights workers in Troy. He could feel her tensing with the turn of conversation.

"Terrible that something like this could happen in our country," her father continued.

"They had no business down there," said Michael blandly. "And neither did Sarah."

"Michael?" said Sarah. "Shut. Up." Carter was surprised by her vehemence.

"What did they expect from those redneck cretins?" Michael continued.

His mother offered Carter the cream cheese. She said she had read in the *Tribune* that President Johnson personally ordered J. Edgar Hoover to flood the area with FBI agents.

"Yeah, well, good luck getting a fair trial down there," Michael said. Then to Carter with mock ingenuousness, "No offense to your old man."

"Were you a civil rights volunteer?" Sarah's mother asked Carter.

"No, ma'am," Carter said, looking at Sarah. He was realizing how little she had told her parents about him. "I work for the newspaper."

"Carter's a friend of one of the Snick fieldworkers I told you about, Daddy. Elijah Knight."

"Some of his best friends are *schvartzes*," Michael said. He made a little moaning sound as he chewed his bagel.

Sarah gave her brother one of those "you gotta laugh" looks that conveyed both distaste and amusement. "Carter just drove Lige and another Snick guy to Atlantic City for the convention," she said. "They're challenging the state's regular party delegates for seating."

"With LBJ a lock for the nomination," Michael said, "I suppose the convention needs some phony drama." He pointed to the cream cheese in front of Carter.

Carter looked at Michael's finger and then stared directly at him.

"Well, I was an Adlai Democrat and voted for Kennedy," said Mr. Solomon, "but I must say, Johnson's surprised a lot of us."

"How so?" Carter asked. He relented and passed the cream cheese to Michael.

"Signing the civil rights bill," he replied.

"With that accent of his," said Michael. He put on his idea of a Texas drawl. "Mah fella Amurricans. Come let us reason together."

Mrs. Solomon widened her eyes in assent. "I was certainly surprised a Southerner would know the words to 'We Shall Overcome.'"

"Dr. King's a Southerner, Mother," said Sarah.

"You know what I mean," her mother replied.

"Well, LBJ's a Texan, not a Southerner," said Carter. The fine distinction went over the Solomons' heads.

"He deserves credit," said Mr. Solomon. "He overcame his background in signing that bill."

As Carter was wondering if what he was doing was "overcoming his background," Mrs. Solomon shifted back into hostess mode. "Will you have a Bloody Mary, Carter?"

"Oh, no ma'am. Water's fine."

"That was a test," Sarah said. "Mom thinks all goyim are lushes." She turned to needle Carter. "Alcohol's against his religion, Mother."

"I didn't know Catholics didn't drink," said Mrs. Solomon.

"No, I'm not Catholic," Carter replied. He felt the urge to laugh.

"Not all gentiles are Catholic, Roz," said Michael. "Hey, Ma, the Reformation? Martin Luther, noted theologian and anti-Semite?"

"Carter's Baptist," said Sarah.

Her parents looked politely horrified.

"Baptists are teetotalers, Ma," said Michael. "You should be pleased."

Carter wanted to laugh again. "Well, I'm not exactly a teetotaler. I'm Baptist, but I'm not a fanatic. In fact, where I come from, Catholics are as exotic as . . . as—"

"Jews," said Michael.

"Zen Buddhists," said Carter.

"So how did you grow up in a place like that and not share the prevailing racial attitudes?" asked Sarah's father.

Carter was glad that Michael interrupted to spare him from replying. He wasn't sure what the answer was. "He's an Atticus Finch Southerner, Pop. Not a Bob Ewell." He lifted his glass to Carter. " 'Chiffarobe,' " he said in Mayella Ewell's desperate whine.

"My brother thinks everything in life can be reduced to movie clichés," said Sarah.

"And my sister thinks there's justice in this world and the good guys win," he said. "So I guess we both think in movie clichés."

"Michael's our cynic, Carter," said Mr. Solomon. "Pity him."

"Oh, I doubt he's a cynic," said Carter, taking a bite of his lox-draped bagel. Sarah stared at him, waiting for an explanation. Carter finished chewing, then swallowed and said, "He sounds more like a disappointed romantic."

"Oho," said Michael, sitting up in his chair. "The Southern Baptist quarterback has a line on the big-city sophisticates."

"Believe me, Carter," Sarah said. "Michael's the most cynical person I've ever met."

Carter explained the origins of the word "cynicism," from the Greek *kynikos*, the etymological root for "canine." The Cynic school of philosophy held that all values were equally worthless, that no beliefs or mores were superior to any other. So they would defy convention by defecating and fornicating in the road—like dogs. "I was standing up for you, Michael—and complimenting your parents," Carter said. "I just don't think good people like them would have raised a Weimaraner."

Michael listened to Carter with a look both predatory and bemused. "Too-shay," he said, giving the word a respectable Southern diphthong. "I thought the only Greek they taught at Vanderbilt was the Deke secret handshake."

"Michael," his father said wearily.

"Fine," Michael said, tossing his napkin into his plate. "I'm due back at work."

"I still don't know why you needed my iron," said his mother.

"Relax, Ma. I don't need it anymore." Michael's face took on a puckish look. "The wall heater in the stockroom works much better."

"What on earth are you talking about?" his mother asked.

"Why do you think I go to work in the mailroom at six in the morning before anybody gets to the office? So I can steam open all the important mail that came in the previous afternoon." Michael was enjoying the look of shock on his father's face. "To find out what big-shot client's writing what big-shot agent about what big-shot deals," he said casually.

Carter felt that Michael's brazenness was a performance. Sarah pressed the heels of her palms against her eyes.

Her mother still didn't grasp what he was saying. "But why?"

"I guess so I can learn something important to advance my career," Michael replied. His father tucked back into his plate of food, which Carter assumed was his way of dealing with his son's conduct. " 'Live dangerously and you live right.' Isn't that what you always say, Pop?"

His father shook his head in resignation. "*Oy gevalt.* You use Goethe to justify snooping in other people's mail?"

"Hey, don't knock it. I found out that Danny Thomas wants to change agents. I've got a meeting with him next week."

"That's disgusting, Michael," said Sarah. "It's also a federal crime."

"Good God, we've raised a felon," said his mother.

Sarah looked at Carter. "My brother has no conscience."

"That's all right, Sis," Michael said. "You have enough for the both of us."

"Dad!" Sarah tried to enlist her father in her outrage. "He's your son. Don't you care that he's a sociopath?"

"It's show business, Pop," Michael said. "No different from law or politics or anything else, academia included. This is how all the big *schlong*s got where they are."

"Michael, watch your language," his mother said.

Michael stood. Straightening his chair, he announced with exaggerated solemnity, "I don't want to hear any complaints from you when I bring a shiksa home to lunch." He came around the table and offered his hand to Carter. "Just kidding, Gomer. Hope you didn't take offense."

"Oh, I found it bracin'," Carter said, standing and shaking hands like a pro at the net after a hard tennis match.

Michael smiled warmly, as if the conversation had never turned contentious. He winked and said, "It's my Weimaraner sense of humor. You two kids have fun." Then he turned to Sarah and asked, "Do you still want those tickets?"

Sarah seemed surprised. She turned to Carter and said, "How would you like to see your first Broadway show tonight?"

A new show in previews, called *Fiddler on the Roof*, was opening in September, but word was out that it was going to be a hit.

"They'll be at the box office," Michael said, and headed into the living room.

Sarah told Carter, "Zero Mostel's a William Morris client."

"Have you heard of Zero Mostel, Carter?" asked Mr. Solomon.

Sarah gave her father a look. "Dad, Mississippi's not entirely cut off from the world. They have television. They see *Ed Sullivan*."

"I'd love to go," said Carter, though he had never heard of Zero Mostel. Then he called to her brother in the living room, "Thank you, Michael."

Michael waved. "You'll be wearing a yarmulke by the time we're finished with you," he shouted as he wheeled his bicycle to the door.

"Can you get more than two?" asked Sarah.

"What—you're going to invite the entire Mississippi Freedom Democratic Party?"

Sarah turned to Carter. "Do you think Stephen would want to go?"

"Are you kidding?"

"Get three, okay, Michael?"

When the door closed, they all returned to their lunch. Mrs. Solomon sighed. "He's very complicated."

"What's so complicated?" said Mr. Solomon. "He's a putz."

"He's just a Jewish prince," Sarah said. "Everything's gone so well for him, yet he can be so sour."

Mrs. Solomon sipped her tea thoughtfully. "My analyst says it's very common for the oldest son to project his oedipal fears onto other males he perceives as a threat. Obviously he would play out his rivalrous feelings toward his father with Carter."

Sarah rolled her eyes. "Mother, Carter's not interested in your psychoanalysis of Michael."

"Or it could be that our son's just a schmuck," said her husband. "Didn't Freud say 'Sometimes a cigar is just a cigar'?"

"True, but with you, dear, that means a cigar is *always* just a cigar."

Sarah drained her glass of seltzer and got up from the table. "We'd better get going if we're not going to lose the day."

Carter began clearing his plate and silverware to take to the kitchen.

"You must have a good relationship with your mother, Carter," Mrs. Solomon called out to him.

"Why do you say that?" he asked.

"You have such good table manners."

"Oh, it's just the WASP obsession," Sarah said. She took his hand and led him toward her room. On the way down the narrow hallway lined with floor-to-ceiling bookcases, he stopped to look at her swimming trophies, academic honors, and family photos. The books on the shelves included Shakespeare, Marx, Freud, Buber, her father's academic texts, and countless bestsellers. Sarah glanced back down the hallway and then snagged a kiss. "I'm proud of you," she whispered. "I thought my mother would faint when you helped clear the dishes."

"How about your father?"

"He likes you. But he's a little proprietary toward me."

"I like them, too," he said.

As they were saying goodbye to her parents, Sarah had to run back to her room for her purse.

Herbert Solomon shook Carter's hand firmly, gripping his forearm with the other hand, and looked him in the eye. "We're so relieved she got home safely," he said. "Thank you."

An hour later, Carter and Sarah lay entangled in each other's arms on a mattress on the floor of Stephen's bedroom. Their tour of the city had gotten only as far as the lake in Central Park. After watching boaters and other young lovers for a while, they had gravitated toward the shadows of the boathouse. "This is my Naked Tail," she whispered as they kissed. They had had to brace themselves against a tree, and finally, Carter, barely able to speak, had said, "What's the quickest way to Stephen's from here?"

All their intentions of spending the afternoon sightseeing lay in a jumble of clothes on the floor. The dust motes floating on the shafts of afternoon sunlight, the sound of a cellist practicing in the apartment upstairs, and the butterfly touch of Sarah's fingertips tracing circles on his chest suffused Carter with a sensation of infinitude. Even the jackhammers and sirens out on the street sounded like music.

Sarah drew her belly close to his and slung her leg over his haunch. Pulling her face toward his, Carter could feel another rush of desire, even though their heartbeats had not yet subsided to normal. The kissing began anew. He had never before felt a woman's tongue in his mouth. The Southern belle's kissing strategy permitted only the occasional congress of tongues in *her* mouth. He felt as if he were about to jump out of his skin.

Sarah drew back to study him. "Life is so strange," she said. "But I never thought it would be this great."

"I haven't even been in New York a day, and I can't remember who I was before."

Sarah parked herself on top of him and dug her knees into the mattress on either side of his thighs. Then she pulled back and looked at him tentatively. "Are you wondering about who I've been with before?" she asked.

Carter was surprised once again by her straightforwardness. And yes, he had felt a little spasm of jealousy earlier—or was it hurt pride—

when she had pulled away from their embrace and taken her purse to the bathroom to put in her diaphragm. "I am," he said.

"I had a college boyfriend," Sarah said. "But"—and she widened her eyes—"he wasn't a quarterback."

Carter smiled. "Anyone else?"

"No one," she answered, and turned over on her back, affecting a swoon. "Ever again."

"Do you realize this is the first show I will have seen without my mother?" Stephen quipped to Carter and Sarah as the usher took their tickets and led them to their seats at the Imperial Theater. Stephen's entire demeanor seemed to have shifted in the last twenty-four hours.

Sarah pointed it out while he went to the restroom at intermission. "He's more himself in the city," Sarah said. "More effeminate." Carter felt defensive despite himself. Sarah suggested that once Stephen was away from his mother, he took on her mannerisms. When he returned to his seat, Carter could see Nell Marie Musgrove in the arch of his eyebrow, the exaggerated claim of his emotions.

After the show, at Sardi's, where Michael met them for a late dinner, the three confirmed his prognosis for the show: promising. Stephen showed off his uncanny recall of the lyrics they had just heard, rendering "If I Were a Rich Man" in a demented Southern accent. Michael started calling him Dill. Sarah, who had warned Carter that her brother could turn the charm on and off like a spigot, whispered to him, not entirely approvingly, "You passed the Michael test."

After Michael announced that he had to leave to meet some friends uptown, Stephen also bade them good night and headed for the subway. Carter and Sarah hailed a cab for their last stop of the day. On the way downtown, Carter told her to close her eyes and hold out her hand. He slipped a ring on her finger. He had bought it from a street vendor that day.

She held it up to examine in the glow of a traffic light. It was her birthstone, an amethyst.

"Will you go steady with me?" he said.

She answered with a kiss, their lips remaining fused until the taxi stopped in Greenwich Village at Cafe Wha?. It was between sets when they took a table close to the stage. Through the cigarette smoke and the chatter of patrons, they talked about the future for the first time that day.

"How do you like being home?" Carter asked.

"I hate it," Sarah said.

Carter was genuinely surprised. He already loved New York. "What are you going to do now?" he said.

"My father wants me to go back to school."

"What do you want to do?" He leaned in and gave her his best movie-star kiss.

"Come back to Mississippi," she replied with an obligatory bat of the eyes.

"You're just saying that." Carter smiled. "Besides, the summer's almost over."

"Lige said Snick needs a full-time person in Ellis County. He offered me the job if I want it."

"No kidding," Carter said. "A white Yankee girl breaks into the inner circle! But what do your parents say?"

"They don't know. This is going to take some persuasion. But if I can talk them into it, I'll be back in September—October at the latest. I felt so bad about leaving everybody. Especially the kids I worked with at the church. I couldn't believe how the little ones would just crawl all over you and want to touch your hair."

Watching her face soften from the memory, Carter felt a twinge of envy.

"You know, it's funny how I didn't really have any perspective on what I was experiencing there till I got back," she said. "The workshops Snick put us through before sending us down to Mississippi mostly focused on how to deal with the hostile white people—the danger and all that. But in a way, the biggest shock when we got there was the Negroes. I think we all envisioned these noble Negroes standing at attention in the cotton fields, just waiting for their chance to march to the Promised Land. But the reality was so much worse—and so much better—than anything we could imagine."

"Which part of it?" Carter said.

"Well, I was unprepared for the living conditions down there. So many of the locals were just too scared or too— God, I had no concept of the meaning of 'deprived.' The idea of freedom is something they can't even imagine, much less fight for. They think voting is some mysterious ritual that white people do. 'White folks' business,' they call it. Or the idea of sitting on juries—they don't even understand what a trial is."

Carter was struck by the paradox of having his own home state being explained to him by a New Yorker, as if he hadn't lived there all his life. It brought home the assumptions he had grown up with—that no one, except perhaps the Negroes themselves, was "responsible" for the afflictions of black Mississippians, that segregation was just the natural order of things and therefore pointless to try to change.

"I can't deny that it was demoralizing to be up against such ignorance," she said. "But then to be able to reach the kids before they're totally lost, to be able to have that kind of direct effect, seems like a miracle."

"Do you believe in miracles? That seems like what it would take to change a place like Ellis County," said Carter.

"You can't think of it in those terms. You do something because you must, not because of the outcome. But you know, if ever I want to make myself cry, all I have to do is think about the young Negroes my age who've never been out of Mississippi. Just to get up enough courage to speak in a Snick meeting—let alone how much courage it already took for them to be *at* a Snick meeting—they'd have to get themselves liquored up. It makes everything up here in New York seem so trivial."

Carter found his mind somehow hovering above the conversation. "Wouldn't the chamber of commerce love to know that Troy had it all over New York?" he said with a little laugh. He also couldn't help but think that there might be some Negroes in Harlem living in poverty that Sarah might find equally exotic.

"Reverend Bunt's wife—Celia's mother—calls me her white daughter. She tells me she's praying for me. She, who has so little, worries about me who has so—" She waved her hand as if the whole city were hers. Sarah's voice caught. "The faith these people have is amazing, not like in the Northern churches and synagogues I've been to." She dabbed her eye with the side of her index finger. "It seems like the people actually do love thine enemy. They have every reason to hate the white man. God, I hate the white man. But really I think they don't." She sipped her Cuba libre and looked around the room at the faces of strangers illuminated by candles.

"Then I come back up here," she said, "and find people like my brother. All they do is think, worry, discuss, obsess over their own thoughts and feelings and deep-down psychological motivations." She stared into her drink and started to smile despite herself. "Michael calls his tension with Dad 'my Oedipus,' like it's some precious acquisition."

"His Oedipus?" Carter burst out laughing. "My God, can you imagine Lige going around talking about his Oedipus?"

"Or even Jewish boys like Goodman and Schwerner? And sadly, I think the attention Goodman, Schwerner, and Chaney are getting is only adding to the tensions in the Movement. Because two of them were white."

Carter, proud of his learning curve about Movement politics, couldn't resist flashing the insights he had picked up on the trip to New York. "It sounds to me like the division is growing wider between the North and South, the urban and rural, between the ones like Lige who live by nonviolence and the others like Dexter who don't even think much of it as a tactic anymore."

Sarah seemed to welcome the return to process. "How do you know that?"

"How could I *not* know it, listening to Lige and Dexter argue. They talked nonstop from Atlanta on up." Carter did an impression of Dexter's high-pitched rant. " 'It's too late for nonviolence.' 'Nonviolence can only work if it can reach the conscience. Gandhi and the British.' 'If Gandhi had come to Mississippi, they would have shot that white nigger dead!' 'The Jews practiced nonviolence against the Nazis and were exterminated.' 'Violence has been successful in Africa.' 'Haiti got freedom after violence.' 'We must show white people we're not afraid.' " Sarah was laughing. "And all this with Stephen and me sitting right there in the car," Carter said. "Now I know what Negroes mean when they say they feel invisible."

"That must have been a first for you," Sarah needled him, "not to be the big man on campus."

"I do like Dexter, though," Carter said. "He's really funny. Out of the blue he'd say something like, 'White people are crazy. You got to be crazy to tell somebody to come to the back door.' And then he'd turn around and give Stephen and me the hairy eyeball. I admitted up front that he had a point. But I think it hurt Stephen's feelings. Especially when Dexter said, 'What it's going to take is for a whole *generation* of white people to die.' And then he'd look back and say, 'Not you, Stephen.'"

"So come the revolution, you won't be spared, eh? I must say, Brother Man, you've become quite the dialectician."

"But the split seems serious," Carter continued. "Lige's convictions are rooted in the Negro church. Dexter's and Charlie Lloyd's seem more rooted in their rage."

"But Mississippi's where we find the common will."

"Isn't it funny," Carter said, "that I never really heard you talk about Mississippi like this while we were down there."

"Yeah. It almost feels like I'm describing a dream. You know Randall's famous line: 'When you're not in Mississippi, it's not real, and when you're there, the rest of the world isn't real.'"

"What does that say about me?" Carter said. "Mississippi is practically all I've ever known."

"Well, since you asked," Sarah said with a Groucho Marx inflection, "I have noticed that you tend to experience everything through your brain. Your mind tries to make sense of the things that your heart can't let in."

The comment hit Carter as a revelation, even if he wasn't quite sure what she meant. "Are you saying I don't have any soul?" he teased.

The lights onstage came up in anticipation of the beginning of the set.

"Oh, no," Sarah said with gravity as a disembodied voice announced its pleasure at presenting the exciting new talent and driving guitar of folk music's next generation: Richie Havens. She leaned over and whispered, "Señor Hombre Sincero has a soul *muy grande*."

———

THE TAXI IN FROM LaGuardia dropped Carter off on lower Park Avenue in front of Les Halles, the French bistro down the street from the *Examiner* office. Arriving just after noon, he thought he was early, but he spotted Dennehy at a table along the wall near the back of the dark, cavernous restaurant.

"How was your flight?" his editor asked, fighting off a smile but standing to embrace Carter.

"If there's anything in this country where the spirit of Soviet bureaucracy still lives, it's Delta Airlines," Carter said. He tormented his boss with an extra-demonstrative hug.

The chef emerged from the kitchen in the rear and spotted Carter. He headed over with his hands extended, palms up. "Mr. Ransom Notes," he said, and pumped Carter's hand. "Where you been?" Then he signaled a waiter to bring a bottle of wine.

"Welcome back, hotshot," said Dennehy. "You're looking good for a broken-down old man. I was just thinking on the walk down here how I stole you from the *Constitution*. How long's it been? Eight years? Remember that?"

Carter smiled. "Sure. How could I forget?" Dennehy had hired Carter after he caused a little brouhaha over a widely quoted editorial in the *Tribune* lamenting one of the budgetary crises that made New York City a butt of the late-night talk shows. "And yes," it concluded, "hundreds of thousands of poor people came to New York because we had a bleeding-heart notion that the dispossessed ought not to starve in the lovely hills of Mississippi." Carter responded in his column for the *Atlanta Constitution* that, in return for all the kindness New York had shown his native state, Mississippi should send a Greyhound-load of trained accountants to New York to help the city straighten out its finances. "Fiscal Riders," he suggested. The *Tribune* had been a good enough sport to print the piece on its op-ed page, and after the letters to the editor poured in, Dennehy had called.

Dennehy chuckled at the memory. "Man, did you piss off a lot of people."

"Thank you," Carter said.

"So are you back for keeps?" he asked, buttering a chunk of bread. "No pressure, but our publisher keeps asking when the column's going to reappear."

"That's what I'm here to talk about," said Carter. The waiter poured him a finger of wine to test.

"Good. I figured it was important. You know how I hate to leave the office for lunch." Carter appreciated his editor's willingness to spare him the well-meaning solicitude he would have gotten with a newsroom appearance.

"I want to stay on the Shiloh Church story," Carter said after the waiter poured the wine and disappeared. He watched Dennehy look down at his wineglass and shake his head.

"How can I put this?" Dennehy said. "You have no credibility."

"I've got to write about it."

"Why did I have to learn about the girl by reading it in the *Tribune*? You can't cover a trial of a murderer when you were in love with one of his victims. No wonder you had a crack-up after the museum bombing."

"Alleged murderer, Ed," Carter said. "I'm a columnist. I can have opinions. I can have biases. That's what you pay me for."

"Yes, but now is not the time to be pushing any ethical envelopes, sweetheart. There's been a whole ration of journalistic no-no's since you've been gone, some high-profile screwups involving reporters at the *Tribune* and other papers—mercifully not at the *Examiner*. Reporters have been suspended for filing stories with datelines from places they'd never been, fabricating sources, expense reports, even official documents."

"So what does that have to do with me?"

"Well, as you can imagine, such grievous lapses in protocol prompted the usual circle jerk of sanctimony around town. Ombudsmen were appointed and whatnot. We at the *Examiner*, being pure as the driven snow, have been going after the competition pretty hard in columns and editorials. It had the effect upstairs of making them even more sphincterish about appearances than usual."

"Tell you what—my first column on the Shiloh Church case will be dedicated to revealing all my compromising relationships." Carter ladled a dollop of mustard next to his *frites* and said, "Did I ever tell you I was sports editor of my high school paper?"

Dennehy exhaled and said emphatically, "No."

"Hear me out. I also played football. During one game I threw two touchdown passes, one of them in the final seconds to win the game. Since I also covered sports for the school paper, I had to write a story about the game. It ran as I wrote it, describing the key touchdowns but carefully avoiding any mention of the name of yours truly, the quarterback who threw them."

"So what's your point?"

"It was ridiculous. Would it have been a sin to report my role in the story?"

"But we have a choice. You don't have to write the story. We've got other people who can cover it."

"So send them. I told you to do that. But I want a piece of it, too. This is a big national story. That's why the *Trib*'s got Lovelace and a couple of others down there on it."

Dennehy's face shifted into a smirk. Like most journalists, he was an inveterate gossip. "Speaking of Lovelace, he was one of Wentworth's problems over at the *Trib*—rumors that he made up sources and filed stories from places he never went. But Wentworth was his rabbi, so he had cover. You've run across him down there?"

"Oh, yes," Carter said, and explained that he had been catching up on the case in the local library where *The Troy Times* stored its clips. "When I got to the pages with stories on the original trial, somebody had razored them out with an X-Acto blade."

"Well, for what it's worth, Lovelace seems to believe your father's implicated. That's another conflict."

"Look, we can run a standing head with each column if you want: 'Rancid Notes.' "

Dennehy looked down at his food. Carter could not believe this was happening. "Why don't you let your readers decide if I'm trustworthy? Come on, Ed, this is the first thing that's gotten my juices going."

"Carter, anything but this. There are lots of other stories."

"Like what?"

"For starters, we've got a candidate for mayor who's getting out of rehab."

"Charlie Lloyd?"

"He's cleaning up his act."

"So?"

"He wants to talk to you."

"Me!" Carter scoffed.

"I don't know why, but he let it be known that when he does his first interview when the campaign kicks in after Labor Day, you're his confessional booth of choice."

"It must have something to do with the trial. He was down there, you know, in the sixties."

"How could anyone who's read his campaign biography not know?" said Dennehy. "He won't be out of rehab till after Labor Day."

"The trial will have begun by then."

Carter could tell that Dennehy wasn't showing all his cards by the way he wouldn't look him in the eye. "I want you back here," he said. "As soon as you feel up to it. How long you in town?"

"Just overnight. I'm taking Josh down for a couple of weeks before school starts. You're changing the subject, Ed."

"I'm sending Tommy Flynn down." Dennehy watched as the realization sank in that he was putting Carter's archrival on the story.

Carter felt as if the breath had been knocked out of him.

"You're welcome to share your insights with him if you like. In fact, I'd consider it a personal favor." Dennehy drained his wineglass to indicate that the subject was closed. "You just relax and rest up and take care of yourself down there. And when you're ready to write about something else, something I can use, let me know."

"Ed," Carter said, "you do understand that I may have to quit over this."

That afternoon, Carter picked up Josh at his summer day camp in the educational annex of the synagogue where the museum memorial service had been. The shy dark-haired boy, looking smaller than the knapsack he trundled on his back, appeared at the door with his counselor. When he recognized Carter standing on the street, he broke into tears and rushed down the steps into his arms. The other children and their parents swirled past them on the sidewalk, politely ignoring their tearful reunion. Repairing to a nearby luncheonette, they sat in a booth sipping egg creams. Then they took the long way home through the park to the Baums' apartment, where Carter would be spending the night. Josh seemed alternately glad to see Carter and sad, and Carter wondered if they were making a mistake reintroducing him into the boy's life. The day's logistics were predicated on his and Emily's agreement that it would be better for Josh not to see them together. The two of them had decided that they would postpone their state-of-the union conversation until Carter brought Josh back to New York.

That evening, Josh enjoyed a final meal with his mother and his grandparents while Carter met Marcy Kennamer and Boz Epstein at an Italian restaurant in midtown. They caught Carter up with the progress of their pregnancy and with gossip about friends, as well as giving him the New York take on the Troy trial. Lovelace's piece had been widely read. "I understand the ethical issues," Marcy said when he told them he was off the story. "They ought to be nervous about it. Especially if you're being called to testify, too. But I don't understand why they don't just let you write a diary about the whole experience."

"So do you think your old man could be publicly disgraced by this thing?" asked Boz, washing down a bite of veal chop with red wine. Carter saw him flinch as Marcy knuckled him under the table while staring into her pasta.

Until then Carter had never considered that his father's ethical tribulations might reverberate out into the world beyond the tiny echo chamber of Mississippi. "I don't know, Boz," he said. "I guess your question answers itself."

After dinner, Carter decided to walk from the restaurant uptown to the Baums' apartment. The evening was cool and fresh after a late afternoon shower. He loved the city at night. Its magisterial indifference was awesome in a way that was obscured by daylight's commerce—the ceaseless warfare of men and machinery," as Thomas Wolfe called it.

Along Broadway, storefront neon reflected off the patches of wet pavement. At Lincoln Center, the theater and the opera were letting out, and crowds flooded the streets of the Upper West Side. The young singles cruised their watering holes, and couples ate in sidewalk cafes along Columbus. He felt again the ache of aloneness that had been muffled by the weeks in Mississippi.

As he made his way up Broadway past the Beacon Theater, Fairway Market, and Citarella, he saw a flower stand outside a Korean market and a young Asian man meticulously arranging the display to accommodate a fresh shipment of daisies. Suddenly he decided to veer over toward Amsterdam and a limestone building with a red awning he had avoided during his years living in New York. At the entrance, he discovered that the doorman had been replaced by a second glass door and a call box on the wall next to it. There he found the name he was hoping was still there, the typed letters faded and barely legible in the slot next to the button. He pushed the buzzer. No answer. He checked his watch. It was eleven-fifteen—too late to be barging in on an old man. But he pressed the button again. Just as he was about to leave, a voice came on the scratchy intercom speaker. "Who is it?"

He pushed the speaker button and answered, "Mr. Solomon?"

"Yes," said a shaky voice. "Who is it?"

"It's me, Mr. Solomon. Carter Ransom."

17

WELL, I GUESS the chickens have come home to roost," Carter said. Carter fumbled in his pocket for a cigarette while looking around the room. It was the first time he had been back in his psychiatrist's office in Atlanta since leaving for the Washington bureau, ten years earlier.

"What does that mean for you?"

"All my defenses. They're not working for me so well anymore."

"Good."

"Easy for you to say. All I see lately is how childish I am. How immature."

"How human?" Dr. Abernathy was writing in his yellow legal pad.

Carter tapped a cigarette in his hand.

The doctor looked up. "I'd say that's a pretty good definition of maturity."

"How?" Carter asked.

"Understanding how immature we are. Psychopaths never think they're crazy. Childish people never think they're childish. Adolescents try to prove they're mature—smoking, drinking, driving too fast—and wind up proving their immaturity. It takes a certain maturity to recognize our immaturity."

Carter stared at the doctor, reminded once again of why he had made the appointment. "Mind if I smoke?" he said.

Dr. Abernathy leaned over and clicked on the air filter next to his chair.

Carter knew the routine. He stood and opened the vents above the sofa. He sat back down with his pack of Winstons. "I quit for a while," he volunteered, and caught himself seeking approval. He lit up, inhaled deeply, and blew the smoke toward the ceiling vent. He took another drag and looked around the room. "I see you've still got that hideous painting." Exhaling, he said, "I guess you know I've been back home for a while. Back in Troy."

"Yes. Your sister called and told me."

"Did she tell you my girlfriend dumped me? I thought about calling you then, but . . ." He didn't finish the sentence, shook his head, and picked a flake of tobacco off his tongue.

"Why didn't you?"

"I don't know. The doctors in New York had thrown around a diagnosis, and I really didn't feel like testing a new theory."

"Which was."

"Post-traumatic stress disorder."

"You've always had a tendency to resist labels, and I don't think that's an unhealthy tendency."

Carter felt himself brighten a degree inside. "Eventually the agitation seemed to subside into something I recognized—depression—and I wasn't sure I had anything new to say on that front."

"Oh?"

"You know. Back where I started from: mother's neediness; fears of commitment, exacerbated by Sarah's death. And now Emily's brush with death. Eventually it gets kind of boring."

"You mean it bores in on you?"

"I knew you'd say that."

"Am I boring you?"

"No. I appreciate your seeing me on such short notice." Carter had called from the Baums' the night before, after returning from the Solomons' apartment, and had rescheduled his and Josh's connecting flight from Atlanta to Troy so that he would have a longer layover. Josh was spending the afternoon with the child of an old colleague from the *Constitution*.

"I had a cancellation, so it worked out fine."

"I know it's weird, me calling you like this out of the blue," Carter said, putting out his cigarette.

"Why is it weird?"

"I thought we were finished."

"Finished."

"That we'd, you know, accomplished what we set out to accomplish."

Scribbling on his yellow legal pad, Dr. Abernathy looked up and asked, "And what was that?"

"Getting me open to the idea of marriage."

"Is that what we were trying to do?"

"More ready to commit. You know what I mean."

Silence.

Carter began to fidget. He didn't know where to begin. "Have you ever had a former patient come back like this after so many years?"

"Occasionally. It's not unusual for patients to check back in now and then. For a tune-up, so to speak."

"This isn't about women this time."

The doctor nodded.

"Or just about women, I should say. This church bombing trial coming up—you may have read about it. Last night I talked to Sarah's father. He tried to get in touch with me after the museum bombing, so I went to follow up."

The doctor took a note.

"After Sarah died, I didn't stay in touch with the Solomons. I felt bad about that."

"Why was that your responsibility? You were a boy."

"But it's because of me that she died. If she hadn't come back down to Mississippi . . ."

"Even more reason they should have kept up with you."

"They're retrying the man who probably ordered the church bombing. There's talk that my father may have suppressed evidence in the first trial. He was the judge in the case."

"How does that make you feel?"

"Disoriented. I can't separate what I feel about the trial from my general alienation. I guess everything we talked about all those years that I was running away from is finally calling me out."

"Tell me about that."

"After the museum bombing in New York, Emily found out about Sarah."

"And?"

"And she broke up with me. We'd been together three years, and I never told her about it. She finds out and feels deceived, like she never really knew me."

"Why did you feel you couldn't tell her?"

Carter was not sure. "Maybe I thought I would seem like some bad-luck charm."

"So that's what you say you set out to accomplish in here: getting married without revealing yourself to your wife?"

Carter felt a bit stung and decided not to clarify that he had not actually asked Emily to marry him until the relationship had begun to unravel. He looked at Dr. Abernathy, who was again writing on his legal pad, and realized with brutal certainty that he would never be able to claim that word: wife.

"Some days I imagine becoming a town character like our local village idiot, Hugh Renfro, somebody people point at and say, 'There goes Carter Ransom. He used to be a newspaper columnist in New York City. He's unlucky with women. Everyone who gets involved with him is either doomed or lives to regret it.'"

"Is that how you feel, that you are hurting them?"

"I feel that I can't save them."

Carter paused to acknowledge a free association. It was to Grayson. "My old high school sweetheart's back in town. She's probably available if I was interested."

"Well?"

"I don't know. Maybe I'm still trying to cheer up my mother. Grayson was always my mother's choice for me, that's for sure."

"It doesn't sound to me like you're making much of a sales pitch for her."

There was some silence. "There's another woman."

"Good."

"I keep having thoughts about this prosecutor. Nothing's been broached. She has a boyfriend."

"Is this prosecutor responsible for punishing Sarah's killer?"

"She may also be bringing my father down. I'm thinking about testifying."

"Testifying? Declaring?"

"I don't know."

"Matters of the heart in the courtroom, your father's domain."

"I don't know if it's because I want the approval of this woman, the prosecutor. There's something fascinating about her."

"What is it about her?"

"She's still in the game."

"And you're not."

"Hell, no."

"But you find that attractive in her."

"Yes. Very much. She's still got her disappointment ahead of her."

"I'd think you would be delighted with that. Your disappointment came so early it skewed the natural arc."

"She's pissed off everybody else in town, but I feel like myself around her." A pause. "My childhood nickname was Pross."

"You're smiling."

"I pissed her off."

He smiled back at Carter uncertainly.

"I called her zealous. She wanted to whip my ass."

There was the encouraging silence.

"That wasn't exactly the quality of my relationship with Emily."

"How would you describe that?"

"Kind, mature, doing the right thing, taking care of her and her son. I'm bringing Josh down to Mississippi with me for a while."

"Moving into the father's role."

"I'm now having those feelings activated by Grayson—she's also divorced, with two kids. That she's kind of perfect for me on paper."

"It seems important to you to be able to be a consistent, dutiful person. You set a lot of store in being moral, with Grayson and Emily—even with the Solomons. You want to do an honorable job of dealing with the hand dealt you."

Carter grew still but was percolating. "Emily was lucky she wasn't killed at the museum. I could have been, too. I missed her phone call that morning. She wanted me to meet her there."

"So you're lucky, too."

"I guess."

"Yet never seem to think in terms of saving yourself."

"I don't understand."

"Maybe that's what love is: not saving someone else, but allowing yourself to be saved." He put down his pad and leaned forward. "The truest things are paradoxes."

18

T HE TRIAL OF Samuel H. Bohannon opened on a clear, bright
Tuesday morning the day after Labor Day. Carter felt strangely
liberated at the prospect of experiencing the event as a human being
rather than as a reporter. He had dropped off Josh and Willie at Sally's
bookstore before heading over to the courthouse. In the week that Josh
had been there, the boys had taken to each other like twins, sharing a
sibling claim on Riley, Emily's transplanted golden retriever. They were
delighted to hang out downtown at the Book Nook and Wad's and
points in between, playing video games, sipping cherry Cokes, and
trolling for intrigue.

When they all arrived at the store, Sally was standing at the front
window, watching the television vans and satellite dishes lining up on
the square down the street. "Are you going to the trial?" Carter asked.

Sally, looking haggard in a Junior League sort of way, shook her
auburn bob in disgust. "I'll check out the circus later."

Carter offered to come by at lunch and take the boys over to
Grayson's pool. He hugged Josh and Willie, slipping them a few bucks
for ice cream and Pac-Man.

"Stay clear of Simon Lester's film crew camping out on the square,"

Sally warned Carter. "Bradley was in here yesterday fishing about whether you'd do an on-camera interview for them."

"What'd you tell her?"

"I told her I stopped speaking on your behalf in junior high when I ordered the wrong Girl Scout cookies and you never let me forget it."

Carter looked at his sister scowling out the window. "What's the matter, Sal? You seem kind of down."

She glanced at the boys to make sure they were out of earshot, and she lowered her voice. "Oh, the loathsome ex called, ostensibly to inquire about Willie's back-to-school needs. He couldn't wait to inform me that, by the way, a mammoth bookstore chain—he can't say which one—is scoping out local real estate for a new store." Sally mouthed the word "Fuck!"

"How does he know?"

"Graysonite owns the buildings they're looking at. Daddy says I should just sell them the store and take the money and run."

"Speaking of the judge," Carter said, "has he said anything about the trial?"

"Not a word. That damned prosecutor. I can't believe I let her into our house."

"She's just doing her job, Sal." Carter didn't tell her he had been trying to reach Sydney Rushton since he got back from New York, but she had been out of town.

Sally searched his face suspiciously, then let the subject drop. She turned back to the window and watched another TV satellite truck rumble past, heading for the courthouse. "I'm going to ask the sheriff to put extra security on the house until this is over."

Despite the blazing September heat, the lawn on the square when Carter arrived had taken on the convivial bustle of a street fair. Bradley Crawford drifted among Simon Lester's film crew like a Macy's Thanksgiving Day float, greeting lawyers and media types with sorority shrieks. She was dressed in some sort of African tribal garb, a brightly colored caftan proclaiming her devotion to racial justice. As Carter crossed the lawn toward the courthouse, he heard Bradley use the word "genius" three times—once to describe the prosecutor, again in reference to a reporter from *The Boston Globe*, and finally to recommend a local cook at the Starlite who was famous for her pecan pie. Meanwhile, her bearded husband voided his wife's promiscuous cheerleading with ex cathedras on the trial's prospects.

Just as Carter started his ascent up the courthouse steps, Lonnie Culpepper slipped up behind him and hooked his hand under his elbow. "What's this about Coach Boutwell?" he asked. Lonnie looked tense, and lines creased his tanned forehead. His jacket was draped over his shoulder, and perspiration stains already bloomed from the armpits of his white shirt.

"I don't know, Lonnie," Carter replied. "I was kind of hoping you could tell me."

"It's ridiculous. Coach was no Kluxer."

"I guess that it's up to Ms. Rushton to prove that he was," said Carter.

"All I know is she's under a lot of pressure. There's a lot of folks watching this thing who are interested in the outcome."

"Besides the media?"

"Sure—investors, corporations looking at Mississippi for the first time in my lifetime for growth potential. WunderCorp, for starters. Helmut Schlank told the mayor he's worried about how this trial is going to play with his board of directors. Opening a can of worms like this is risky. I just hope she can get the lid back on." As he spoke, Lonnie was watching a crew unload camera equipment from one of the network vans. "Look at those vultures swooping down on this town. No offense, Pross, insulting your colleagues like that, but Jesus."

Carter checked his watch. It was quarter of nine. Court would open in fifteen minutes. "Who's the brass?" he asked, indicating a tall man in uniform next to the Confederate Memorial who was answering questions from a reporter.

Lonnie replied, "Pete Callahan told me one of the military colleges—Virginia Military Institute, I think—is considering honoring one of its alumni who had come down here. They sent an observer to the trial."

"VMI?" said Carter. "That's where Daniel Johnston went to school."

"Who?"

"Danny Johnston. One of the Freedom Summer workers, remember? The Episcopal seminarian who died at Shiloh Church."

"I remember. He was at that picnic at Naked Tail—played the banjo. Nice guy."

"Reminds you of what a charnel house it was around here back then."

"Come on, it wasn't any worse than anywhere else," Lonnie said.

"It was worse than we knew at the time."

"Worse here than Neshoba County?" Lonnie said.

"Thank God for Neshoba County," said Carter. "They got Schwerner-Goodman-Chaney; we merely have Shiloh Church."

"I just don't understand why an entire community is held responsible for the actions of a few lunatics. It's not right. Like Dallas after the Kennedy assassination."

"What's not right?" asked Jimbo, sidling up beside them with Doc Renfro and Pete Callahan in tow. Pete, his brush cut now totally gray, cuffed Carter gently on the back and looked at him with the same intelligent eyes that had once cut through his copy like a buzz saw. "Carter" was all he said.

"Hey, we should get credit for holding the trial," Jimbo said. "We're interested in righting wrongs, even if it is just to spruce up our image. That's got to count for something, right, Doc?"

Ray Renfro smiled and waved, but he and Pete kept moving with the crowd toward the steps heading into the courthouse. Jimbo called to the elderly physician, "See you inside, Doc."

"Will he be all right?" asked Carter. The doctor was looking his age, like the judge, although moving a little slower.

"Doc's solid as a rock," said Jimbo. "He took me fishing a week ago. On the way over here he told me about a lynching held right here on the square when he was a boy. People turned out to see it like it was the county fair."

"I'm surprised Doc came," said Carter.

"He had to be here." Jimbo's face turned solemn. "He's concerned about the trial bringing up his son's FBI testimony. He's protective of Hugh, even now."

"This thing opens up a lot of old wounds," said Lonnie. "Look at those people." He pointed to an elderly black couple moving up the steps. "The families of the church bombing victims. You think they want to relive this thing?"

"Hey, at least they know what happened to their boy," Carter said. He pointed to a couple on the steps. "I think that's Dexter Washington's parents."

"Which one was he, the guy you drove to Atlantic City?" Jimbo siad.

"Yeah, with Stephen and Lige," said Carter. "He was one of the older Snick organizers. He'd worked community relations for A&P in Chicago before coming down here, and he was always ranting about the local customs." A couple of months after the Atlantic City convention, Dexter disappeared.

"Right, they never found his body," Lonnie said.

"We did," said Jimbo.

"Shut up, Jimbo," said Lonnie. "You don't know that."

Carter turned to head up the steps. "What a magical time."

———

HALLOWEEN WAS the last day of frog-gigging season. Jimbo cut the engine halfway up the river, and Carter, Stephen, and Lonnie paddled the johnboat close to shore. After the sun went down, the chorus of peeps, croaks, and hums along the banks of the Little Chickasaw had risen to a crescendo.

"The love song of J. Alfred Bullfrog," Stephen said.

"Shut up or you'll scare them all away," Jimbo said as he crammed another chaw of Red Man into his cheek and swept his floodlight along the shore. Late spring and summer were the ideal weather for frog gigging, but in south Mississippi the opportunity extended well into autumn. It was the only outdoor sport Jimbo could ever talk his three friends into, and October 31 was their final opportunity of the year. Halloween frog hunts had been a ritual of their youth, and they'd been harder to arrange after college pulled them away, but this year Carter was back in town, Lonnie home to interview for a summer internship with Judge Ransom, and Stephen had come back on a break from Juilliard.

It was a moonless night, and Lonnie and Stephen wore miners' helmets with carbide lamps. Jimbo, in waders, operated the oversize spotlight, which was most effective for isolating pairs of red bullfrog eyes and mesmerizing them long enough to move in for the kill. The challenge in gigging frogs was to get close enough to them along the shore without scaring them away. The object was to spear them with the eight-foot pole, pin them to the riverbank or muddy bottom, and reach down into the water to nab them.

Lying at Carter's feet was a Louisville Slugger that Coach Boutwell had let him keep after graduating from Little League. He brought it along to use on the occasional water moccasin, coiled around branches in the bushes along the banks, that could drop into the boat. Cradled awkwardly in Stephen's lap was Jimbo's .22 pistol. Frog gigging was a team sport. Carter, with the surest, quietest stroke, paddled while Lonnie and Stephen scoured the shore with flashlights. Jimbo stood ready with the gig. Carter paid close attention to the croaking sounds, moving the boat toward the lower register hums and listening for the basso profundo of the bullfrog.

A pair of red eyes appeared, and the beams of all three flashlights converged over the white throat of a croaker. There was a climactic pause, a moment of frozen anticipation just before the kill, when the hunted could look upon the hunter and the outcome was not certain. Jimbo lunged and caught the belly with the points of the four-pronged gig they had spent an hour sharpening on sandpaper blocks. Lonnie followed with another gig because one was usually not enough to kill a bullfrog of any serious size. After each trophy was deposited in the five-gallon bucket with a slit inner tube stretched across the top, they celebrated with a beer from the cooler in the hull of the boat.

"Remember the time we made it all the way up the river to Bohannon's fish camp?" said Jimbo. "Nearly drove his hog dogs crazy seeing us out on the river."

"Same big red eyes in the dark," Carter said. "We should've gigged one of them ugly dogs and brought it back to fry."

They drifted downriver, beginning the process all over. Jimbo said, "Shhh. Over there."

Carter turned and saw a light glowing in the distance across the river. "It's a campfire."

"Who'd be camping up here on Halloween?" said Stephen.

"Wait. It's moving," said Lonnie.

Jimbo said, "No, dumbass, that's us. The boat's drifting on the current."

The glow of the fire seemed to shift, and again they couldn't tell if it was the light or the drift of the boat.

"Wait. Isn't that our lagoon?" asked Lonnie.

"Yeah," said Carter. "Naked Tail."

Another light flared on the shore. "There's more than one campfire," said Jimbo. "And damned if they're not moving." The lights moved erratically like giant fireflies.

"Let's go check it out," said Carter.

Jimbo switched on the ignition.

"No. Don't turn on the motor," Carter said. "We'll paddle."

The rowing was slow going, and as they made their way across the river, the firelight receded. At the sandbar that defined the lagoon's outer rim, Carter navigated by the lightning tree's limbs, which reached out of the water like the fingers of a drowning man. By then the firelight was disappearing into the trees. Carter let the craft drift toward the shore. They listened for any sound of campers. The trees beyond the shoreline were silhouetted in darkness, but Carter thought he saw shapes moving into the forest.

"They're gone," Lonnie whispered. "Whoever it was skedaddled."

"We were making a racket," said Jimbo.

"Turn on the big light," said Stephen.

Jimbo lifted his floodlight and shone it toward the shoreline. The beam caught the deep autumn reds and yellows in the trees. Nothing could be seen in the recesses of darkness. They all shimmered the surface of the water with their lights. When Lonnie turned to grab the oar that had slipped into the bottom of the boat, his helmet light swept across the lagoon and up the promontory. Something caught Carter's attention.

"Jimbo, shine your light toward the oak," he said.

Jimbo turned his spot on the promontory. A dark shape in the foreground startled them, hovering just a few feet over the water. "Jesus Christ!" said Carter.

Jimbo's spotlight rose slowly to reveal a dark figure suspended over the water like a scarecrow. A pair of work boots swung lazily a few inches above the water. Dangling from the knotted rope swing off the limb of the oak was what appeared to be the body of a man. His back was to the boat, and his hands were tied behind his back. His shoulders were draped in burlap—a feed bag had been slipped over his head and covered his shoulders. The body swayed slightly. They couldn't see the face.

"Lord God," said Lonnie. "Let's get the hell out of here."

"Shouldn't we check it out?" said Stephen.

"Yeah, maybe it's a dummy," said Jimbo. He swept his light up through the woods again. "Whoever did it may still be here. Let's go tell the sheriff."

"What if it is just a Halloween prank?" Stephen said, then turned to Jimbo and said accusingly, "All right, did you tell anybody we were going gigging? If this is one of your—"

"Hell, no!"

Carter squinted into the darkness, trying to make out the face of the figure that had slowly twisted around, but it was shadowed by the burlap cowl. "Come on, let's get the sheriff," Lonnie said. Jimbo started the motor and, circling around, sped off downstream toward the fork where the Little Chickasaw joined the Big Chickasaw.

They returned with the sheriff's deputy on duty, Peyton Posey. Arriving by car after midnight, they trudged from the highway through the crunching leaves of the autumn woods, guided by flashlights. When they arrived at naked Tail, there was no body hanging from the rope swing and no sign that there had ever been one. The rope dangled over the water from the limb of the oak tree on the promontory as it always had. Posey looked at the boys expectantly.

"Somebody took it down and moved it," said Carter.

"We swear it was there, Peyton," said Jimbo. "We all saw it."

"I told you it was a Halloween prank," said Lonnie.

"You did not, Lonnie," Stephen said.

"Trick or treat, boys," said Peyton Posey. "Y'all been played for fools." They got sent home with a lecture on the dangers of mixing boating and alcohol.

The next day, SNCC's field coordinator, Elijah Knight, reported to the Troy Sheriff's Department that one of the workers at Magic Time was missing. Dexter Washington was last seen buying MoonPies at Scarborough's grocery store late on the afternoon of October 31. He was by himself, which would have been against the rules the previous summer. The police said he had been arrested on suspicion of Halloween vandalism early that evening and held in jail for a couple of hours, and then Peyton Posey had released him. A search was ordered by Sheriff Mizell, but with no witnesses to his movements after he left the jail on foot, the local authorities gave up after a couple of weeks and turned the case over to the FBI. Carter kept Dexter's disappearance before the reading public for months in *The Troy Times*, but the body was never found.

———

CARTER OFTEN PUZZLED OVER how he could have kept that memory beneath the surface of consciousness in the ensuing years, how he had somehow indulged the fantasy that the swinging body at Naked Tail was a Halloween trick and that Dexter would turn up any day. If he could find the explanation for his own capacity for denial, then he would probably solve the mystery of the Good German. For the past few days, since recalling the evening he came upon Glen Boutwell's Klan regalia, Carter had been searching his mind to figure out how the import of that discovery could so easily have slipped by him. At the time, he was just beginning to awaken to the sin of his people, but if he was honest with himself, he would have to admit that he had not experienced collective guilt over the fates of Schwerner, Goodman, and Chaney. That crime was the work of the Other—a Mississippian, perhaps, but from a couple of counties away, not someone whose catfish dinners were the local culinary treat. It reminded Carter of the way New Yorkers rationalized the danger around them, calculating the slim odds of their being at a subway stop where there had recently been a murder—at the same time, on the same line, going in the same direction—contingencies sliced as thin as it took to achieve exemption.

But there was more to it than magical thinking. When an event dislodges from the jumble of daily life and claims the foreground of history, it drives out the human particulars, the "stuff" that defines a person's actual experience. And so from now on, that whole chapter in Carter's youth would be about Glen Boutwell's Klan robe. It was only a flash in time, but would henceforth blur the true preoccupations of his life then—the stress at home, the uncertainty about his future, the mastery of a new career, and the irresistible force of hormones. Carter's mission had been falling in love, and what were the tides of history compared with that?

But there was an even simpler reason why Carter had not drawn any conclusions from the fresh red dirt stain on Glen Boutwell's robe: he knew Glen Boutwell. And the Boutwell he knew, the beloved coach who taught him the verities of good sportsmanship, team spirit, and fair play, the dignity of hard work and discipline and personal sacrifice, was every bit as real as the Boutwell who was now being implicated in crimes against humanity committed under the cover of a white sheet. And that, Carter suddenly realized, was what he could not explain to Emily. In her orderly humanistic world, progress was measured in tidy increments, and who a person was could not be separated from what he did. But in the South, being had always transcended doing; faith trumped works. The region had leveraged a cult of chivalry out of slavery, after all. How to describe to anyone outside the South the ways love and evil were entwined and fused beyond the means of interpretation or reason? How to account for loving the sinner when the sin was so despicable?

"What are you doing here, Ransom?" asked Rasheed Lovelace. Carter had been having a last cigarette before entering the courthouse when Lovelace broke away from his conversation with Wendell Rawls, the Atlanta bureau chief of the *New York Tribune*, to intercept him.

"Flynn told me he and your national reporter are covering the trial for the *Examiner*."

Carter shrugged, flashed his notebook, and headed into the courthouse. He made his way upstairs to take a seat in the balcony amid the usual suspects from the print crowd. There were Southern correspondents for the *Los Angeles Times*, *The Boston Globe*, *The Washington Post*; old-timers who had earned their bona fides reporting on the civil rights movement for the newsmagazines; and representatives from the state and local papers like the Jackson *Clarion-Ledger* and *The Troy Times*. Harold Bernhardt, columnist for the local alternative weekly, *The Barricade*, was practically levitating with self-importance and territorial paranoia. Carter felt awkward as hell being there without marching orders from his newspaper and the adrenaline drip of the deadline. Especially when everyone treated him as if he were there on the story just like them. Without his journalistic armor, he finally had no choice but to accept that he was part of the story.

He surveyed the recently remodeled courtroom's vast acreage of walnut paneling. The victims' families filed in and took their seats in the balcony opposite the press. Carter had not seen Randall Peek's mother and sister, well-dressed representatives of the black bourgeoisie, since he attended Randall's burial in Atlanta. He also recognized Reverend Bunt's elderly widow and Celia's surviving brothers and sisters, their own children in tow. Besides Daniel Johnston's mother, a diminutive gray-haired retired elementary school principal, the only other white relative present was a tall, handsome man in an Italian-cut suit, with thick salt-and-pepper hair slicked back into a ponytail. Carter smiled to himself as he watched the man leave the front row of the gallery to kibitz with Simon Lester, whose film crew was setting up in the balcony.

Down on the courtroom floor, the lead defense lawyer, Arthur Puckett, was talking to his co-counsel. Across the aisle, Sydney Rushton conferred with her team at the prosecution table, looking efficiently no-nonsense in glasses, her blond hair pulled back in a twist. Carter had never seen her in full battle array, complete with a fashionable dark business suit, but he found his admiration doused by the sight of the star witness, Lacey Hullender, seated behind her. It was the first time Carter had seen Hullender in decades, and the years had not been as forgiving as the state was apparently prepared to be. Hullender looked twitchy and depleted in his brown corduroy suit, as if life had blown through him like a thunderstorm.

The atmosphere in the courtroom was oddly festive, like a family reunion, with press colleagues who had been veterans of the civil rights story, lawyers on both sides, and witnesses all greeting each other like long-lost relatives. Family members of some of the victims reacquainted themselves, having bonded in a fragile intimacy at the first trial twenty years earlier. The cacophony of voices subsided to a murmur when the doors swung open and a tall black man in a white short-sleeved jumpsuit pushed in the wheelchair that held Sam Bohannon. The defendant was slumped over, his white hair combed neatly and the sideburns anachronistically long. He wore a herringbone jacket, an American flag pinned to one lapel and a Mickey Mouse button on the other. The black nurse wheeled his chair through the spectators toward the defense table up front. All that remained of Bohannon's old panache was the glad hand he waved at the faithful catfish eaters he recognized, as if he were still working the room at Sambo's.

Carter stared at the man he knew was responsible for Sarah's murder, and he felt the same numbness he always had. He was not sure if it was a glaze of denial or the protective carapace of habit that had allowed him to function in the world without collapsing.

Among the entourage around Sydney, Carter recognized some of the aging FBI agents who had interviewed him long ago. In one of the middle benches, Sheriff Mizell sat with some other retired law enforcement officers, looking feeble and wizened. Dr. Raymond Renfro sat beside Jimbo in the last row, his son Hugh's keeper beyond death. Carter's eyes swept the pews. His father's absence suddenly hit him. The jargon of psychotherapy intruded upon his reportorial accounting. How could his father not be there for him? Never mind the professional connection with this case. What about his duty as a father? This trial was about the loss of the girl who was his son's first love. Carter suddenly saw clearly the assumptions he had labored under his entire life, the unspoken shibboleth that could never be challenged. No matter what life threw at Carter, it would always end up being about the judge. And so, until this moment, he had been worrying over his father's feelings about the trial, even though the reckoning was his. Carter's emotions, so dutifully submerged, coalesced into three words: fuck the judge.

"All rise!" the bailiff called out. The Ellis County circuit court judge Robert D. McDonnell entered through a door to the left of the bench. Judge McDonnell had a reputation for fairness, toughness, and suffering fools not at all. He was built like a sumo wrestler, and his wide-set blue eyes seemed mounted on his temples. If he found anything out of the ordinary about facing a courtroom crawling with local muckety-mucks and the national news media, he gave no indication of it. His eyes remained fixed on the large venire of prospective jurors sitting expectantly in the well of the court.

"Thank you for agreeing to serve your country today," he addressed them. "Regardless of what you may have seen on the news or read in the paper, this is, as far as you are concerned, a murder trial, nothing more and nothing less.

McDonnell proceeded with the mundane protocols of justice, explaining to the members of the jury pool that for the foreseeable future, their time would belong to the lawyers in the case. As the questioning of the jurors got under way, some of the lay spectators made furtive departures. Carter moved to the front row of the balcony, where he had a clear view of Bohannon's face. Again he thought he should feel something visceral and violent, but all he felt for the little white-haired invalid in the wheelchair was contempt. The *New York Daily News*'s Southern correspondent leaned forward and whispered, "Flynn tells me you were pulled from the story. I can't believe you're missing this, man. I was looking forward to reading your shit. I had no idea you'd lost a girl-friend in the church. Do you mind talking to me about it? Off the record, of course. Or on, if you want. Your call."

Jury selection went on for the rest of the morning, and after the first break Carter went outside for a smoke. Bradley Crawford was working the crowd, and her husband, Harold Bernhardt, held forth to an audience of out-of-town reporters on the steps of the courthouse. Flynn was among them, looking professionally skeptical. Tommy had been cordial and deferential on Carter's turf, but he clearly considered his presence a nuisance. Carter spotted Rasheed Lovelace on a pay phone inside, reading from his notes as he called in his teaser.

As Carter stood on the courthouse steps taking in the scene, a member of the prosecution team, a pinched young bespectacled man he had seen hovering around Sydney, approached. "Mr. Ransom? Sydney Rushton says she can see you now."

Carter followed him up to the second-floor suite of the district attorney's offices. They passed a room where Hullender was sitting at a desk talking on the phone. He looked up impassively just as Carter walked by. Their eyes met, but Carter saw no flinch of recognition. Every nerve ending in Carter's body stood at full attention, and his paranoia glands were activated.

"How's it going?" he asked, standing at the open door to the office.

Sydney motioned him in, handed the folder back to her assistant, and asked that he close the door behind him. She offered Carter a chair. "Won't know till the juror questionnaires start coming back. I've got other things to worry about. I called you last week, but your sister said you were out of town. Did she tell you I called?"

Carter didn't answer and pretended to be studying the papers on her desk. Sally had mentioned nothing.

Sydney leaned over and shuffled some file folders into a drawer. "I figured she didn't. I wanted you to know when you'd be testifying. Maybe Friday of next week. Or Monday at the latest."

"I have to fly out on Friday," Carter said.

She looked up, concerned. "Where are you going?"

"New York again. I've got to take Josh back before school starts."

"I'm glad you told me. I'll try to get to you before then. I really need your testimony, especially now."

"Why especially now?"

"We are off the record, yes?"

"No problem. I'm not covering the trial." Carter didn't feel the need to explain why he had been taken off the story. "I talked to my father about the Sovereignty Commission report, by the way. He told me who the businessman is that Hullender will name."

She studied his face. "Did he."

"Glen Boutwell was my Little League coach."

Sydney leaned back in her chair and propped her legs up on a nearby trash can. "I was hoping to circumvent the Baby Huey business altogether and avert any mention of your father. That's one of the reasons I called you. But I'm afraid we've had a setback."

"What happened?"

Sydney had had a witness who was all set to name Boutwell and implicate Bohannon, but he'd died the previous night in his home. Suicide—a self-inflicted gunshot wound.

"Who was it?" Carter asked.

"A former Klansman named Reggie Curlee. He was terrified about testifying."

"That's a tough break. What are you going to do?" A part of Carter wondered whether Bohannon's sphere of influence still encompassed hit men.

"Peyton Posey's ex-wife could back up Hullender's story, but we've turned up a history of mental problems. Puckett would have a field day. I don't think I can put her through that."

"So?"

"I thought I should warn you. I may have to call your father as a witness."

Carter felt strangely unconcerned by the idea of seeing his father up on the stand. "You have to do what you have to do. Do you have anything else?"

"I've got some physical evidence I'm still working on. There was a threatening letter sent to Magic Time in care of Scarborough's store just before the bombing. The FBI finally coughed it up. It wasn't 'available' in the first trial." Carter remembered all the threats that used to come to Scarborough's, having relayed the contents of one of the letters to Lige. Hullender had told Sydney that Bohannon typed the letter and asked

Hullender to mail it. Sydney had gotten hold of Bohannon's typewriter, which had also been used to type up his *Klan Ledger* mimeo sheets, and she had experts who could match the type.

"It's promising," she said. "Other threats were typed on it, too, but any number of people had access to that typewriter, and there were no fingerprints. So Bohannon will say he doesn't know who typed the Shiloh letter. You know, the 'unauthorized mission' defense. God, it's frustrating." She looked at the photographs on her desk that Carter had been staring at. They were of the victims. He looked up in time to see her face freeze. There was a good deal of kindness in her expression. "I'm sorry," she said. "I didn't mean to leave those lying around."

"You forget I identified the body. It can't get any worse than that."

"Did you know that her brother, Michael, is here?" she asked, gathering up the photos and returning them to a manila folder.

"I saw him. Is he one of your witnesses?"

"I couldn't risk putting someone like that on the stand. He's too slick, too Hollywood—ponytail and all. He's some studio hotshot now, involved with the documentary they're shooting. Way too much for Troy. That's why you're my oracle."

"Did Michael tell you I saw Mr. Solomon in New York?"

"He mentioned it."

Carter described his visit with Herbert Solomon. His health was failing, the hour was late, and their reunion was awkward there in the apartment Carter had visited as a young man. The conversation did not last long. But before Carter left, Mr. Solomon explained the reason he had come to the newsroom after the memorial service: a man had called him claiming to know something about Sarah's death. The caller had read about the upcoming trial in the Pascagoula newspaper. He was crying a lot and hard to understand. He said he was sorry for what he had done and wanted to make it right.

"When did this call take place?" Sydney's metabolism seemed to have quickened.

"Apparently not too long before my 'hiatus.' Mr. Solomon thought I would know what to do with the information. But I disappeared, and he couldn't get the paper to tell him where I was. Then I showed up on his doorstep."

Her face clouded. "God, I've got no time. And everybody on my staff is up to their asses in alligators. How did this man find Solomon?"

"New York City directory assistance." Carter paused a beat to savor the frustration on Sydney's face. Then he produced the yellow Post-it that he had stuck to his palm. "The caller gave Mr. Solomon his number." He handed it to Sydney. "I could talk to him if you like," he offered.

"For the paper?"

"I said I'm not working."

She looked at him. "I'm just trying to come up with a strategy for following up on this. The trial's already under way, and I'm short-handed. If we had a Democrat in the White House, I'd have the entire staff of the Mississippi FBI at my disposal."

Carter gave her a lazy look. "I already took the liberty of checking him out." When he got up and backed out of the office, Sydney was still staring at him, but with faraway eyes, preoccupied now, as he was slowly beginning to appreciate, with trying to bend the world to her will.

19

WHENEVER CARTER MADE the hour-and-a-half drive from Troy to the Mississippi Gulf Coast, the salt-air smells, the nabob architecture, the Spanish moss drifting from the trees, always gave him the feeling that he had abandoned his fledgling middle-class state for some subtropical banana republic. But the part of Pascagoula he was now entering existed on the margins of that vacation idyll, resembling rather some of the nether regions of hardscrabble Ellis County.

It was midafternoon when Carter pulled up next to a blue Plymouth parked in front of a green and white double-wide in the Sea Pines Trailer Park. Emerging from his car, he could smell a charcoal grill on a nearby patio. Chickens pecking the sandy coastal dirt in the yard scattered as Carter approached. A small black mongrel on a chain in the backyard roused from a nap and barked hysterically.

The front door was open, and through the screen door Carter could hear the mumble of a television. He knocked. An overweight middle-aged woman appeared on the other side of the screen. Her hair, a Clairol shade too dark, and her makeup were done up as if she were expecting company, and her plastic slides matched her blue terry-cloth sweat suit.

"Is this where Mr. Thigpen lives?" Carter asked.

"Lawrence," she called, turning away from the door, "somebody here to see you." The formality of the name clashed endearingly with the surroundings.

"Who is it?" a voice drawled from somewhere inside the trailer.

"Carter Ransom," he shouted. "The reporter who called. I'm a friend of Mr. Solomon's."

"Ransom. Come in." In the living room of the trailer, a rangy slab of a man in a T-shirt that rode up on his gut rested in a Barcalounger that foreshortened his long-legged frame. The small TV set had been muted but was still on.

"Bring me a Heiney, woman," he called good-naturedly to the hostess standing by the door. Thigpen's most memorable feature besides his red hair—a comb-over swirled onto the crown of his head like a scarlet honey bun—was the large crescent-shaped birthmark down his cheek that was a deep shade of oxblood. Bushy gray sideburns stood guard before his jug ears. Thigpen turned surprisingly fierce blue eyes toward Carter and, indicating the bottle in his hand, said, "Want one?"

"No, thanks."

The woman was searching the refrigerator in the cramped kitchen, occasionally eyeing Carter. "We're all out," she said.

"Well, go fetch us some at the Jiffy then, Inez," Thigpen said. "The menfolk got to talk."

Moving slowly and sighing loudly, Inez freshened her lipstick without benefit of a mirror, lifted a set of keys from an ashtray on top of the TV, and minced out the front door.

"I ain't got long." Thigpen glanced at the clock over the stove in the kitchen. "I work the swing shift at Ingalls, so I got to get moving directly." Ingalls shipyard was one of the major employers in the state's southeast corner, building everything from battleships for the U.S. Navy to luxury liners. Shipbuilding had been a pastime on the coast since the 1700s, when the region's piney woods had provided the timber, turpentine, tar, pitch, resin, and desperate men required of the trade.

Carter worried that he might not have enough time to establish the trust necessary to find out what he had come for. He did not want to seem overly aggressive. He allowed Thigpen to lead the discussion, which meandered from the Atlanta Braves' prospects to Ole Miss football to the last hurricane that came through and rearranged the trailer park. "We won't living here then," said Thigpen. "Me and Inez—she's my common-law wife—had us a nice brick ranch in a development between here and Moss Point, but that's when my troubles started."

"Troubles," Carter prompted.

"Gambling. Lost my life savings—over thirty thousand dollars in six months this past year. That's when I started going to my meetings."

Carter wanted to reach for his notebook but didn't.

Thigpen finished off the last of his Heineken. "I been off it about five months now. No blackjack, no slots, no roulette. Twelve-step program saved my life."

"Mr. Solomon said you mentioned the gambling when you called him."

"The recovery program. You're asked to make amends to someone who you caused to suffer." Thigpen's face fell, and his speech faltered. "It's been over twenty-five years." He hesitated as he reached for the words. "I felt like I could have done something to stop the church bombing up there in Troy. I been feeling real bad about it now for a long time."

"What was your connection?"

"I won't a Kluxer," he said a bit defensively. "But at the time, I was working for Sam Bohannon. I overheard Mr. Bohannon talking about bombing the church. I felt like I should've gone to the police." The dangerous blue eyes teared up. "She was a pretty girl, the one that died. And nice, too. I remembered her from that day with Hullender on the river."

Carter felt the blood drain from his face. He studied Thigpen's expression, but the man's eyes were averted, unreadable. The red hair was the unmistakable signature, reiterated in the flushed red blood vessels of his face. And that birthmark. When Carter had last seen him, Thigpen had been an aging juvenile delinquent, the tagalong member of Hullender's squad at Naked Tail on a summer day in 1964. Strawberry.

Carter removed his pen from his jacket. Strawberry snuffled and rubbed the heel of his hand over his eye. "Lacey never got over that. He swore he was going to get the nigger that made us jump in the water if it was the last thing he ever done. The one that run for Congress."

"Elijah Knight," Carter said gingerly. He decided that he was not going to acknowledge their previous acquaintanceship unless Strawberry brought it up first.

"And the other one. The Jew. I remember we done some damage to his daddy's store." Strawberry would still not make eye contact. "I was just along for the ride. That graffiti won't Klan business. Hullender was settling scores. But the church bombing—that was ordered."

"And you had nothing to do with the church bombing?"

"No sir, not me. But I knew who did."

"Why didn't you come forward before?"

"Scared, I reckon. I felt bad about it after the first trial. I was still in Troy then and knowed the truth wouldn't come out. Mr. Bohannon seen to that."

"How was that?"

"He got to the jury. Phone calls during the trial, telling them it was important certain things be done, and if not, they'd better check under their car hoods." Strawberry stared at the television screen. "Cain't say I was sorry Posey got sent up, though. Him and Hullender both. They deserved what they got. Tell you the truth, I was sorry to hear Hullender got out."

"I thought you and Lacey were friends."

"We run in the same crowd when we was younger, but we won't never asshole buddies. He just got crazier and crazier over the years, and meaner and meaner." Strawberry paused to suppress a belch. "And that's saying something." He idly stuck a callused index finger in the neck of his beer bottle. "I never told nobody this before, but I'm about to give you a scoop, Ransom. When we was younguns, no more'n twelve or thirteen years old, a bunch of us used to go swimming out on the Chickasaw River, diving off the railroad trestle. Some colored boys come around one day watching the horseplay, like they wanted to join in."

Lacey told them they would have to dive off the bridge if they wanted to play with the big boys. When they got up there, he ordered them to dive off the other side—where the swamp started and the water was only about a foot deep. Lacey egged them on, and the first black boy dived off headfirst.

"We liked to died laughing and carrying on when he landed in a heap in that shallow water," Strawberry said. "Lacey thought that was about the funniest thing he ever seen. We hightailed it off into the woods when we realized he was probably dead, but I've always felt bad about it."

Carter composed his reporter's face to indicate placid encouragement.

Strawberry stared at the screen door in a trance of recall. "I never trusted Posey," he said. "I seen how he was as a cop. One time me and a friend got drunk and was raising hell over at the Dairy Queen parking lot. Posey come over there and beat us with his nightstick. And he enjoyed it, bragged about it later. I still got the scars." He rubbed the back of his head. "He was working all sides, too. For the Klan and the FBI. That's why Bohannon didn't trust him. Bohannon may have had him sent up."

Carter finally got out his notebook.

"You writing this for the paper?" Strawberry asked.

"No. Just taking notes."

Strawberry looked disappointed. "I thought you was a reporter."

"I am. I'm just not on this story."

"Then why are you here?"

"I'm trying to help a friend."

"Look, I just want to get my life straight," Strawberry continued. He looked embarrassed, as if something painful was still close to the surface. "I'm lucky to have this job I got now. The foreman down there's been real good to me—he's a nigra—and I'm sick to death of living like this. I got to go through with this thing."

The mutt out back began barking, and Strawberry got up and went to the door.

"Kimberly!" he shouted. The dog wouldn't stop barking. "'Scuse me a second," Strawberry said, and pushed open the screen door. He lowered himself down the rickety steps and disappeared around the double-wide. Carter could hear him admonishing the dog. When Strawberry reentered, the little black fice clambered up the steps on a short leash behind him. "Just let little Kimberly smell of your hand and she'll be all right," he said, though he choked the dog back on her leash as she pushed her black snout toward Carter's tentatively extended hand. "It's all right, Kimberly. He won't mess with you. Now set. Set."

With Kimberly curled up on the floor next to the Barcalounger, Thigpen resumed. "I'd been wrassling with this for a while," he said. "Then I read about the trial coming up. I wanted to get my story out to the family, but I didn't want to go to the authorities."

"Why was that?"

Strawberry snorted. "Redneck peckerwood like me with my record? Are you shittin' me? Like I said, I was lucky to get hired at Ingalls. I got laid off from the machine shop at Graysonite back in the seventies for stealing parts. Couldn't get work for a while. Then I worked in garages and filling stations all over south Mississippi till a buddy of mine finally got me on with Ingalls. Me and Inez bought the house. Then the gambling took over. I ain't exactly been reliable. Who's going to believe somebody like me?"

"How do you know Sam Bohannon?"

He shook his head. "I worked for him from the time I was fourteen. He and my daddy was friends, and after my daddy died, he give me a job busing tables at his restaurant in town. Then out at his fish camp on the river. I was good with animals, and he let me work with his dogs, too. I used to run errands, train the pups, whatever was needed. Mr. Bohannon would learn how to do something real good, then get somebody else to do it for him. He taught me all about dogs and how to raise them." Thigpen reached down and stroked Kimberly's ear.

"So how did you happen to know the Klan's business?"

"Mr. Bohannon formed the White Knights at his fish camp." At first, he explained, they used to just sit around and talk politics and religion. Bohannon gave them free beer, even though he didn't drink himself. When he got a little wound up at the Klan meetings, he would always end up talking about his favorite book. "It was something called *Animal Farm*," Strawberry said. "And he couldn't stop talking about it. He called it the greatest book in the English language."

Carter looked up from his notebook to see if Thigpen could be putting him on. The notion of the Klan sitting around discussing Stalin and Trotsky was not in the vast catalog of Southern stereotypes. "Bohannon was reading *Animal Farm* by George Orwell?"

"Well, like I says, his book was called *Animal Farm*. That's all I can remember. Mr. Bohannon was a real brainy type. Read everything. And real religious. He had lots of books about the Bible and prophecy and the like. He was a little bit peculiar. Kept to hisself. I don't know if he ever married. Some said he had a woman when he was young who broke his heart. I reckon he was married to his work. Anyway, when he found out typing was my best subject in high school before I dropped out, he bought me an old typewriter and let me type up his *Klan Ledger*s."

Strawberry got up and went into a bedroom in back and returned with a mimeographed copy of the *Ledger*, now yellowed and coffee-stained. Carter remembered seeing them around town when he was a teenager. He read the poem printed on the front page:

> *Now listen you COMMUNISTS, NIGGERS, and JEWS*
> *Tell all your buddies to spread the news,*
> *Your day of judgment will soon be nigh*
> *As the Lord in His wisdom looks down from on high,*
> *Will this battle be lost, NEVER I say,*
> *For the Ku Klux Klan is here today.*
> *Here Tomorrow, Here Forever!!!*

"Typewriter was pink." Strawberry smiled ruefully. "Mr. Bohannon said he got it from a pawnshop."

As Carter paged through the document, Strawberry described how he mimeographed the papers for Sam and threw them on lawns around town and passed them out in restaurants and Laundromats.

"I did a lot of hauling for Sam, too. I didn't know what I was hauling. It could have been guns or dynamite. I don't know. I never took the oath for the Klan, but I considered myself part of it. If they had asked me, I probably would have joined. Once, I asked Sam why he never let me play a bigger role. He just grinned and said I was the 'minister of propaganda.' "

Carter kept jotting down notes.

Strawberry was lost in his memories. "I overheard a lot of conversations, though. Sam and Peyton Posey and Hullender. They was upset about the polling bit in Troy."

"Voter registration," Carter said.

Strawberry nodded. "That's it. Talk about somebody worked up over that nigger Knight. Excuse me, that 'black.' Sam Bohannon and Lacey Hullender—they used to bad-mouth him and all of them who stayed out at that juke joint."

"Magic Time."

"I thought Mr. Bohannon was gonna blow it up hisself. But that ain't his way. Like I said, he gets others to do it. He never liked to get his hands dirty. Just like he run the restaurant." Strawberry retrieved his train of thought. "Anyway, the Klan meetings up at the camp got bigger and more regular during that summer—what year was that again?"

"Nineteen sixty-four," said Carter.

"At one meeting with everybody there—Posey, Hullender, all of them—Mr. Bohannon said, 'Something's got to be done about that nigger from Troy.' And he slapped the counter and said, 'Put a Code Four on him.'"

"Code Four?" Carter said, as if he didn't know the term.

"Kill him," Strawberry said. "Code Four was murder."

"Would you testify to that in court?"

Strawberry hesitated and stared at the silent television screen. "I don't know," he said. "Step nine in my recovery says that I have to make direct amends for those I wronged if it's possible to do so without causing injury to others. I don't want to injure my old friends. Mr. Bohannon was always good to me. Treated me like his son. I don't know—"

"The trial's already started. Time's running out. Are you still afraid?"

Strawberry shifted in his chair. "No, not no more. Not from Mr. Bohannon anyways. He was never going to do nothin' to me. The one I was afraid of is dead."

"Who?"

"Sam's shotgun. The one they called The Man. The Grand Dragon, that was his official title."

"Who was that?"

"I cain't say for sure. He was Sam's right-hand man. But he was always in his robes. I never seen his face. And he hardly ever said nothing.

Never went to rallies. Rumor was he was some big shot in town. But Sam Bohannon would never let nobody know who he was. That's how he protected hisself." Strawberry jiggled his empty bottle while Carter wrote.

"Are you talking about Glen Boutwell?" Carter asked without looking up from his notepad. Out of his peripheral vision he could see Strawberry start.

"Who told you that?"

"It's going to be brought out in the trial."

Strawberry sat up in the lounger and leaned forward. "I never heard nobody say it out loud before, I reckon. He might have been the Grand Dragon. I suspected as much when Sam gave Boutwell the pick of the litter of his hog dogs. That's when I thought maybe they was in cahoots."

"Was Glen Boutwell at that meeting the night Sam put a Code Four on Elijah Knight?"

"Well, the man I assume was him was."

"Were you at Shiloh Church the night it was bombed?"

Strawberry looked away. "No, sir."

Carter didn't believe him, but he wasn't going to press it. He aimed for the most passive tone he could and said, "If you would testify at the trial, it would be the best way for you to get your story out into the newspapers and on the record and a way to make amends that would make a difference. I hope you don't mind, but I gave your phone number to Miss Rushton, the prosecutor."

Strawberry shook his head. "Naw, I ain't talking to no prosecutor. I got enough troubles. I thought if I could just set this straight between me and the family of that girl, maybe get it wrote up, that would be enough. I don't want to be the reason Sam Bohannon goes to jail."

"There's other testimony. You wouldn't be the only one. Besides, if the story gets out, she could subpoena you anyway." Apparently, Strawberry had been absent from civics class that day.

"The prosecution lost a key witness over the weekend," Carter continued.

Strawberry looked blank.

"You might know him. Reggie Curlee?"

"I know Skeebo."

Carter felt a tingling emanate from his temples. There always came a point in the reporting of a story when a bit of information contracted a seemingly random universe of data to its elemental coordinates. Carter would feel it in his body before his mind registered it consciously. He had never known that Skeebo, the third man in Hullender's posse at Naked Tail, had a last name or that his real name was Reggie.

"He's dead," Carter said. "They say he committed suicide."

"Shot hisself?" asked Strawberry.

Carter nodded. "I think so."

Strawberry shook his head. "Just like Lacey's daddy."

Carter felt another wave of numbness. The Hullender family had served the same function for the children of Troy that the Radleys' sordid background had in fictional Maycomb. Old man Hullender used to get drunk and sit out on his front porch with his pistol and make like he was taking target practice at the cars passing on the highway, sometimes even squeezing off a round or two. Sheriff's deputies would have to make regular trips to the Hullender homeplace in response to complaints from terrified motorists. It was a miracle nobody had gotten shot. On one particular day when Hullender's wife tried to discourage him from taking up his gun, the old man slurred, "Don't worry, darlin', it ain't loaded." Then he put the barrel up to his head to demonstrate, pulled the trigger, and blew his brains out right there in front of his wife. Supposedly, Lacey had had to help his mother clean the porch.

Strawberry dispassionately affirmed the Freudian connections forming in Carter's mind. "Skeebo didn't commit no suicide," he said. "Skeebo don't have enough sense to kill hisself."

A car pulled up in the yard. Carter knew Inez was back and the conversation was probably coming to a close. Strawberry was checking the clock in the kitchen, and Carter realized he'd lost him.

"I want to get the story out in case something happens to me," Strawberry said. "I want to do at least one thing in my life that ain't selfish."

Carter was momentarily paralyzed by the pathos of the scene, by

Strawberry's unblinking acceptance of Skeebo's death and an equally unsentimental acceptance of his own expendability—yet, for all that, a determination to transcend his worthlessness.

Strawberry cleared his throat and looked away. "And while I'm apologizing, Carter, I'd like to say to you personally that I'm sorry for what happened to that little Jew girl." His voice softened to a whisper. "She shore was a pretty one."

20

S ARAH AND CARTER HAD BEEN inseparable since she came back
to Mississippi at the first of the year. Parental resistance had delayed her return until after Christmas, and throughout the fall they had
kept up their romance by mail and telephone. At the end of each work-
day, after everyone had cleared out of the *Troy Times* newsroom, Carter
stayed late pretending to go over his copy, but he was actually writing
long, intimate missives to Sarah on his Remington. Each morning he
would mail his letter at the post office and pick up the company pouch
on his way in, plucking hers to him from the office mail.

Most of the student volunteers had gone home at the end of Freedom Summer, but the core of the Student Nonviolent Coordinating
Committee's paid staffers at Magic Time—Lige, Randall Peek, and
Daniel Johnston—remained in Troy. Charlie Lloyd had requested a
transfer to Hattiesburg after the disappearance of Dexter Washington.
Carter had grown increasingly restless living at home, where the tension
with his father had gotten worse. He didn't know what irritated
Mitchell more—his involvement with the outsiders or his regular byline
in the local newspaper, a public reminder of the father's failure to pass
on to his son a healthy sense of filial duty, public service, and higher ambition. Carter's only solace through those slow months of waiting for

Sarah had been his deepening interest in his work and, with it, the search for wider venues for his writing.

When Sarah finally returned in January as a SNCC fieldworker, her primary responsibility was running the Freedom School at Shiloh Church. Reluctant to stay with the Bunts, as she had during the summer, she rented the garage apartment behind Stephen's house. Sarah could come and go inconspicuously, parking her secondhand Volkswagen among the magnolias, crepe myrtles, and bamboo that kept it hidden from the street. Stephen agreed that his mother didn't need to know about Sarah's job, and Miz Nell thought her tenant was a student at Troy College. Nobody would suspect the town music teacher of harboring a civil rights worker.

Carter spent more time in Sarah's garage apartment than he did at home. Their clandestine domesticity was a parallel dimension of libido, which mixed sex, music, secrecy, and world saving into some headlong urgency that Carter had experienced only once, during a hurricane on the coast. In the evenings after work, Sarah and he would take turns cooking, listen to Dylan and the Yardbirds, or watch *The Man from U.N.C.L.E.* and *Rawhide*. More often than not, they read books—Carter's most recent, *The Moviegoer*—toes touching on the sofa.

On a Sunday night in March, Carter and Sarah had made some popcorn and were watching the ABC Sunday Night Movie, *Judgment at Nuremberg*, about the Nazi war crimes tribunal. At nine-thirty, Frank Reynolds broke in with a news bulletin from Selma, Alabama. Carter and Sarah looked at each other with dread. SNCC had been running a voter registration campaign in Selma for many months, and Lige had gone there that weekend: Martin Luther King's organization, the Southern Christian Leadership Conference, had hastily called a march from Selma to Montgomery to vent over the death of a young black man—a local volunteer named Jimmie Lee Jackson—at the hands of the Alabama state police. Even though Selma had been its baby, SNCC wasn't backing the march, partly out of fear for what might happen to the protesters and partly because it was an SCLC event and King would, as usual, snake all the credit away from the young people in the trenches. "A march led by King will do more for SCLC than for the people of Selma," Charlie Lloyd had said.

There had been a bitter debate among SNCC's Mississippi organizers about whether to join in, and Lige broke with his SNCC comrades. "If the people of Selma want to march," he said, "who are we to deny them our support?" He went to Selma at the last minute, although not in his official capacity as a SNCC staffer. Lloyd, who had been challenging Lige's leadership in south Mississippi, used the disagreement within SNCC as a way to curry favor and rally support to oust Lige. Throughout the organization the Gandhian stalwarts were being mocked by the militants, and since Dexter's disappearance, Charlie had grown vocally impatient with Lige's philosophy of forbearance, calling him a house nigger.

The march had been scheduled for that Sunday. As it turned out, Martin Luther King had remained in Atlanta that day, leaving the front-line honors to SCLC's Hosea Williams and to SNCC's John Lewis, who, like Lige, had bucked his colleagues' decision to boycott the march. And now Carter and Sarah sat before the television transfixed by the footage of the state troopers charging the Negroes at Selma's Edmund Pettus Bridge. At one point you could hear the sheriff, the infamous Jim Clark, shouting, "Get those goddamned niggers" and "Get those goddamned white niggers, too." Watching as John Lewis was felled by a billy club, Sarah and Carter assumed that Lige was among the lead marchers taking the brunt of the blows. The grotesque mismatch of heroes and villains—in scene after scene of police on horseback beating people to the ground with sticks—was drawn with such operatic vividness that Carter had to remind himself that it was real life he was watching. By ten o'clock he was on the road, driving through the night north toward Meridian, then east on Highway 80 to Selma.

"What is the name of the patient?"

"Elijah Knight."

The Negro nurse on duty behind the admissions desk checked out Carter suspiciously, then said, "Just a moment." She turned to consult with a white nun in a small office behind her.

The nun emerged from the office and approached the window where Carter was standing. "May I help you?" she asked.

It was amazing how reassuring a white face could be in Selma, Alabama, on March 7, 1965, even if that face was boxed in the exotic black-and-white habit of Catholicism. As a reporter, Carter was now used to finding his way in unfamiliar territory, but his foray into black Selma in the wake of an assault by armed white authorities on defenseless Negroes magnified any ordinary awkwardness he might have felt into paranoid self-consciousness. Suspicious eyes had greeted him when he pulled up at Brown Chapel, a brick Methodist church with twin cupolas and sweeping arches, architecturally incongruous in a nondescript housing project on the colored side of town. There had been a mass meeting there that night after the aborted march ended with Sheriff Jim Clark's posse on horseback driving the Negroes back to the steps of the chapel. Some of the injured were still being tended at the parsonage next door, which had been turned into a first-aid center to treat cuts, bumps, bruises, tear-gas burns, and nausea. It was there that Carter learned that the more seriously wounded had been taken by ambulance to Good Samaritan Hospital, run by white Catholics but staffed mostly by black doctors and nurses.

Carter was inordinately relieved now to be dealing with this inquiring pink Irish countenance. "A patient was brought here," he explained to the nun. "A Negro named Elijah Knight. He was beaten on the bridge. His mother's very worried about him. Can you tell me anything about his condition?"

She studied Carter's face, then examined the paperwork on the clipboard the Negro nurse was holding. "We had many of the injured brought in from the march," she said. "Most were treated and released."

Carter pressed her. "Could you check your records?"

The inverted U of her mouth furrowed even deeper into her jowls as she took the clipboard from the nurse. "Elijah Knight, yes. He was admitted this afternoon."

"Is he okay?"

"He's suffered a severe head trauma." She told Carter he was in critical condition.

"Can I see him?"

"He's in a coma."

"Please, ma'am. I drove three hours to get here," Carter said. "Please. I've got to tell his mama I saw him."

"It's very late. Let me talk to the doctor on duty."

As Carter stood there waiting for the nun to return, he noticed the bandaged people who were sleeping in the darkened waiting room. Then he realized that the chemical odor he was smelling must be tear gas saturating their clothes. He supposed they had dozed off waiting for word on friends still being treated. Finally the nun reemerged. She nodded to Carter and led him through the swinging doors and down the hall to intensive care.

Lige was nearly unrecognizable. He was wrapped like a mummy. Tubes ran from his nose and mouth. His eyes were swollen shut. Next to his bed hung drips from bottles containing blood. A monitor beeped steadily beside him. Carter stared at Lige's bluish waxen complexion, his hair matted with blood, wishing he could communicate something through the bloody bandages.

He sought out the doctor on call, a young Negro who could have barely been out of medical school, and was told little more than what the nun had conveyed: contusions, hematoma, concussion. Prognosis vague, uncertain. The coma could last for a matter of hours or weeks or forever. Or Lige could die. The nurses wouldn't let Carter linger. After a few minutes he made his way back to the waiting room. He called Sarah on the pay phone and asked her to tell Nettie what he had learned.

Fueled on truck-stop coffee, Carter drove into the dark Alabama night, feeling as if he had finally left his blinkered small-town experience behind and entered the South that the rest of the country was growing regrettably familiar with. Now he knew how the Germans must have felt watching *Judgment at Nuremberg*. He was struck with a powerful urge to write down everything he had seen and experienced. He figured Pete would run wire copy on the march in the *Times* the next day. He would talk to him again about letting him do something on Lige as a follow-up.

To keep himself awake and fix details in his mind, he delivered an imaginary soliloquy to Sarah. They had been apart only a few hours, and he missed her already. They had become pretty creative at keeping their romance under the radar of others, including Carter's parents. When they did go out on a real date, they would drive out of town to shop or take in a movie in Hattiesburg, where they could blend in with the student population at the University of Southern Mississippi. Carter knew that dating on the sly couldn't last and wouldn't, and he didn't want it to. He had found himself behaving like an outcast in the hometown that he had owned during his starry high school career.

He hadn't forgotten his invitation to Sarah the previous summer, annulled by her return to New York, to be his date for the dance at the Troy Country Club. The club's annual Spring Fling was coming up and would offer the perfect opportunity to proclaim to the world, or Troy's small corner of it, that this was the girl he wanted to spend his life with. On the long drive back home he rehearsed his preemptive indignation over the reaction he expected he would get from his parents. They were going to have to deal with it.

It was nearly four in the morning when Carter got to Troy. He had decided to go to his parents' home, since he knew he would have to enlist them to get Nettie to Lige's side in Selma. Hoping to slip in the back door without waking anyone, he stepped inside and carefully closed the screen and bolted the lock. A voice startled him. "Carter?"

His father switched on the kitchen light and stood there looking bleary-eyed in his burgundy bathrobe over pale yellow pajamas.

"Dad," said Carter, "what are you doing up so late?"

"I could ask you the same thing."

"I just got in. Sorry if I kept you up waiting."

"I heard the car pull into the driveway. Where have you been?"

"I was out of town."

"So I heard. Nettie called. She heard from your girlfriend."

Carter blanched when he heard his father refer to Sarah so impersonally. "Sarah?" he said, and held his father's gaze. "I asked her to call Nettie." He told his father that Lige was in a coma and the doctors didn't know if he would regain consciousness.

"Good God," Mitchell said. "I told you it would come to this. Lige is going to get himself killed. And you should stay away from that mess."

"I'm just sorry I wasn't there to cover it."

"You would've been behaving irresponsibly if you were. You could have been hurt, too."

"Dad, it's the biggest story of my generation." Carter didn't mention that he was now stringing for the Nashville *Tennessean*, which had published a profile he wrote of Lige.

"And there are plenty of others to cover it. You'd risk your life, and for what?" Mitchell's face soured at the thought.

"If Lige doesn't make it, at least he'll have died for something he believes in."

"Anarchy. Violence."

"Excuse me, Your Honor, but Lige is nonviolent. You know that."

"He may be well intended, but he provokes violence. Can't you see that? I don't expect him to understand that, but surely you can."

"Your rule of law is violent, Daddy. Or did you miss the film of the Alabama state troopers?" Seeing his father's eyes glaze over, Carter shook his head and turned toward the dining-room entrance. He stopped and looked back at Mitchell. "And the saddest part of it all is that you're the best the South has got." He added gratuitously, "How very tragic."

Mitchell's voice went dangerously low. "How dare you speak that way to me, young man."

"I'm tired," Carter said, resuming his dramatic exit. "I want to go to bed."

"Well, maybe this will wake you up." His father reached into his bathrobe pocket. He tossed a letter onto the table. Carter read his name in the address window. The envelope was ripped open on the end.

"You opened my mail?"

"I knew what was in it," Mitchell replied. "Just read it." He stood there watching Carter scan the official-looking document. He couldn't resist repeating what it said. "Greetings. You've been drafted. You're to report for your physical in Meridian next month. Just like I told you."

Carter did not want his father to see how much this news upset him, so he took out after him on a phony offensive. "You opened my mail, Dad. Don't you have any respect for my personal belongings?"

Mitchell ignored the gambit. "I'll talk to Colonel Bradshaw at the local draft board. We served in North Africa together. But if you were in law school, you'd have a deferment."

"Well, I'm not. And you're ignoring the issue here. Privacy."

His father waved him off. "I'm not interested in scoring debating points with you, Pross. As long as you live here and get mail at this address—"

"Fine," Carter interrupted. "I'll move out."

"And go where? Move in with your girlfriend? Sarah," he said, as if remembering a dental appointment. "That girl's the one who put these crazy ideas in your head. Questioning the rule of law, provoking hooligans, tearing at the fabric of civilization."

"Oh, I thought it was Lige who corrupted me. Now it's Sarah. Admit it, Judge, you just want me to date who you want me to date. Don't tell me you and Mama weren't upset when Grayson and I broke up after I didn't take her to the dance last summer."

"I couldn't care less who you take to the dance."

"Oh, really."

"Besides, I was never crazy about you going with Grayson Boutwell in the first place, if you want to know the truth. Your mother may have had designs in that regard, but not me."

Carter stared at his father and saw a flicker of some unidentifiable emotion in his eye. "Don't get me wrong," the judge said. "She's a nice girl. But—"

"But what?"

His father reversed field. "Well, she's certainly preferable to some civil rightser."

"You mean some Jew." Carter knew he was jumping on bait not offered, but there was something enraging about his father gunnysacking a disapproval of Grayson all those years.

His father eyed him furiously. "Don't you take that tone of voice with me, Carter. You know good and well I'm not anti-Semitic."

"You just wouldn't want your son to marry one."

Mitchell Ransom shook his head and sighed. "Is it that serious?"

"I'm inviting her to the spring dance at the club. Or don't they let Jews in your glorious shrine to the fabric of civilization?"

Judge Ransom stared at Carter but ignored his question. "It's late," he said wearily. "Go to bed. You don't know what you're talking about."

"Dad, let me spell it out for you. You want me to stay here in this town and become a part of it just like you. A pillar of the community. If I stay here, I'll become a—a—a village idiot. Like Hugh Renfro."

His father acted with the swiftness of a lineman off the snap. He slammed into Carter, pushing him back against the doorjamb. "Don't you dare make fun of someone less fortunate than you!" Carter's breath was knocked out of him. "I didn't raise you to ridicule the feeble-minded. Hugh Renfro may have the mind of a child, but the Scriptures say his soul is every bit as worthy as yours and mine."

In all the years of Carter's childhood, Mitchell Ransom had never lifted a hand to his son. The force of his reaction surprised him as much as it did Carter. Only when Carter looked down did he notice that his father had grasped the lapels of his coat with both hands. They stood nose to nose. Mitchell Ransom breathed heavily, pressing his son with the full weight of his body to the wall.

"Would it be as worthy if his skin weren't white?" Carter whispered.

His father didn't move.

"Mitchell?" His mother was calling from the stairwell upstairs. "Is that Carter? Is he home?"

The judge slowly released Carter's lapels, backed off, and turned toward the door. "He's home, Katharine. Go back to bed."

Carter stared at his father, waiting for the shutting sound of their bedroom door, then moved quickly past him toward the stairwell and up to his own room.

———

IT WAS DARK by the time Carter returned from the coast and his interview with Lawrence "Strawberry" Thigpen. When he got to Grayburn to pick up the boys, hot dogs had been ordered from Wad's, and Grayson persuaded Carter to have a drink by the pool while the kids finished eating and watching a Disney video. She seemed subdued as they sat watching the reflection of pool lights flickering on the water. The fragrant mix of chlorine and tea olive was soothingly familiar, yet disconcerting by being so, reminding Carter of the many nights he had spent out there as a teenager.

"Where's your mom?" he asked as she handed him a coaster for his vodka tonic.

"Upstairs in her room. She's pretty upset. I suppose you've heard they're putting Daddy on trial."

Carter didn't know what to say, so he decided to find out how much she knew. "What do you mean?"

Grayson cut him a look that telegraphed her disappointment. "Well, it's a bit hard to conclude otherwise when a bunch of state investigators show up at your door with a search warrant." Carter tried to strike an expression somewhere between surprised and shocked. "I called Lonnie when they got here, and I had to hear it from him. He said Hullender's going to claim that Daddy was in the Ku Klux Klan, that he was involved with the church bombing." She seemed dazed, as if under heavy sedation. "And that your father was protecting him in the first trial."

She looked at Carter for a reaction. He was still absorbing how fast Sydney had acted on the information he had given her. He had called her after leaving her office that afternoon, before heading down to Pascagoula, to report the recollection he had forgotten to mention earlier, about seeing Glen Boutwell's Klan robe as a young man.

"Can you imagine?" Grayson said. The question dissipated in the air. She took a sip of her drink and fixed her eyes on the pool, then uttered with conviction, "I guess libel laws don't apply to the dead." She sniffled and reached into her pocket for a Kleenex. "I'm sorry," she said, dabbing her nose. "Maybe it was the way Lonnie told me, with such condescension, as if I were his charity case." She blew softly into the Kleenex. "When I think of how Daddy was so good to him, how he taught him how to field a grounder and to choke up on the bat, it makes me so mad." Carter was taking some nostalgic pleasure in the memory of Boutwell's coaching when Grayson turned her bitterness on him. "So what's your excuse for holding out on me about this?"

Carter felt infinitely inadequate. "I was hoping it wouldn't be necessary for you to find out," he said. "Apparently there's some question about whether parts of Hullender's testimony—his allegations against your daddy—will be allowed. Or be needed."

Grayson took a drink of her vodka tonic and stared at the shimmering pool. Her face softened. "Lord knows Daddy had his problems. But, my God, the Klan—" There was a question in her inflection, as if she were considering the possibility that it might be true.

Hearing the grief in Grayson's voice, Carter couldn't quite believe that he had just spent the afternoon trying to persuade a man to publicly reveal Glen Boutwell's Klan connection.

"You know Daddy," Grayson said. "He was a driven man. He came from a rough background." She applied her tissue to the condensation on her glass. "I didn't know some of this—about his childhood—until after he was dead; that's how protective he was of me. And I think he was always a little defensive about where he came from. But Mother filled me in." She took another sip of her drink, as if fortifying herself. "Daddy grew up in vicious poverty in south Mississippi, over in Amite County in—I guess what the talk-show hosts today call a dysfunctional family. The mother was a drunk and a little crazy. At any rate, she was more interested in the booze than in raising her five sons."

They had been tenant farmers, moving around from plantation to plantation and taking up quarters in abandoned slave cabins to farm the land for hire. During the Depression, their mother died of liver disease and their father moved them into a turpentine camp. Sixteen-year-old Glen took charge of his younger brothers, and always claimed that he raised the family.

"Remember having to read 'Barn Burning' in high school? Mother said the Boutwells were a lot like the Snopeses," Grayson said. "But Daddy took a lot of pride in withstanding hardship. Physically, as you know, Daddy was huge—and fearless."

The turpentine camps, though a rough existence, were perhaps a step up from where they started. Glen worked his way up into the

306 _____ DOUG MARLETTE

sawmills and brought his brothers along. It was when his brother's arm was mangled by a saw blade that Glen found the entrepreneurial drive to enter the prosthetic limbs business.

"I try to imagine what it must have been for him meeting Mama, the heiress to a sawmill fortune," Grayson said. "How he probably had no idea what he was in for, the world he was entering."

"It must have been intimidating, but it's hard to think of Coach being buffaloed by anything. He seemed so much larger than life, yet he fit in seamlessly."

Grayson gave Carter a pitiful little smile. Then she took a gulp of breath and exhaled slowly. "Carter," she said tentatively, "Daddy was horrible to Mama."

Carter felt an urgent desire not to hear what was coming. "How?"

Grayson paused, as if debating with herself whether to continue. "You know how they were always the life of the party?"

"Yeah. I remember seeing *The Thin Man* in college and thinking your parents were Mississippi's answer to Nick and Nora Charles."

"When they came home from any social event, there would be terrible scenes," Grayson said. "Daddy would humiliate Mama, tell her there was nothing cheaper than a tipsy woman."

"And you witnessed this?"

"Oh, I was an essential part of the dynamic. I was so identified with Daddy that I blamed Mama—you know, for not being who he wanted her to be."

"So you got to be who he wanted."

Grayson burst into tears. "Down to my fucking name: unisex, you know. Looking back, I realize that his behavior toward Mama was abusive. But I was actually on his side. And Mama just got more and more isolated, sipping her Tabs all day long until it got late enough to add the double shot of bourbon."

"Grayson, all families have secrets," Carter said. "Still, it's hard to see how the Klan fits into that profile." He wondered if he would have to tell her how their family secrets intersected, the rumors about his father.

"So you believe it," Grayson said sharply. Then she composed herself and turned contemplative, as if trying to reconcile the contradictions of her upbringing for the first time. "It doesn't add up, Carter. He hated it if anyone did something to embarrass the family. I'd say his chief motivation was this sad drive for respectability. Which he got when he married Mama. But then, of course, to be truly respectable, he had to show he wasn't beholden to her family and their money. What could he possibly have gotten out of the Klan?"

"A way to humiliate Sheppy to her core and remain loyal to his own father?" Carter said. "I don't know, Grayson. I'm not a shrink. But maybe the Klan was the only social group he could feel truly ascendant in." He took a sip of his drink. "I'm sure your dad felt he was defending everything he had worked so hard to get. Hearth and home. The cunning of the South is that we act on our worst instincts and convince ourselves they're our best."

Grayson's eyes focused on the middle distance. "He did drive Mama crazy by calling blacks coons and jigs and niggers. But Daddy didn't like his own kind, poor whites, any better. He wanted to get away from them. Yet he was always going off hunting with Sam Bohannon."

"Everybody who hunted wild boar went to Bohannon for their dogs, just like they did for catfish," Carter said. "Jimbo went with him a couple of times."

Grayson smiled. "Daddy would go on these expeditions with his brothers out into the swamps. Something left over from his boyhood. He belonged to a hunt club in Wiggins where they exclusively hunt boar. I went along once to see what it was all about." Her face scrunched at the memory. "Primitive. But it was as if he had to go back to remind himself of what he'd escaped." Grayson reached for her Kleenex and blew her nose. She suddenly seemed self-conscious about dominating the conversation. "When do you testify?" she asked.

"I don't know. Maybe next week."

"Are you nervous?"

"No."

She breathed what she said next so softly that Carter nearly missed it. "And now there's talk about exhuming his body."

"What?"

"Disinterring my father," she said, reaching for another Kleenex.

"I had not heard that," Carter said truthfully. "Jesus God."

"Something about matching his DNA for evidence."

"That does seem awfully extreme." And desperate, he thought. He would have to ask Sydney about it.

"That's what I told Lonnie. It's so upsetting. He's going to speak to them. Now you understand why Mama's taken to her bed."

"I'm so sorry, Grayson." Carter genuinely felt for her, yet he was growing fidgety.

Grayson sensed his retreat. "Thanks for listening, Carter. Your father's been a help, too, with Mama. I don't know what we'd have done without him." She shifted in her chair and picked her glass up from the table. "Hey, I know you've got to get the boys home to bed. Sally's going to shoot me if they come home all wired."

The sound of giggles and movement upstairs signaled that the video was over and the kids were playing. Carter stood and started toward the stairs to call the boys.

"Carter," Grayson said, catching up to him before he reached the steps. He turned back to her. "Are you going to be at the Nature Conservancy fund-raiser for Congressman Knight when he comes to town to testify?"

"I don't know anything about it."

"It's Jimbo's idea. You know, Elijah may be in trouble for his opposition to the WunderCorp development, and Jimbo talked Sally into letting them have it at her store."

"Then I guess I will," he said.

"Tell him we'll be sending in our contribution. I wish I could be there, but I doubt I'll be doing much socializing while this trial is going on. I can hardly stand to go to the Piggly Wiggly."

She held out her arms and gathered him into a hug. He stood there holding her lightly. She looked up at him. He could see the tears on her eyelashes. She pressed her mouth onto the corner of his. "Thanks for listening," she said.

Carter turned his lips onto the familiar topography of hers and lingered there just a beat beyond regret.

21

I T WAS a little after 10:00 p.m. on a cold March night. Unit Four, Ellis County White Knights of the Ku Klux Klan, arrived at Shiloh Baptist Church in three cars and a truck. They came armed with pistols, shotguns, twelve gallons of gasoline, and the will to destroy human life."

Thus began Sydney Rushton's introductory remarks in *The State of Mississippi v. Samuel Holifield Bohannon*. She spoke in a grave voice to the jury of seven whites, six blacks, and one Asian-American. The two alternates among them would be named before deliberations began. It was a portrait of diversity by Mississippi standards, chosen through a selection process that had taken a whole tedious week. She painted a picture of what happened that night when the Klansmen arrived at Shiloh Church. The commencement ceremony for Freedom School "graduates" had just broken up there, and remaining inside were civil rights workers from Magic Time and a few of the honorees. Four of them died when a confrontation with the intruders ended in gunplay and firebombs, transforming a time of celebration into a nightmare of murder and devastation. Sydney described the weapons the Klansmen used in the assault that preceded the blast, and she traced the responsibility for the bombing of the church to Sam Bohannon. He sat impassively in his wheelchair, eyes half closed, a perhaps involuntary smirk playing on his lips.

Carter could see that Sydney was a dramatist of superior gifts as she guided the jury back to the night of March 20, 1965. She introduced the victims: Randall Peek, the sensitive, intellectual young apostle of non-violence from Harvard by way of Atlanta; Daniel Johnston, the white seminarian and former cadet at Virginia Military Institute who graduated at the top of his class, underwent a religious conversion, entered seminary, and felt called to come south; Celia Bunt, girlfriend of Randall Peek and oldest daughter of the Reverend Curtis Bunt, who had never considered college a possibility until her Freedom School experience; and Sarah Solomon, the pretty Barnard College English major who had learned at such a young age one of the most honorable of life's lessons: to regard her own advantages as a gift to be shared. Sydney produced pictures of the victims, which had been enlarged and mounted on poster board, and she passed them around to the jury. Also on display were the police photos of the scene, showing the damage to the church and property. Smaller prints were handed to the jurors. Sydney identified them as the coroner's close-ups of the maimed bodies left behind in the wreckage.

From the blunt facts, Carter saw, Sydney was setting up themes that would speak as much to historical conscience as to criminal justice: the sudden savage attack by brutal men upon the young and the innocent, the shotgun blasts and Molotov cocktails inflicted on the helpless and undeserving, "the vicious end to a hope-filled commencement." The architect of what she called "this holocaust of hate" had gone unpunished for a quarter of a century. Sydney ended her opening statement by noting with a catch in her voice that September 10, that very day, would have been Celia Bunt's forty-fifth birthday.

Arthur Puckett had listened attentively and respectfully during the entire hour Sydney spoke, lapsing only occasionally to clean his glasses with his handkerchief. He rose to present his opening statement in defense of Samuel Bohannon. Looking dapper in his gray Italian suit, indigo-blue dress shirt with white collar and cuffs, and red silk tie, the defense lawyer confronted the horror of the crime head-on, declaring the revulsion he felt when as an undergraduate at Ole Miss, he learned of the bombing of Shiloh Church while watching the evening news in his dormitory. At the time, he thought about how the victims were not much older than he and how he hoped that whoever committed the crime would pay the ultimate price. But for all his disgust at the killers, he had also since developed a keen sense of justice and due process, and he had learned that punishing the wrong person would only compound an injustice. He went on in that vein, stressing the achievement of the first trial in bringing the real killers to justice. After outlining the contributions Sam Bohannon had made to the civic life of Troy as a restaurateur and dog breeder, Puckett pointed out that on the night of the crime, his client was a hundred miles away in Natchez, visiting his ailing mother. Understanding that the jurors' attention span had already been tested by the state's lengthy opening remarks, Puckett kept his statement brief. As the defense lawyer talked, Carter observed Sydney casually watching the jury and occasionally checking out Bohannon with cold eyes.

"You want to try to see the congressman before he testifies?" Jimbo asked Carter as they exited the courthouse for the lunch recess. The afternoon's star witness, Elijah Knight, was standing with his mother on the courthouse steps, surrounded by the media's cameras and mikes. Carter was struck by the irony. There, on the very spot where Lige had been beaten and bloodied as a nonperson, he now contended with the slings of celebrity. The condition, in turn, not only insulated him from the voiceless people he represented but alienated him from the "authenticity" that had brought him his fame.

Ever since getting elected to the U.S. House of Representatives in the early 1980s, Lige had been returned with landslide margins by an enthusiastic constituency of black and white voters. His seat had been considered safe for years. Carter was in awe of the distance his friend had traversed over twenty-five years, from Freedom Rides to fact-finding missions with the president on Air Force One. His career was a tribute to the best of the democratic process Lige had fought so hard for, but it was also a reminder of how beholden that process was to corporate whim. Lige's opposition to WunderCorp had put his seat in jeopardy and necessitated his first fund-raiser in years.

"I'll catch him tonight at Sally's," Carter said to Jimbo after sizing up the clamor around Lige. The two headed down the street to Wad's for a sandwich, betting that the courtroom crowd would be at the Starlite for lunch.

The first witness Sydney called after the recess was Sheriff Lawrence Mizell, now a husk of the Central Casting Klan-sympathizing bully he had been as one of the first lawmen to arrive at the crime scene. At lunch Jimbo had filled Carter in on the sheriff's progress through the years—from brute enforcer of the segregationist codes to evenhanded upholder of the law, one of those redemption sagas that the American South had a way of offering up in contradiction to every expectation. His authoritarian personality had also concealed a clear sense of right and wrong and a strong religious bent, which he exercised on the Methodist church's board of stewards alongside Doc Renfro. Mizell had gone through some conversion. Jimbo believed it began with his father's store. Saul Stein and Sheriff Mizell used to have breakfast early every morning at the Starlite Cafe, and when Saul's store got defaced with anti-Semitic slurs after the showdown at Naked Tail, the sheriff felt personally affronted.

"It looked like a war zone" was how Mizell described the crime scene from the witness stand. "I hadn't seen nothing like it since serving in the Pacific during World War Two. Half the church was completely demolished, and what was left was burning up. Volunteer fire department showed up, but it was too late. Two bodies were lying on the ground outside the door. A Caucasian male and a black female."

On a screen adjacent to the jury box, Sydney's assistant projected slides of photographs of Daniel Johnston in his clerical collar and Celia Bunt's high school yearbook photograph.

"They had both been shot at close range with a shotgun," Mizell said, with a reflexive professionalism that contradicted his wizened state. "The other two bodies were found inside—their remains anyway."

The slides of Randall Peek in his horn-rimmed glasses and Sarah Solomon's frank, open face, taken from their SNCC files, were flashed on the screen. To his surprise, Carter did not feel the urge to look away from Sarah's large brown eyes shining out from the musty college photograph. A flicker of mischief subverted the mask of institutional photography and made his heart leap across a quarter of a century.

"Let the record show," said Sydney Rushton, "that according to the coroner's report, Randall Peek and Sarah Solomon both died of gunshot wounds and asphyxiation."

Sydney spent most of the first day establishing the crime. Among her lineup of witnesses were the retired pathologist who prepared the original coroner's report; tearful members of the Bunt family, who lived in the parsonage next door and gave accounts of the raid; and aging retired FBI agents, who supplied technical descriptions of the type of explosives used.

The state called Congressman Elijah Knight late in the day. Lige, who had been seated next to his mother, Nettie, during the opening statements, strode out the witness room with languid grace. Middle age had marked him greatly, with lines etching his forehead like beveled mahogany. A dark blue suit accentuated his still-lanky frame; on its lapel was an American flag pin.

"Thank you for being here today, Congressman," Sydney said. "Sir, you have seen and heard the descriptions of the four who died at Shiloh Church. Did you know the victims?"

"They were friends and colleagues."

Sydney asked him to describe his role as a fieldworker with the Student Nonviolent Coordinating Committee and how he came to know the victims. Lige launched into a thorough but succinct description of the kind of work he and the others had done at Magic Time. He spoke in the same no-nonsense staccato many in the courtroom had grown accustomed to hearing over the years at his press conferences or when he was a guest on television news shows discussing such mundane topics as tax rebates and farm subsidies. When he finished outlining the work of SNCC and the Freedom Summer programs at Shiloh Baptist Church, Sydney asked if he was aware that he was the target of the attack on the church.

"Yes, I was."

She produced a photocopy of a letter that she said had been sent to

SNCC on the day of the bombing, in care of Scarborough's grocery. It arrived the following Monday, two days after the crime. She asked the court to enter it into evidence as State's Exhibit Number 4. She then handed it to Lige and asked him to read it. " 'Dear Snick,' " he read. " 'By the time you get this letter, nigger Knight will be dead.' " Lige lingered slightly on the "nigger." " 'He is a traitor to his community. This will teach you that the South means business. Go home, Jews and Communists. The white, God-fearing Christian citizens of Ellis County don't want you here.' "

It was signed, "The White Knights of the Ku Klux Klan."

Sydney asked Lige if he had ever seen the letter.

"Yes, I have."

She then asked him if he was at the church the night of the bombing.

"I was scheduled to talk there at the meeting. It was a graduation ceremony of sorts, for some of the youngsters at our Freedom School. But I wasn't there."

"Where were you instead?"

"I was in the hospital in Selma, Alabama."

"Would you tell the jury why you were there?"

"Objection, Your Honor," Puckett called out.

LIGE'S EYES OPENED and slowly focused on Carter, who was sitting in a chair next to his bed at Good Samaritan Hospital. "Brother Man," he said, smiling weakly. Lige had been in a coma for more than a week. Nettie had stayed by his side, until finally he woke one morning and asked her what was for breakfast. Much of the swelling around his eyes had gone down, and the bandages had been removed from his face, but he was still hooked up to monitors and drips. "Where's Mama?" he asked Carter.

"Take it easy, buddy row." Carter handed him a glass of juice. "We thought we'd relieve her for a while and let her get something to eat in the cafeteria."

Sarah leaned into his field of vision. "Hey, Preacher. Remember me?" Carter saw her lip quiver as she fought the need to cry.

"Sarah Sunshine," Lige said.

"Look who else is here," Sarah said. Randall Peek, Celia Bunt, and Daniel Johnston gathered in around his bed.

Lige's smile vanished, and his eyes went flat. "Now all we're missing is Dexter," he said.

There was a solemn moment of silence before Carter spoke. "You're looking better than the last time I saw you," he said.

Sarah filled Lige in on the controversy over the march in the week since he had gone unconscious, how the nation, including her and Carter, had learned of what happened at the Edmund Pettus Bridge in the middle of watching *Judgment at Nuremberg*. Women and children being attacked by armed men on horseback? Impossible. Not in America. People now were flying into Alabama from all over the country.

"All the others now feel bad that they weren't there," said Sarah. SNCC fieldworkers from Mississippi and staffers from Atlanta had rushed to Selma the next day after "Bloody Sunday," as the media were now calling the aborted Selma march.

Carter took up the commentary. There was a lot of pressure on the leaders to act after Bloody Sunday, he reported, and the debate over what to do next was intense. The state of Alabama had gotten an injunction to prevent further marches, and federal judge Frank Johnson was to rule on it. But with Johnson's hearing a few days off, nobody wanted to wait and risk losing momentum. So on Tuesday, Martin Luther King had led two thousand people to the Edmund Pettus Bridge, where they faced the troopers again. But instead of a confrontation, King prayed with the protesters, and after they sang "We Shall Overcome," he turned them around and marched back to Brown Chapel. The young SNCC leadership—militants like Charlie Lloyd—were livid at King's effort to finesse the situation in what they were calling "Turnaround Tuesday." They had been ready to march to Montgomery, and they felt betrayed.

"I thought we had settled the argument back in Birmingham over whether to obey an injunction against marching," Lige said with annoyance.

"Well, Frank Johnson's a decent guy, and the feeling was he might rule in our"—Carter caught himself—"your favor." He ran down other major developments. A young white Unitarian minister from Boston named James Reeb had been beaten by whites with a baseball bat and had died in the hospital. Governor George Wallace went to the White House to plead his state's case against the protestors, but President Johnson emerged from the meeting and announced that he was sending legislation to Congress to protect voters. He then went on television in front of seventy million Americans and called for a federal voting rights act. Carter took his notebook out of his pocket, shuffled the pages, and read the president's words.

" 'At times history and fate meet at a single time in a single place to shape a turning point in man's unending search for freedom. So it was at Lexington and Concord. So it was a century ago at Appomattox. So it was last week in Selma, Alabama.' "

And then the rest of Lige's visiting party began reciting the speech's most memorable challenge: " 'Their cause must be our cause, too. Because it is not just Negroes, but really it is all of us who must overcome the crippling legacy of bigotry and injustice. And we shall overcome.' "

No one spoke for a moment. Then Danny Johnston said, "You were a lot luckier than Brother Reeb, Lige."

Lige looked thoughtful, abashed. "Did Mama tell you Dr. King and Ralph Abernathy came by for a visit?" he said. "Or so I'm told. I was still unconscious. Mama nearly fainted."

Celia was impressed. "Dr. King came to see you?"

"It's not like that," Lige said. "John Lewis had a bed down the hall. They really came to see him. He asked them to look in on me. Mama met Dr. King, though."

"So what did De Lawd have to say?" asked a deep voice behind them.

They all turned toward the door, where Charlie Lloyd stood, wearing a dark overcoat and shades. His beard was fuller now than it had been when Carter last saw him, and his hair had grown out thicker.

"Charlie Lloyd," said Randall, "what are you doing here?"

"Paying my respects to the shut-ins. Hello, Elijah."

"Charlie, come on in," Lige said.

"Don't let me interrupt your prayer meeting," Charlie said. "What I got to tell you can wait."

"We can't wait," said Lige. "Isn't that what Dr. King says?"

"Maybe it should wait, Charlie," said Sarah. "Lige isn't up to full strength yet."

"Then what are you doing here, Sarah Soda Cracker?" Charlie moved into the room to the foot of the bed. "Oh, I see," he said, looking at Carter. "You're with Mr. Cracker."

Randall could use his quiet reserve to intimidate and subdue, and now he dropped his voice to the level just above a whisper. "Lige doesn't need any of your static right now, Charlie."

"Just a courtesy call, Randall. Atlanta staff's appointed me the new interim representative for Snick in southeast Mississippi—until Lige gets back on his feet. I heard he was out of the woods and thought I'd drop by and let him know we're marching on Sunday."

"What?" Lige said, and made an unsuccessful effort to sit up.

"Ain't you heard?" Lloyd asked. Carter noted that he was once again using the language of the street.

"Heard what? We just got in from Troy and came straight to the hospital," Danny said.

"The good Judge Johnson done issued his ruling," said Charlie. "The march from Selma to Montgomery is on. King announced it last night at a mass meeting."

Randall broke character and shouted, "All right!" The room burst into applause.

"It wasn't all 'Balm in Gilead.'" Charlie smirked. "Forman caused quite a stir."

"Jim's been frustrated for a while. What happened?" asked Lige.

"Jim Forman got up, bless him, and said, 'If we can't sit at the table of democracy, we'll knock the fucking legs off!' You should've seen King's face."

Lige's expression did not reciprocate Charlie's amusement.

"Oh, yeah," Charlie persisted.

"That's not the message we want to send out," Lige said.

"Fuck the message you want to send out," Charlie said breezily. "It's past time for your little Sunday school lessons."

Sarah gave Carter a barely perceptible shake of the head as he was about to chime in. "What in the world are you squabbling for?" she said to the others. "This march is a wonderful victory for the Movement. Maybe thousands of people will be there Sunday from all over the country."

"Sarah's right," said Randall. "I mean, did any one of us ever think we'd see a president saying 'We shall overcome' on national TV?"

"Forman said LBJ spoiled a good song that day," Charlie Lloyd said, and cackled.

"What's the staff position on the march, Charlie?" asked Lige. He tried to lift up from his pillow to his elbows.

"That's what I came to tell you. While you were knocked out, Snick decided not to wait around for no injunction. We've been laying siege to the capitol in Montgomery all week long."

Carter had heard about the series of demonstrations SNCC had organized in Montgomery since the march, taunting, provoking, clashing with armed policemen.

Danny explained SNCC's frustration. "SCLC ran a full-page ad in *The New York Times* to raise money, and they used a picture of John Lewis getting beaten up."

"Hell, yes," said Charlie. "Our guy gets the concussion, and King's organization gets the publicity and the donations."

"And what have you done, Charlie?" asked Randall. "Snick lost the moral high ground by not supporting the march. Lewis had to march 'unofficially.'"

Sarah said, "And now you're claiming Lige and John Lewis as your own again, right, Charlie. Just like 'De Lawd.'"

"Hell," said Randall, "Snick's getting just as bad as SCLC."

Carter reached for his notebook.

"Hey, this is off the record, Scoop," Sarah said, jostling him playfully.

"If I'm going to write about Selma, I've got to write about the conflict, don't I?"

"The Movement's not a house divided," said Lige. "We've never been one voice. SCLC and Snick are different expressions of the same spirit."

"We're more like a family," said Randall. "Arguments take place in a family."

Charlie eyed Carter suspiciously. "Shit," he said, "you can get cut in my family."

Partly to get under Charlie's skin, Carter continued jotting notes.

"What the hell is it to you anyway, Ransom?" Charlie demanded, and turned to Sarah. "This is your fault for fraternizing. We should have known you white folk would go native once you got down here."

Sarah gave him a look that would strip paint. "Yeah, Charlie, I've been going native running a Freedom School while you've been working on covering up your fine Howard education. And Stuyvesant High School to boot," she added, injecting a bit of New York fellowship.

Lige looked pained. "That's right, the Freedom School graduation ceremony is Saturday night, and I've got to somehow be back here for the march on Sunday."

Charlie watched Lige sink back into his pillow. A look of secret satisfaction challenged Charlie's scowl, in recognition of the obvious fact that his rival wasn't going anywhere anytime soon. "Well, I plan on being on the Edmund Pettus Bridge representing southeast Mississippi whether you can make it or not," he said. He started toward the door but stopped next to Sarah. "You and Miss Celia are still looking mighty fine, Sarah." Charlie eyed Carter as he spoke. Then he leaned back and leered at Sarah's backside.

Carter nearly leaped out of his bedside seat, but Sarah spoke coolly, "Well, you need to come back and see us sometime so you can clean out your stuff from Magic Time, Charlie. Your little treasure trove of press clips is a fire hazard cluttering up my workspace." Sarah had told Carter that Charlie was the leading self-archivist in the Movement, keeping souvenirs, mementos, and scrapbooks of every article—including Carter's—ever written about SNCC that spelled his name right.

"You get ready, then, 'cause like I always said, darlin', the only position for women in the movement is prone." Then, looking around the room at their offended faces, he said, "See y'all in Montgomery?" As he exited, Charlie pumped his fist above his head and said, "We *shall* overcome."

Lige seemed to be losing his concentration, struggling to maintain eye contact. Sarah looked at Carter and signaled the others that they should be leaving. "We'll go down and find Mrs. Knight," she said. "Carter, why don't you stay here until she gets back up?"

After the farewells, Lige lay with his eyes closed. Carter, listening to his friend's steady breathing and the bleep of his monitor, thought he was asleep. When Lige spoke, Carter was startled. "Hey, I see you're in the big time now, Pross." He pointed to the copy of the Nashville *Tennessean* on the bedside table. "Mama showed me the story you wrote."

"They cut too much."

"Hey, you quoted me right. Most of them don't, you know. You could have stressed my good looks some more, but other than that, I got no complaints."

Carter smiled. "Well, in my line of work, if your subject doesn't squawk about something, you've done something wrong. I guess the *Tennessean* liked the piece, though. They asked me to help cover the march on Sunday."

"Mazel tov," he said, and opened one eye to shoot him a droll look.

"My father said if I cover it, I might as well not come home. I may have to stay with Sarah."

"Congratulations. You needed to get out of that house and out of that town."

"Yeah, well, I may get my chance soon. I got my draft notice. I've got to report for a physical in Jackson next month."

Lige opened both his eyes and lifted his head off the pillow. "So ol' selective service retaliated against you before they did me in. I guess it's more disturbing to the status quo for a white judge's son to get mixed up in 'the mess' than for a black nigger like me."

It had not occurred to Carter that his notice was anything more than bureaucratically motivated. He carried Lige's vengeance theory a step further and wondered if his own father might have initiated the draft process in order to get him back into law school.

"Would you go over there if they drafted you?" Carter said.

"I don't agree with this war in Indochina. Or any war for that matter."

"Except the one you're fighting in now," Carter said. He got up to leave. "I'll be back next week to cover the preparations for the march."

"Well, I won't be here, Pross," Lige said. "Don't tell Mama, but I'm going back for the Freedom School graduation Saturday night. I'll be back here Sunday morning for the march to Montgomery if I have to drive all night."

Carter listened to Lige's commitment talking but knew his body would not cooperate. "You're not going anywhere if the doctor tells you to stay put," he said. "Besides, did Sarah tell you about the threats they've been getting? Somebody sent them a clip of my *Tennessean* story about you, and it had obscenities scrawled all over it."

"We get threats all the time," said Lige, closing his eyes again.

"It said something cryptic, too, on the envelope."

"What?"

" 'School's out for you.' Sarah wonders if it's a reference to the Freedom School ceremony this Saturday. She thinks it might be good if you're not there."

"Well, I'm not going to miss the graduation. Or the march."

"Lige, it may be safer for everyone if you're not in Ellis County."

"Carter, if we let threats of violence stop the Movement, then we don't—"

"I know the speech, Lige; it's in my story," Carter interrupted. "But sometimes I can't tell whether it's your ego moving you or the 'spirit of history.' " The *Tennessean* had headlined his profile of Lige AT ONE WITH THE "SPIRIT OF HISTORY," after one of his quotes in the article.

"That's a good question, Pross. But I'm still going to march." Lige opened his eyes again. "You'll be there at the bridge, too, right?"

"I'll be there with my notebook."

Lige smiled, cut Carter a look, then turned his head away as if he were going to sleep. "If I don't make it, you'll just have to lay down that notebook and take my place, Brother Man." Then Lige fluttered his fingers, widened his eyes, and whistled in mock terror. And Carter for the first time appreciated the absurd gap between the dilemma he faced and the trauma that had been Elijah's from birth.

ON THE WITNESS STAND, Congressman Knight delivered an eloquent tribute to the four who died in his place at Shiloh Baptist Church
on the night of the Freedom School graduation. Carter understood Sydney's strategic intent in having Lige speak on the first day, to give the
imprimatur of the United States Congress to the testimony that would
follow—powerful validation of the sacrifice made by Sarah and her
friends at Shiloh a quarter of a century earlier. The impact of Lige's testimony on the obviously stunned jury seemed inversely proportional to
the calm, almost flat manner in which it was delivered. Carter watched
Lacey Hullender and Sam Bohannon as they listened, but they registered
little. Bohannon kept his head bowed in silent contemplation, looking
up occasionally and only briefly in the direction of the witness stand.
Hullender stared at Elijah as if responding to something unsaid by the
congressman. When Judge McDonnell asked the defense counsel if he
had any questions, Puckett declined; there was little percentage in taking on an icon. The judge adjourned court until the next day. Carter
watched Sydney as she crisply put away her file folders. In her face,
though it was composed to reveal no emotion, he could see a glint of the
killer instinct.

22

O H, CAHTUH! I'm so worried about Grayson." Bradley Crawford pushed her bosom into Carter's arm the moment he entered Sally's bookstore for the fund-raiser for Elijah Knight. "I didn't know her daddy, but the family must be mortified. Nobody's seen Sheppy for weeks, and Grayson doesn't return my calls." The veneer of concern was as thick as Bradley's lip gloss. Before Carter could answer, another voice called to him.

"Opening day went well, don't you think?" said Lonnie, who was hovering behind Bradley, a drink in one hand and the other hand in his pocket. His tie was loosened. "Sydney happy?" he asked.

"I wouldn't know," Carter replied, puzzled by the implication that he should.

"Oh, I thought you two were consulting regularly on this case," Lonnie said, raising his glass to his lips. Carter assumed that the whiskey was not his first.

Bradley suddenly sobered up. "Are Carter and our brilliant little prosecutor an item? My, don't we work fast?"

Carter wearily shook his head in disavowal. Lonnie downed the rest of his drink and said, "He better put the moves on her pretty quick, though, because this trial's going to be over before you know it, and she and her three-ring circus will be gone."

Sally slipped up beside Carter and hooked her arm under his. "May I borrow my brother for a second?" she said.

Bradley stalled them. "Cahtuh, I begged your sister to let me host this soirée at my house, but she was ruthless."

"It's fine, Bradley," Sally said, spinning her brother away and discreetly rolling her eyes. Sally was diligent about paying proper tribute to Troy's very own bestselling writer, although to Carter, privately, she referred to Bradley's novels as "hysterical fiction," full of cinnamon toast, lavalieres, and quirky but indomitable middle-aged women lamenting the tragic waning of their mythic girlhoods.

"God, she's been insufferable since the trial started," Sally whispered. She took in the crowd jammed into her narrow, high-ceilinged retail space, which had once been a feedstore. "I'm going to kill Jimbo. He told me to expect a hundred. There's twice that many already. We're going to run out of wine."

"I'll go pick some up." Carter was delighted with the opportunity to make himself scarce.

"No," Sally said. "You stay and help me play host. Stephen's already volunteered. I just wanted to ask you to check on Daddy when you get home. I'll probably be late cleaning up. He's watching the boys, but I worry about how he's holding up with Hullender testifying tomorrow."

They made their way to the service area in back, where caterers were arranging finger food on trays. Nettie showed up at the delivery entrance with baskets of her famous ham biscuits.

"Lige won't like it if you get caught coming through the service entrance, Nettie," Carter teased. "How's he doing? I haven't been able to break through the media shield to talk to him."

"Good as gold," she said. "He don't get home as much as I like, but he's got responsibilities, you know. He tells me he's been traveling overseas with the president. He saw the Crown Prince of Syria." Carter wondered if Nettie was as attuned to her son's cloudy reelection prospects as everyone else in town. She showed off a pair of sapphire earrings Lige had given her. "Lige always bring his mama back a little something on them—what he call—junkets." She howled at the word in one of her hearty guffaws. "I always told him he better not stay gone too long from his younguns. He gonna miss they babyhood." Carter had been an usher in Lige's wedding to his college sweetheart, a girl from Alabama whom he met in Nashville at Fisk. She was then performing with the Jubilee Singers and had gone on to a long and successful career as an antitrust lawyer. They now had two young children. Nettie clucked her tongue in mock disapproval. "Politics—Elijah live and breathe it."

"Nettie, get on out there and mingle," said Sally, escorting her away from the hors d'oeuvres table she was trying to arrange. "You're Lige's secret weapon." Sally followed her back out into the crowd, brandishing a REELECT ELIJAH KNIGHT poster in one hand and a staple gun in the other.

"Where *is* Lige?" Carter asked as Sally bustled by. The crowd now spilled out onto the sidewalk in the relative cool of the evening. Many of the usual suspects were there—Troy's social and literary set, local politicos and activists, as well as a number of out-of-towners who were in Troy for the trial. Some of the relatives of the Shiloh Church victims were talking to the national reporters Carter had seen in the courtroom press gallery. He hoped to see Sydney but wasn't surprised that her prosecution team would stay away from a political event. Anyway, she was probably working late on the case. He spotted Jimbo entertaining a group of print and TV types, as well as Simon Lester, the British filmmaker documenting the trial.

"Mr. Ransom," said a black woman in a caftan and a brightly colored turban, escorting an elderly white-haired woman. "My mother wanted to speak to you today in court, but you got away before we could reach you."

Carter extended his hand. "I'm Aurelia Bunt," said the younger woman. "Celia's sister. I was just a baby when it happened. Daddy died a few years ago, but Mama remembers you."

The tiny, frail woman, clinging to her daughter's arm, pulled Carter to her and in a hoarse whisper said, "I was reminded today of what a beautiful young girl Sarah Solomon was. She was such a sweet child. And she loved you very much."

Carter was taken by surprise, and all he could manage was, "Thank you. It's good to see you again, Mrs. Bunt. Thank you. Sarah loved you, too."

The old woman and her daughter moved on when Sally appeared. "Don't look now," she said, nodding toward the front window to indicate the couple out on the sidewalk, "but Lonnie and Loretta are having a fight."

Lonnie seemed unsteady on his feet, and Loretta was mouthing angry words at him. He reached for her arm, and she pulled away and stalked off.

Sally said, sotto voce, to Carter, "Keep an eye on him, Pross."

"Nice party, Sally." Jimbo had walked up and laid his head on her shoulder. "Thanks for donating to the cause."

"The least I can do," said Sally.

"Quite a turnout. Even a celeb or two. Besides Carter. Have you spoken to Lige?"

Sally informed them that the congressman was over in Nonfiction.

Carter and Jimbo picked their way through the crowd to where Lige was greeting well-wishers, Pete Callahan among them.

"Pross," Lige said to Carter. They embraced, and Lige pounded Carter on the back.

"How's the only living saint in history ever welcomed into Dante's seventh circle known as the United States Congress?"

Lige laughed. "Coming from Troy's own nationally certified pundit and prophet, that's quite a compliment."

"I heard your testimony today, Preacher. Nice job."

"Seems like only yesterday, doesn't it?" Lige searched Carter's eyes. "How are you holding up, Pross?"

"I'm all right. How about you?" Carter asked.

Lige sighed. "Well, at least revisiting all that puts what I'm going through now in perspective. It's going to be a tough campaign. The money is mostly migrating into my opponent's war chest."

"WunderCorp," Pete Callahan explained. He was standing off to the side, as befit a gray eminence, puffing on his meerschaum, ever present since he gave up cigarettes in the seventies. That morning the *Troy Times* had reported that Lige's Republican challenger, a white pharmacist, was closing in on him in the polls. The national Democratic Party was starting to put pressure on Lige to back off WunderCorp. Carter started to ask about it when someone shouldered in front of him and squared off in front of Lige.

"Excuse me, Congressman," said Rasheed Lovelace. "*New York Tribune.* Can we talk now?"

"Can we set up something for later, Rasheed?"

"I see you have time for the competition," said Lovelace, indicating Carter.

"We're old friends," Lige said. "He's not interviewing me."

Carter saw something flare in Pete Callahan's ancient eyes as he drew close. "Excuse me, young fella, I don't believe I caught your name."

"Lovelace. *New York Tribune*," Rasheed said, offering Pete his hand.

"Oh, yes," said Pete, refusing to introduce himself. "You're the one who wrote that horse manure libeling Mitchell Ransom."

"I stand by my story, mister. Although I'm not surprised some local revisionists might be upset by it."

"See, that's just the kind of arrogance that made your story so amateurish." Pete turned and made his way through the crowd to the bar.

"What's up with the geezer?" Lovelace said, as if he'd just been accosted by a panhandler.

"He has standards, 'Sheed," said Carter. "Something you may have read about in J-school."

"Cheap shot, Ransom. But I understand. You got to stand up for your old man, which probably explains why I beat you on your own story. That's got to hurt the professional pride, man."

Carter shook his head and smiled at Lige. "My tribe," he said, but with a sinking feeling. How was Pete going to feel if the trial proved that even someone with Rasheed's standards was occasionally right?

"Welcome to my life," said Lige. Then to Lovelace, "Okay, Rasheed, two minutes."

Lovelace proceeded to lecture Lige about the historic significance of Magic Time, having appropriated the substance of the congressman's testimony earlier that day. Then, in a seeming non sequitur punctuated by the usual snuffling, he said, "I'd like to sit down and talk to you about why you're so attached to saving it even if it means hurting your district. You're opposed to WunderCorp's plans for Troy, are you not?"

"I don't think the development of one of the last pristine wilderness areas in the world helps my district," Lige said, warming immediately to the subject. "And I doubt a petrol chemical plant dumping hundreds of thousands of gallons of untreated waste into the Little Chickasaw does either."

"I saw all the environmental impact studies. They met all the state standards."

"Down here, our environmental protection regulations are such that if it's impossible to meet the standards, they don't have to be met."

"What does that mean?" Lovelace asked.

"The laws are written so that if a chemical is created that cannot be broken down, it can be dumped. WunderCorp comes to Mississippi for the same reasons they went to Africa. We're like a third world country. One: they want a monolithic political structure they can grease to get what they want without a lot of red tape and hassle. And two: cheap labor."

"Any other reasons you oppose them?"

"The ecosystem of the Little Chickasaw directly affects the Shiloh Church community. A lot of them are fishermen. It hurts their way of making a living by killing off the catfish. WunderCorp's intention to dismantle Magic Time is symbolic of their disregard for the entire community out there."

"But WunderCorp is willing to build a civil rights museum, state of the art," said Rasheed. "Schlank showed me the plans and models. It's pretty impressive." WunderCorp was going to keep Magic Time intact and move it cinder block by cinder block to the museum's memorial gardens along a Freedom Walk that ended up at the Troy courthouse.

"I'm sure they're going to have tour guides dressed up as authentic Negroes," said Lige.

Lovelace seemed to undergo a painful moment of self-reflection; then he took his leave of the group after offering his services to Knight as a ghostwriter for his memoirs. "My agent can get us a book deal tomorrow."

Stephen and Jimbo approached Carter with a long-haired young man whom they introduced as Tom Thames, a professor of American studies at Troy University.

"Right," said Carter. "We met at the judge's party." He was the folklorist interested in restoring Magic Time.

"Hey, Lovelace," Jimbo called to Rasheed, who was chatting up one of the pretty servers, "whatever happened to that piece you were going to do about saving Magic Time? The *Trib* could get behind Tom's idea of a retirement home for blues musicians."

Lovelace turned to face Jimbo. "WunderCorp is all over that, too. Schlank's already hired his own folklorist."

Thames was aware of the WunderCorp consultant, a former professor of his at Yale. "A lot of the blues old-timers had substance abuse problems," he explained. Instead of getting them treatment, the Yale folklorist indulged their pathologies—drugs, alcohol, wife beating. "He considers it all part of their blues mystique," said Thames.

Carter found himself suddenly intrigued by the idea of stopping WunderCorp. "What kind of tricks have you got up your sleeve, Jimbo?"

"Just something a little birdie told me," Jimbo said. "Long shot." He was still working on getting the river declared a nature preserve.

"Maybe if you can get catfish declared an endangered species, Sam Bohannon will help you out," Carter said.

"Cahtuh! Look who's here!" Carter turned to see Bradley Crawford ushering a guest toward him, sweeping along her husband in their wake. "It's the editor of the *New York Tribune*," she cried. "Haynes Wentworth, here in our little Troy."

"Carter," Wentworth said with earnest sympathy, "I hadn't realized your connection to the Shiloh case."

"Hello, Haynes," Carter said. "Here for the trial?"

Carter's editor, Ed Dennehy, had bet that Wentworth would show up in Troy at least once before the trial was over. "He can pose for a photo that may be useful someday for his memoir," Ed had said.

Wentworth lowered his baritone confidentially. "I hope your father took that piece we did on the trial in the spirit it was intended."

Carter looked at Haynes noncommittally and said, "I'm sure my father took it in the spirit it was intended."

Wentworth returned to small talk and asked Carter if he had gone back to work yet. Carter said vaguely that his editor wanted him back in the city to do a local story. He was impressed at how easily Wentworth guessed the assignment.

"If you're thinking of getting Reverend Lloyd to talk, good luck," he said, sipping his Heineken. "We've been trying to get a post-rehab interview for weeks now."

"We'll see," Carter said blandly.

Wentworth turned back to the solace of Bradley's décolletage.

"Haynes," she said, "this is Harold Bernhardt, my darling husband and an outstanding local columnist."

"I demanded that the Confederate flag be removed from the Mississippi state flag," said Bernhardt. "I was the first in the state to call for it."

"Excuse me," said Wentworth sorrowfully to Bradley's chest. "I need another drink."

Jimbo happily took Wentworth's place at Bernhardt's side to point out that the offending emblem in question was not the Confederate flag, but the battle flag. "You wouldn't recognize the flag of the Confederacy if it was shoved up your ass. Nobody would."

"It doesn't matter, Stein," said Bernhardt. "I didn't hear you 'heritage-not-hate' apologists for the Old Confederacy complaining when the Klan hijacked your flag for their ugly little purposes."

"Good point, Blowhard. But I'm just as skeptical of secret Stalinists like you, revising history on your whim in the name of public virtue. I'm not surprised you're pimping for WunderCorp in your columns."

Bradley seized upon an opportunity to shift focus. "Oh, look, y'all," she squealed. "Here comes my producer, Simon Lester, from Hollywood." The British filmmaker, in his Birkenstocks, approached gingerly, sensing a debate was under way. "Can you believe I called you my producer, Simon," Bradley said, pulling him into the circle. "This man is such a genius," she announced. "You know Carter Ransom, don't you, Simon?"

Simon smiled his guileless yellow smile. "I'm hoping to catch you for a sit-down soon." Before Carter could tell him he would be out of town, Simon said, "You must know this fellow here now, don't you?"

Standing behind Simon was the tall, handsome man Carter had seen in the courtroom earlier, wearing shades, with the graying ponytail. He looked elegantly out of context in tan Hugo Boss, his sleeves pushed up above his wrists. "Yes, we met years ago," said the man. "Hello, Carter."

"Hello, Michael." Carter felt simultaneous pleasure and dire dread.

"You know each other?" said Simon.

"Yes," said Michael, and his voice shook with emotion. "I would not be an only child today if it wasn't for Carter Ransom."

Carter's smile vanished.

"It was foolish of Sarah to come back down here after Goodman, Schwerner, and Chaney," Michael said to Carter, as if he'd waited for years to unload this observation. "She wouldn't have done it if it weren't for you. That's not an accusation, just a fact."

Carter tried to maintain his composure. "I saw your father in the city recently," he said.

"Yes, he told me."

"Michael's the executive producer on our documentary on the church bombing," explained Simon, grinning desperately.

"Hardly," said Michael. "I put them in touch with some financing."

"You're with a studio now?" asked Carter.

Simon squeezed Michael's arm. "Head of production at Warner. They made the movie of Bradley's novel."

Bernhardt interjected. "You know, if you ever decide to do a treatment on the Shiloh Church bombing case—I don't know how familiar you are with the case, but—"

Jimbo interrupted. "His sister was one of the victims, numb-nuts. Does the name Sarah Solomon ring a bell?"

Lonnie inserted himself into the group and said a little too loudly, "Well, now, this looks like the party's epicenter. What's up, Jimbo?"

"Bernhardt's going to see Doc Renfro to have his foot surgically removed from his mouth," Jimbo explained.

Michael graciously let Bernhardt off the hook. "Actually, I am thinking of the Shiloh Church case as a feature."

Carter wasn't sure he was hearing correctly. "You're thinking of doing a movie on your sister's death?" he said.

Lonnie broke in, oblivious. "Saturday night, Carter. We thought we'd take the out-of-towners to Sambo's for catfish. Right, Bradley?"

"Wouldn't it be a hoot?" she said.

"I'll be in New York Saturday," Carter said.

"What's in the goddamned city?" Lonnie demanded.

"I'm taking Josh back."

Belligerence slipped up on Lonnie like a cowl whenever he had too much to drink, and Carter always knew to retreat into a quiet solicitude in dealing with him.

"What's the matter with you, Carter?" Lonnie continued. "The editor of the *New York* goddamned *Tribune* will be there."

"Whoa, Lonnie," said Jimbo, draping his arm over his friend's shoulder. "Settle down, son."

As he gave in to Jimbo's gentle maneuvering, Carter could hear Lonnie muttering, "So he gets the sympathy vote just because he never got over his Jewish girlfriend dying. He won't have no problem getting laid. Right, Jimbo? He's already hitting on the prosecutor."

"What the hell was that all about?" Sally whispered to Carter as she followed in their wake. He had excused himself from the guests who had witnessed Lonnie's display, and he was circling through the stacks. Heading for the service entrance to make a discreet escape, Carter felt a tap on the shoulder. He turned around to face Sydney Rushton. He had an autonomic twinge of guilt, and he glanced to see if Lonnie was observing the encounter. To his relief, Jimbo and Stephen were escorting their soused friend out the front door.

"What are you doing here?" Carter said.

"I'm looking for you," she said.

"Here I am," he said. "Can I get you a glass of wine?"

"Oh, I didn't come to socialize. My bosses wouldn't look kindly on any show of partisanship."

"So what's up?"

"I'm having my usual panic attack on the eve of my star witness's testimony."

"What are you worried about? Your congressman came through for you on the stand today, didn't he?"

"Lacey Hullender is no Elijah Knight," she said. "Sometimes you don't know if your star witness will help or hurt you. Hullender is the kind of witness that trial lawyers dream of destroying on cross."

"So did you track me down to talk shop? Don't you have boyfriends for that?"

Sydney gave him an unperturbed look. "Do you think you could come back to my office to talk about something?"

Carter found himself enjoying Sydney's "panic attack." "It seems like you need a drink. I'll buy you a beer at Knotty's."

"Is that the kind of place we might be seen—by Lonnie, for instance?" Sydney said.

"Oh, so you've gotten the treatment, too," Carter said. "No. Lonnie's too much of a yuppie to go to a roadhouse dive like Knotty's anymore. The chamber of commerce might swear out a warrant for his arrest."

Sydney and Carter took separate cars to the ramshackle honky-tonk on Highway 17 south of town; it was nestled in the kudzu and scrub pines just beyond the county fairgrounds. They were the only linen jackets—his wheat-colored, hers celadon—in the fashion show of Diesel caps and Lynyrd Skynyrd T-shirts.

"Any luck with Strawberry?" Carter asked, after the waitress, a retired WAC Carter recognized from the last time he had been there—in 1985—brought them their Millers on tap.

Sydney looked at him blankly.

"Thigpen," he said. "Lawrence Thigpen."

"Oh, I don't know yet. I'm still working on that. Thanks again for contacting him for me—driving down to the coast and all."

"No big deal. You know, this is the kind of thing reporters do in their sleep."

"Yeah, well, I wish I could return the courtesy. That's really what made me find you tonight. Guilt."

"What about?"

"About what may come out tomorrow, about your father. I feel terrible."

"A girl's got to eat. I have a stake in seeing Bohannon convicted."

"Well, believe it or not, I'd like to limit the collateral damage."

"How's the evidence gathering?"

"It could be better. But then it always could be. That's why there are more famous defense attorneys than famous prosecutors."

Carter thought about that for a beat and then siad, "Got any more search warrants out? Like for the Ransom family home?"

She squinted at Carter quizzically, as if trying to figure out who his other sources were. "We had to search the Boutwell place to see if we could find any of his old Klan gear, but apparently the widow had auctioned off all his memorabilia," she said. "You know, people in the community are going to have a hard time accepting that he was even a member."

"Why do you need to exhume the body?"

Sydney looked baffled. "I've never seriously thought about that. For one thing, it would delay the trial too much."

It occurred to Carter that Lonnie might have raised the possibility of exhumation with Grayson in order to buff his role as rescuer and protector.

"You're not Sheppy's favorite person in the world," Carter said.

"How do you know?"

"Her daughter told me. We used to be close."

"Ah, your source."

Carter wondered if he detected a feline tone. "Initially I thought she didn't like you because you were from a tacky place like Birmingham."

"Well, we can't all have Glen Boutwell's stellar pedigree, now, can we," Sydney said with weary sarcasm.

Carter toasted her with his beer mug and said, "Quick on her feet."

She did not reciprocate. "Carter," she said, all seriousness. "Remember—I'm now going to be calling you last. You'll be back from New York early next week, right?"

He raised his glass to her again. For the first time in his dealings with a woman since Sarah, he felt more wanted than needed.

"Would you like another beer?" he said.

"No. I'm getting a headache." She closed her eyes and massaged the bridge of her nose.

The WAC appeared at their booth.

"I'll have another draft," Carter said, "and for the lady, a couple of Bayer." Then he turned to Sydney, lit a cigarette, and leaned back against the pew. "Seriously, why the empathy about my father? I thought that was specifically forbidden by the professional oath."

"Are we sparring, or do you really want to know?" Sydney said.

"I really want to know."

"I had a moment of truth like you're having, only mine was with my grandfather. I adored him when I was a little girl. He was a city father and all that, who could do no wrong in my eyes. He was always being written up in the local papers as a military hero in the Pacific. And then one day a real journalist comes along and prints a story about how Pops had worked the 'security' detail for the big steel companies during the thirties. Which essentially meant that he had coordinated the Klan's attacks on the union organizers who came south during the New Deal."

"Why would the Klan be going after labor?" Carter said.

Sydney explained that the unions were beginning to organize blacks and whites together at that point, and the industrialists were putting the Klan up to dirty work through intermediaries like her grandfather. "Pops personally participated in some of the attacks—you know, hitting strikers-who-happened-to-be-black upside the head with rifle butts, abducting union officials and flogging them to within an inch of their lives. They called their little adventures 'fishing expeditions.' "

"No kidding," Carter said. "Race always seems to camouflage money, doesn't it?"

Sydney had been in college up North "trying to catch the last 'vibes' of the counterculture" when she found out about her grandfather's early career. "It made me physically ill," she said. "I didn't realize how much family pride I had, and it made me just want to crawl into a hole when I went back home."

The WAC put down a beer mug in front of Carter and handed Sydney a dose of aspirin, individually wrapped in Bayer's trademark brown and yellow.

"In Birmingham, busting heads will get you a street named after you, won't it," Carter said.

Sydney studied him for a second. "It's true," she said. "No one was fazed. Not even Pops." U.S. Steel, Birmingham's major industry, had repaid her grandfather's loyalty by setting him up in business as a sort of middleman between it and the clients.

"And that's how you became the Blond Avenger," he said.

"Yes. But how did Glen Boutwell become the Grand Dragon?"

"Beats me. Return of the repressed—the call of the trailer park?" After that evening by Grayson's pool, Carter had taken some of his Faulkner off the shelf at home and reread "Barn Burning." The image that had stayed with him was old man Snopes deliberately stepping in horseshit and then smearing it across the fancy rug in the big house of his plantation boss.

"How did you know they would have aspirin?" Sydney asked.

"Damsels in distress are my specialty, even though you do not appear to have much functional familiarity with the genre."

"Thank you." She gave a minxy little smile, adding, "But the night is young." Her expression drifted. She was back to sincere eye contact. "Are you a professional knight in shining armor?"

Carter felt his head go light from the rush of emotion, and he was unable to speak for several seconds. "If I am," he said, "I seem to have failed spectacularly." He sensed himself being drawn down into the suffocating feeling of bungled responsibility, the conviction that Michael Solomon had spoken the harsh truth earlier that evening. Carter managed to find Sydney's eyes. They were limpid, brimming with tenderness and competence.

23

S YDNEY RUSHTON HAD PROCEEDED in the task of prosecuting Sam Bohannon with the systematic and relentless efficiency of a jackhammer. After three days of producing witnesses, photographs, and physical evidence to establish the crime, she was ready to bring forth the people who linked Bohannon to the bombing of Shiloh Church. Much of the testimony had already been heard the first time around, twenty years earlier. But not all.

Lewis Powell was the retired FBI agent who had originally interviewed Hugh Renfro about the night at Shiloh Church—the testimony that was not allowed by Judge Ransom in the original trial. Powell was razor thin, dressed in a dark suit and bow tie, with a high, bulbous forehead and thinning white hair. Slow-moving now, in his seventies, he walked with a cane but otherwise seemed alert and sharp.

"Mr. Powell, on or about August 6, 1965," Sydney began after swearing him in, "did you have a conversation with Hugh Renfro about the Shiloh Church bombing?"

"I did."

"Can you describe who Mr. Renfro was?"

"He was a mentally challenged man who was well known to the community."

"How old was he at the time, approximately?"

"My recollection is that he was around eighteen."

"Did you record that conversation with Mr. Renfro?"

"I did."

"Your Honor, I'd like to approach the witness."

The judge nodded, and Sydney continued. "Mr. Powell, does this tape appear to be the taped conversation you had with Hugh Renfro?"

After he ceremonially examined the label on an old-fashioned reel and affirmed that it was, Sydney entered the tape into evidence.

"Your Honor, at this time we would like to play a dub the FBI lab made of this tape for the jury," she said.

"That would be allowed." The judge glanced at Puckett, who had spent the better part of two days in pretrial arguing against the admissibility of the tape.

"Your Honor, we've made transcripts for each of the jurors to follow along. Would the bailiff hand out the transcripts?"

As the bailiff passed out pages to the jury, the judge instructed the jurors that the transcript was not itself evidence, only a listening aid.

Sydney's audiovisual people cued up the tape, and the scratchy hissing eventually produced Hugh Renfro's high-pitched singsong voice answering the questions of the much younger Special Agent Lewis Powell.

"Hugh, did you recognize anyone else of the others there at the church?"

"Yes, sir. Señor Lacey Hullender. Señor Peyton Posey." There was a pause. Carter smiled when he realized that for the interview Hugh was lapsing into his José Jiménez impression, the timorous Hispanic monotone of Bill Dana's comic persona who had been a fixture of the time on *Red Skelton* and *The Ed Sullivan Show*.

"And Coach," said Hugh's voice.

"Coach?" said Powell's voice.

"Coach Boutwell. He coach me in Little League. He was wearing a costume."

"What kind of costume?"

"Sheets. I say, 'Coach, why you dress like a ghost? He say, 'Be quiet.' "

"Was his face covered?"

"Yes. He talk through eyeholes. I know how Coach sound."

"Was there any other way you recognized him, even though he was in costume?"

Hugh did not hesitate. "His shoes. Florsheim loafers with topstitching, size ten, brown. He dress sharp. I know shoes. I know everybody shoes in town."

"What else did Coach say to you?"

"He say go back and get in truck. I ask when the fireworks."

"What made you ask about fireworks?"

"I heard Lacey and Peyton say they going to have fireworks at church. I ask Coach when they start fireworks."

"What did he say?"

"He say he'll get me a ghost suit like his if I stay in truck. He say he let me throw fire bottles if I sit in truck and watch the gas needle. Make sure it no move."

"And what happened?"

"I watch for a while, but I get tired. I see them talking in front of church. I want fireworks to start. I no like watching needle. I brung my own—cherry bombs and firecrackers, some nigger chasers. So I light a string of firecrackers with car lighter and fling it out the window."

Sydney stopped the tape at the firecrackers, before the real fireworks. As Carter listened to the rambling, incoherent testimony his father had disallowed in the first Shiloh Church trial, he wondered if the judge had really based his ruling on Hugh's unreliability. Anybody who knew Hugh would know that he was legendary locally for identifying people by their shoes, like the five-year-old boy who can deduce the make and model of a car from the flash of a taillight. So perhaps the testimony was too reliable, and Mitchell had reason to be concerned for Hugh's safety. And for Glen Boutwell's hide. Had he suppressed the evidence for Sheppy's sake? Or was the main person he was protecting himself?

After the lunch recess, the court overflowed with the biggest crowd since the trial started. The media were crammed in their corral in the balcony. Carter found a seat next to his sister in the gallery across from the press, along with the victims' families. From where he sat, he could see Sydney conferring assiduously with her colleagues, oblivious to the man sitting next to the defense table just beyond. Sam Bohannon sat motionless, hunched over in his motorized wheelchair. The faint shadow of a cannula could be seen running from his nose to his ear, tracing the curve of his hollow cheekbone before it disappeared into the wispy white strands of hair over his collar and attached to the portable oxygen unit on the back of the chair.

"The state calls Lacey Hullender to the witness stand," Sydney said with what Carter thought was theatrical casualness.

Hullender emerged from the witness room. He walked deliberately, as if uncertain of his footing. His ill-fitting gabardine suit and cheap tie made him look more like a defendant than the man designated to redeem the soul of Mississippi.

"Mr. Hullender," Sydney said after he had been sworn in, "you were a member of the White Knights of the Ku Klux Klan, were you not?"

"Yes, ma'am."

"And you served twenty years in Parchman prison for your part in the crime we are revisiting today?"

"Yes, ma'am."

Carter had never seen Lacey Hullender so meek, almost abject. He didn't trust it.

"Mr. Hullender, you pleaded not guilty in the first Shiloh Church bombing trial; yet you were convicted. Do you still feel that you are innocent?"

"No, ma'am."

"Would you tell the court why you changed your mind?"

Hullender chose his words carefully. "Because back then, the way I thought at the time, I believed I was innocent. I didn't think what we done was a crime. But that was before I got saved. I was lost and hadn't invited Jesus Christ into my life as my personal Savior." Sydney nodded for him to continue, and Hullender added, "And because we was told to plead innocent 'cause we'd never get convicted by a white jury."

"Who told you that?"

"Our lawyer. Mr. Turner." Jess Turner had been the local Klan lawyer.

"And Mr. Turner was your attorney as well as Sam Bohannon's personal lawyer?"

"Yes, ma'am."

Hullender's affect seemed strange to Carter. His answers lagged a beat behind, as if he were distracted, floating, his mind wandering; then suddenly he would snap out of it and come to himself. Lacey had always been wound tightly, and prison had taken something out of him, but Carter could not tell if this new personality was any improvement.

"Mr. Hullender, did you know Sam Bohannon before you joined the White Knights of the Ku Klux Klan?"

"Yes, ma'am. I used to mind his dogs some for him. A friend of mine worked for him raising his hog dogs, and I used to help out."

"You knew he was the Imperial Wizard of the Mississippi Klan?"

"Yes, ma'am."

"Mr. Hullender, tell the court and this jury who ordered the bombings at Shiloh Church on March 20, 1965."

"Sam Bohannon."

"And if Sam Bohannon ordered the bombing of Shiloh Church, why did you not say so before? Why didn't you name Mr. Bohannon in the first trial?"

"We didn't think it was our business to do that."

"Were you afraid of what might happen to you if you did?"

Arthur Puckett interrupted in the languid way that defense lawyers affect indifference to the state's case. "Objection," said Puckett. "Leading." The judge sustained him.

"Were you afraid of Mr. Bohannon?"

"I reckon."

"And are you still afraid?"

Hullender looked directly at Bohannon. "No, ma'am."

"Would you tell us in your own words what happened on the evening of March 20, 1965?"

Hullender rearranged himself in the chair, smoothed his hair back, and cocked his good eye toward the jury. "Me and Peyton Posey drove out to Shiloh Church in my truck, the one I hauled lumber in."

Sydney asked him to identify Posey for the jury.

"He was an acquaintance of mine in the sheriff's department who was in the Klan. We done time together for this at Parchman."

"Let it be stated for the record that in 1970 Peyton Posey was also sentenced to life in prison for the Shiloh Church bombing, along with Mr. Hullender. Mr. Posey is now deceased," said Sydney. "Proceed."

"We pulled up along with some others under some pecan trees down a ways from the church. When we got out, the Grand Dragon told us there'd been a change of plans."

Sydney interrupted Hullender to ask him to explain to the jury what the Grand Dragon is, and he described him as "like the foreman, or vice president."

He continued. "So like I says, the Grand Dragon said they changed their minds, that instead of a Code One—that was a cross-burning—Bohannon now wanted a firebombing. That was a Code Three. And he also wanted a Code Four."

"What was a Code Four?"

"A killing. We was supposed to kill Elijah Knight."

"And what happened next?"

The right side of Hullender's face twitched, the good-eye side, and he rotated his neck and shifted in his seat. He settled back and folded his hands, then dipped his head toward the jury as if he were going to tell them a bedtime story.

"The Grand Dragon opened the trunk of a car," he said, "and there was all this gasoline and bottles for Molotov cocktails. And rifles and shotguns and such. There was a commotion among the others and some questions because some was way skittish about bombing the church with people in it."

"You knew there were people inside?"

"Yes, ma'am. They was singing and carrying on. You could hear them from where we was."

"And was there any other reason to be skittish, as you put it?"

"Also because by Klan rules only Sam Bohannon could order a Code Three or Code Four. We come out there on what we thought was a Code One till the Grand Dragon changed the order."

"But you went along with the Grand Dragon's new order. Why?"

"Because he spoke for Sam Bohannon."

"Objection to leading, Your Honor."

"Sustained," said the judge.

"Did you know who the Grand Dragon was?" asked Sydney.

"At the time, no. I never seen his face. We heard he was a big deal in town. But Sam Bohannon protected his identity at all costs. He talked to the Grand Dragon, and the Grand Dragon give us the orders."

"Mr. Hullender, things seemed to go awry with your plans that night, did they not?"

"Yes, ma'am."

Hullender adjusted his tie and folded his hands and sat up primly. "Next we crossed the parking lot and lit up the cross, and the Grand Dragon shot off his shotgun in the air. The singing inside the church stopped. Peyton Posey got on the bullhorn and says to Elijah Knight to come on out—'You got one minute to step outside.' The lights inside the church went off. We waited, and there was no sound. Posey calls Elijah Knight again—'You got one minute to step outside.' Still no sound from inside the church. Posey said it again. Then from inside the church finally somebody yelled, 'Elijah Knight ain't here.'"

"And you didn't know Elijah Knight was in the hospital in Selma at the time?" asked Sydney.

"We didn't know it. We had some bad intelligence. The Grand Dragon was looking at me and Posey 'cause we was responsible for knowing. So this was a little embarrassing. But Posey won't about to let on that we screwed up. Posey says, 'He better come on out, or we'll come in there and drag him out here.' Nothing. The Grand Dragon looked at us and says, 'Are you sure he's here?' 'Positive,' said Posey. 'They lying.'"

Hullender described how the Grand Dragon signaled for him and Posey to follow him down to the front door of the sanctuary. Posey pounded on the door and stepped back and yelled again for Elijah Knight to come out.

"Then one of them, the white boy, come out the front and said, 'He ain't here,'" said Hullender.

"Is this the white boy who appeared, Daniel Johnston?" Sydney nodded to her assistant, who flashed the slide of Johnston on the screen.

"Yes, ma'am. I recognized him as one of the ones at Magic Time. Then Posey said, 'You lying,' and called him a name." Hullender looked at Sydney sheepishly. "Should I say it?"

"Go ahead."

"N-word lover."

Carter glanced at his sister, needing to share the triumph of Mississippi's much-belated reconstruction. Sydney continued to walk her witness through the escalating pandemonium. As Daniel Johnston stood facing the Klansmen, Celia Bunt had tried to escape from the church past him and was talked back in by her frightened comrades.

"All of a sudden we hear this popping sound from the pecan trees behind us," said Hullender. "Like gunfire. Lacked to scared us to death. We don't know what it is. We wonder if somebody tipped the FBI."

"Did you subsequently learn the source of the sound?"

"Hugh Renfro setting off firecrackers."

"Do you know how Mr. Renfro came to be at the church?"

Hullender said, "He had stowed away on my lumber truck."

"And you had no idea he was there?" asked Sydney.

"We discovered he'd tagged along from town when we got there, but the Grand Dragon dealt with him. Told him to stay in the truck. We didn't know he had brought fireworks."

"What happened next?"

"We panicked, thinking somebody was shooting at us, till somebody said it was Hugh. But then somebody fired a shot at us from inside the church."

"Did you see who it was?" Sydney asked.

"Nah," said Hullender. "We didn't know they had any weapons. Until the bullet winged Posey in the thigh. They was supposed to be nonviolent."

A .38 Smith & Wesson had been entered during Mizell's testimony earlier as the state's Exhibit 3. Sydney identified it as the firearm found inside the incinerated church building.

"That's when the Grand Dragon's gun went off," said Hullender.

Carter leaned forward. He realized he had never heard an eyewitness account of the shootings.

"Did he hit anyone?"

"The Johnston boy stepped in front of the colored girl to put his body between her and the Grand Dragon, and he got shot and so did she. Then all heck broke loose. We all turned our guns on them and whoever was shooting at us from the doorway."

"And what happened next?"

"The Grand Dragon opened up on the ones in the doorway and drove them back inside the church. Then he used the ax handle to bar the door."

"There was no other way out?"

"Well, I reckon some of the others got out the back door, but it wouldn't have been no help to the ones that had been shot. Then the Grand Dragon signaled the others to toss the firebombs."

Sydney paused to let the information settle in. Then she asked, "Mr. Hullender, where did you get your orders to raid Shiloh Church that night? From what individual directly?"

"I reckon that was Peyton Posey. At the time I done what Posey told me to do."

"Mr. Hullender, how did you know Mr. Posey originally?"

"He was with the sheriff's department, so most people in town knew him. Later on I learned he worked for Mr. Bohannon. He was active in the Klan, but I didn't get to know him real well till we was in prison together."

"Was it in prison that Posey told you he had heard Sam Bohannon give the order to burn the church and murder Elijah Knight?"

"Yes, ma'am."

"And why did you believe Mr. Posey?"

"Because he was in the Klan longer than me and higher up in it and was at all the important meetings. He knew all the secret inside stuff."

Sydney led Hullender through a description of the Ellis County Klan hierarchy as he understood it, and the tight-knit, paranoid management that passed out information on a need-to-know basis. Posey, the free-lancer, who worked intermittently for the police, the Klan, the FBI as an informant, and the state Sovereignty Commission, was the conduit between the brass and the ground troops, like a master sergeant over his platoon of miscreants and malcontents.

"And who sent Posey to the church that night?"

"Sam Bohannon."

"Objection, Your Honor," Puckett said wearily. "Hearsay."

"I'm going to sustain that," said the judge just as wearily.

"You got your orders from Posey," Sydney resumed. "And he got his from the Grand Dragon, who got his from the Imperial Wizard."

"Objection," Puckett called out with unprecedented insistence.

"Sustained." Judge McDonnell didn't look up.

"Did you learn the Grand Dragon's name?" asked Sydney.

Hullender then described how he and Posey heard on the radio in prison that a big, important businessman from Troy died. "That's when Posey told me he was the Grand Dragon."

"What was the businessman's name?"

"Mr. Glen Boutwell."

There was a stir and whispering among the locals in the courtroom. Hearing the name spoken by a flesh-and-blood witness seemed to affect the audience differently than the disembodied jabbering of the late Hugh Renfro. Carter saw Jimbo look at Doc Renfro next to him, but Doc just stared straight ahead, registering nothing. Pete Callahan lowered his head and stared at his lap.

"Did Posey tell you anything else about Mr. Boutwell's relationship with Mr. Bohannon?" Sydney asked.

"He said Boutwell was the one who set us up to go to prison. That we was scapegoats to protect him and Bohannon. Posey used to say, 'Ain't it funny that Bohannon didn't get convicted and the Grand Dragon—Boutwell—never even got indicted?' "

"Were you aware at the time of Mr. Boutwell's position in the community?"

"For most of us young people in town he was just known as Coach."

Carter looked over at his sister as she tried to digest what was being said.

Sydney Rushton retrieved something from the evidence table. "Mr. Hullender," she said, "have you ever seen this letter?" She handed him

State Exhibit 4. Simultaneously a copy of it was flashed on the slide screen. It was the letter sent to Magic Time on the day of the bombing, saying that Lige Knight would be dead by the time they read it.

Hullender examined it. "Did you write this letter?" Sydney asked.

"No, ma'am."

"Do you know who did?"

"Sam Bohannon."

"How do you know Sam Bohannon wrote it?"

"I saw him type it and heard him read it at his fish camp."

Sydney asked Hullender to explain why he was there.

"It was on the morning of the Saturday that the church was bombed. Posey called me up early. Woke me up. I had a bad hangover. He told me to get over to Bohannon's fish camp pronto. When I got there, him and the Grand Dragon and Bohannon was there, and Bohannon was typing up the letter. And the Grand Dragon asked me to drop it in the mail before noon, when the post office closed."

"Glen Boutwell?"

"Objection," said Puckett, and was again sustained.

"He was in his robes," said Hullender, "but it was the Grand Dragon's usual voice. He asked me to mail it. I mailed lots of stuff. Posey made the phone calls. I handled the postal."

"Do you see the man who wrote this letter in this courtroom?"

"Yes, ma'am."

"Would you point him out for the jury?"

"Yes, ma'am." He stood and pointed at Bohannon, who stared back at him levelly, with a condescending smile.

The courtroom was buzzing after Judge McDonnell called a recess. Carter ducked out in a hurry to catch a plane to take Josh back home to New York. He missed the last of Hullender's testimony, but that night he called home from the Baums', and Sally filled him in on the rest of the day's proceedings.

"Mainly more of what Posey told Hullender about Bohannon and corroborating testimony from the transcript of the earlier trial," she said.

"Nothing came out specifically about Pop?"

"No," said Sally. "How did we dodge that bullet?"

Carter asked his sister if their father had inquired about Hullender's testimony. "He muttered something about the Sovereignty Commission's general sorriness," said Sally. "Then he watched a baseball game with Willie. He just kills me with his stiff upper lip."

"What do you expect him to do? Spill his guts about his fling with Sheppy Boutwell?"

"I don't think 'fling' is the word, I'm sorry to say, Carter. God, I'm so grateful Mama's not alive to hear this."

"Don't you think she knew?"

"I can't think about it. Apparently, Sheppy's taken to her bed."

"When does the defense cross-examine Hullender?" Carter asked.

"Monday. You'll be back, right?"

"If I finish my story."

After hanging up, Carter dialed the number for the Pinehurst Hotel. He figured it was late enough for Sydney to be back in her room.

"Do I owe you one?" he asked when she picked up the phone. "Sally said Dad didn't come up in your direct after I left today."

"Oh, you made it," Sydney said. "One plane trip down, one to go." As it turned out, she didn't need to drag in the judge in order to introduce Lacey's contention that the state had not gotten the big guys. But if Puckett went into specifics of Bohannon's first trial in his cross-examination of Hullender, then she might have to bring up Mitchell's alleged role in throwing the case. "Don't break out the Millers yet," she said, "or whatever they're drinking in Manhattan these days."

"You've put your weight back on," Emily said. "You look good." She appeared relaxed, subdued, her summer tan set off by a coral silk blouse.

"Thanks," he replied. "So do you." They had arranged to meet for lunch at a favorite Italian restaurant near her office in SoHo. He had been a little apprehensive, but to Carter's relief her smile was as uncomplicated as the house pinot grigio. He gamely let down his guard.

She thanked him again for hosting her son in Mississippi, and their conversation flowed naturally from Josh's adventures in Troy to her father's keynote at the Peabody Awards ceremony. By the time they ordered coffee, he was beginning to wonder if the entire lunch would play out without their addressing the obvious.

When the cappuccinos arrived, Emily took a sip, regarded him tenderly, and said, "Carter, I don't want to add to your pressures, but I didn't want you to misinterpret my request to let Josh visit. You know how much that meant to both of us, but I also want to let you know where I am now about us."

"Sure," he said. Emily's gesture in allowing Josh to visit had somehow freed him of his obligation to her, and he felt ready to hear what she had to say. Even so, he was shocked if not surprised when she stated it bluntly.

"I know we're not going to get back together."

"Emily—" he began, looking down to compose his thoughts. He wasn't sure if what he was feeling was truly dismay.

"You may not have reached that conclusion yet, but I have. I've known for a while that if we ever were, I would have heard from you by now."

"I'm sorry, Emily, I didn't—"

"No apologies. It's been good for me to have this time apart. First, let me say that I'm glad you're going to testify in the trial. I think it'll be healthy for you to face what that girl meant to you."

Carter closed his eyes and let out his breath. "I wasn't trying to deceive you, Emily."

"I know. I don't hold that against you." She gave him a sympathetic look, as if to say he still didn't get it. "But it could never be a level playing field for me. How could I compete with a saint, a martyr, someone—maybe the love of your life—who was cut down in her prime? How could I compete with someone who never got crow's-feet or postpartum? Or figured out that there was no such thing as happily ever after?"

Carter set down his coffee. "I wanted to be with you and Josh. I told you that after the museum bombing."

"Because you thought I was gone."

"No."

"Carter, the operative words here are 'you and Josh.' Yes, *you* and Josh. The truth about us—and it's taken me a while to see this—is that what you loved was not me, but some idea of me, me and my son, to certify that you were finally a grown-up." She gave a little laugh. "It's so ironic and circular. You look to me as a way to get beyond your past, and I end up delivering you right back to it so that you truly can get beyond it. And in doing so, I lose you."

Carter stared at the entrance to the restaurant as if he expected someone to arrive to rescue him from the conversation; then he glanced down at the foam in his cup. Anywhere but into Emily's hurt eyes. For one thing, he was afraid that if he looked at her, she would see all she was saying confirmed in his eyes.

"Emily, I don't know what to say" was all he could muster.

"It was apparent early in our relationship that I wanted to have more children and you were happy just to be a stepfather." She seemed to realize that what she said was wounding Carter, but she couldn't reverse field. "Look, the only reason I can discuss this now—besides months of therapy—is because I've sort of been seeing someone."

Before responding, Carter paused to ask himself if he really wanted to know. "Who?"

"Haynes Wentworth."

Carter took a moment to recover from the blow to his ego and then fought back the urge to make his case against Wentworth. He had no standing to do so. And he wasn't surprised that Wentworth had sensed an opportunity with his exit to Mississippi and moved on it.

"I don't know where it's going," Emily said, "but Josh will need a male in his life. His dad's more involved now, but you know—that's a mixed blessing. That's one of the reasons I thought it would be nice for him to visit you."

They sat silent as Carter absorbed the information. She stared at her empty cup. Her eyes glistened, but there was a look of purposefulness that trumped tears. "I loved you, Carter. And in a way I love you even more now that I know who you really are. Because of that, I feel I need to say this to you. The reason I ultimately wasn't able to act on that love was, I was not going to let it go unrequited."

Carter looked at her blankly. He didn't quite grasp what she was saying, but he knew she was articulating something important. "Unrequit-edness" was one of his tropes, but not something he necessarily used in connection with women. His unrequitedness was bigger than romance; it was the pose of the misunderstood genius whom the world could not possibly reward adequately. Emily had sometimes tweaked him about it, calling it a form of vanity.

"Do you remember how we used to talk about the way people seem addicted to their *meshugaas*?" Emily looked at Carter imploringly. "That people like their neuroses, that we seem doomed to reenact our childhood frustrations."

Carter had spent endless hours on the couch with Dr. Abernathy in Atlanta discussing just those kinds of internal dynamics. The appeal of the familiar, the "comfort food" of neurosis, the "good ol' corn bread and black-eyed peas of childhood" was what Dr. Abernathy called them.

"The wounds that deform us emotionally when we're young. We find ways to return to them," he said.

"You told me when we first started dating that you had been in a se-ries of relationships with women," she said, "but that you were always the one who broke them up. Never the other way around."

"Until now," Carter said with a rueful smile. But she was right. Dur-ing his long bachelorhood he had gone out with lots of women, gotten involved, and been serious a few times throughout the years. But he had always managed to find the kind of woman who he knew would let him down somehow, who wasn't quite up to code. Until he met Emily.

"I think your attraction, contradictory as it might seem, is to unre-quited love."

"You think I wanted to lose Sarah?"

"No, of course not. But I think your loss of Sarah must have reiter-ated your past somehow—not that the tragedy wasn't bad enough. And I don't know what that is, Carter. Over the past few months I've gone over what I knew about you—to convince myself that I really did know you, even if you had withheld such an important part of yourself. And what I realized was that I had no concept of your mother. I didn't have a visual image. Was she blond, brunette? I didn't even know her first name."

Carter could feel himself shutting down as she spoke. The familiar lurch and grind of the gears engaging in his mechanisms of defense was what told him she was getting close to something important.

"I don't know, Carter, but the word that kept occurring to me when I thought about your relationship to your mother was 'ruthless.' It was as if you had just 'disappeared' her." Emily's voice went a little quavery. "That's a little how I felt. As if I no longer existed for you."

Carter remained quiet. "You may be onto something," he finally said. "And I know that's not very gallant of me to say."

Emily reached across the table and picked a crumb off his cuff. "Carter, I know now that it wasn't meant to be between us. But I wish this for you: that you will thank your Baptist God I didn't die in the museum and you will use that as an opportunity to let go of your self-imposed life sentence—of duty, of grief, of all that noble stoicism that we Jews find so fascinating. I know there's someone out there ready to be requited. And I wish it could have been me."

The Reverend Charles Lloyd had requested that Carter come to his Harlem apartment on Strivers Row, at 138th Street off Seventh Avenue. Carter arrived there just after four on Saturday afternoon. The clean and sober mayoral candidate, fresh out of rehab, greeted him at the door of the spacious brownstone wearing not his clerical collar but green jogging sweats and a surprisingly warm smile. "Carter Ransom," he said. He looked skeletally thin but more relaxed than he ever had in news photos or at press conferences. Losing the facial hair made his face appear young, the flecks of gray in his modified Afro the main indication of creeping middle age. His eyes were old; all the Movement survivors' were.

"How's Mississippi treating you?" he asked.

"Can't complain, Reverend." It seemed surreal to be exchanging pleasantries with someone who understood how charged that question would have been thirty years ago. Carter's suspicion of Lloyd's motives, the fact they had never gotten along, and his basic dislike for the man now seemed anachronistic if not trivial, up against the fact that there were not many people in the world who shared their history.

Lloyd looked at Carter quizzically, as if trying to discern if there was any irony in the honorific. "Come on, Ransom, call me Charlie," he said, escorting Carter through the entrance hall and into the sumptuous high-ceilinged living room. He indicated the cup and saucer balanced in his hand and asked, "Hot tea?"

"No, thanks," said Carter. He took in the spacious walls adorned with an array of African art objects, bright canvases, and colorful woven tapestries. He walked over to the bookcases lining one wall; Ellison, Wright, Baldwin, Hurston, Hughes, and Morrison were tastefully interspersed with carved wooden totems and sculptures of teak and ivory.

"I'm new to it myself," said Charlie, turning toward the modern stainless steel kitchen that opened off the living room. "It's one of my 'substitute' oral fixations now that I'm off the hard stuff."

Carter sensed that no one else was in the apartment, not even the usual aides-de-camp that shadowed politicians of Charlie's aspirations like suckerfish trailing in the wake of great whites. He wondered if Charlie's wife was still with him after the tabloid saga about his drug-dealer mistress.

"Did your editor tell you I requested you for this inquisition?" Charlie called from the kitchen.

"I must say I was a little surprised." Carter was examining a Romare Bearden print over the fireplace. "I haven't been exactly supportive of your political ambitions in my columns."

The teakettle back in the kitchen began to whistle. "Relax, Ransom," Charlie said. "We may disagree, but you've always been fair, even when you were a little pissant reporter in Mississippi. I deserved some of the flak I got. I brought it on myself. If I'm going to turn all that around in time for the election, I figure I should start with somebody in the media who everybody knows likes to stick it to me." Carter entered the kitchen as Charlie poured the steaming water into a cup over a tea bag, then wrapped the string tightly to secure the bag to the spoon like a heretic to the stake. Watching Charlie stir in lemon and honey with sacramental devotion, Carter supposed the ritualistic deliberation was a remnant from his freebasing days. "Besides," Charlie said, "we go back a ways."

Carter stared out the French doors off the kitchen to a terrace over-looking a housing project. Charlie continued dunking his tea bag. "I can't believe they reopened the Shiloh case," he said. "I never thought I'd see the day that bastard Bohannon would be held accountable."

"None of us did," said Carter, turning to face Charlie Lloyd and head off any bonding over mutual enemies. Nor did he generally feel like engaging in any heart-to-hearts about Shiloh. "So how does it feel to be out of rehab, Reverend?" he asked, reaching inside his jacket for his notebook.

"Taking it one day at a time," Charlie answered, ignoring the abruptness of the change of subject. "Every day's a struggle. I'm sure I don't have to tell you about that."

Again, Carter felt Charlie's search for common ground between them. He let the comment pass.

"You may not believe this," Charlie continued, undeterred, "but I al-ways admired you, Ransom. Even though I knew you didn't care for me. Even back in Mississippi. I guess that would make sense, though. I had a crush on Sarah. She wouldn't give me the time of day. When she took up with you back then, it was hard for a brother like me to swallow. Then Shiloh Church." He poured more honey into his cup. "Last spring, when I was in the middle of my 'troubles' and I saw your columns on the museum bombing . . ." He shook his head. "Then you went missing af-ter that. Even through my crack haze I was able to put two and two to-gether."

Charlie's stabs at reconciliation were all the more unsettling for seeming sincere. And Carter knew from friends who had struggled with addiction back in the early eighties about the horrors of cocaine detox. "Why do you think you got into drugs?" he asked.

Charlie looked at him questioningly. "You still cut to the chase, don't you, Ransom?"

"That's what the voters are going to want to know," Carter said.

Charlie sipped his tea. Then pulled a chair up to the counter and of-fered Carter a seat. "So I guess you think this is just part of my reper-toire—opening up to you like this?"

"I think it's shrewd. Eight weeks until the election, taking the bull by the horns, putting your own spin on the story. People will forgive politicians their foibles as long as there's a genuine confession—and repentance. They don't like being played."

Charlie shook his head and grinned, staring down at the cup in his hand.

"What?" Carter asked.

"Back in Mississippi, when you were writing your stories and we were getting our heads busted and people were getting killed, who would have thought things would turn out this way? Me and you sitting here for a campaign interview. Me a minister, for starters."

"I got to admit I was a little taken aback by the clerical collar at your first press conference," Carter said, smiling for the first time.

"So was I," said Charlie. "But I came late to some kind of faith. It wasn't like Lige and Randall, some of the others." He sniffed. "There was no way I was going to fall for all that God talk back then."

He told Carter something of his life since Mississippi, how he had slipped into a depression after the assassination of Dr. King, the man he had criticized so flippantly. As the Movement unraveled, he had felt rudderless through years of what felt like futile social activism—running community programs, registering people to vote with little resistance but their own. He had finally gone to law school, then dropped out. A decade-long tailspin was reversed by a lucrative stint as a Popeyes chicken franchise owner in the early eighties. The money he made allowed him to enter the ministry in search of some world that needed saving, but it also supported an expensive cocaine habit. Nevertheless, with a few well-chosen high-profile "community" battles, he parlayed his congregation into one of those political constituencies that swing elections.

"So why do you think you've had these struggles?" Carter asked.

Charlie looked interested in the question. "I don't want to say anything that sounds like I'm making excuses, because I'm not. But I think, for all the romanticization of the sixties—our storied youth and all that—the truth is that a lot of us were robbed of our childhoods, and some of us have been trying to make up for it ever since. I know I have."

Carter exhaled, not unsympathetically.

"How old were we back then?" Charlie asked. "Early twenties?

That's when you ought to be sowing your wild oats, drinking and carousing, being carefree and irresponsible, not wrestling with the powers and principalities."

"So you think you've been making up for your lost adolescence."

"Somewhat. That's not the whole story. I've got my personal demons. And I know a lot of crackheads who don't need an exalted excuse like that to throw their lives away. I just know I found it a whole lot easier to live life as a crusade than the way it's been since."

Carter jotted something in his notebook. "You sort of experienced life the opposite of the way it usually goes. You know that line from T. S. Eliot: 'We had the experience but missed the meaning.' It was hard to miss the meaning of what we—you—were doing."

Charlie sipped his tea. "I don't know about Eliot, but life's a helluva lot easier when you've got an enemy, a 'big problem' out there to define you. 'The Man,'" he said, shivering his voice melodramatically. "Or now, for me, an election. Then, it's like a video game, and you can just fire away at the alien invaders and get lost in the battle, never stopping to grapple with yourself."

Charlie Lloyd sounded more contrite and thoughtful than Carter had expected. Ultimately, it had been his own "demons" that brought him to his knees rather than the nightsticks he had so cagily avoided during the Movement.

"I never thought I'd say I missed Mississippi," Charlie continued, "but I've got to admit, life's been a little dull ever since. I know I've been looking to recapture that freedom high my whole life. Politics is the closest I've come to it. And believe me, it's a pale imitation."

He got up from the counter and led Carter down a hallway and up a stairwell to his study off the second-floor landing. There were shelves of books, walls filled with campaign posters, and pictures of Lloyd with black politicians and with Stokely Carmichael, Adam Clayton Powell, Muhammad Ali. Charlie picked up one of the photographs in a frame on his desk and handed it over. Carter's heart stopped when he saw it. It was from that day of the picnic at Naked Tail. Sarah, Celia, Randall, Danny, Dexter, and Charlie with the football. Jimbo had taken it with Randall's camera. Charlie sighed elaborately as Carter, fearing the onset of tears, examined the photograph. "That was one of the happiest days of my life," Lloyd said.

"I'd never have guessed," Carter said. Then he smiled. "I didn't realize you finally got the station you were looking for on that transistor radio."

"Would you have guessed I'd be the only one in that picture from Magic Time who survived?"

Carter looked at the photo again. "Survivor's guilt," he said. "There's a reason to take drugs."

"I do know that they were all better than me," Charlie said. "Every one of them in that picture. I didn't deserve to carry their laundry." He took the photo from Carter and stared at it. "I wish I could be there to see that bastard Bohannon get prosecuted for murder," he said.

"Why don't you come down for closing arguments?"

Charlie looked at Carter as if to confirm that the invitation was sincere. Then he set the photo back on his desk and said, "I saved a lot of souvenirs from that time. I'm a bit of a pack rat. I've got all kinds of memorabilia." He pointed to file cabinets lining one wall. "The archives," he said. He opened one of the drawers and removed a folder. He flipped through it and handed Carter a mimeographed sheet. It was a copy of *The Klan Ledger*, like the one Strawberry had shown him. Carter read the lunatic headlines on the front page, so bizarrely out of place in this Harlem apartment.

"I kept it all," said Charlie. "Here's my Movement papers. All organized by year and campaign. Freedom Rides, Mississippi Summer project, Magic Time, Selma. Someday I'll donate all this to Howard University or the King Center. That is, if I can stand to part with any of it. I've got tons of clippings, letters, papers, write-ups, leaflets, memos."

Watching Charlie Lloyd flip through file folders of untold historical value, Carter thought back to how they had all smirked at his habit of self-commemoration. "I guess you finally cleaned your clutter out of Sarah's office at Magic Time."

"I even kept the hate mail we got at Scarborough's."

"You've got that?"

"Well, after the bombing, the FBI took those letters." Charlie riffled through the file. "Most of what's in this folder is from later in Hattiesburg. Remember the last letter they sent threatening Lige? I'm the one who picked it up at Scarborough's when we all rushed to Troy after the bombing."

"That was State Exhibit Four, I think, in the trial."

"Well, they got the letter, but . . ." He held up a soiled yellow envelope addressed to "Knight's Coon School c/o Scarborough's Grocery." Carter took it and examined the postmark. Troy, Mississippi. March 20, 1965. The day of the Shiloh Church bombing. Scrawled on the back of the envelope in faded pencil were the words "No More Teacher's Dirty Looks."

Charlie explained, "When the FBI was collecting evidence after the bombing, I turned over the letter to them, but I couldn't find the envelope. I found it later in the pocket of a jacket I left in Atlanta. I figured if it was important, they'd come back looking for it."

Carter stared at the envelope. "I wonder if you'd mind if I borrowed this from you, Charlie. I'd like to show it to the prosecutor."

"Sure, if it would help nail Bohannon. Nothing I'd like better. But what about the interview?"

Carter made true eye contact with Charlie Lloyd for the first time that afternoon. He smiled. "This was the interview."

24

C ARTER WAS BACK HOME by Monday morning, in time to hear
Sam Bohannon's attorney, Arthur Puckett, begin his assault on
Lacey Hullender's credibility. Like a paunchy archangel ticking off a list
of cardinal offenses, Puckett questioned Hullender on his lengthy rap
sheet—from arrests for childhood petty larceny, including bicycle theft
in the sixth grade, to teenage armed robbery, to felony assault and murder. He inquired about other Klan crimes Hullender had been connected with, even the death threats he had sent to Judge Ransom from
Parchman prison. The picture he painted of Hullender was of a liar, a
thief, a murderer, and a criminal sociopath. When confronted with his
legacy of brutality and deceit, Lacey Hullender was serene in his defense. "Everything you say about me is true," he agreed. "I was all those
things you said I was. I was a sinner, but all that is forgiven. It don't matter what you think about me. It just matters what God thinks."

Through his clever cross-examination of Hullender, Puckett was
also able to lay waste to the memory of Peyton Posey, whose record of
treachery was as impressive and well documented as Hullender's. Even
some observers in the courtroom who were already familiar with his
multifaceted career let out gasps when Hullender mentioned under

Puckett's questioning that Posey had also helped the FBI wiretap his buddies in the Klan, including Sam Bohannon.

As Carter read it, Puckett's emerging defense strategy was two-pronged: to discredit Hullender's and Posey's claims against Bohannon, and to suggest that it was Glen Boutwell alone who had masterminded that night's mayhem by Unit Four of the White Knights of the Ku Klux Klan. Not only was Boutwell, as a heretofore unknown suspect, a convenient scapegoat; he possessed the added allure of being dead.

So while Sydney Rushton was working hard to link Bohannon to the crime through his right-hand man, Puckett sought to stop the buck at Boutwell. His simple goal was to establish Bohannon's alibi and to suggest that the Shiloh Church raid was a rogue operation conceived and orchestrated by Grand Dragon Glen Boutwell without the knowledge of Imperial Wizard Sam Bohannon. According to Puckett, the Grand Dragon was the power behind the throne, authorized to act without Bohannon's go-ahead. Though the lawyer conceded that his client was no Mother Teresa, he argued that Bohannon was not responsible for the crime, was moreover out of the county on the night it ocurred. By suggesting a broken chain of command, Puckett portrayed Bohannon as a hands-off macro-manager who didn't know what his right hand was doing. All that was required of the defense was to raise a reasonable doubt in the minds of the jurors.

The judge adjourned court early that day at the state's request so that Sydney could figure out how to adjust her game plan to include the present Carter had brought back to her from New York. And apparently the defense strategy had spared the Ransom family. Puckett had decided not to revisit the first trial in his takedown of Hullender, and Sydney had not needed to bring up Mitchell's role in it on redirect. As she dropped the files into her briefcase, her face was unreadable.

Carter had somewhat reluctantly agreed to join Stephen aboard Jimbo's modified Montauk seventeen-foot runabout Boston Whaler for what was billed as a cocktail cruise on the Little Chickasaw. When they met late in the afternoon at the Front Street marina, Carter was surprised to find Grayson Boutwell on board, helping Stephen set out a picnic basket of boiled shrimp, pepper jelly and cream cheese, and French bread. "We asked Grayson to come along and help civilize this little outing," said Stephen.

"Hi," said Carter, kissing Grayson somewhat formally on the cheek. He had not seen her since that night he returned from the coast. He was curious as to how she was holding up after Hullender's testimony, but he sensed that ignoring the subject would be the best solace. "What's with the sound system?" Carter asked, indicating the amplifier and gigantic speakers taking up deck space.

"You'll see," Jimbo said as he cast off the lines from the dock and maneuvered the sleek new craft onto the river. "I borrowed my shop's floor models."

The afternoon sun danced on the water, and the Boston Whaler's flat bottom slapped the waves as Jimbo wound the ninety-horsepower Johnson out of the marina and onto the gently moving Chickasaw. Carter sat on the other side of the console from the starboard pilot seat, facing Stephen and Grayson, who were in the aft bench seats. Stephen looked tanned and happy. Grayson's sun-flecked brown hair was pulled back in a pink silk scarf that whipped and snapped in the breeze along with the American flag unfurled across the bow. The wind pressed her blouse against the soft curves of her chest. Her sunglasses hid her eyes, but her smile conveyed relief to be out. "Why didn't Lonnie come along?" she asked.

"I think he's embarrassed about what happened at Sally's party," said Stephen.

Jimbo snorted. "If he's going to stay home every time he's an asshole, he'll never get to work on that tan."

"Wait'll he hears you and Carter were here together, Grayson," said Stephen.

Carter looked off at the receding shoreline. The monitoring of his alleged love life was wearing thin.

Jimbo cut the engine, and his craft drifted across the sandbar into the cove at Naked Tail. The sun had reached the tree line, and the late afternoon palette was muted in the shadows along the shore. The lagoon was inviting in September, just past the sun-sapped apathy of summer.

"What are we looking for?" Stephen asked, raising the binoculars.

"*Picoides borealis,*" Jimbo answered, setting up the two large speakers on the fish chest in the bow of the boat, facing the shore.

"Say what?" Grayson asked.

"Red-cockaded woodpecker," said Jimbo. He fumbled with the cassette and inserted it into the tape deck hooked up to the amp and speakers.

"Are you sure it's here?" Stephen said.

"No. But it can't hurt to try to find out. I've been out here several times this past week in the early morning. Now I want to try it at sundown." He pointed to the cassette. "A friend of mine, an ornithologist with the Audubon Society, lent me this copy of a recording made from an Edison wax cylinder." He switched on the boom box and punched the play button. "Shhh. Listen." The noise emanating from the speakers was the drumming sound, the unmistakable signature of a woodpecker, punctuated momentarily by a harsh, discordant cry. "*Yank yank,*" followed by a "*srrrripp*" sound, boomed over the cove and into the trees. It had been recorded on a loop, and Jimbo let it play several times, then turned it off. They looked at the stand of pines along the shore and listened, but the only sound returned was the quarreling of sparrows and jays and the lapping of water against the hull of the boat.

"Remind me again why we're looking for Woody Woodpecker," said Stephen.

"Shhh," said Jimbo. He rewound the tape and punched the play button, and the ancient recorded call of the red-cockaded woodpecker echoed across the lagoon. Still no reply. Jimbo turned to his guests and explained, "It's our only hope to stop WunderCorp. If we can prove that this is the natural habitat of a rare species thought to be extinct, we might be able to get the area declared a nature preserve."

"Jimbo, we spotted that bird twenty-five years ago," said Carter. "What makes you think it would still be here?"

"The roosting and nesting cavities they make in pine can be used by generations of red-cockadeds, some for forty to fifty years. They probably retreated here in the first place because of all the logging."

"I don't understand why WunderCorp needs so much land," said Grayson. "Their manufacturing facility couldn't take up all that much room. Why'd they have to buy up half the county?"

"Probably so they can do what they want without having to hassle with neighbors over mineral rights and easements and rights-of-way," said Carter.

"Why don't you look into that, Mr. Investigative Reporter?" said Jimbo.

"Hey, can't we just relax and enjoy the river?" said Carter. "This all seems pretty far-fetched."

They sat back and drank their wine and watched Jimbo go on intensely about his experiment, replaying the recording a number of times. After a while, even he grew discouraged, and they gave up on woodpeckers and sat talking and snacking on boiled Gulf shrimp. The sun sank far below the ridge of the treetops above the lagoon.

Grayson patted her brow with her napkin. "Mississippi," she said. "It's still warm even though the sun's gone down."

"Welcome home," said Jimbo.

"Let's go swimming," Stephen said.

"I didn't bring a suit," said Grayson.

"We can go skinny-dipping," said Jimbo with a lascivious grin. "Like the old days."

"I'm game," said Grayson. She looked at Carter.

"Last one in is a rotten egg," said Jimbo. He stripped off his shorts and dived off the bow beyond the sandbar, his hairy backside disappearing beneath the water. "Not as cold as it used to be," he said when he surfaced.

Stephen followed, and Grayson ducked behind the console, reappearing wrapped in a towel. "No peeking," she said to no one in particular, strategically dropping the towel as she slipped over the railing on the side of the boat opposite the other swimmers. "It feels refreshing," she said when she came up, pushing her hair out of her eyes. "Are you coming in, Carter?" For some reason, his usual enthusiasm for the water had deserted him.

"Come on in, Carter," shouted Stephen. "The water's a perfect temperature."

"I'll pass," said Carter. Something felt off to him.

Jimbo hooted. "Carter Ransom, you chickenshit. What's come over you, boy?"

Carter stared at the trees beyond the promontory. Above them the moon hung like a mirror in the sky. "I'm just not feeling aquatic today."

Grayson treaded water as she listened to their exhortations and finally turned away from their exchange, but not before Carter caught the disappointment edging her eyes. The awkwardness did not end until the bathers emerged from the water, dried off, and put their clothes back on.

"So this is Naked Tail," said Grayson, teeth chattering. She hugged her knees to her chest, stared at the lagoon in the twilight, and sipped her wine. "I've heard a lot about it, but have never been up here before. I think Daddy used to go hunting for wild boar somewhere in these parts."

"No, that's further upriver," said Jimbo. "Beyond Bohannon's fish camp, where the Little Chickasaw opens out into Lake Juniper in one direction and the Bogue Homa swamp in the other."

"I've never been up there either," said Grayson.

"Come on, I'll show you," said Jimbo, setting the speakers and sound system down in the hull. He returned to the console and fired up the engine, slowly letting out on the throttle, and swung the boat around in a wide circle as they headed upriver. "Doc Renfro and I used to go up there quail hunting." Jimbo was shouting now to be heard over the motor. "And we hunted boar with Coach Boutwell once in the Bogue Homa."

After a mile or two, at the point where the river opened up into the lake, the Bohannon fish camp appeared like a freighter on the horizon, a ramshackle, low-slung building, not much more than a weather-beaten collection of clapboard, pilings, whitewash, and rusted tin roofing, now dark and deserted in the moonlight. Jimbo cut the engine, and they drifted about fifty yards from shore past the small abandoned marina until they could see the dog pens in the shadows. Beyond a series of wooden outbuildings were eight-foot chain-link fences with razor wire around the top.

Jimbo lowered his voice. "This is where everybody met before the wild boar hunts."

Grayson's mouth tightened. "I hated it when Daddy would come back from those hog hunts covered with blood."

"They don't hunt hogs with guns," said Jimbo, oblivious to Grayson's sensitivities. "Just long knives, which, on one hand, gives the hog a fighting chance. But it's pretty bloody. You have to kill it by sticking the knife in its guzzle."

"Guzzle?" Stephen said distastefully.

"Where the Adam's apple would be, if the hog had one. Not a slice of the throat, but a quick, deep jab." Jimbo imitated the thrust. "Same way you kill a goat before you dress it. Hit the artery, and a stream of blood shoots out."

They all groaned.

Jimbo shrugged. "It's supposed to be more humane. The knives look like the ones the SS wore in Germany. Long and sharp. Your daddy wore his in a pouch on his belt, Grayson. Anyway, the hogs can swim, so you sometimes have to chase them across the river. If they turn on you there in the water, you're in trouble."

Jimbo proceeded to tell them what it was like on the boar hunts, the importance of the dogs Bohannon raised. "You usually have a little fice—like a tough little Jack Russell—to worry the hog, bite it around the face, the way a mongoose worries a snake. While it's distracting the hog, the other dogs go into action—and never walkers or hounds or beagles. Boar hunters use pit bulls and curs, like Ole Yeller. They don't have the big jaws, but they're used for their bravery and smarts. If you have a dog that's cowardly, the other dogs will back off and the hog will get the upper hand, usually a big old boar with tusks, who can kill a dog or a man. The curs go in and the fice, then the bulldogs that are called catch dogs. The 'ass dogs' go for the rear of the hog and the 'nose dogs' for the front, and they get a grip and hang on till the hunter wades in and sticks him in the guzzle." He paused for a swig of the beer he had taken from the cooler, his eyes alive with enthusiasm. "Those catch dogs are so tenacious that sometimes you have to crack open their jaws with a stick to make them let go. Or even sedate them."

Grayson shuddered.

Carter said, "Sport of kings."

"Bohannon's prime hog dog was a white pit bull named Samson," Jimbo continued. "That was one mean dog. He gave Coach one of the pups Samson sired."

"Sounds like the one Bohannon has now," said Carter.

"That's a descendant of Samson, but just as mean. He names them all Samson."

"Lovely tradition," said Grayson.

"Your daddy sure knew what he was doing, especially with the dogs. He kept his out here at Bohannon's kennels."

Again, Jimbo's heedlessness caused Carter and Stephen to shift in their seats, but Grayson seemed unfazed. "He must have learned all that growing up," she said.

Jimbo shook his head in sympathy. "On that hunting trip, your daddy talked some about the turpentine camp he grew up in. Bleeding the sap from pine trees for turpentine and resin was hard, shitty work. It was like peonage in those camps, for whites as well as blacks—just a step up from slavery. Coach told about the time during the Depression when the Communists came down and tried to organize."

"Communists?" Grayson said skeptically.

"You mean there were Communists in Mississippi before the evil red menace of the civil rights movement?" said Stephen. "I thought the Communists were just a figment of the late great Senator Eastland's fevered imagination."

Jimbo squinted. "It's been a while, but as I recall, Coach said his father was a union man. He lost his job in the turpentine camps because of joining. Folks don't realize the South was fertile ground for labor organizers and Communists in those days. Your daddy said he and his brothers were punished for leafleting for the union. That's how his brother lost his arm."

"No," said Grayson. "Uncle Jack lost his arm in a sawmill accident."

"Your daddy said it was no accident. Company thugs did it. He still sounded bitter about it. Those timber barons were rough men. They weren't about to let the union get a foothold."

"Daddy always had a soft spot for the working poor," said Grayson. "Whenever he heard they were laying off men at Graysonite, he'd bring them over to work on the house, landscaping or painting."

"So that's how Grayburn became such a showplace," said Stephen.

Grayson laughed. "He couldn't stand to see them out of work. So he just kept adding patios and terracing."

"What gets me," said Jimbo, "is how the children of those left-wing union men could become such virulent racists."

Grayson had begun to snuffle. Carter thought about Sydney, and how her union-fighting grandfather's exploits had turned her into a crusader.

"I'm sorry, Grayson," Jimbo said. "I wasn't referring to Coach."

"No, it's all true," she said, patting at her eyes with a cocktail napkin. "At least according to Lacey Hullender."

"You weren't in court today," said Stephen, "but Bohannon's lawyer Puckett cast some serious doubt on Hullender's credibility."

"It doesn't matter," she replied. "Hullender's done his damage. But how can anyone listen to someone like that?"

"He's found Jay-ee-zus," said Jimbo. "But who knows, maybe he's just using our Lord and Savior Jesus Christ." He shushed himself. "Shhh. I thought I heard something." He shone his flashlight on the docks but saw nothing. "The dogs have been awfully quiet. We used to come up here frog gigging, and any little thing would set them off. Maybe he moved them."

"This is where they say Daddy had the meetings with Bohannon," Grayson said meekly.

"Well, like I said, this is where everybody had to come to pick up their dogs," Jimbo said.

"It's where they made plans to kill Lige," Carter said, "and burn Shiloh Church."

"Boys of Troy," Jimbo said suddenly, steering the conversation back from treacherous shoals. "I feel a hymn coming on." He turned to Carter and Stephen and raised his beer can.

"You'll wake Bohannon," said Carter.

"Nobody's in there. Come on, let's show them dogs what we got. '*So sings my soooooul,*'" Jimbo began, and Carter and Stephen both dutifully filled out their harmony parts. "'*My Savior God, to Theeeeee . . .*'" As their voices lifted over the water, dogs moaned in answer. from the blackness of the pens.

"'*How great Thou arrrrrt . . .*'" their voices boomed as Stephen and Jimbo's high harmonies swooped over Carter's baritone. "'*HOW GREAT THOU ART!*'"

From the pens the dogs barked a descant, their howls echoing across the lake. Suddenly a floodlight came on at the dock. "Holy shit," cried Jimbo. "I thought nobody was out here during the off-season except to feed the dogs." He started up the engine, made a wide sweep into the lake, and headed down the river.

Carter looked back and thought he saw someone moving on the dock in the moonlight. From a window in the abandoned restaurant overlooking the river, a cigarette lighter flared.

When Carter got home that night, the slight adolescent buzz he felt from the boating escapade flattened as soon as he found a message from Sally on the kitchen counter. Sam Bohannon's lawyer had called and left his number. Carter reached Arthur Puckett at his room at the Pinehurst. Puckett told Carter that Sam Bohannon had requested a meeting.

"What for?" Carter asked, immediately wary.

"I don't know," Puckett replied. "My client simply asked me to deliver this request. He'd like you to meet him tomorrow evening after court lets out."

"Arthur, I doubt whether you got to where you can command the fees you do by letting your clients talk to reporters without knowing what they're going to say."

"Maybe he has nothing to hide." Ah, thought Carter, always on the job, as the great Southern lawyers inevitably are. "He wants you to meet him at his fish camp up on the river, where he's staying. He's on oxygen, so he hopes you won't mind coming to him. Do you need directions?"

"I know where it is," Carter replied.

"Frankly, I don't approve," said Puckett.

Carter decided to let it pass. Knowing Bohannon, he figured Puckett might be telling the truth. "Is this an interview?"

"He says it's personal."

"I don't understand."

"He told me to tell you he wants to talk to you about your father."

Carter held his breath for a second. "What about him?"

"I don't know. I'm just relaying the message. He insisted on seeing you alone. If you're worried about safety—"

"No, it's not that," Carter said, and strangely enough, it wasn't. The thing about criminals of Bohannon's ilk was that they weren't a danger to the community that had granted them the tacit permission to commit the crime.

"If you'd like me to tell him you're unavailable—"

"No. I'll be there."

Sydney Rushton had already presented the forensics portion of her case, having introduced expert witnesses on the causes of the deaths, fingerprint analyses of the weapons, and autopsy reports by the medical examiner. The next morning the judge sent the jury out while she argued for submitting her newest evidence as an addendum to State's Exhibit Number 4. "Your Honor, the state has located the missing original envelope in which the threat was mailed to Scarborough's grocery on the day of the Shiloh Church massacre. We apologize to the court for not presenting it earlier, but this information came to light a few days after we started the trial. We have sent it to the lab and are waiting for the DNA results."

"Objection, Your Honor." Arthur Puckett stood and spoke with his eyebrows raised condescendingly at Sydney. "The defense has not had an opportunity to examine such evidence."

Carter knew that Sydney's use of the envelope from Charlie Lloyd's archives would be controversial. She was counting on new DNA technology to link the letter to Bohannon through analysis of the saliva on the stamp. The judge called Sydney and Puckett into his chambers. When they emerged from the conference after half an hour, Carter could tell that Sydney had been thwarted. Judges sometimes divvied up the spoils between prosecution and defense on close calls, and Sydney had won the main pretrial victory, over the admissibility of an FBI wiretap that predated federal wiretap laws. There was a fierce set to her jaw.

"Put 'em back in the box," Judge McDonnell said, to summon the jurors.

After they had taken their seats, Sydney said, "Your Honor, the state will now recall agent Lewis Powell to the stand."

Judge McDonnell said, "Agent Powell, we will remind you that you are still under oath. Proceed."

Powell, in his dark suit and bow tie, with wispy strands of white hair over a high forehead that gave him the appearance of an amiable lightbulb, moved to the stand slowly, but this time without his cane.

Sydney had dropped the daughterly demeanor she had shown in her earlier questioning of Powell. "Mr. Powell, at the time you served as a special agent, did the Federal Bureau of Investigation ever tap Mr. Bohannon's phone?"

"Yes, ma'am."

"Do you remember when the wiretap was initiated?"

"After the disappearance of Schwerner, Goodman, and Chaney."

"Did you install the wiretap yourself?"

"No, ma'am."

"Who did?"

"One of our freelance field operatives."

"Did you know his name?"

"Yes, ma'am. He was a Troy sheriff's deputy named Peyton Posey."

"How long did Mr. Posey work for the FBI before the Shiloh Church attack?"

"Several months. Maybe a year."

"So was Peyton Posey working undercover for the FBI on the night the attack was planned?"

"Yes'm. He was supposed to report all activities."

"Did he report the planned attack on Shiloh Church?"

"No, ma'am. That's the reason we let him go later. He was unreliable."

"Was he still working for the FBI on the night he participated in the attack on Shiloh Church?"

"Yes, ma'am. I'm afraid so."

"He was still on the FBI payroll as a paid informant while murdering civil rights workers?"

Powell did not wince. "Like I said, he was unreliable."

Laughter erupted in the courtroom. The judge pounded his gavel for order while Puckett lofted a halfhearted objection.

Sydney, looking mildly irritated at the commotion, signaled for her assistant to hand out another sheet to the jury. "Mr. Powell, the state is going to play an FBI recording of a telephone conversation that took place between Glen Boutwell and Sam Bohannon on March 10, 1965, ten days before the bombing. I will ask the jurors to follow along on their transcript."

The courtroom fell silent as everyone again strained to make out the words on the rough tape recording.

"Hello?"

"Hey, it's Sambo. Just wanted to let you know, Mr. Boutwell, that we are planning another hunting trip right soon."

"Is that right?"

"Yeah, I been trying to get organized around here. You know, the season's picking up again after all that business over in Alabama."

"So I hear."

"I just wanted to let you know I got a mongrel you said you might be interested in."

"What kind?"

"Black-mouth cur. I'm thinking it might need some special attention. It's been foaming at the mouth, stirring up trouble with the other mutts. I think I'm going to have to put it down."

"He's the alpha. Take care of him, and the others will just back off," said Glen Boutwell's voice.

"Can you take care of it?" Bohannon asked.

"Might need some help. If you can round up the others."

"I'll see what I can do. When's the hunting party?"

"Saturday night," said Boutwell. "The twentieth. Twenty-one hundred hours."

Sydney's assistant shut off the recording.

Sydney then verified that it was FBI practice for agents to take down license plate numbers at Klan rallies and meetings and that Powell himself had been monitoring Bohannon's fish camp on the night of March 16, six days after the taped conversation and four days before the church bombing. She entered as evidence an FBI list of tag numbers Powell had collected, which he confirmed was in his handwriting.

"Would you read the license number of the Pontiac Firebird here at the top?" She handed him the list.

He read, " 'Mississippi. 15-6832. Nineteen sixty-five. Ellis County' "

"And according to the 1965 State of Mississippi Department of Motor Vehicles records, to whom did that license number belong?"

"Mr. Glen Boutwell," said Powell.

There was a murmur in the courtroom.

"Thank you, Mr. Powell. That is all," Sydney said, and Powell stepped down.

Sydney returned with her folders to the defense table. She and one of her assistants consulted briefly. Then she announced, "The state calls Lawrence Thigpen." Carter was surprised, not having expected Strawberry to consent to testify. He wondered if Sydney had had to subpoena him.

Strawberry walked to the stand stoop-shouldered, eyes straight ahead, though he couldn't help glance at Bohannon—seeking forgiveness, Carter assumed. Bohannon showed no reaction, maintaining the expressionless stare Carter had seen every day since the trial started.

"Mr. Thigpen," Sydney said after he had been sworn in, "were you present at the Shiloh Baptist Church on the night of March 20, 1965?"

"Yes, ma'am."

"Were you a member of the White Knights of the Ku Klux Klan?"

"No, ma'am. Not official. I guess you could say I was honorary. I worked for Mr. Bohannon taking care of his dogs and such."

"Would you describe Sam Bohannon as a friend?"

The witness seemed to ponder the question for a moment before saying, "He was like a daddy to me."

"You were not an official member of the White Knights," Sydney continued swiftly, not allowing the emotion to land, "but you went along that night?"

"Yes, ma'am."

"Now, Mr. Thigpen, I am going to play for you the tape recording of the conversation between Mr. Bohannon and Mr. Boutwell the jury just heard, and I would like to ask you some questions about it." She then requested that her assistant replay the recording.

When it was over, she asked Strawberry, "Mr. Thigpen, did that tape have any special significance to you?"

"Yes, ma'am, it did."

"Because you took care of Mr. Bohannon's dogs?"

"No, ma'am. That conversation won't about dogs."

"What was it about?"

"It was code. Whenever Mr. Bohannon talked about a Klan raid, he dressed it up in dog talk. Black-mouth cur was a nigra troublemaker. A white fice was a white civil rights worker. A mongrel was the target for annihilation. Hunting party was a raid. There was a whole language Mr. Bohannon worked out for hiding what he was talking about from wiretappers."

Sydney then played the conversation back one more time, stopping it strategically to ask Thigpen to define certain terms.

"Mr. Thigpen," she continued, "you have stated that you were not a member of the White Knights, but you were there the night of the Shiloh Church raid."

"Yes, ma'am, I went along for the ride that night. Like everybody else, I thought it was going to be a Code One. A cross-burning. I'd seen those before. But when we got there and the Grand Dragon said it was a Code Four, I wanted no part of it."

"Objection, Your Honor." Puckett looked furious that Strawberry was being allowed the indulgence of expiation.

"Overruled. Proceed."

"Did you participate?"

"No, ma'am. When I seen what they was up to, I went back and sat in the car. I would've left, but I rode out there with Skeebo Curlee. It was his car."

"But you saw everything?"

"Yes, ma'am. I seen it all."

———

THE WHITE CLAPBOARD CHURCH STOOD solitary in the clearing amid the scrub pine and sweet gums. The windows of the sanctuary were lit up like a jack-o'-lantern. It was a clear night, and the cicadas were already announcing that, despite the March chill in the air, spring was on its way. Strawberry and Skeebo, who was already an official member of Unit Four of the White Knights, met the caravan at the railroad crossing north of town and followed it out to the edge of the Caldwell community of trailers and farmhouses and tar-paper shacks where the church was situated. They pulled up behind the cars and a truck that were parked under a pecan tree. After slipping into the burlap hoods Skeebo brought along, they got out. Several other men, dressed in work clothes and coveralls, were hanging around their vehicles. Hoods were pulled over their heads, with eyeholes cut out of the burlap. The Grand Dragon was the only one fully robed in Klan regalia. He carried a flashlight and growled muffled orders at the others.

Strawberry balked when he heard him say there had been a change of plans, that this was no longer a routine Code One. It was now a Code Four. Strawberry knew what that meant. "What's going on?" he asked Skeebo.

"New orders," said Skeebo. "It happens sometimes. Relax." The Grand Dragon swept past both of them and opened the trunk of one of the cars, where guns, bottles, and gasoline were stored. Strawberry's stomach flopped when he saw the Grand Dragon handing out shotguns.

Skeebo stepped forward to take a weapon. Strawberry looked around for a way out without humiliating himself. Instead of letting on that he was too yellow to take part in a Code Four, he decided to challenge the Grand Dragon on procedural grounds. Strawberry asked him if Mr. Bohannon had ordered the change, and the man in the white robe responded that any Klansman worth his oath lived for the day he got to carry out a Code Four.

A high voice called out from the flatbed of the lumber truck. Strawberry recognized it as belonging to Hugh Renfro, Baby Huey. "Hey, y'all, wait for me."

"God Almighty," said the Grand Dragon. "How the hell did Hugh get here?"

"Goddamn him," said Hullender. "He must've stowed away in my truck. He was pestering us at the Starlite, but we run him off. You want me to take care of him?" he asked the Grand Dragon.

"Hold on," said the Grand Dragon.

"When's the fireworks?" said Baby Huey in his high-pitched whine. He leaned over the railings of the flatbed, where he had been hiding. "Hey, y'all. When's the fireworks?"

"Somebody get him the hell down from there and out of here," said the Grand Dragon. But Hugh was already scrambling off the back of the truck and heading toward them. Hullender started moving toward Hugh, who pushed past him toward the Grand Dragon. "Coach. Is that you, Coach?" Hugh said. "What you doin', Coach? Why you dressed up like that?"

The Grand Dragon personally spun Hugh around and ushered him back around behind the truck. Strawberry could hear them talking. He couldn't hear what the Grand Dragon was saying, but Hugh's voice was loud and distinct. "But when's the fireworks, Coach?"

The louder Hugh got, the quieter the Grand Dragon spoke. He talked to Hugh in a calm, paternal voice, and Strawberry heard him promise Hugh fireworks if he would pipe down. After a moment, Hugh lowered his voice. Then the Grand Dragon led him around and opened the door to Hullender's truck and sat him in the passenger's seat. With

Hugh finally appeased, the Grand Dragon returned to the group, and they all stood under the pecan trees for a moment and listened to the singing from the church. A single male voice accompanied by a banjo was soon joined by others. *"We are not afraid,"* they sang. *"We are not afraid."*

The Grand Dragon nodded to the other men, and they began lighting torches and crossing the parking lot, moving toward the sanctuary. Strawberry told Skeebo he had to take a leak, and he disappeared behind one of the pecan trees. "I'll catch up with you," he said before he shrank back into the shadows of the trees and the parked vehicles. He wanted to leave, but Skeebo had the keys to the car, so he stood and waited behind Hullender's truck, out of sight of Hugh and the rearviews. Strawberry wondered how he would hold his head up if the others found that he had chickened out. He could hear Hugh humming to himself inside the truck.

The Grand Dragon led the remaining Klansmen to the church entrance. As they drew near the front door, he signaled them to halt. Hullender fired his shotgun into the air. The singing inside the church stopped. Peyton Posey, whose voice Strawberry recognized even though his head was covered in burlap, used a bullhorn he had apparently lifted from the Troy Sheriff's Department equipment locker—along with the nightsticks some of the others carried—to address the ones inside. "Come on out, Elijah Knight." His voice was harsh and metallic through the megaphone. "You have one minute to step outside."

The lights inside the church were doused. The hooded men waited, and there was no sound.

"Elijah Knight," Posey repeated over the bullhorn. "You have one minute to step outside."

Still no sound from inside the church. The Grand Dragon nodded, and two of the hooded men stepped forward and planted in the churchyard a gigantic cross swaddled in oil-soaked rags. Then they lit torches and set the cross on fire. The swoosh and flare of sudden ignition forced them backward as flames leaped high into the night sky. While they all were distracted by the intensity of the blazing cross, Strawberry noticed through the trees a yellow light blink on the front porch of the house next to the church, beyond the parking lot. Then he heard a male voice from inside the church cry out, "Elijah Knight isn't here."

Posey said it again. "Elijah Knight, come on out."

The front door of the sanctuary opened slightly, and from the darkness inside, a girl's voice said, "He's not here."

"He better come on out," Posey said, "or we'll come in there and drag him out here."

Silence.

Then the door slammed shut again. Posey looked at the Grand Dragon, who checked his watch.

He signaled Posey and Hullender to approach the front door of the sanctuary. They pounded on the door and stepped back, and Posey shouted, "Did you hear me? Send nigger Knight on out here. Or we'll come in and get him."

Silence.

The door slowly opened again, and a white male wearing a preacher's collar stepped out into the moonlight. "Elijah's not here," he said. Strawberry recognized him as the banjo player he had messed with the previous summer."

"You're lying, nigger lover," said Hullender. "You better send him out here. Your minute's about up."

"I'm telling the truth," said the white preacher boy. "He's out of town."

"Come on out of there, Knight," shouted Posey.

The slam of a screen door was heard from the parsonage beyond the parking lot. A Negro man, the pastor of the church, bounded down the front porch steps and crossed the yard at a fast clip. The Klansmen spread out to intercept him. "Don't you mess with my girl," the man shouted, and a woman behind him screamed from the porch, "Curtis, don't."

"My daughter's in there," he announced as he drew closer. "Let her go." They could see from the light of the fiery cross that he was waving a shotgun.

"Daddy," cried a voice from the open doorway of the church.

"Celia!" said the Negro preacher. He rushed toward the three Kluxers standing there at the door, oblivious to the weapons they carried.

Hullender drew a pistol from the holster under his arm. The girl stepped out from the doorway, screaming, "Daddy!"

Posey shouted, "Shut up, you black bitch."

A white girl behind her cried out from the doorway, "Please, let her go to her father."

Posey turned his shotgun on both the white boy and the colored girl and said, "Get your asses back inside."

As the Negro preacher drew closer, Hullender cocked his pistol.

The white girl's voice from the door shouted, "Please, no."

Before Hullender could fire, one of the hooded men slipped in behind the preacher and brought an ax handle down on the back of his head. There was a sickening thud, and the man crumpled forward to the ground, dropping his shotgun. His daughter screamed, "Daddy!" and tried to push past the white boy to run to her father lying on the ground. Grabbing her by the arm as she passed him, the white boy pulled her back, saying, "Celia, no. Get back inside."

The white girl at the doorway cried out to her as well. "Celia, come back."

"You heard them, black bitch," Posey said to the distraught colored girl. "Get back inside." She was straining to get free of the white boy, who had her by the waist now. Posey stepped in front of her as she flailed to get to her father.

"Leave her alone," the white girl in the doorway pleaded. "Elijah Knight's not here. This is a school."

"Go back in, Sarah," said the white boy. He called to the Negro now standing next to Sarah at the door. "Randall, take them back inside, and get the children out the back."

"Send that nigger Knight out here, or we're coming in after him," screamed Hullender.

Suddenly a popping sound was heard from the pecan grove behind them. All the Klansmen whirled around. "Jesus Christ," said the Grand Dragon. Then another quick succession of loud pops, erupted like gunfire.

Celia lunged forward toward her father, and Posey stepped forward with his shotgun, shouting, "I said back inside." Then a shot was fired from inside the church, and all of the Klansmen turned their guns on the doorway. Celia stopped abruptly, and the white boy caught up with her and stepped between the girl and the Grand Dragon's shotgun when it went off. Posey and Hullender pumped the doorway full of smoking shells.

The white girl, Sarah, turned her back to the Klansmen. She dropped to her knees, put her face in her hands, and then rocked back on her heels with her face tilted skyward. Hullender was screaming, "Get Knight, get Knight!" like a crazy man. Sarah toppled against the mild-looking man in glasses they called Randall, who had fired the Smith & Wesson .38 into Peyton Posey's leg before the spray of pellets reached his own face.

A falsetto singsong mimicked Hullender from the direction of the grove where the flatbed truck was parked. "Good night, good night!" Hugh Renfro keened as he scampered into view. He rushed up to the Grand Dragon and said, "Coach, did the fireworks start?" The Grand Dragon draped his arm around Hugh's shoulders and turned him aside before he could get a look at the carnage in the doorway.

"Let Hugh have his fun," the Grand Dragon called to the others as he led his charge to the side of the church. He handed Hugh a Molotov cocktail and then pantomimed intense pitching instructions.

"I can do it, Coach," Hugh promised. Then the Grand Dragon lit the kerosene-soaked wick. Hugh stutter-stepped backward and heaved the first firebomb through the window of Shiloh Baptist Church.

————

LAWRENCE THIGPEN'S EYES WERE FULL, and his cheeks were wet. "Then Hullender barred the door with an ax handle. And the others flung their bottles of gasoline through the windows. There was a big explosion, and the whole church went up in flames."

Carter noted the discrepancies with Hullender's version of events. It was Hullender who barred the door, according to Thigpen, not Boutwell. Strawberry's shoulders were quaking, and he blew his nose in a tissue Sydney offered him.

"Mr. Thigpen," she asked, "were you fearful about testifying today?"

380 ___ DOUG MARLETTE

"Yes, ma'am," Strawberry said. "I didn't want to have to go through with this."

"Why not?"

"Objection," Puckett said. "Irrelevant."

"Sam Bohannon was good to me. I don't want to cause him no trouble."

25

T HE PARKING LOT outside Sambo's On-the-River was deserted
except for a dusty dark blue Buick Park Avenue. Carter pulled in
just before eight as the sky was losing its shaggy September light, and
the same copper-colored moon from the night before hung low above
the treetops. Dogs began barking in the near distance as soon as his tires
crunched gravel. There was a long, low shed adjacent to the restaurant,
and the baying and yapping came from the darkness beyond. The fish
camp operated from Memorial Day to Labor Day as a restaurant, and
the ramshackle main building now appeared deserted, closed for the
season. The only light in sight was a neon Budweiser beer sign, flickering and buzzing in the window next to the front door.

The door opened before Carter could knock. Behind the screen door
stood the tall, burly black man he had seen before and assumed was Bohannon's chauffeur or nurse. Without speaking, he escorted Carter into
the empty main dining room, where upturned benches were stacked on
top of the picnic tables. A small black-and-white TV was on behind the
cash register, and a half-smoked cigarette smoldered in the ashtray. The
man led Carter back to the kitchen area, wanly lit by a fluorescent tube
above the stove.

There Bohannon sat in the dark, staring out the window at the river.

His motorized wheelchair whined as he pivoted to face Carter. Bohannon looked shrunken, gaunt, and hollow-eyed, his white hair slicked back on his high forehead. The cannula ran from his ear to his nose and back to his oxygen source on his chair. He wore pressed denim jeans and a light blue T-shirt bearing the yellow Warner Bros. icon of Tweety Bird. Draped over his lap like a comforter was his white pit bull, who eyed Carter but did not move.

Bohannon spoke in a quavering, uninflected drawl. "I would shake hands, Mr. Ransom, but—" He held up the gnarled fingers of his right hand. "Arthritis." He returned to dandling his dog's neck. "Yessir, ole Arthur's the meanest one of them Ritis boys." He then indicated a Styrofoam cup on the picnic table beside him. "Would you care for some coffee, Mr. Ransom? Billy will bring you some." Carter was aware of the large black man hovering in the doorway behind him.

"No, thank you," Carter said.

Billy returned to his post by the television set in the dining room.

Carter studied the kitchen. The picnic table in the corner was covered with a red-and-white-checkered oilcloth like the ones on the tables at Sambo's Catfish House in town. There was a complete set of condiments on the table—salt, pepper, hot sauce, horseradish, and an open jar of Sambo's famous baby gherkins.

"I realize it was an inconvenience to meet me out here," said Bohannon, "but as you can see, I don't get around as well as I once did."

Bohannon's shriveled exterior showed little hint of the radioactive core that had fueled his long career as Imperial Wizard. Carter had learned much about Bohannon on his recent trips to the library: the faded gentry background—tracing his lineage through his mother, the daughter of a wealthy planter and three-term U.S. congressman, all the way back to the Virginia House of Burgesses. Bohannon definitely did not fit the stereotype of the redneck vigilante. Although his father was a car salesman and his mother worked as a secretary in the Mississippi state archives in Jackson, he was extremely proud of his aristocratic antecedents, as well as of the Methodist bishop and the banker on the family tree. His parents divorced when he was fourteen. As a rebellious youth, frustrated by what he called "adult imposition," he entered the military during World

War II and was honorably discharged as a machinist mate first-class just after V-J Day. His acquaintances said that when he got back from the Pacific Theater, his garden-variety racism had twisted into a weird obsession with Jews, whom he blamed for causing the war. Bohannon studied mechanical engineering at Tulane on the GI Bill before returning to Troy to try his hand at various business ventures. After he started up the catfish restaurant, he got interested in Nazi and racist philosophy, as well as theology and the novels of George Orwell and Thomas Dixon, including *The Clansman*, which D. W. Griffith turned into a movie, *The Birth of a Nation*.

"What do you want to talk to me about, Mr. Bohannon?" Carter had hoped not to let his emotions show, but there was already an edge in his voice.

"I won't waste your time," said Bohannon, wheeling away from Carter and facing the window again. His features, in three-quarter view, were cast into darkness. "I hope you don't mind the low lighting, but my cataracts are acting up and I have trouble with the glare." He abruptly shouted into the dining room, "Billy, bring Mr. Ransom a chair." Then to Carter, "These benches are hard on the back."

Billy appeared at the door with a metal folding chair and set it up next to Carter, facing Bohannon. Carter sat.

"I invited you here to help shed light on something that I'm sure has been troubling you. The first thing you should know about me is that I have total hatred for the academy and the pagan media. I hope and pray that both implode under the force of their own corruption and stagnation."

"Then why see me, a representative of the pagan media?"

"The Holy Scripture says the truth shall set you free, and I want to share what I know about some of what we've heard lately in that temple of lies called the Ellis County Courthouse."

Carter had always wondered how he would feel if he found himself alone with Sarah's killers, but now that the moment was here, he felt very little. As a young man, Carter had often seen Bohannon in his role as fastidious host and greeter of customers at Sambo's, but he could not connect that persona with the man seated before him now. He was struck by Bohannon's odd courtliness, the stilted manner of speaking, and primarily by his almost dainty physical presence. If he had expected to encounter a modern-day Kurtz, a larger-than-life antagonist there in his lair on the river, he was disappointed. Bohannon seemed more like Uriah Heep.

"My lawyer won't let me testify," Bohannon continued. "Which is probably for the best. But it is not easy to have to sit there day in and day out and listen to such mendacity, prevarication, and untruths, such distortion from wicked and iniquitous charlatans and poseurs like Lacey Hullender."

Carter knew that there was an element of pure snobbery in Bohannon's contempt for Hullender. Bohannon considered the White Knights of the Ku Klux Klan part of a tradition of aristocratic and intellectual racialists, former Confederate officers banded together originally by the military genius of Nathan Bedford Forrest in resistance to the reign of terror that was Reconstruction. But alas, most of Bohannon's early recruits were working-class men from the sawmills and the Graysonite factory. Secretly, he despised them. "The typical Mississippi redneck doesn't have sense enough to come in out of the rain," Bohannon once confided to an FBI informant. "I have to use him for my own cause and direct his every action to fit my plan."

"Why tell me all this?" Carter asked.

"I know you have many, shall we say personal, ties to this trial and that it weighs on you. I want to offer my deepest condolences for the unfortunate death of your girlfriend."

Carter was taken aback that he would speak of it so brazenly.

"I know you think I was responsible for her death." Bohannon looked him in the eye as he spoke. "But I can assure you I was not. The men responsible, Hullender and Posey, have more or less paid their debt to society. They took it upon themselves that terrible night to annihilate her and the others out of their obsession with Elijah Knight."

"Mr. Bohannon, with all due respect, I'm sure you're less motivated by compassion for me and more by concern for your own hide."

Bohannon wheezed a chuckle. "Believe me, I'm beyond all that. I surely do not feel compelled to avoid personal injury for the sake of attacking the false gods that keep America from fulfilling its Abrahamic promise. I resigned myself long ago to my role as scapegoat. But I want someone to know the truth about what is being discussed down there. And what I'm going to tell you might bring some solace"—he pronounced it "sollizz"—"to you and your family in this difficult time."

"I'm assuming you don't want me to write about this."

"Absolutely not. I instructed my attorney to tell you that this conversation would be strictly off the record. I expect you as a Southern gentleman to honor that request."

"What makes you think you can trust me?"

Bohannon's mouth formed a thin, slightly upturned line of amusement. "Frankly, I'm surprised you're not more enthusiastic about our dialogue, Mr. Ransom. Your colleague has been trying to get to me for weeks now."

"What colleague?" He had a feeling he knew.

"The African gentleman. From the New York paper."

"Lovelace."

"Yes. Mr. Rasheed Lovelace. Now tell me, Mr. Ransom, as a journalist of distinction. Do you honestly believe Mr. Lovelace got his position on the great *New York Tribune*—right out of journalism school, leapfrogging over more experienced white reporters—on his own merit?"

"He's got talent." Sam Bohannon was perhaps the only person on the planet who could back Carter into defending Lovelace.

"But morally flawed. A drug addict. The kind who was born on third base due to the color of his skin and thinks he hit a triple." A small smile played again on Bohannon's thin lips. "I may grant him an interview."

"Why did you ask to see me?"

"As I said, I imagine this has been a difficult time for you. And I thought you might want to know a few things."

"About what?"

"About your father, for one thing, the topic du jour for speculation by media vultures like Rah-sheed." Bohannon reached for his Styrofoam cup. "My fate is in the hands of others." He sighed. "At my age I know that there's no justice for someone like me this side of the River Jordan. I gave up on that long ago—when I was put in federal prison for crimes I did not commit." His breathing was labored, and he had to pause every few sentences to catch his breath. "Those who are set on putting me away again, they know not what they do. Anyone can see that this is a Communist-type show trial. It's about nothing more than the political ambitions of the state attorney general who wants to run for governor. The girl, his prosecutor, she's just his whore. Hullender and Posey were Judases. They sold out the innocent white people of the South to the Communists and the Jews."

Carter didn't know if it was some form of dementia, but despite his respiratory problems, Bohannon seemed to launch into political, theological, and philosophical declamations at the slightest encouragement. Carter had known some editorial writers like that.

"Sarah Solomon was a Jew," Carter said.

Bohannon looked up.

"And in case you haven't noticed something about your Communist conspiracy, the Berlin Wall was torn down, the Soviet Union is no more, and Communism is dead."

Bohannon smiled in concession. "You're the reporter. Perhaps I should allow you to lead this interview. What would you like to hear from me?"

"Tell me about Glen Boutwell."

"What about him?"

"Was he your Grand Dragon?"

"Unfortunately, I'm not at liberty to comment with a trial on. He was a business associate. Many years ago I received help financing my catfish restaurant from him. Occasionally we hunted together. I helped him with his dogs. It was the kind of collegial business relationship that goes on every day on the golf course at the Troy Country Club, which, by the way, my grandfather was a charter member of. Boutwell and I were businessmen. Nothing happened between us that wasn't business."

"You do admit that you were the Imperial Wizard of the White Knights of the Ku Klux Klan."

"Yes, of course," Bohannon said, taking a sip from his Styrofoam cup, seemingly oblivious to Carter's sarcasm, "but our work is largely educational in nature. We make every effort that sober, responsible

Christian Americans can make to persuade atheists and traitors to turn from their ungodly ways. We are under oath to preserve Christian civilization at all costs. We operate solely from a position of self-defense for our homes, our families, our nation, and Christian civilization."

Carter's reaction to being in the presence of such casual fanaticism was an urge to laugh. "But you are not opposed to violence," Carter said, attempting to draw Bohannon out on an overlooked tenet of his spiritual mission.

"As Christians, we are disposed to generosity, affection, and humility in our dealings with others. As militants, we are disposed to use physical force against our enemies. How can we reconcile these two? The answer, of course, is to purge malice, bitterness, and vengeance from our hearts. If it is necessary to eliminate someone, it should be done with no malice, in complete silence, and in the manner of a sacramental Christian act."

"So you admit eliminating your enemies."

"I try to love my enemies."

"You sound like Congressman Knight." Carter was constantly amazed that the same Gospel could speak to two men as different as Sam Bohannon and Elijah Knight. He thought of the old Southern canard of "extremists on both sides," which equated Bohannon's Christian militancy with Lige's Beloved Community.

"Your congressman, not mine," Bohannon said.

"Lige Knight is a Christian, just like you. You tried to kill him."

"He was a dupe of the international Communist conspiracy and Jewish banking cartel bent on destroying Christian America through the mongrelization of the white race."

"As I recall, you said something like that about my father once during your first trial."

"Yes. The judge was a dupe of the liberal Jewish Communist conspiracy, but at least he was honest. Misguided, perhaps, but he does not deserve to be slandered by the likes of Mr. Rasheed Lovelace of the *New York Tribune*."

"Then you don't believe my father withheld evidence to protect Boutwell?"

Bohannon shook his head. "I doubt your daddy would have gone out of his way to help Boutwell. There was no love lost between them. I don't know about your daddy, but I do know that Glen Boutwell was real jealous of Judge Ransom."

"Why?" It was only now that Carter found himself entering into the ritual dance of mutual manipulation between reporter and source. Carter realized that Bohannon knew a great deal about what had gone on between Boutwell and his father, between his father and Sheppy, and Carter had to decide whether to pretend to know more than Bohannon did or less. He chose. "I never saw any indication of that growing up," he said.

"For years Glen Boutwell suspected his wife of being in love with your daddy. I know that in his mind he had some proof or evidence of this, but he would not say what it was."

"How do you know?"

"On occasion Glen would take a drink. I do not drink. His tongue would loosen, and I would learn things—things he perhaps would not have told under circumstances of sobriety. Unfortunately, Posey heard the same things I heard and revealed them to other, less discreet, less compassionate ears."

"Like the Sovereignty Commission." Carter tipped his hand.

"I have nothing to say about that."

"You talk about Hullender's lies. What lies?"

"For instance, trying to blame the Grand Dragon for shotgunning that colored girl and white boy, as he did in the courtroom the other day. The Grand Dragon never carried a weapon. Except for a hog blade." Suddenly Bohannon produced a nine-inch knife, seemingly out of nowhere. "Like this one." Carter's heart skipped a beat. In the shadowy recesses of the poorly lit kitchen, he couldn't tell where it came from. Bohannon began cleaning his nails with the blade. "And he never used it," Bohannon continued. "He gave orders. It was not for him to carry them out."

"What else?"

"Boutwell was too proud to let out his belief of being a cuckold to anybody, much less Judge Ransom. I think your daddy made a decision about not calling that retarded boy to the witness stand for his own sound legal and humanitarian reasons. Not because Glen Boutwell was blackmailing him."

"You know, Mr. Bohannon, a lot of folks besides Hullender think the reason you got away with murder twenty years ago while the errand boys got convicted was that you got to the jurors."

Bohannon sneered. "Pure speculation."

"Ah, I don't hear a denial. They say you intimidated them. Threatening phone calls to their homes. Afterward, one juror said she felt the Klan would firebomb her house if she voted to convict you. For six weeks after the verdicts, U.S. Marshals guarded her home."

"I know nothing about any of that."

"At least Hullender's served his time."

"Not enough time, if the truth be known," Bohannon said. "What's the name of the prosecution's witness who died? My defense lawyers were so looking forward to his testimony."

Carter had an intuition that they were finally getting to the reason Bohannon had summoned him. "Skeebo Curlee."

"Ah, yes. Reginald 'Skeebo' Curlee." The contempt rose in Bohannon's voice. "The poor so-called suicide. So terrified of testifying against Sam Bohannon that he took his own life."

"Are you saying he didn't commit suicide?"

"Ask yourself who might have motive to stop him from testifying."

"You."

"I couldn't care less."

"You're saying Lacey killed him?"

"Hullender had good reason. He was afraid he might spill the beans."

"On what? Lacey's not on trial."

"More of his freelance 'civil rights' work. Things nobody can say I had anything to do with."

"Like what?"

"Who was that colored boy that disappeared?"

"Dexter Washington."

"That was another occasion when Hullender and his friends, through their lack of discipline, followed their own lower impulses. You're a reporter. Why don't you investigate that little incident? Posey was in the sheriff's department at the time and helped cover it up. He may have even helped carry it out. Why do you think the body was never found? I bet you wouldn't have to look far for the remains."

"Meaning?"

"Do you know the expression, Mr. Ransom, 'hiding in plain sight'?"

"Why are you telling me this? I could go to the authorities, and you'd be facing another inquiry."

"Because, my friend, I will never breathe another free breath again once this trial is concluded," said Bohannon, smiling through yellow dentures.

"I thought you said you were innocent."

"History demands a conviction," he said, "and the forces of history always checkmate the forces of justice."

Carter stared at the Imperial Wizard, trying to figure out what he was up to.

Bohannon coughed again. "Now if you'll excuse me. My doctor insists I keep to his regimen." Carter looked up and saw Billy at the kitchen door looking at his watch. As Carter stood to leave, Bohannon said, "You know, Glen Boutwell was always quite fond of you."

"Excuse me?"

"He was very disappointed you didn't marry his daughter." Carter was somehow offended by this turn of the conversation. Bohannon continued. "I always thought he was trying to get back at your father by stealing his son. You were his hope for an heir. The crown prince. He was quite upset when you got involved with the civil rightsers. And his daughter was replaced by one of them."

"I don't know what the fuck you're talking about," Carter said, although there was a boiling of comprehension in the pit of his stomach.

"It's really none of my business. I always thought Glen was paranoid when it came to the judge. He was convinced your mother's depression was due to your daddy's affair with his wife."

Carter looked blank.

"Oh, I'm sorry," said Bohannon. He sounded genuine this time. "I've spoken out of turn. You didn't know about your mother's breakdown. Of course they wouldn't have told you why she was in the hospital. You were probably just a boy."

"I'm really not following you," Carter said. He felt disoriented.

"I've said enough." Bohannon drained the last of his coffee. "You're an intelligent young fellow. You don't need me to explain." His cold eyes peered out at Carter from beneath his unruly gray eyebrows. "I've handed over the dog. It's up to you to get it to hunt." His wheelchair whirred as he steered it around again to face the window. With his back turned, he said, "Billy, will you show Carter to the door?"

26

S ORRY TO CALL so late." Sydney sounded irritable. "I need to talk to you. Can you meet me at Knotty's in fifteen minutes?" Carter had just gotten back from his session with Sam Bohannon. He was still digesting the encounter and wanted to call Sydney to fill her in, but he had hesitated because it was past eleven.

When he got to Knotty's, she was there, sitting in the same booth as before, looking out of place in a silky T-shirt and a short skirt. A boozy squadron of amorous Bubbas was checking her out, looking eager to relieve her of her loneliness. Carter slid into the bench opposite her, and the guys slunk into the penumbra of the pool tables and pinball machines. Hank Williams was on the jukebox, singing about the silence of a falling star lighting up a purple sky. Sydney had already ordered Carter a Miller.

"I got the results back from the lab," she said when he sat down. "Guess who licked the stamp on the death threat letter."

"Hullender."

"Bohannon. We matched his DNA."

"Congratulations."

"I don't think we can use it." Sydney tossed her crumpled napkin on the table. "The defense has the right to vet all evidence beforehand.

Arthur'll call for a recess to have his own experts look at it. He'll send it to an independent lab, which will take time. He could delay the trial for months. The jury couldn't be held, and he'd ask for a mistrial. So we've got to bag it."

"Well, look on the bright side," said Carter. "At least you have the comfort of knowing you're trying to put away a guilty man."

Sydney paused from gnawing the corner of a manicured fingernail to give him an "I am not amused" look before changing the subject. "The *New York Tribune* wants to do a photo spread of all the principals in the case for their Sunday magazine. Should I do it?" She seemed to be talking to herself more than to him, and before he could answer, she said, "Even though you'd think that would be like a dream come true, the idea of it kind of makes me sick."

"It's never what you want when you finally get what you want," Carter said.

"Besides, what if I lose the case?"

Carter had never seen Sydney show doubt. He was charmed. "What happened to old Bear Bryant Rushton?"

Sydney shrugged off his attempt to jolly her. "I practically fainted when Strawberry said it was Hullender who barred the church door. God, I can't believe I didn't pick that up in the pretrial interview. They're probably spiking the ball and strutting in the end zone over at Puckett's suite right now." She paused for a second and smiled in spite of herself. "You know, Coach Bryant didn't let his players celebrate in the end zone. He said, 'Act like you've been there before.'"

Carter could see that for the first time, Sydney had some serious concern that she might lose the case. "I made a big mistake opening with Hullender," she said. "Lacey should have followed Thigpen."

"But Strawberry didn't turn up till the last minute," said Carter. "You're a little sensitive right now."

She looked up at him. "That's what my father always said about me. 'You're too sensitive to be a good lawyer.'"

"Sounds like my father," said Carter.

"He was hard to please," Sydney said, looking around for the waitress. "Especially after my brother died."

When she turned back to Carter, he had composed a look of sympathetic anticipation of an explanation. "It was the summer Maris and Mantle were in that home-run race, and my brother had become a huge New York Yankees fan," Sydney said.

Their father was driving them to Howard Johnson's for an ice cream, with Sydney in the backseat and Robbie up front. He had on his Yankees baseball cap. He had rolled down his window, and the wind caught the cap and blew it onto the busy street.

"Daddy stopped the car," Sydney said, "and before anyone could react, Robbie had jumped out to get it and was hit by a car. I watched it all from the backseat. He was dead by the time the ambulance arrived. It tore my father up. My mother blamed Daddy. They divorced a year later."

"God, I'm so sorry."

She smiled weakly. "You asked that time about my Freudian motivations. Well, my brother was the golden child—athlete, scholar, worldbeater."

"And you thought you wouldn't measure up," Carter said. "Do you think that was why you were so close to your grandfather?"

Sydney looked startled, as if she had never considered that before. Tears sprang to her eyes. She stared at him for a moment and then began craning for the waitress. "Who do you have to subpoena to get a drink around here?"

Carter flagged the waitress.

After they ordered, Sydney continued. "And now from the tragic to the cheesy, I just got word that my boyfriend's coming in for the summation. Talk about pressure."

Carter felt a slight injury to his Y chromosome. "Well, I've got something you might find interesting," he said, but he realized the gleanings from his talk with Bohannon were only going to put her further off-balance.

She listened intently to his report about Bohannon's brief on Hullender, squinting occasionally. "He's trying to spin it," she said. Her certitude seemed to have returned. "Shift blame. It's the same thing his attorney's doing in the courtroom—turning it back on Hullender, Boutwell, anybody but himself."

"But why tell me?"

"Because he knows you'll tell me," Sydney said matter-of-factly.

Carter shifted in the booth. He sensed that she was referring to something going on between them beyond his connection with the case, and the challenging wide-eyed look she was giving him did not discourage that impression. He was embarrassed to think that this might be apparent to Bohannon.

"If he goes down," she continued, "he's going to take down with him the ones who took him down."

Carter fiddled with the bowl of boiled peanuts on the table. He felt truly disappointed that the evidentiary assistance from Charlie Lloyd hadn't borne more fruit. When he glanced back up at Sydney, he found that she was looking at him fondly.

"You're sweet, you know," she said. "Yes, I realize that's the worst thing you can say to a guy, but I'm assuming your ego can take it."

"What do you have in mind?" Carter said.

"I'll never be able to repay you for finding Thigpen for me and softening him up. He's a gold mine. He confirmed most of what I got from Skeebo Curlee."

"Bohannon suggests that Lacey had something to do with Skeebo's suicide."

Sydney looked ceilingward, as if she didn't even want to think about the possibility that her star witness was capable of something like that—yet she clearly had. Then she jumped slightly, as if shocked by one of her synapses. "Hey," she said, "Skeebo told me about something he and Lacey were involved in that I wasn't aware of before I got this case." She started rummaging through her briefcase, picking up audiotapes and checking their labels. "Have you got a cassette deck in your car?" she said after palming one of the tapes. "You're not going to believe this."

"Sure," he said, and fished some bills out of his pocket to leave on the table. They headed out to his sister's Mercury Grand Marquis parked in the lot. Carter turned the key in the ignition as Sydney slid into the passenger seat. She dunked the cassette into the player and fumbled with the fast-forward to queue it up. She turned up the volume until her voice, interviewing the late Skeebo Curlee, could be heard.

"Did Sam Bohannon send you to Shiloh Church?"

"Yes, ma'am."

"Did you know you were on a mission to assassinate Elijah Knight?"

"No, ma'am. I wouldn't have gone if I thought we was supposed to kill somebody. After they changed it from a cross-burning to a Code Four, I wanted out, but didn't know how to get out of it. I'd had enough of that mess. Ever since what happened at the river."

"What happened?"

There was a pause.

"You can tell me," said Sydney's voice. Carter recognized that same offhanded guile that he had used a million times on sources who, for their own sake, shouldn't have been talking to him.

"It was Halloween. Mr. Bohannon sent Hullender and some men out to make some mischief—burn crosses, rough some folks up. Mr. Bohannon wanted me to take Strawberry along to show him what it was like to be part of the Klan. We rode with Posey in his squad car and cruised by Magic Time a couple of times, then went over to Scarborough's.

"We followed this colored boy pulling out of the parking lot. We recognized him as one of the outside agitators. Posey'd been casing them out there at Magic Time, and we knowed he'd slip off and go to Scarborough's by hisself. We pulled him over, and Posey arrested him for speeding and locked him up for a couple of hours back in town. Then Posey let him go."

"And that was it?"

Skeebo paused again. Then he said, "Naw. The others followed him back out into the county and forced his car off the road. Pulled him and a box of MoonPies out of the front seat."

Long pause.

"What happened then?"

Another pause and the sound of a muffled sob. "They strung that boy up. Out on that swing on the river. We was just supposed to scare him. But then it got out of hand. When they cut down the body, they made all of us that was there touch it. They wanted us all in on it. So we wouldn't tell."

"Who's 'they'?"

Silence.

"Who did it?"

"It was Posey and Hullender's idea. They cut off his fingers with a hog blade and handed them out as souvenirs. Hullender used to brag about having a thumb he kept in his pack of cigarettes. He tried to force me to take one, but I wouldn't do it. That's when I had to get out of there. I stumbled up the rise through the trees and threw up. Nearly got lost in the woods in the dark because they had all the torches. I had to find my way back to the road and hitchhike home."

"Did Sam Bohannon order the murder?"

"I don't reckon so, because Mr. Bohannon was mad when he found out from Strawberry what happened. He didn't mind there was another dead nigger. He just wanted to be in charge of what was going on."

"What did they do with the body?"

Silence.

"Did you know?"

"I heard the Grand Dragon arranged for the disposal when he found out about it." Another pause. "And I don't know where it is."

"Did the Grand Dragon know about the plan in advance."

"I wouldn't have known, since nobody knew who he was."

Sydney switched off the cassette player. "That was the Washington 'disappearance.' They lynched him."

"I knew Dexter," said Carter, and he told Sydney about the execution he had nearly witnessed but had convinced himself was a Halloween prank. "We took Posey back to Naked Tail that night and he tried to have us believe we were hallucinating. And that son of a bitch had been there."

"I guess I should have played this for you sooner," Sydney said. "I had no idea this case was so well known around here. All you hear about is the church bombing."

"So that much of what Bohannon told me was true," Carter said.

"Sounds like you might have to reopen another case, so don't get too attached to Lacey."

"I love it when I get caught in a testosterone cross fire," Sydney said sarcastically.

Carter laughed at the thought of Lacey as her suitor. "So many rivals for your affection. But seriously, will the judge allow the lynching as evidence in this one?"

"Doubtful. Court rules bar most evidence of other crimes."

"Probably just as well."

"Yes, it could hurt me more than help me. More damage to Hullender's credibility. Plus Puckett could use it to support his claim that the Klansmen went off on rogue missions. Tomorrow, he's going to try to destroy Thigpen on cross." Sydney cleared her throat and looked away. "That's why I wanted to talk to you. We need to go over your testimony. The state is probably going to rest day after tomorrow. You're my last witness."

Carter studied Sydney's profile. She was still not looking at him, as if out of respect. It had been a long time since he had sat in a dark car with a beautiful woman, and it was remarkable how a pastime so obsolete could still evoke longing and possibility. He thought of the abrupt termination of his own adolescence, and of its delusion of immortality, and how it had ironically led to this reprise of the inchoate peak emotions of youth, decidedly stripped of innocence, yet, as Carter was surprised to realize, never of hope.

Still refusing eye contact, she said, "I'm going to have to ask you about the autopsy report."

"I know," said Carter.

Finally she turned toward him. "And there's another thing," she said. "Michael Solomon brought me something at the beginning of the trial. I wasn't going to mention it to you in case the judge didn't allow it. But he gave his ruling today, and I'm going to put it into evidence when you testify."

Carter had not seen Michael since the fund-raiser for Lige, and they had not had a chance for a real conversation. He could not imagine what he had that would be relevant to Sydney's case.

She reached across the front seat to hand Carter an open envelope containing a small ziplock bag. When he took it from her, she did not withdraw her hand, but pressed it onto his flank, as if to brace him.

Sydney was right. Arthur Puckett set out to demolish Lawrence Thigpen on the stand, following the same plan of attack he had used on Hullender. He dredged up every mistake the man had ever made, reaching far back to his arrest record for burglary, his firing at Graysonite for stealing, and his gambling addiction. He portrayed for the jury a man who could not control his impulses, who had a pattern of betraying those who had placed their trust in him, including Bohannon. Thigpen's company insurance records at Ingalls indicated that he had been referred for psychiatric evaluation several months earlier, and according to those records, he had been put on medication for depression.

Strawberry drooped under the assault and nearly broke down at several points. Judge McDonnell recessed the court for lunch, when Inez, Strawberry's common-law wife, burst into hysterics in her seat in the gallery and began to scream for God's help. As Inez was being escorted from the courtroom by a bailiff, Sydney caught Carter's eye and gave him a glum look that seemed to say, "Why do I put people through this?"

That night, Carter found his father in his basement workroom tinkering with one of his clockfaces. Mitchell Ransom looked pale and drawn. "Dad, I'm going to be called to testify tomorrow." Lawrence Thigpen's ordeal had concluded following the recess that afternoon. As it turned out, in the course of his evisceration Puckett strategically ignored the discrepancy between Hullender's testimony and Strawberry's over who barred the church door. Strawberry's claim that it was Lacey rather than Glen Boutwell, after all, did not advance Puckett's scenario of the Grand Dragon running his own franchise.

Carter straddled a bench opposite the judge. "Did Sally tell you I talked to Bohannon?"

"She did," his father said without looking up.

"I'm not sure why he wanted to talk to me, but he told me some things about Glen Boutwell." He watched for his father's reaction. There was none.

"What else could we possibly learn about poor Glen Boutwell that we don't already know?" his father said with weary sarcasm.

"He said you and Coach Boutwell had some tension between you," Carter said, picking up a Phillips-head screwdriver and examining the grip. "I never knew that."

"And why would you listen to a crackpot like Bohannon?"

Carter was coiled and ready for the first dismissive flick from his father. "Dad, did you cover up evidence in the first Shiloh Church trial?"

Mitchell Ransom peered over the rims of his glasses at Carter. "Did Sam Bohannon tell you that?"

"No. He said he didn't think you did."

"Well, he's right about that." Mitchell went back to work on the tiny moving part he was oiling.

"Apparently, Bohannon was close to Coach Boutwell, though. He knew him pretty well."

The judge continued working without reaction, almost as if he wasn't listening.

"Dad, did you have an affair with Sheppy Boutwell?"

Mitchell continued oiling the part but said, "So he told you that? You didn't have to drive out to Sambo's fish camp to hear that. You could have gotten that from the Sovereignty Commission."

"Did you?"

"No."

"He said Coach was obsessed with you. He thought Sheppy was in love with you. He said Mama's sadness was related to that."

"For a man facing life in prison, Sam Bohannon seems to have a lot of opinions about other people's business. For a man with the blood of four innocent young people on his hands, it seems like he'd be more concerned about the beam in his own eye."

"You need to talk to me, Daddy."

Judge Ransom stopped what he was doing at the nostalgic sound of "Daddy" and removed his glasses to massage the bridge of his nose. "Glen Boutwell was a complicated man," he said. "For all that chamber of commerce, hail-fellow-well-met business, he was a deeply resentful man. He came from extreme poverty and had to take charge at a young age and practically raise his brothers by himself. He never went to college, and I think he never got over that. I think it also weighed on him being married into a family like the Graysons. I knew he was troubled, but I had no idea he would be mixed up in the Klan or that he was close to Sam Bohannon. But when you get to be my age, you learn not to be surprised by anyone's secrets. And in a strange way, I think Glen probably felt that his Klan work was an extension of his Jaycee and Little League activities, protecting his family, society, civilization."

Normally Carter would have snorted at such rationales, but he had known Boutwell. "What about your secrets, Daddy? What about Sheppy? Did you have a relationship with her that Coach Boutwell should have been concerned about?"

His father stared at the parts on the table before him. "Sheppy and I are old friends. I met her through old man Grayson when I first came to Troy. Before I met Glen. He wasn't even back from the war. She was already engaged to him." Mitchell put down his tools finally. "Over the years she would consult with me about personal matters. I would advise her. That could be the source of some of these rumors. I have learned that you cannot control what people say about you. And when you're in a position of influence, they will say anything." He sighed and returned to his clock. "Did you tell Sally what Bohannon said to you?"

"Yes."

His father looked pained. "I loved your mother more than anything. There are things that happen that we can't control. You know that too well. But as long as your mother and I lived together as man and wife, I never did anything that I would be ashamed to tell her about. Her 'sadness' was something neither I nor her doctors nor you nor your sister could do anything about."

The basement door squeaked open, and there was a clamor on the stairs. The voice of Carter's nephew could be heard. "Grandpa?" Willie stood at the top of the stairwell. "Hey, Uncle Carter," he said. Then, to his grandfather, "Grandpa, you promised me a story."

"I'm sorry, Daddy," Sally called down, "but he won't go to sleep until you tuck him in."

"Tell me about the war, Grandpa," said Willie. "About the POW camp."

Mitchell took off his glasses and stood slowly. He looked at Carter, who was sitting in the path to the stairwell. Carter stood to let his father pass. As he walked by, Mitchell Ransom reached over and caressed his son's neck and said, "Good luck tomorrow."

The next day, a story under Rasheed Lovelace's byline ran on the front page of the *New York Tribune* stating that evidence now available, which had been ignored by Judge Mitchell Ransom during the first Shiloh Church trial, suggested that prominent Troy businessman Glen Boutwell had orchestrated the assault on the church and that he may have personally gunned down two of the civil rights workers, Sarah Solomon and Randall Peek. It said that Sovereignty Commission reports corroborated the evidence and suggested that Boutwell may have escaped prosecution in the earlier trial because he was blackmailing the judge, who had had an affair with Boutwell's wife. The story intimated that this new evidence raised questions about the culpability of Imperial Wizard Sam Bohannon and could lead to yet another failed attempt to convict him.

Carter was confused as he read the story over coffee that morning. He felt a surge of fury that a shitbird like Lovelace would be trying to take down his father. Yet he couldn't confidently say the story wasn't true. In Carter's experience as his son, it was inconceivable that Mitchell could lie. But in the absence of any truly compelling explanation for why his father had ruled out Hugh Renfro's testimony, it had a certain ring of truth. Sydney had kept his father out of the trial, but now Lovelace had undone all that. Had Bohannon ended up giving Rasheed his interview? Or was it Sydney's own witness who was talking to reporters?

If the structure of a prosecutor's case can be compared to the movements of a symphony, the last day of state testimony from friends and relatives of the victims might be heard as the final minutes of Tchaikovsky's *Pathé-tique*, when the string section produces an uncanny sound of anguished human voices. Though the legal justification for the testimony is to identify the bodies of the victims or describe their last living moments, its real purpose is to bring the jury to tears.

During her turn on the witness stand, Aurelia Bunt managed to convey that her big sister Celia would have been the first in her family to go to college. Daniel Johnston's mother worked in her husband's death in World War II as a decorated war hero. And Dorothea Peek spoke of her brother Randall's academic gifts, a genius that showed up when he began doing algebra in fourth grade and led him to Harvard's graduate department in philosophy.

Court recessed for lunch. Then it was Carter's turn.

After he took his place on the stand, he looked out at the courtroom and was surprised to see that it was packed. The spectators had fallen off since Lacey Hullender's testimony, but now the locals outnumbered the national media. Following Sydney's suggestion, Carter wore a coat and tie and khaki pants, neither too casual nor too fancy. When he raised his hand to be sworn in, his eyes went to the jury. They appeared exhausted but attentive and dutiful. He then looked at Sam Bohannon, in his usual position beside Arthur Puckett. Bohannon stared back at Carter inscrutably, his expression blank, showing no acknowledgment of their recent exchange.

Carter swept the room again as he was seated and saw the victims' families in the balcony. Michael Solomon had returned. Carter also spotted Elijah Knight, who had told him he was coming back after a roll-call vote in Washington. Sitting beside him was Nettie, fanning herself with a copy of the free alternative weekly that had just endorsed Lige's opponent in the election. On Lige's other side, to Carter's astonishment, sat a clear-eyed Charlie Lloyd, looking relaxed and happy to be there. Doc Renfro, who had not been back since Hugh's taped testimony, was there again, sitting with Pete Callahan, Jimbo Stein, Stephen Musgrove, and Lonnie Culpepper.

The press gallery was overflowing with national correspondents from the networks and all the major dailies. Carter recognized Curtis Wilkie from *The Boston Globe*, Chuck Stone from the *Philadelphia Daily News*, Murray Kempton from the *New York Post*, Heidi Evans from the *New York Daily News*, and Kristy Schumaker from the *Los Angeles Times*—all present for the state's final act. Rasheed Lovelace, aglow with the self-esteem of someone who had just published a 1-A story in the *New York Tribune*, was seated next to the editor who hired him, Haynes Wentworth. Harold Bernhardt hovered nearby: he had written the sorrowful endorsement of Lige's opponent in *The Barricade*. His wife, Bradley, giddy with public-mindedness, sat with Simon Lester, whose crew was documenting it all from the heights of the balcony press gallery. WunderCorp's Helmut Schlank was seated toward the back of the courtroom, bland-looking and expectant. Carter searched for Sally, who said she would be there with Willie. Seated next to her was the last person Carter expected to see. There he was, proud and stoical, trying hopelessly to blend into the mahogany: Judge Mitchell Ransom.

Sydney made eye contact as she approached Carter. Then she turned and faced the jury.

"Mr. Ransom," she began, "did you know any of the victims of the Shiloh Church bombing?"

"I knew all of them."

"Would you tell the court how you came to know them?"

"Elijah Knight was a friend of mine. His mother worked for my family. He introduced his colleagues to me when he came to work for Snick, registering voters in Ellis County."

"Did you know any of the four victims better than the others?" Sydney never looked at Carter as she asked her questions.

"I knew Sarah Solomon the best."

"Mr. Ransom, would you describe your relationship with Sarah Solomon?"

"I was in love with her." Carter had never said those words out loud before, and the effect on him was invigorating.

"Where were you the night the Shiloh Baptist Church was bombed?" she asked.

"I was out of town, in Selma, Alabama."

WHEN CARTER RETURNED to Selma on Saturday afternoon, March 20, 1965, thousands of people from all over the country were pouring into town, including reporters from the major media. The Nashville *Tennessean* had booked a room at the Albert Hotel for him to share with their photographer. The second attempt to march to Montgomery was to begin the next day. Carter almost hadn't made it. He and Sarah had had a fight the day before that left him so desolate he actually thought about asking the *Tennessean* to send someone else as its second man. The argument had been about marriage, and Carter had used her refusal to go with him to the Spring Fling at the Troy Country Club to rain doubt upon whether they would ever be able to fully accept each other's worlds. That morning, as a peace offering, she had made him some rugalach to take on the road.

"Separation anxiety," she had said, to explain away their fight, and she had given him a goofy, melodramatic kiss goodbye.

His father had been less than enthusiastic about his assignment when Carter called to tell his parents that he would be gone for a few days. "Covering it, my ass! You might as well be marching," Mitchell Ransom shouted before Carter hung up on him. Carter seldom went home now, having virtually moved into Sarah's garage apartment.

When he arrived in Selma late Saturday afternoon, he drove straight to the hospital to check on Lige and found him sitting up in bed in his room, his bandages removed, the bruises fading, and the swelling down. "The doctors say I can go home in a couple of days," he said. "It's killing me not to be at the march. And I'm missing Mrs. Bunt's caramel cake at the Freedom School graduation tonight, too."

Carter filled him in on Sarah's plans for the ceremony. She had been up late doing the hand calligraphy for the diplomas. "You've come a long way for the whitest white boy in Ellis County," Lige said. "Who'd ever believe you'd be at the march instead of me. You'll be my eyes and ears. And feet. I want a full report." As Carter was leaving, Lige removed something from his side-table drawer and said, "Brother Man, do me a favor tomorrow. Take this and wear it." He held out the chain and St. Christopher medal his mother had given Carter to take to her son the summer before. "Carry it for me, ramblin' man. It's the patron saint of travelers, Christ-bearer. It protects you against lightning, toothaches, and the Alabama State Highway Patrol."

Carter looked askance at Lige and said, "Oh well, two out of three ain't bad."

Lige laughed. "Well, I don't know if even God would be much good against the troopers." Carter lifted the silver medal and chain over his head and let it drop around his neck.

Carter drove over to Brown Chapel, where more than two hundred people were preparing to spend the night. There he ran into his new roommate, the *Tennessean* photographer Bill Hennessey, a friendly, flush-faced middle-aged man dressed in a plaid jacket, white shirt, and tie loosened at the collar. He caught a ride with Carter back to the Albert, where they convened with the other out-of-town newsmen at a couple of tables in the hotel coffee shop. Carter recognized some of their bylines: Roy Reed from *The New York Times*, Jack Nelson from the *Los Angeles Times*, Richard Valeriani from NBC, Gay Talese from *The New York Times Magazine*. Carter couldn't believe he was in the company of some of the nation's sharpest journalists. He sat in as if he belonged, smoking, complaining, and swapping local apocrypha in anticipation of the march the next day. The reporters who had been there for weeks covering the voter registration campaign bemoaned the accommodations at the Albert, having concluded that the only good food to be found in Selma was at the Tally Ho, the segregated club out on the edge of town. In the bellyaching world of journalism, cynicism had evolved to a science, in which every observation was offered with a pin through the thorax. As a result, the South's culinary shortcomings somehow took on the same weight as the cattle prods Sheriff Jim Clark liked to use on demonstrators.

As they discussed the prospects of another confrontation on Sunday or a sniper attack along the highway, it was clear that the national press was sympathetic to the marchers. The shoptalk turned to the resentments of the younger Negro activists toward Martin Luther King's SCLC for trying to steal their thunder for the Selma campaign, and

Carter said knowingly, "Yeah, well, why do you think the Snick guys call SCLC 'Slick'?" Carter wondered, though, if his colleagues' grasp of Movement politics was matched by their reporting on the other side. Did the national press have as much of a feel for the complexities of white resistance? He could sense a flatness in their view of the segregationists, a lack of understanding, especially among the Northerners, of the forces that would create such defiance, and he sensed an opportunity. Whatever his personal sympathies, he wanted his reportage to fill in that gap.

Back in his room, Carter tried calling Sarah at home to tell her about his hobnobbing with the big boys, but he got no answer. He figured she was with the kids, celebrating their graduation. He would try again in the morning.

"AND DID YOU TRY to call Sarah the next morning?" Sydney asked.

"I did. But there was no answer at her apartment."

"Was that unusual?"

"I thought she could be having breakfast with her landlady, Mrs. Nell Musgrove. She did that sometimes. But I felt funny not talking to her before I went to work. We stayed in constant contact whenever I was on the road. We used to joke that we were like Laurel and Hardy, Abbott and Costello, Burns and Allen."

"Romeo and Juliet." Carter glanced up at her, unsure if that was a spontaneous or calculated remark. But Sydney was still facing the jury. Puckett did not bother to object. "Mr. Ransom," she said, "when did you next see Sarah Solomon?"

MORE THAN THREE THOUSAND MARCHERS had gathered at Brown Chapel that Sunday morning. An array of Americans, black and white, ranging from schoolteachers to movie stars, had come to Selma from far-flung parts to join the locals in the march to Montgomery. A TV truck, with lights and cameras, was setting up at the head of the march to record every step of the way. The mile or so stretch of road from Brown Chapel to Highway 80 was lined with National Guardsmen and state troopers. Some of the same troopers who had beaten the marchers two weeks earlier were now there to ensure their safe passage out of town and along the fifty-four-mile route to Montgomery. Carter became energized when he saw the crowd at the church, the media presence, and the precautions of the authorities. Today he would cover his first national event for a major metropolitan daily. The crowd was peppered with VIPs and civil rights leaders whom Carter recognized—Dr. King, John Lewis, Dick Gregory, Harry Belafonte. As he surveyed their faces, he heard a voice shouting his name.

"Ransom!" said Hennessey, the photographer from the *Tennessean*. "The city desk got a message from your sister to call home. She said it's an emergency."

Carter's mouth went dry. He ran back to his car to drive downtown to look for a phone. His first thought was his mother. Her health had been poor lately, and she had had extended bouts of melancholia. Along the streets now lined with guardsmen and state troopers, he frantically searched for a phone booth. Inside one shop, the owner, after a brief appraisal, identified him as a troublemaker and refused to let him use the public phone. Finally he located a pay phone inside a drugstore. He called home collect and was relieved when his mother answered.

"Oh, Carter! Thank God you called!"

"Mother, what is it? Is it Daddy?"

"No, no. There was a fire at the colored church outside of town. Your friend Sarah's been hurt."

"She's been hurt? How bad?"

"It's bad." His mother began sobbing. "It's bad."

Carter heard his father saying something in the background, and then the judge was on the line. "They're dead, son."

"What?" he screamed into the receiver.

"Four of them died in the blaze. Your girlfriend was among them. Sarah."

Carter felt the oxygen being pulled out of his body. He crumpled to his knees. He could hear his mother crying in the background.

"I'm so sorry, son," his father said softly. "I wish we could be there with you."

Carter could find no words.

"Nettie contacted Lige already. I don't know what your situation is there," his father said hesitantly, "but Doc called this morning." Carter stared through his tears at the cosmetics counter of the drugstore, astonished that there were people in the world going through their ordinary transactions. "He wanted to know if you could come over to the county morgue. They're looking for someone who can identify the bodies."

"I'm coming," Carter finally managed to say.

"Drive carefully, son" was the last thing his father said. "We'll be here."

———

SYDNEY LOCKED IN on Carter with her eyes for the first time since she had begun her questioning. He found something comforting about the compassionate detachment of her gaze, realizing that she encountered people at the limits of human experience every day on the job. She would not flinch from the story that had always isolated him in a condition that somehow felt like shame. He now felt pleased with himself for finally opening up his heart to her, yet glad that he had not done so with anyone before. Because to her he was just another witness, he was for the first time able to reclaim his story from the pity of others.

"And what did you do when you got home to Troy?" Sydney asked.

"I went straight to the county morgue."

"What did you see there?"

Carter exhaled, and his voice broke as he said, "They were all burned and mangled beyond recognition."

"But you identified Sarah?"

"Yes," he said.

Sydney paused before she asked him the next question. "How could you tell it was Sarah?"

"I recognized the ring she was wearing," Carter said.

"Was there anything particular about the ring?"

"I had given it to her in New York, the first time I went there."
Carter cleared his throat. "It was still on her finger. The stone had been
blown out of its setting."

Sydney then produced the plastic bag holding the ring with the gem-
stone missing, the object that had been in the envelope she presented to
Carter in the parking lot at Knotty's, now State Exhibit Number 9. She
showed it to Carter and, avoiding his eyes, said, "Is this the ring?"

"Yes," Carter said without looking at it.

Sydney handed it to the jury foreman, who began circulating it
among the jurors.

She drew closer to Carter. "As we saw earlier, the coroner's report
showed that Sarah had suffered gunshot wounds but died of asphyxiation."

"That's right."

"Did the medical examiner reveal anything else about the results of
the autopsy?"

"Yes."

She now spoke in a soft voice, yet clear enough to be heard by everyone in the courtroom. "Would you tell the jury what that was?"

Carter inhaled and said it out loud for the first time. "She was
pregnant."

Sydney asked, "And was she carrying your child?"

"Yes, she was carrying my child."

Sydney let the words settle over the courtroom as she returned to the
prosecution table. "That is all," she said without looking at anyone.

"I have no questions, Your Honor," Carter heard Puckett say in the
solicitous tone of a minister on a house call. With the courtroom completely silent, Carter departed the witness stand. He looked at his father, whose eyes remained downcast. The hush resounded even after
Judge Robert McDonnell gaveled the day to an end.

———

AFTER LEAVING the coroner's office, Carter went home and collapsed
in the bedroom of his childhood home. He slept fitfully the rest of the

day and into the night. His parents and sister checked on him but respected his grief. That night, after everyone else was asleep, he woke up and left the house. He drove to the garage apartment behind Stephen's house and let himself in with his key.

He spent the next couple of days alone among Sarah's things.

The aroma of the recently baked rugalach still lingered in the air. Sarah's clothes hung in the closets, as if she would arrive at any minute to claim them. Her toiletries littered the bathroom. Books and magazines she had been reading cluttered the coffee table. Notes and articles and snapshots decorated the mirrors and the refrigerator. A small photograph of her and Carter at Naked Tail sat on the nightstand next to the telephone. Their unfinished game of Scrabble was left set up on the kitchen table. Carter thought about how competitive Sarah was. And now he wondered for what.

Over the next forty-eight hours he didn't shower or shave. He didn't go out or talk to anyone. He sat staring at soap operas and game shows on the television set. He leafed through books he found open on the floor by Sarah's side of the bed. He didn't eat, and he slept sporadically. He thought about Sarah and the child, their life force as a couple.

He would lie on the mattress on her side of the bed, his head on her pillow, and stare at the ceiling as the afternoon shadows lengthened. Her dog-eared copy of *The Second Sex* was on the nightstand. Sarah had been obsessed with Simone de Beauvoir and her relationship with Jean-Paul Sartre. She had introduced Carter to Sartre and Camus, and they had endless conversations about existentialism and "authenticity" and "freedom," and the idea that living fully and authentically was easier during wartime and times of crisis than in "bourgeois" periods of peace and stability. How much an indulgence those abstractions seemed now. He realized that Sarah had not been "the second sex"—that it was his life that lacked authenticity and "commitment." Reticence had marked him as a coward and a phony. At moments he felt he hadn't deserved her love and wished he could change places with her. He was impatient with the absurdity of his survival. He decided that he would not wait for the draft, but would rush out to the nearest army recruitment center and sign up for Vietnam, hurl himself into the war zone. He tugged on the St. Christopher medal and wondered if it would protect him halfway around the world. He wondered if it would have protected Sarah.

Sometimes he would plot revenge on Sarah's murderers. Other times a spiral of self-recrimination would lead to dark, self-destructive thoughts. He went over all the ways he could have changed things. If only he had stayed at home and gone with her to the church instead of to Selma. Carter had truly not grasped that his people were capable of what Sarah knew they might do. He had averted disaster once before, when Mizell and Posey were harassing them; if he had been there this time, maybe he could have done it again. In the maelstrom of regret that kept him awake, the thought he kept returning to was, if only he had asked Sarah to marry him.

The next day, Sally brought him soup and sandwiches. She told him that arrangements had been made to fly Sarah's body back to New York for burial the following weekend. On the third day, Pete Callahan dropped by. Carter hadn't read the paper, but Pete told him about the news out of Alabama, the march to Montgomery, how it was going relatively smoothly and would be over the following morning. Then he handed Carter a small brown envelope. "Sheriff Mizell found this in the rubble at the scene. I asked him if I could give it to you." Inside was the amethyst birthstone from the ring Carter had given Sarah.

That night Carter awakened at 3:00 a.m., showered, and shaved. He got into the car and headed for Montgomery. From there he would go to New York for the funeral.

He drove four hours into the sunrise and joined the throng of marchers on a pristine morning at the Catholic complex of St. Jude's outside Montgomery, the campsite from the night before. The crowd had grown to fifty thousand, Carter learned from one of the reporters he sought out. He wanted to take notes and maybe give Pete something he could use in *The Troy Times*. He nodded to Hennessey and some of the writers he had met at the Albert back in Selma. But as he stood watching the crowd pass him by on the road into the capital of Alabama, he put away his notebook.

He thought of the concatenation of events that had led him to be with these thousands of souls at this moment, a series of contingencies that in his own case went all the way back to a new Duncan yo-yo mesmerizing a boy preacher in the shade of the Troy courthouse square: two sons joined by the need not to accept the future their parents had planned for them. Carter multiplied his and Lige's story by all the other lives represented here on this bittersweet spring morning in a city known as the Cradle of the Confederacy. And now all those life experiences were ordered and branded with meaning, made random no more by this event, this moment in history.

Sarah had always been drawn to Thomas Merton's story about a child hit by a car in a Latin American barrio. A priest appeared on the scene to administer the last rites, and through that ancient ritual of absolution, the child's suffering was placed in a sacred context, connecting it with the agony of Christ and the martyrs throughout history, of all who had gone before, so as to redeem it from pointless absurdity. Carter, the Baptist, had come to see religion as one of the quirks that disconnected his region and his people from the secular urgencies of the day, as a force of division rather than continuity. But Sarah, the agnostic Reform Jew, had insisted on the necessity of ritual, of gesture, of the act: the demonstration.

Today Carter decided to do something that violated every withholding, self-regarding, parsimonious instinct of his journalist's soul. He stepped off the curb where he had been standing with the other reporters, and he joined the marchers. If he could not overcome his inhibition on his own behalf, he would march for Lige in the hospital, for Randall and Celia and Danny, and for Sarah. Self-consciously at first, he moved into the crowd, and with each step he felt himself enlarged by his own anonymity. He became just another one of the thousands who rambled the six miles into downtown Montgomery, the simple act of walking belying the complexity of the forces that compelled them. In the rising heat he became aware of the St. Christopher medal sticking to his chest, and he pulled it outside his T-shirt. The marchers reached the fountain on Court Square, where slaves watered their masters' horses in antebellum days, and moved up Dexter Avenue past the church where Dr. King had begun his pilgrimage nearly a decade earlier as the green young leader of a bus boycott. Finally, they reached the silver and white capitol building, from whose domed top the state of Alabama flew the battle flag of the Confederacy.

Carter began to smile. And then he began to laugh. It was a euphoric kind of laughter that resolved into tears. Up on the speakers' stand, in the shadow of the capitol, Dr. King preached of the long season of suffering that had brought them there to that place, and the tears continued to stream down Carter's cheeks. He turned his face to the sun, accepting the baptism.

Dr. King's words poured over the crowd like honey and fire.

"I know some of you are asking today, 'How long will it take?' I come to say to you this afternoon, however difficult the moment, however frustrating the hour, it will not be long, because truth pressed to the earth will rise again.

"How long? Not long, because no lie can live forever.

"How long? Not long, because you will reap what you sow.

"How long? Not long, because the arc of the moral universe is long, but it bends toward justice.

"How long? Not long, because mine eyes have seen the glory of the coming of the Lord. He is trampling out the vintage where the grapes of wrath are stored. He hath loosed the fateful lightning of his terrible swift sword. His truth is marching on.

"Glory Hallelujah! Glory Hallelujah!"

When Carter returned to Mississippi from Sarah's funeral, the first thing he did was report to the U.S. Army recruitment office in Troy and volunteer his services for the war in Vietnam.

27

B UT YOU DIDN'T END UP going to Vietnam, did you?" Sydney
asked. Carter had called her that Saturday evening at the Pinehurst, and they had been on the phone for nearly an hour. The luxuri-
ous, fuguelike quality of the conversation, along with the fact that he
was conducting his end of it in his childhood home, had given him an
autonomic shimmer of adolescence.

"I didn't," said Carter.

"What happened?"

"I failed the physical. I was classified 4-F."

"You had a physical problem?"

"Not really," Carter said, "but I love it when you direct-examine me."

"Oh," Sydney said.

"Psychiatric grounds," Carter said. "My father made sure."

"How?"

"I passed all the physical exams, but somebody insisted on a psychiatric examination and determined I'd been under 'too much stress.'
Their words. I found out later that the judge pulled strings."

"Oh." This time the inflection had the up-lilt of keen sympathy. To
his amazement, Carter kind of liked it. There was a comfortable silence. Then Sydney whispered, "Thank you for testifying."

"You're welcome," he whispered back. "So then," he said in his normal voice, "how was the first day of the photo shoot?"

"Surreal," she said. "Creepy." That weekend, one of the most lavish and expensive spreads in the *New York Tribune Magazine*'s history was being shot on location at Magic Time and Shiloh Church, scheduled to run after the verdict was handed down. The celebrity photographer Jill Jaffe, famous for her stark, "edgy" glamour portraits of celebrities and politicians, had arrived from New Orleans on Thursday night in a fleet of vans and trucks full of lights and equipment and a crew of stylists, makeup artists, set designers, and assistants. They were in a cluster of suites at the Pinehurst.

"Then why'd you agree to it?" Carter asked.

"Look," she said mock defensively, "it's the *Tribune* Sunday magazine. Do you know how many lawyers would give their left nut for that kind of publicity?"

"You don't have a left nut."

"I know. That's a direct quote from the attorney general, who insisted I participate. Believe me, I didn't want to. That's all I need: to tempt fate before the verdict comes down."

Judge McDonnell had not allowed the jurors—or whoever among them was willing to participate—to be photographed, so the shoot had focused only on the principals in the trial. The "class portrait," as Jill Jaffe called it, had been taken that morning at Shiloh Church. Congressman Elijah Knight and New York mayoral candidate Charles Lloyd were there to represent the surviving SNCC staffers, Lacey Hullender and Lawrence "Strawberry" Thigpen the Klansmen. Some of the victims' relatives were included as well—Celia Bunt's sister Aurelia, Randall Peek's surviving siblings, Daniel Johnston's mother, and Sarah Solomon's brother, Michael. Even the defendant, Sam Bohannon, showed up with his bodyguard and his lawyer. Getting Bohannon to cooperate had not been easy, but, Sydney gathered, the *Tribune*'s editor, Haynes Wentworth, had pulled out all the stops, persuading Puckett it would help "humanize" his client. Since Carter had declined to participate and refused to intercede with his father to sit for a portrait with Judge McDonnell, Wentworth had Robert Kennedy, Jr., call Judge Ransom for a personal favor, to no avail.

"I know you already passed," Sydney said, "but they asked me if I'd talk to you about letting them take your picture. Jill Jaffe was bugging me about it all day."

"It feels unseemly. Or what was your word? Creepy."

"Unseemly," Sydney said appreciatively. "Sounds like something from another time and place, like spats or snuffboxes, or dignity."

"Fundamentally, I wouldn't be able to live with myself."

"It's amazing you're the only one who feels that way."

"Besides my father," Carter said. "Well, you know, with the fall of Communism, the only 'ism' we have to fear is show bizm."

"Well, I guess I'm part of the problem, too," she said with a not altogether sincere sigh. "But Carter, as a professional observer of the human spectacle, you really should have been there." Bradley Crawford, Harold Bernhardt, and some of the other camp followers of the trial had made a pilgrimage out to Shiloh Church that morning to watch the show.

Sydney went on to describe the day's highlights, including Jill Jaffe as a photo dominatrix. "She's this downtown chick, dressed completely in black, Hermès scarf, pierced nostril, peroxide-white pixie do, with leathery orange skin, a slash of bright red lipstick, and big aviator glasses. When I asked her if she was burning up in those clothes, she said"—here Sydney found her adenoids—" 'Look, I'm a Noo Yawkuh. I wawk fast, I tawk fast, I dress in black, and I say "fuck" a lot.' "

"Wick-ed," Carter said.

"But she's a pro," Sydney continued. "The shoot was organized like the half-time show at the Super Bowl." Each set of "subjects" arrived in shifts and moved in and out like clockwork. The relatives of the victims first; then the "assailants," as Jaffe called them. Some of the survivors were at Shiloh Church for the first time since it had been rebuilt. "Even Jaffe had to be moved by it, although she has the maternal instincts of a black widow spider. The families of the victims kept breaking down during the setup."

"How'd Jill handle that?"

Sydney, back in accent: " 'Jeezus H. Chrrrist, it's like they never had their pictures taken before. So friggin' hysterical. Streisand was like that. But I've never had nobodies act this way.' "

"Sounds like a nightmare."

"Hullender was acting weird, too. The trial's set him off. And now this photo shoot. He seems agitated. I think he may be on drugs or something."

"I guess Jesus must have lost His healing powers," Carter said. "Oh, well. It'll all be over soon."

"Tomorrow she wants another group shot of the Magic Time crew, Knight and Lloyd, and of the 'assailants'—Strawberry, Hullender, and Sam Bohannon. And me."

"I'm surprised she didn't ask you to dress up as Blind Justice."

"God. She's probably got the scales and blindfold in her wardrobe van. You should have seen her trying to make over some of the others. Dress Congressman Knight in 'period' overalls. Putting shadow on Hullender's bad eye. Insisting that Strawberry smile so she can see his wretched teeth. I wonder what's in store for us tomorrow afternoon. 'Magic Time at Magic Time' she's calling it. Something about the light."

Carter knew that the hour of golden light in late afternoon was known in photography circles as magic time or the magic hour because the shadows melt away and there's a lustrous richness to the light that can transform a photograph into something mystical and otherworldly, and seems to conjure forth a human subject's essence.

"Do you have plans for dinner afterward?" he asked.

Sydney went silent. "Are you asking me out on a date?"

"I just asked you if you had plans, not if you wanted to have dinner with me," Carter teased. "Bring your boyfriend along. Has he arrived yet?"

"He's coming Monday afternoon—to be here for closing arguments. I doubt Puckett's defense is going to last more than a day."

"My friend Stephen wants to have us over for a home-cooked meal before you break camp."

"Oh, I see." She sounded confused.

"It'll give you one more chance to talk me down after our big moment together." Carter was referring to his time on the witness stand and testing to see whether it had shifted Sydney's psychic coordinates as well.

"Oh, so this is it?"

"Disappointed?"

"A little." Then she said, "I shouldn't be acting like this."

"How are you acting?"

"You know," she said.

"How?" he persisted.

"Flirty," she said.

"That's default, isn't it?" Carter said.

"I didn't realize you thought so little of yourself," she teased back. Carter could hear her inhale, and he braced himself slightly. "This kind of thing is pretty common, though, during trials."

"What kind of thing?"

"Well"—she searched for the right phrase—"these sort of fateful attractions."

"I guess it's like on movie sets. The cast comes together in artificial but turbocharged circumstances. They pair off, and it feels like kismet."

"The theatrical analogy is apt," said Sydney drily. "Plus, in the courtroom you're dealing with life in extremis, the suddenness with which it all can be ended. The passions get churned up." She was quiet for a moment. "This is making me feel sad," she said. "So what time?"

"Six-thirty. Sunday's a school night." Then he added gratuitously, "And your boyfriend's coming."

Sydney sighed. "Pick me up at Magic Time. We'll be wrapping up that damned shoot. I'll catch a ride out there from the hotel with Jill Jaffe. She says it won't go much later than six."

The parking lot at Magic Time was emptier than Carter expected when he pulled up late Sunday afternoon. The photographer's rental utility van was parked out front, its rear cargo door open and lighting equipment on the lift. The black-and-white patrol car belonging to the sheriff's deputy assigned to escort Bohannon was parked next to the van, and a Ryder truck was next to it. A minivan for shuttling subjects from town explained the scarcity of vehicles.

The old cinder-block building was blistered with age and peeling paint, shrouded now in weeds and kudzu, though the front door and window were freshly painted and distressed for authenticity, and the Magic

Time sign had been retouched. The vintage Jax beer sign and Dr Pepper thermometer were still there. Highway tar and the buttery lemon fragrance of tea-olive blossoms mixed with the smell of the paint. Carter hadn't anticipated an emotional reaction to a place he had passed countless times on the highway in the years since, but as he approached, he was hit by a phantom feeling of loss.

The front door was ajar. Carter heard no sound from inside. "Hello?" he called through the screen door. "Anybody here?"

One of the photographer's assistants appeared on the other side of the rusted screen, a pale, anorexic girl in jeans and a T-shirt, with no makeup and black spiked hair, like a refugee from another dimension. "They went into town for dinner," she said with a hysterical flutter. "We haven't eaten all day." There was something off about her tone, non sequitur.

"Who?" Carter asked.

"The other staffers."

"Are Ms. Rushton and Congressman Knight here?"

The girl looked blank. Then her eyes shifted nervously to her right before answering. "Um—yeah."

Carter stood there awkwardly, waiting to be asked inside, but he realized that the assistant was a New Yorker, and he opened the screen door to let himself in. He stepped into the damp, mildewed interior, blinking as his eyes adjusted to the darkness.

He felt cold steel at his temple.

"Well, welcome," said the familiar voice of Lacey Hullender. "Just in time." Carter did not risk turning to look at Hullender, but could smell the alcohol on his breath. He nudged Carter with the muzzle of his gun to follow the girl, who threw him a look that said, I tried.

"What's going on, Lacey?" Carter's heart thundered in his chest.

Voices could be heard from the back, and Hullender shouted, "Y'all behave now." Then to Carter, "We're having us a prayer meeting, that's all." Hullender, dressed in the same coat and tie he had worn to testify, signaled him with his gun, a Glock semiautomatic, past the dilapidated pool table and the grimy jukebox. Dust lifted beneath Carter's loafers as he moved across the pinewood floor past a canvas drop that partitioned off the set in back. Peripherally, he caught the outline of two figures lying on the floor in the shadows of the drop, blood puddling beneath one of them. Bohannon's nurse, Billy, and his police deputy escort.

Rounding the corner onto the lighted set, Carter saw Lacey's hostages lined up in front of a white paper backdrop. They turned anxiously toward him as he entered. "Look what the Lord sent us," Hullender announced. "His wonders never cease."

"Carter," Sydney called, "he's got explosives."

"That's right, Ransom," Hullender said. "I got a little equalizer right here." He held up a device that looked like a video game joystick. "I trigger this little gizmo, and there's a Ryder truck full of dynamite, diesel fuel, and ammonium nitrate outside ready to blow. That way I make sure none of y'all get funny on me till I'm done." He blinked his one-eyed squint. "'Vengeance is mine, saith the Lord.'"

Carter took in the tableau Hullender—or maybe it was Jill Jaffe's composition—had arranged. Sydney stood behind Elijah Knight and Charles Lloyd, who were seated in folding chairs. Next to them sat Bohannon in his wheelchair, with his dog on his lap. Strawberry stood awkwardly behind the old man. So many people would be a challenge for Hullender to keep in line by himself, and Carter was already calculating the odds against his success. As if reading his thoughts, Hullender reminded him, "All I got to do is push this little red remote button. Boom." A strange light shone in Lacey's eye. Carter did not think it was just the alcohol, or drugs.

The group was lit like a nativity scene by light stands on both sides with two umbrella reflectors attached to each. Carter noticed for the first time the unmistakable Jill Jaffe, standing impatiently behind her Gitzo tripod, haloed by a cloud of cigarette smoke. She sighed and crossed her arms, then let them dangle, then crossed them again, as her assistant cowered behind her. "This is outrageous," she said to Carter, as if he were responsible.

"Silence, please," said Lacey.

"So what's going on, Lacey?" Carter tried to sound friendly.

"He's hijacked my shoot," Jill Jaffe answered for him. "That's what's going on."

"I'm just trying to see justice gets done here," said Hullender. "What y'all don't understand is it's out of my hands. It's God's business now. I'm just a instrument. And right now the Lord wants some pictures of His handiwork." He nudged Jaffe with the muzzle of his gun.

"He's ruining everything," she complained. "And my assistants will be back from dinner any minute now."

"The more the merrier," said Hullender, holding up the remote in his left hand.

Hullender's manic enthusiasm for his enterprise suddenly bated as he gazed at the two bodies on the floor. "They was just part of God's plan. Bystanders like the guards that was slain, forcing Shadrach, Meshach, and Abednego into the fiery furnace." Then, as if awakening from a dream, he took in his surroundings and turned back to Carter. "All the folks who dogged my ass all those years right here under the same roof at Magic Time. How could the Lord let an opportunity like this slip away?" He took in the room and sarcastically declaimed, "Snick headquarters."

Lige looked at Carter and widened his eyes slightly.

"Lacey, you were doing so well with your parole," said Sydney, trying to break the weird spell.

Hullender's face clouded. "You already blew it, sweet lady. This trial's a joke. Bohannon's going to get off again, and I'm going to get stuck holding the bag for the Afro-American strung up at the river."

"I don't know what you mean," Sydney lied.

"Nuh-uh. No way," said Hullender, shaking his head. Then he studied Thigpen. "Strawberry, you always was a pussy." He turned back to Carter. "I'm glad you showed up, Ransom. I really am. God is good. I wanted a record of today, and I might need some assistance taking pictures, since this one here"—he pointed at Jill Jaffe, who was drawing on her filtered cigarette—"is definitely not a blessing." She turned her back to him. "You know how to run a camera, don't you, Ransom? I seen your pictures in *The Troy Times*."

Jill Jaffe whirled around and stepped toward Hullender. "Nobody uses my cameras but me, you fucking redneck. Do you hear?"

In a deft, swift motion, Hullender backhanded the handle of the Glock against the side of her head.

Jaffe's assistant rushed to break her fall. "Oh, my God," the girl screamed, looking up at Hullender, her eyes white with terror.

"Jesus, Lacey," said Strawberry.

"I can't believe I was dumb enough to come back to Mississippi," Charlie Lloyd muttered, lowering his forehead into his hand.

Hullender continued his sermon. "Now, before you showed up, Ransom, we was having a little discussion about whether our congressman here was the saint they say he is." He stopped before Lige and gave him a look. "Now me—I say that only the Lamb of God is perfect and that His peace, the peace that passeth understanding, is for Him and Him alone. Not for sinners like us. And that those who would act like Him, to pretend they're blameless, who don't recognize their own sinfulness, are blasphemers and self-idolaters and need to be shown the error of their ways."

"We are all sinners, Lacey," said Lige wearily.

"But I say the only way to test it is to test it." He stood in front of Sam Bohannon.

Bohannon peered up at Hullender through a thicket of eyebrows, contempt in his gaze. He started to say something, but his voice caught and he began to cough.

Hullender addressed Lige. "Now face it, Congressman. Sambo here's the one who had your friends killed. Ain't that right, Miss Sydney?"

Lacey waved Lige to get up. "Move!" Hullender fired his pistol into the ceiling.

Lige stood up and faced Bohannon's wheelchair. "Okay, that's more like it." Hullender held out the gun. "Now, I want you to take this instrument of divine retribution, Mr. Congressman"—he offered Lige his gun—"and put a bullet in Sam Bohannon's head."

Lige just stared.

Hullender held the gun out to him by the barrel. "Come on, you know you want to," he said. "Put a bullet through his brain." Hullender's head pivoted to allow his good eye to take in his surroundings. "You know Ransom would do it. But he don't pretend to be a saint, Congressman." He waved the gun under Lige's nose.

"You are one sick fuck, Hullender," Charlie Lloyd muttered.

"Watch your language!" Hullender glared at Charlie and added with disgust, "Reverend!"

"He's high, folks," Charlie explained. "In case you haven't noticed. Probably on crank or blow."

"What if I am?" Hullender laughed and swiped his hand across his nose.

"What do drugs have to do with Jesus?" said Charlie. "Ain't that a sin?"

"You're just pissed 'cause you ain't got none. I know all about you, Charlie. That Afro-American reporter told me all about you and your junkie thing for blow."

"Who, Lovelace?" asked Carter.

"Yeah, ol' 'Sheed scored me some shit for tellin' him the straight lowdown."

Carter glanced at Sydney. She looked crestfallen.

"And it was bad shit," Hullender said with a laugh. "Cut with Ajax, more than likely." Then, turning back to Lige, "I'm waiting, Knight. Go on and take your shot."

Lige shook his head, refusing the weapon again.

"How do you know he wouldn't use the bullet on you, Lacey?" said Carter.

Hullender held up the detonator. "Because here in my other hand is my insurance policy. If I push the button, we all go up."

Bohannon was seized with a hacking cough. Hullender became irritated. "Now the Imperial Wizard here seems to be having a little trouble breathing." Bohannon's wheezing had increased considerably over the last few minutes.

"It's all the dust in here," said Strawberry.

"And what do you call this here doohickey, Sambo?" said Hullender, indicating the inhaler Bohannon was clutching in his left hand.

Bohannon coughed and struggled to answer. "A nebulizer," he croaked, his voice hoarse and weaker than it had been at the fish camp with Carter.

"Nebulizer." Hullender rolled it over on his tongue. "Yeah, I seen you sucking on that thing in the courtroom. Keeps you alive, don't it?"

Bohannon continued to cough.

Hullender reached for the nebulizer. A growl rumbled from somewhere deep in the throat of the dog in Bohannon's lap. Hullender pulled his hand back. "Now, Sambo, you got a leash on that mutt, don't you?" His drug-fueled swagger subsided in the presence of the animal, and he held up the detonator like a crucifix. Bohannon, still wheezing, moved the swollen knuckles of his arthritic fingers to reveal a studded collar around Samson's thick neck and a short, sturdy chain that ran back to the base of the wheelchair. "As long as he's chained up nice and tight," said Hullender. "I don't want to have to shoot him. There's nothing that upsets me more than cruelty to animals."

He turned back to Lige and said, "Okay, so you don't want to shoot nobody neither." He pointed to the tank rigged up on the back of Bohannon's wheelchair. "Now, this here's his oxygen. Take it away from him." Hullender circled Bohannon's wheelchair. Samson growled. "I'll start you out," said Hullender casually. As he passed behind the chair, he flicked the cannula from Bohannon's nose and handed it to Lige.

"Leave him alone, Lacey," said Strawberry.

"You keep your mouth shut, you snitch," Hullender said to Strawberry. Samson snarled again, and Hullender pulled back. "Sambo, make that dog shut up. You keep it quiet now!" He held up the detonator to supply the "or else." Bohannon soothed Samson. "Strawberry, you help keep that dog under control, too, now!" said Hullender. Strawberry reached over to stroke Samson behind the ears, as he had undoubtedly done to Samson's forebears.

Hullender turned back to Lige and ordered him to twist open the valve on Bohannon's oxygen tank. When Lige did not move, Hullender kicked off his loafer and, in a pirouette-like move, wrenched the oxygen valve open with the toe of his shiny stockinged foot. The contents escaped with a loud hiss.

"This is not helpful, Lacey," said Sydney.

Hullender looked at her with a pleading expression, like a little boy caught in some minor transgression. "If the congressman here is a godly man, then he's going to make sure that Bohannon gets the fate he deserves. Isn't that what we want, sweet lady?"

Lige said with a lavish fatigue, "What do you want with us, Hullender? Obviously, your problem is still with me. Let the others go."

Hullender shook his head. "No. Huh-uh. To every thing there is a season. A time to be born and a time to die. A time to kill and a time to heal. We're going to have us our own little judgment day. I'm the judge and jury this go-round. And I'm going to say who lives and dies."

" 'Judge not, lest ye be judged.' " Sam Bohannon had found the strength to confront Hullender.

"We already have a trial, Lacey," said Carter. "You just don't like the way it's going."

"That's right, Ransom. So I figured it was up to me to bring ol' Sambo here to justice. Render unto Caesar the things that are Caesar's, but render unto God the things that are God's. And if Caesar screws up"—he looked at Sydney—"God will provide." He held up his pistol in one hand and the detonator in the other. "I'm just the sword of His retribution. And we'll have the pictures all taken for the six o'clock news."

Carter was beginning to see the outlines of Hullender's logic. He was God's anointed. And now he was going to see justice done by His lights. And have it all validated by the only judge that mattered in this world, the camera's eye of the outside media.

Lacey addressed them all. "Okay, now, picture time. Let's get started. Now it's y'all's turn to take off your clothes."

Charlie Lloyd and Lige looked at each other.

"I don't understand," Lige said.

"Take 'em off." Hullender's temper seemed to be shortening as the afternoon wore on and the drugs wore off. "First, the black gentlemen. And Ransom. You, too, Little Miss Attorney General."

"She wasn't at the river that day, Lacey," said Carter.

"But she's here today." Hullender winked at her. "Too bad that little Jew boy ain't here," Hullender added. "He's the one who needs to be put right with the Lord. Like we got even with that one on Halloween. Right, Straw?"

"Dexter," said Charlie Lloyd. He stared at Hullender bitterly.

Carter realized that Lloyd hadn't known about his friend's ultimate fate.

Lacey furrowed his brow in mock concern. "Yeah, him and his MoonPies." He smiled and cocked his head to look at Thigpen. "You'll never guess where that one is."

Bohannon wheezed as he rearranged his body in the wheelchair and spoke. "There's your story, Ransom."

"Shut up, Sambo!" Hullender exploded. "You got no right to say nothing about it. That was the Grand Dragon's business. He's the only one could get things done. And if Baby Huey hadn't messed things up at Shiloh Church, it wouldn't have got so ugly. You wanted Knight, and he won't there. The Grand Dragon wanted the Jew girl." It took a split second for Carter to realize what he was talking about, and only then did it hit him that Glen Boutwell, whom he had chosen to regard as a tragic figure, was a ruthless murderer.

Bohannon hacked painfully but rose to the argument, gasping out each sentence, raising himself up magisterially in the chair. "You never had any discipline, Hullender. You were always a loose cannon. And you still are."

Lacey stared at Bohannon, his expression curdling from some memory. "What, do you think I wanted to drop the damned pistol?" he finally blurted. "You think I done it on purpose? It was a accident." His voice turned whiny and adolescent. "You was always blaming me for anything that went wrong."

Bohannon sank into his chair and stared at the animal in his lap.

Suddenly conscious of the others, Lacey recovered and collected himself. "Yeah, well, the Grand Dragon knew how to take care of business, didn't he? None of your mumbo jumbo. Why don't you tell them where he put that one, Sam?"

Bohannon looked away. "I know nothing about it."

"Why don't you tell them, Strawberry. You was with us when the Grand Dragon got Culpepper to take care of it for us. You probably think about it like I do every time you go in that courthouse."

"What's he talking about?" Sydney directed her question at Strawberry.

Strawberry shook his head and muttered, "Skeebo could've told you they hid the body in plain sight."

"What does the courthouse have to do with it?" asked Carter.

"Check out the cornerstone," Hullender crowed. "We done it when they was renovating down there. All we needed was access to the site and somebody to run the mixer. MoonPie Man is in the cornerstone of the new courthouse annex." He watched the information sink in and cocked his head toward Carter. "Lonnie Culpepper's daddy done nice work, don't you think, Ransom?"

Carter looked at Bohannon.

"I told you I had nothing to do with that," said Bohannon. "Zero." He choked out his words, the effects of his oxygen loss growing more apparent. "That was Posey and his renegades. Boutwell got dragged in after the fact because Posey had the information on your daddy and your brother."

Carter was feeling nauseated now. And he couldn't make out what Bohannon was saying through the rasp and wheeze. Did he hear him correctly? He thought he said something about his mother again.

Hullender was growing impatient. "We ain't got time to listen to you, old man. We got pictures to take. So what are y'all waiting for? Take off your clothes!" The varnish of religious restraint had chipped away to reveal the crude Lacey Hullender of old. He approached the anorexic assistant, who had been cowering in the corner, and put the gun to her head. He turned back to the others and said, "Do it now!"

Lige, Charlie, Carter, and Sydney looked at one another, then slowly began undressing.

Hullender watched, paying particular attention to Sydney. Circling around them, his head swiveling, he slipped up behind her while she was folding her jacket over the chair. She straightened up. Using the muzzle of his pistol, he began lifting the hair off the back of her neck. "Like I said," Hullender whispered loudly in her ear, "I don't plan on getting caught again, Counselor." Sydney stood frozen. "I learned a lot in prison. A lot more than you knew." He traced her lips with the steel of the barrel as if it were a tube of lipstick. "And there's more ways into Mexico than the wetbacks or border patrol's got any idea about."

"Leave her alone, Hullender," Carter said.

"You didn't think I was going to let Skeebo or Strawberry get away with nailing me, did you, pretty lady?" Hullender continued.

"Besides"—he now aimed the pistol at Carter—"I don't plan on leaving no witnesses."

Sam Bohannon spoke up, his voice ragged. "'Ye have heard it was said by them of old time, Thou shalt not commit adultery: But I say unto you, That whosoever looketh on a woman to lust after her hath committed adultery with her already in his heart.'" Then Bohannon began coughing again and clasped the nebulizer to his lips.

"Uh-oh," Lacey said. "Look at what the congressman's done to our poor defendant. He's run out of oxygen."

"Stop torturing the man, Hullender," said Lige.

Lacey turned to Carter. "We got some pictures to take, Ransom. Before we lose Sambo to the croup. Get over there behind that camera."

Carter, who was down to socks and underwear now, made his way over to the tripod. "Someone's going to need to show me how this works," he said.

"Go ahead, assistant," Hullender said. "Start assisting." The poor anorexic began showing Carter the equipment. "And the rest of y'all keep stripping off them clothes." Sydney finished unbuttoning her blouse and removed her top. Lige and Charlie Lloyd, too, were down to their underwear. "Come on, Ransom," he barked. "We ain't got all day."

"Just a minute," Carter said as the assistant showed him the Mamiya RZ 6 x 7.

Lige and Charlie were the first to get completely naked. Sydney was taking deep breaths, scrunched in the chair in her underwear. Lacey studied the two black men. "Whoo-eee!" he leered. "I ain't seen anything like this since Parchman." He circled them in candid appraisal. "You ever done it doggy-style, Congressman? You and the mayor make a right cute couple."

"Get this over with, Hullender," said Charlie Lloyd.

"What you complaining about? I'm going to make you an adult entertainment star. Are you ready, Ransom?"

"Not yet," said Carter. He adjusted the light balance and managed to say, "All set."

"All right. First, let's put the white girl together with the colored gentlemen on each side. Like a Oreo." Hullender instructed Sydney to sit in the chair between Lige and Charlie. "Squeeze in there real tight between them with your head about crotch-high. Make a little prosecutor sandwich." He framed the shot pretentiously with his hands. He stood back and looked at them. "You ain't completely undressed, lady. It'll look a whole lot better when you're nude. And I want me in this picture, too." He returned to the tripod, moving Carter and the assistant aside to peer into the viewfinder. "Let me see where to stand." Grinning smugly, he strode back over to place himself in the shot directly behind the seated Sydney. "Go ahead, Ransom," he commanded, "tell us when to say cheese."

"Hold on," said Carter. He and the assistant fussed with the sync cord running to the camera from the battery pack.

"Shoot it, Ransom. We got rolls of film to go. And we're not leaving till we get the money shot." He nodded at Jill Jaffe, who was prone on the floor. "That's what she called the most important picture she took yesterday. The money shot."

"And what would that be?" Carter said wearily, holding up his hand to signal that they were almost ready.

"Sam Bohannon meeting his maker."

Carter pressed the shutter, releasing the camera's motor drive. "Smile, Lacey," he said. The gigantic Octabank Softbox suddenly lit up the room to the stark candlepower of a supernova. It produced the kind of intense light against the white backdrop that would bring up every detail of the subjects' faces, all the way down to the pores of their skin. Blue and pink dots the size of beach balls floated in Carter's field of vision.

Hullender clawed at the air, then covered his eyes with his forearm. "What the fuck!" he shouted. The flashing continued. Carter's finger held the shutter down. The strobe effect of repeated flashes was like being trapped inside an electrical storm. The loud click-whoosh-click-whoosh-click-whoosh of the sustained flickering megawatt flash drove Bohannon's dog crazy. Samson was growling and barking madly.

Carter chose that instant to rush Hullender. He broke out from behind the camera and dived over Sydney, propelling himself off her chair and scattering Lige and Charlie in the wake of his lunge. He hit Lacey high like a middle linebacker, and they both tumbled to the floor. The gun discharged, then dropped from Hullender's hand and skittered across the pinewood. Somehow Hullender held on to the detonator, but Lige went for the gun. Strawberry slumped to the floor next to Bohannon's wheelchair, holding his shoulder where Hullender's stray bullet had struck him. Hullender caught Carter across the eye with his fist, then broke free long enough to scramble to his feet. Lige had the pistol now, and he and Lacey squared off.

Carter picked himself up off the floor and crouched between them, third party to the standoff. Lacey held out the detonator, threatening the armed and naked Elijah Knight with his thumb on the red button. "So now we ain't fucking around," gasped Hullender, panting heavily. "We going to find out some answers, huh, Congressman."

Sam Bohannon was doubled over in his wheelchair, struggling for air, with Strawberry collapsed on the floor, his hand on his wound, blood seeping through his fingers.

Hullender circled Lige, taunting him to use the weapon. "Now's your chance, Knight. Be a saint!"

"Toss me the gun, Lige," said Charlie Lloyd, clutching his jacket against his crotch. "The fucker lynched Dexter. I have no problem shooting him."

"Put the bomb down, Lacey," Carter said. "You don't want to die."

"What have I got to live for? I ain't going back to Parchman, that's for sure."

"Lacey," Sydney said. "You haven't been charged with anything yet. Just calm down and think about what you're doing."

"Come on, Lige, let me have the gun, man, please," Charlie said. "Let me do it."

Lige shook his head and kept his eye on Lacey.

"This ain't about me," Lacey said. "This is the Lord's business. If I go, I'm taking all of y'all with me. Even if you shoot me, I'll have the last word."

As Hullender circled and talked, he backed closer to Bohannon's wheelchair. Samson growled deep and low as Lacey drew closer. "Shut that dog the fuck up, Sambo," he shouted. "Or I'll blow this place to kingdom come."

With great effort, Bohannon lifted his bleary eyes to peer up at Hullender, then lowered them to the snarling Samson.

"I mean it, Sambo, shut him up!"

Bohannon lowered his head to whisper in the dog's ear, simultaneously unhooking the clasp at his collar.

The white pit bull bolted from the wheelchair and in a single bounce off the floor crashed into Hullender's chest, sending him sprawling backward.

Screaming as the dog snapped at him, Hullender managed to whack Samson on the snout with his elbow and launch the animal across the floor. But Samson righted himself and, legs churning, barreled back at Hullender and pounced on him before he could get up. Although trained to go for the throat, Samson settled for the closest unprotected area. Carter witnessed the moment when, wedged between Lacey's legs, Samson rolled his eyes back in his head and snapped his pincerlike jaws down on Hullender's groin. Carter was astonished that Lacey still managed somehow to hold on to the detonator as he backpedaled while climbing to his feet. When he finally stood up, howling, Samson hung from his crotch.

"Get him off, Strawberry!" Lacey screamed. "Get him off!"

As Charlie Lloyd began to charge toward Lacey, the wounded Strawberry, curled up on the floor next to the wheelchair, warned him, "Get out of sight. You don't want to distract the dog. Samson don't like niggers."

Lloyd backed off.

Carter shouted to Sydney and the photo assistant, "Get out of here." Sydney gathered up her clothes, and they both scrambled for the exit. Sydney remained in the door, watching. Carter gave Lige an imploring look. Lige hesitated, then handed him the pistol. Lacey reeled and stumbled in circles, screaming, as Samson dangled from his pants like a ham.

Carter took aim, and for the first time in his adult life pulled the trigger of a gun. The sound pierced the pandemonium.

Hullender grabbed his wrist, his hand still clasping the detonator. Behind him Carter heard the click of another gun being cocked. He followed Hullender's eyes to the door. There by the curtain, standing next to Sydney, was Stephen Musgrove, clasping a pistol in both hands, arms extended, legs spread in a marksman's stance, just as Jimbo had taught him at the firing range.

"Drop it, Lacey," Stephen said. "Right now."

"Go home to Mama," Hullender said dismissively, without looking at him. "I don't take orders from little faggots." Then he struggled on his knees over to Bohannon's wheelchair. "Goddammit, Sambo, in God's name, call the fucking dog off!"

The bullet Stephen Musgrove fired buried itself in Lacey Hullender's abdomen. Hullender looked down at the blood spreading across his upper torso. With his shirt soaked red, he braced himself on the wheelchair and lifted up the detonator before Sam Bohannon.

" 'Be not deceived; God is not mocked: For whatsoever a man soweth, that shall he also reap,' " Hullender declared, with his thumb poised over the red button and a crazed, unhinged look in his eye. "Fuck all of you. I'll see you in hell, Sambo!"

But the old man had reached under his pant leg and was palming something shiny. Cold steel flashed. With both hands and a heroic burst of strength, Sam Bohannon drove a hog blade straight up into Hullender's guzzle.

28

A T THE PINEHURST HOTEL, where Carter had driven Sydney after the police took their statements at Magic Time, neither could
say good night. On their second bourbon neat, Sydney had reached her
hand under the table and rested it palm up on his knee. He engulfed it
in his hand and was still holding it at last call. The bartender allowed
them to remain at their corner well booth past the ridiculously early closing time.

"You look nice with your clothes on." Carter tried to joke, but he
could barely fathom the joy he felt simply seeing her sitting across from
him. After midnight, Sydney invited him up to her room for a nightcap
from the minibar.

Standing outside her door, fiddling with the old-fashioned room key,
she turned to him. She held his gaze for an uncertain moment and said
in a small, resolute voice, "Nothing's going to happen."

The emotions he felt were too complex for him to argue with her.
The fact of her boyfriend seemed like a glitch compared with the mor-
bidly ironic circumstances of their finding each other and the encounter
with death they had just survived. He was happy enough to be crossing
the threshold into her personal domain, even if it was only a hotel room.

Inside, Sydney kicked off her shoes and lay down on the bed, patting the spot next to her. He stretched out beside her, feeling as if he were easing into an out-of-body experience. They lay side by side facing the ceiling, only their hands touching, their pinkies hooked tightly.

Carter spoke first. "You know the argument I had with Sarah the night before she died?"

"Yes."

"It was about the baby. We knew she was pregnant."

Sydney adjusted her hand so that it covered his. They lay in silence for a few more moments. Carter heard her swallow.

"I wasn't sure I was ready. She knew that, and she offered to see a doctor in New York. We were so young."

"I know," Sydney said.

"I wasn't enough of a mensch to ask her to marry me."

Sydney turned toward him, her eyes closed tightly, and pressed her forehead against his chest. "Oh, sweetheart," she whispered.

The next thing Carter was aware of was a blade of dawn slicing the curtains. He and Sydney were still fully clothed, facing each other. His hand cupped the back of her head, her face burrowed under his chin. Her foot was wedged between his calves.

He pried himself up and watched her profile for a long time, then pressed his mouth to the bridge of her nose before sliding out of bed. As he let himself out the door, he turned back to confirm one last time that she existed. She had not moved, except to lift her hand in a stationary wave goodbye.

To Carter's amazement, Hullender's hijacking of the photo shoot did not void the *State of Mississippi v. Samuel Holifield Bohannon*. Judge McDonnell acted quickly to sequester the jury so that news of the death of the star witness at the hands of the defendant wouldn't jeopardize the conclusion of the trial. Sydney and Arthur Puckett spent Monday in closed session with the judge while the defense hit McDonnell with motion after motion for a mistrial. The judge decided this one in Sydney's favor, though she told Carter afterward that the underlying purpose of Puckett's hissy fits had been to establish grounds for an appeal.

The defense's case was brief, as Sydney speculated, and centered on

Bohannon's alibi for the night of March 20, 1965: He had been visiting his mother in Natchez. One of the three witnesses Puckett called was Bohannon's sister, a mousy, henna-haired retired RN who, in the course of confirming his story, managed to mention that her brother had gotten his famous catfish recipe from the family maid. As the case went to closing arguments, the buzz around the trial finally reached a decibel level equal to its pretrial fanfare, and the courtroom was standing room only.

Sydney Rushton was able to regain her focus and to rise to the "call of destiny," as she put it to Carter, in her way of joking but not really. On Wednesday morning she began her summation by somewhat relentlessly reconstructing the crime. Then she softened. The second half of her closing arguments was a leisurely, almost intimate imploring of the jury to honor the humanity of Celia, Randall, Daniel, and Sarah. They, the jurors, she said, were the last chance, if not for redemption, then for justice. These jurors now stood between those heroic young people and the shotguns and Molotov cocktails and firebombs sent by Sam Bohannon that tragic March night; they were poised to veer history into a different direction, however belatedly. The offhanded delivery, almost as if she were thinking out loud, provided a nice tonal counterpoint to the big abstract themes of good versus evil.

Arthur Puckett, who in his opening statements had stressed that "this is not a popularity contest between the civil rights workers and Sam Bohannon," chose not to dwell on his own client. Affecting pity more than indignation, he lacerated the character and reliability of the state's chief witnesses, Hullender and Lawrence Thigpen. When he referred to Hullender's "mental instability," he shot Sydney one of Jack Benny's "Well?" looks. Carter thought he saw Sydney trying to suppress a smirk. She had indeed dodged a bullet. If Lacey's breakdown had occurred a week earlier, Bohannon would have walked.

The main thrust of Puckett's speech was the alternative case against Glen Boutwell: he was at the crime scene, with the will and the authority to act unilaterally. In an ingeniously bold touch, Puckett argued that Boutwell was an example of how unimaginably bad it was back in those racist days of yore—proof that the most upstanding citizens in the community, men like Boutwell, were party to this heinous crime. "Bohannon is being scapegoated," he declared, and then made an egregious appeal to the blacks on the jury. "If you pretend that he was a freak," he said, "if you pretend that Sam Bohannon was segregation's Satan, then you are denying the systemic brutality inflicted on our country's black citizens a mere twenty-five years ago. To convict Mr. Bohannon would be to disregard the full extent of the crime of segregation. It would dishonor the memory of the victims at hand."

Carter was impressed by Puckett's specious logic, spellbound by its cynicism. He glanced at Sydney. Her eyebrow cocked and her lips pursed, as if to say, We'll see about that.

Now Puckett's cadences turned sorghum thick, signaling to Carter that the summation to follow was not necessarily original with this case. Puckett started in on a fairy tale, the Hans Christian Andersen story "The Emperor's New Clothes." He suggested that the government's arguments had been as flimsy and immaterial as those fairy-tale garments. The kingdom in the story had been convinced that the "good" citizens could discern clothing that did not exist. The jurors should not be made to feel, he said, that seeing through the prosecution's elaborate imaginary wardrobe somehow made them "bad." He gestured to the media, reminding them of the burden of history the jury shouldered. "Don't give in to it," he said. "There is no dishonor in saying to the government, 'I'm sorry. Try as I might, I cannot see your new clothing. I just don't see your fanciful outfit. There is no case. The emperor has no clothes.'"

Puckett took off his glasses and polished the lenses on his lapels. He then peered at the jury through nearsighted eyes. "That's the reason the trial by jury is a sacrament of our democracy, ladies and gentlemen," he said, his voice towering reverently. "Because in our society, it behooves the government to prove its case in order to satisfy history. And in America, history is written not by the state but by . . . the people."

The consensus of the press was that the prosecution had not made its case beyond a reasonable doubt. Sydney knew she was constructing a slender, rickety bridge of circumstantial evidence, without solid support of physical proof. But she made up for its shortcomings with rhetorical leading-by-the-hand and brazen emotional appeal.

In her second closing argument—the prosecution had the last word—Sydney also invoked the totems of childhood. Her metaphor was a jigsaw puzzle. Even though some pieces were missing, you could still make out the picture: Sam Bohannon, church bomber. Building up to her pièce de résistance, Sydney folded her hands prayerfully and brought them to her lips as she paced. Her technicians flashed an image on the slide screen. It was a stained-glass window showing Jesus surrounded by children in shades of royal purple, violet, and pink. It had been the rose window at the front of Shiloh Baptist Church. Sydney explained that it had been a gift from a northern Baptist congregation wanting to help atone for the sins of its white Southern brethren; a humble wooden church like Shiloh would never have been able to afford such a work of art. The wall in which it was mounted was the only one left standing after the fire, and the window remained intact except for one piece: the face of Christ had been blown out of its leaded frame.

"Like that magnificent image of the Savior," Sydney concluded, "so it is with our case." She paused and let the image sink in. "Although the face of Christ is missing, you still know who it is, and you know what Jesus represented to all the children of the world, red and yellow"—she paused again—"black and white." All the stained-glass children were white.

Carter took in the dumbstruck faces of the jurors, then glanced around the courtroom, trying to figure out which of the spectators might be Sydney's boyfriend. Carter looked back at her, thinking she might have sought out her sweetheart's face for an "attagirl." Instead, those preoccupied eyes of hers were staring straight at him.

The case went to the jury late that afternoon.

Carter joined Lonnie, Jimbo, and Stephen for fries and cherry Cokes at Wad's. "The longer they're out, the less likely Bohannon gets convicted," said Lonnie. He had lain low since his performance at Sally's party. And now he was dealing with the revelation, spreading along the local grapevine, that the Klan had enlisted his old man to operate the cement mixer that entombed the remains of Dexter Washington. Although Mr. Culpepper had died of liver disease years before, a parent's capacity to humiliate was everlasting.

As their food arrived, Carter looked across the table at Stephen, who had helpfully monopolized most of the media attention for thwarting Hullender's scheme. He seemed in his modest way to enjoy the celebration of his marksmanship. "I got worried when my friends didn't show up on time for dinner," he told the press. "You can set your watch by Carter Ransom."

Stephen said to Carter, "Lonnie and Loretta arrived, and I asked them to watch the bouillabaisse while I drove out there to see what was holding you up. Lucky I heard a gunshot when I got to the door, or I might have walked into Lacey's movie."

"And lucky you kept your target pistol in the car," said Jimbo.

Jimbo was annoyed that he had missed the showdown. "Did he really call me that little Jew boy?" he asked. "You know, I got some anonymous anti-Semitic e-mail at the store, and it crossed my mind that it could have been from Hullender."

"Lacey online?" said Stephen. "I doubt he was wired into the information superhighway."

"Maybe he had computer classes in prison," said Lonnie.

"Can you imagine?" Jimbo said, shaking his head. "Thank God the Nazis didn't have computers."

They had finished their snacks and pushed their ketchup-smeared plates to the center of the table. The conversation moved to the verdict and how it would affect the community, either way.

"How's the judge doing?" Jimbo asked Lonnie. Mitchell Ransom had been spending most days downtown at the office.

"He's unreadable," said Lonnie. "He seems a little distracted."

"He seemed more upset about the deer he hit on the way home the other night," said Carter. "He was rushing home from his book group at the country club to beat sundown, and he hit a buck. Bloodied the grille and nearly totaled the car. He's been morose ever since. It seemed to have broken something in his spirit."

Just then one of Sydney's staff appeared and announced to the table, "Jury's coming back."

Carter joined his sister, his nephew, and his father on a pew down in front next to Nettie and Lige and his siblings. Mitchell Ransom looked somber and uncomfortable among the spectators in the courtroom where he had so long reigned. Carter knew it was not easy for a man like the judge to show up at a proceeding that implicitly questioned his handling of the case. But Carter also knew the testimony could have gone a lot worse for his father, given what little damaging material came out in the trial, how few locals read the *New York Tribune*, and what remained buried with Hullender and the Sovereignty Commission files.

Lonnie, Jimbo, and Stephen took their seats a few rows behind them, next to Doc Renfro and Pete Callahan. Reporters now filled the upstairs press gallery to capacity, their numbers spiking because of the Magic Time hostage-taking incident. Some media latecomers had been forced to watch from closed-circuit monitors in overflow rooms down the hall. Haynes Wentworth, frustrated that his photo shoot had been disrupted, had inserted himself in the *Tribune* coverage by taking a seat next to Rasheed Lovelace, ostentatiously whispering instructions to his star reporter and taking notes whenever Rasheed repaired to the restroom, as he did frequently.

The victims' families filled the gallery in the balcony across from the press—the Bunts, the Peeks, the Johnstons, and Michael Solomon, who had flown his father in for the verdict.

Carter had met Herbert Solomon at the Pinehurst that morning for breakfast and thanked him for helping locate Strawberry for the prosecution. Michael joined them and, by way of apology for his behavior, told Carter he had not really understood until now the implications of Sarah's pregnancy. By which Carter assumed he meant: since none of us ended up having any children. Carter thanked him for returning the ring setting. Michael then informed them that he was not going forward with a plan to film the Shiloh Church case. "What's the story?" he asked, trying to figure out whether to put syrup on his grits.

"You're right," said Carter, offering the butter, salt, and pepper. "Definitely no story there."

Carter watched Sydney as she shuffled papers and conferred nervously with her staff in an effort to remain calm.

The courtroom audience rose as the jury of six whites, five African-Americans, and one Asian-American filed in.

"Ladies and gentlemen, have you reached a verdict?" said Judge Mc-Donnell.

"Yes, sir, we have," the foreman answered in a barely audible mumble.

"Hand it to the clerk, please."

The clerk took the piece of paper from the foreman and delivered it to the judge, who studied it for what seemed like forever before he said, "It appears to be in order." Then he looked at Sam Bohannon. "Will the defendant please rise?" In anticipation of the verdict, Bohannon began emptying his pockets and removing his wristwatch and billfold and other belongings and placing them in a box on the defense table. Then, with the help of a black deputy, Bohannon struggled to lift himself up from the wheelchair, supporting himself by leaning on the table next to him. His nurse, Billy, was now gone. Once he was on his feet, Bohannon waved the deputy off and stood on his own for the first time since the trial began.

A few of the women jurors, black and white, began to sniffle and remove Kleenex tissues from their purses. Judge McDonnell gave the piece of paper back to the clerk, who handed it to the foreman. She announced that the jury had reached a verdict. "As to each count of the indictment of Samuel Holifield Bohannon, for murder in the first degree in the deaths of Celia Bunt, Daniel Johnston, Randall Peek, and Sarah Solomon—" She paused to collect herself. "We find the defendant guilty."

The courtroom exploded into quickly truncated applause. Shouts of "Hallelujah" and "Praise Jesus" erupted from the balcony, where the families hugged and buried their heads in one another's arms. Bohannon lowered himself into his wheelchair and began sucking on his nebulizer.

Judge McDonnell pounded his gavel lightly and said, "Order, order in the courtroom!" but he seemed content to let the commotion play out for a little while.

After calm returned, the defendant indicated that he had nothing to say before Judge Robert McDonnell read the sentence: life in prison at the Parchman correctional facility. Three black sheriff's deputies led Bohannon away. The judge declared the court adjourned.

Sydney was embracing each member of her staff. Passing by Puckett, who was consulting gravely with the defense team, she cuffed him on the back of his shoulder, then made her way to the families of the victims, who had flooded downstairs to envelop her. Surrounded by Aurelia Bunt, the Peeks, the Johnstons, and Herbert and Michael Solomon, Sydney burst into tears.

Carter tried to fix everything about this moment in his mind. Then he rose and turned to hug Sally and Willie. The judge gathered his grown children to him along with his only grandchild. Behind them Lonnie shook hands with Doc Renfro and Pete Callahan, while Jimbo and Stephen were hailing everyone in sight. Bradley Crawford wept on the shoulders of "her" producer, Simon Lester, whose film crew documented the scene for posterity.

Carter felt a hand on his shoulder. Charlie Lloyd introduced Carter to his wife. "Thanks for getting me back down here," he said. "And for the piece you wrote. It got the press to take me seriously again."

"I never write anything I don't mean."

"So I've noticed," Charlie said drily. He had missed an important mayoral debate in order to be in Troy, and Carter knew he had gotten a lot of criticism in the New York media for it. The *Examiner*'s columnist, Tommy Flynn, wrote that Charles Lloyd's decision to be in Mississippi for the trial, to dwell in the past instead of grappling with the problems facing New Yorkers today, might cost him the mayoral election. But Charlie appeared happier than Carter had ever seen him. "Even with the Hullender crap," Charlie said, "it was worth it."

Carter wanted to thank Sydney, but she was surrounded by her staff, fielding questions from a pack of reporters. The network reporters, distinguishable by their expensive suits and haircuts, were pressing her out toward the courthouse steps to get their bite for the evening news. Finally Carter saw the boyfriend, his hand resting proprietarily on the small of her back. He was tall and confident-looking, with dark, intelligent eyes and a thick head of brown hair. Carter turned away to find Lige, who had been swamped by political supporters. The two men reached their arms to each other over the bodies separating them.

Lige looked sad.

"You may be the only man here who feels bad for Sam Bohannon," Carter said to his friend. "Surely you're not upset he got convicted?"

"No," Lige protested uncertainly. "I wanted justice for Randall, Danny, Celia, and Sarah, but—"

"But what?"

"We're all caught up in forces we don't understand." Lige looked away and stated categorically, "That's why Jesus never liked to see any man imprisoned."

That evening, Carter sat in the porch swing, smoking a cigarette and listening to the muffled sounds of late-night Troy—cicadas chirping, a dog barking in the distance, the occasional muted swoosh of a passing car. Most of the lights in the house were off, and the porch was pitch-black in the moonless night. The glow of the streetlight at the foot of the driveway provided the only exterior illumination. Sally was upstairs in the back bedroom, reading Willie a story. A faint iridescence seeped out of the ground-level basement window, where his father was in his workroom.

Carter was too wired to sleep, so he languished on the front porch, absorbing the reverberation of all that had happened. He had heard from many of his New York friends after the Shiloh Church verdict appeared on the news—Marcy Kennamer and Boz Epstein, Jim and Louise Lassiter. They had offered their congratulations and gestures of affirmation, and also asked about his father. Earlier, Ed Dennehy had weighed in and told him that the suspects in the bombing of the Institute of Modern Art, a radical Islamic terrorist cell out of Brooklyn and New Jersey, had been indicted. Their trial was expected to start after the first of the year. The Baums checked in, too, and also Emily. Her expression of joy for him over the outcome of the trial somehow sealed the blessings of requitedness that she had wished on him at their last lunch in New York. She put Josh on the phone so that Carter could fill him in on how his golden retriever, Riley, was doing. Carter invited him down to visit Riley and Willie after Christmas.

In the midst of all the big gestures and historic resolutions, Carter had been diverted by that dull, exquisite ache of incipient love lost. He wondered if he might be sharing the moment with Sydney now if he had been less reticent and declared himself at the Pinehurst on Sunday night. He kept trying to push from his mind the visions of Sydney celebrating with her boyfriend. By now, Carter figured, they had worked their way through a bottle of Moët at La Residence, the only place in town that served real champagne. Then it struck Carter that the last time he had had the indulgence of sexual jealousy was when he wondered about the boyfriends Sarah had before him.

As he took a final drag on his cigarette, a car pulled up on the street in front of the house and the door opened and slammed shut. He couldn't see the make of the car or who had gotten out, but he heard the click of high heels coming up the sidewalk. He knew that from the sidewalk, all that could be seen in the gloom of the porch was the red eye of his lighted Winston. He didn't want to frighten the visitor heading for the front door, so he coughed and got up out of the swing and crossed to the steps to greet her.

Sydney's face materialized at close range. "I can't breathe," she said.

They rushed together, his mouth instantly on hers. And in that second Carter experienced his sorrow blazing through his consciousness in images of Sarah forever young and immaculate, yet suddenly, finally, too infallible for the man he had become. All his emotions, the past that had perpetually mortgaged his future to regret, merged in a blur of longing and hope until he could feel nothing except this woman, this moment, and, most miraculously of all, himself. As the kiss became more insistent, Sydney drew gaspy little intakes of breath from his mouth. He bore down, feeling a compulsion to consume her. And then she pulled away.

"What am I going to do?" she said.

Carter blinked her into focus. Her eyes were slightly wild. He brushed her hair away from her cheek and then put his arms around her again, low across the ribs, and picked her up and hitched her against his torso. After he set her back down, he gently pulled her toward the house. "You're going to come up and sit on this porch with me and tell me why you're not out toasting yourself with your boyfriend." He sat on the swing and took in the vision of her standing before him. She had on the short black cap-sleeved dress she had worn to the judge's birthday party. He patted his lap. She climbed on it, and they resumed their kiss. Carter's hands traced the curve of her back down the hourglass of her waist and hips, his touch like an archaeological search for a missing rib or a prehistoric ancestor or evidence of a lost tribe. They looked at each other in the dark for long, silent moments, Sydney's eyes holding wonder, incredulity, and pain; then they plunged back into the search.

"May I finally properly thank you for curing my amnesia," he said. He felt the tears threatening, but it was she who broke down. He covered her eyes with his hand while she sobbed softly.

Then she took a deep breath to compose herself. "May I thank you," she said, "for revealing to me why I do what I do." She drew back, looked at him, and sighed with resignation. "You're so beautiful," she said.

"Thank you," Carter said. "Why do you make that sound like a bad thing?"

"Because I don't love Warren."

Carter traced the crease at the back of her knee as the confession landed.

"Those are the happiest words in the English language."

She collapsed back against his shoulder. "I've invested so much in Warren. And the thing is, there's no rational reason for me to be bolting right now. I wish he would do something unforgivable, but he was perfect through the trial. And tonight he seemed so proud of me."

Carter twisted around so that he could look into her face. "So what's the problem?"

She started to smile. "Are you fishing for compliments? You mean, aside from you?" She snagged another kiss but stopped before committing. "All evening I found myself worrying about when it was going to sink in with him that I had just tried the case that will, you know, lead my obituary."

Carter had always been sympathetic to the dilemma of intelligent women, the "problem" they posed for ambitious men, and so he answered a question that hadn't really been asked.

"No one could be too smart for me." He grinned at her, pleased that he was putting himself in the game.

Sydney gave him one of her sly double takes. "Are you sure you're a member of the male species?" she teased. She cupped his groin to confirm.

Carter hiked her body around, pulling her dress up to her hips so that she could straddle him. "You know I'm proud of you, too," he whispered. "But right now I think I have to ravish you."

He pressed her into him. The making-out resumed.

Finally, she said into his ear, "I need to feel your weight."

They pulled themselves up from the porch swing and walked to her Ford Taurus. Carter felt lighthearted, exalted by a sensation that felt strangely like youth. The smell of the rental car triggered a secondary flashback, to one of his favorite parts of being a journalist—riding into a strange place on borrowed wheels and imposing his personality on the environment. "Take off your shirt," Sydney breathed when they had scooted onto the backseat. Carter closed the car door and pulled off his T-shirt, then lowered himself onto her. Sydney torqued her body under him. And with their glazed eyes locked, he began moving against her in a rhythm as old as the species.

Lights from the interior of the house flooded the driveway, and the porch light switched on. The screen door flung wide open, slamming against the wall. At the front door, Sally was screaming, "Carter, come quick. It's Daddy."

29

M ITCHELL RANSOM WAS ADMITTED to the emergency room of the cardiovascular unit at Troy Memorial Hospital. He was unconscious on arrival.

"He was downstairs in his workshop and came up to watch the ten o'clock news about the verdict," Sally had explained to Carter and Sydney in the ambulance on the way to the hospital. He had begun rubbing his chest, saying, "I think I'm having one of those accelerated fibrillations," and then he slumped against the sofa. Sally got him stretched out on the floor and called 911. Then she gave him mouth-to-mouth. By the time the medics got there, he had slipped into a coma.

During the first day the judge was in the cardiac intensive care unit, Nettie helped relieve Sally, who had to mind the store and tend to Willie. But Nettie got so upset seeing the judge incapacitated that she cried and cried and could hardly keep it together when she was around him. After that, Carter took over full-time. Mostly, he sat on the edge of the bed, holding his father's hand. That night, he and Sally alternated shifts, sleeping on a cot outside the hospital room.

Mitchell breathed shallowly beneath an electronic bramble of life support—monitors, wires, tubes, and drips. A cannula ran from his nose, and a clear oxygen mask was clamped to his face. Feeding tubes and catheters allowed his bodily functions to go on without his con-scious consent. He looked pale, swollen, and puffy around his face, and underneath his flimsy hospital gown there was bruising, purplish spots on his chest where the paramedics had administered the defibrillator cardio pads at the house.

Specialists checked him regularly, exuding professionalism but care-ful not to offer much hope of recovery. His neurologist's speculation was that he could have "shut-in syndrome"—that possibly he could hear but not communicate. His eyes opened up and registered light, and the pupils dilated: he would seem to be seeing in this odd middle dis-tance. Carter thought his father was perceiving shapes, color, form, but not him. Not Carter. Sometimes his father would start, involuntarily moan, jerk around as if he were irritated by something.

When his neurologist suggested that music might have a salutary ef-fect on the patient, Sally brought in her boom box from the store, along with tapes and CDs of her father's favorite classical music—Bach, Haydn, Mozart, and Tchaikovsky.

The waiting room those first couple of days was filled with members of the church and community, sometimes overflowing into the nurses' station and spilling down the hall toward Mitchell's room. Stephen dropped by with comestibles for the family and the other visitors. Jimbo checked in. Old friends of Mitchell's generation, like Doc Renfro and Pete Callahan, stopped in often, and Sally's ex-husband appeared to pay his respects. Lige, who was home frequently now campaigning, showed up with Nettie. The congressman's willingness to take time from his gru-eling campaign schedule reminded Carter and Sally that their father had paid Lige's way to the seminary.

The first night in the hospital, Lonnie had come by late and sat with Carter after everyone else had gone home. He had brought along a cas-sette of Patsy Cline hits, which Carter inserted in the tape deck. "As I re-call, the judge always had a secret jones for ol' Patsy."

As that voice of pure heartbreak poured from the speakers in the corner of the room, Lonnie joined Carter at the foot of the bed, staring at Mitchell. "It's hard to believe he can't hear us," Lonnie whis-pered.

"Maybe he can," Carter replied.

"We used to whisper like this even when he was two blocks away." Lonnie laughed at the memory. Returning to his normal voice, he caught Carter up on the latest fallout from the trial.

The day after the verdict, Helmut Schlank had called a press conference to announce plans for a WunderCorp-sponsored civil rights walking tour of Troy. "Freedom Walk, he calls it," said Lonnie. "It'll start at the courthouse, go by the old Kress's building, and end up at their new civil rights museum."

"So he still plans to incorporate Magic Time into the museum?"

"It's their money. Speaking of memorials, did you see that Virginia Military Institute is going to honor Daniel Johnston with a monument on their campus? It's the only one to a VMI grad not killed in military combat."

"And on the campus where Stonewall Jackson taught," said Carter.

Lonnie whistled. "And Robert E. Lee buried next door at Washington and Lee."

"His mother must be pleased," said Carter.

"I saw the Brit interviewing her about it for his documentary. Did you see there's a bit of an uproar over Lovelace's coverage of the trial?" Lonnie said. "It got out that Hullender was his source on the story that gigged your father."

Carter said nothing, wondering if Lonnie had his own questions about how much of it was true.

"Have you been in touch with Grayson?" Carter asked.

"She's been laying low. Finding solace in the arms of the governor, I hear. She's still smarting over the search of her house ordered by Sydney Rushton. But I'm sure there's no love lost for the *Tribune* either. Looks like Sydney'll be coming back to Troy to look into the Dexter Washington case."

"I know," said Carter. "The girl's on a roll." Carter's long phone conversations with Sydney, who had returned to Jackson after the trial, had been virtually his only connection with the outside world.

Lonnie's and Carter's eyes met. Carter raised his brows ever so slightly, and Lonnie just as subtly shrugged in male concession.

Lonnie walked to the window and stared down at the parking lot. "Now my old man's going to be put under the microscope."

"He was maneuvered into pouring that cement, Lonnie. Nobody's going to believe he was a Kluxer."

"Hullender and Posey and that bunch used to hang around the fireworks stand when I worked on weekends, chugging six-packs with Daddy. Shooting off the profits. But everybody hung out there. I doubt Daddy knew they were Klan." Lonnie let out a sigh, shaking his head morosely. "When I think about Lacey and what he came from, I feel like, there but for the grace of God. I mean, if it wasn't for sports and some-body believing in me"—he nodded toward the judge—"I could have easily ended up like him." Lonnie changed the subject abruptly. "I prob-ably should tell you this before you hear it from the town crier, Smitty Crawford," he said. "Loretta and I are separating."

"I'm sorry, Lonnie."

"I don't blame her. I'd separate from me, too, if I could."

"You're too hard on yourself, son."

"That's what my psychiatrist says." He walked to the door and looked out into the hall, as if to make sure no one was eavesdropping. "I'm seeing a shrink now, if you can believe that."

"Why not? My shrink saved my life."

"You saw a shrink?" Lonnie seemed shocked. "When?"

"In Atlanta. I should have done it sooner."

Lonnie shook his head. "I always sneered at therapy talk."

"Believe me. Everybody in New York is in therapy."

"Mine's a psychoanalyst," said Lonnie, as if he were admitting to consulting with a past-lives channeler. "Loretta made me go to a cou-ples therapist, and I continued treatment with an analyst. I see him twice a week."

"There's an analyst in Troy? No kidding. Is he any good?"

"Well, we'll see, won't we," Lonnie said with a laugh. "I know the trend today is pills and quick fixes. But goddammit, I don't want to feel good. That's what the booze was supposed to be for, and it didn't work. I don't want to end up like my old man."

"The external world is a lot easier to tame than the internal," Carter said. "Even twenty-five years after the fact, you can hold a trial."

"I've underestimated how much that trial upset me. What it was bringing up about the town—your father. But I think I was really worried about what my father had to hide." Lonnie's voice cracked. "My old man was such an embarrassment to me, Pross. I was so ashamed of him. That's why I latched onto the judge. Your daddy was good to me in a million ways I can never repay. He always tried to get me to forgive my old man. But I never could."

"Even when we aren't waiting for the other shoe to drop, it drops anyway," said Carter. "Look at me. It's strange. I'm not embarrassed about what came out about Dad. It almost makes him seem like a man of flesh and blood rather than granite. My problem was that I didn't think my father was flawed enough. And the more I was in rebellion against him, the more I was enslaved. Churchill got it backward: 'Always, always, always give up.'"

"Did you know the judge helped me through law school?"

"Good investment," said Carter.

"He did that for a lot of disadvantaged kids. All he asked was that they make good grades. He's probably responsible for most of the good lawyers active in the state today."

"His firm made a lot of money over the years," said Carter.

"Did you know he bailed out Pete Callahan when a chain tried to buy *The Troy Times*?"

"Really? As much as he hated that I was an ink-stained wretch."

"I know you two had tensions. And I guess I filled out some role for him that you couldn't."

"Wouldn't."

"I can't say I wasn't aware that my competitiveness with you drove me to seek your father's approval. I'm not proud of that, but I want you to know I know." Then he turned to look at the judge lying in silence.

"Lonnie, I always said you were the son my daddy never had. And you don't know how much I appreciated your playing that role. It took the pressure off me."

Lonnie grinned suddenly. "Can you believe a couple of Bubbas like us shrink-talking?"

"Hey, it makes sense to me. Towns like Troy aren't much different from Freud's Vienna: families too much with us, guilt, repression, alcoholism, psychosomatic symptoms."

"Yeah, why shouldn't Southerners have a talent for the talking cure?" said Lonnie. "That's the thing we're really good at."

Carter didn't leave the hospital room all the next day. When the neurologist came by to check the monitors, he looked down at Mitchell's chart, then back at the monitor, and said, "Hmm."

"What?" Carter said.

"There's been a slight change in his brain function," the doctor said.

"Is that good?" said Carter.

"Difficult to say. We have to consider this anomalous unless proven otherwise."

Mitchell's nurse came in to check on him. She began shaving him but, Carter noticed, not quite competently. There were patches of bristle that escaped her attention. His face and neck were cut in places. Something about the intimacy of the act of shaving and the nurse's carelessness brought home to Carter his father's helplessness. The thing that Mitchell Ransom valued the most, his personal sovereignty, had been stolen from him.

That evening, Sally brought Carter his guitar from home. He had hardly picked up his old Gibson since returning to Mississippi, but that night in the hospital where his father was dying, he tuned it up and played for the first time in years. And he played the songs that he could recall were some of his father's favorites. He played old Doc Watson and Ralph Stanley songs, bluegrass gospel, and mountain fiddle tunes, standards from his father's Carolina upbringing. As he sat there strumming and reaching to remember the chords and words to barely remembered songs, he thought of his father's vague discomfort with his musical ability, how the judge feared it was taking Carter away from the serious and important things he was destined for as the only son of Mitchell Ransom. And now here they were.

The next day, when the nurse appeared with the razor, Carter informed her that he would shave his father. The performance of this simple task of grooming—entering the terrain of vanity and pride and self-regard, and tending it with meticulous care—had a gratifying effect. It was like taking care of a baby. His father's conscious presence and force were gone. He was now dependent upon Carter, inverting yet reiterating the ancient bond.

While scraping a swath through the shaving cream, Carter felt something shift in his father's state of consciousness. Mitchell's eyes were open, and there was depth where there had been blankness.

"Dad?"

"Son."

"Daddy."

"Lower your voice in a hospital, son. You'll disturb your mother."

"Okay, Pop." His father was hallucinating. Carter leaned in to hear.

"She's not been herself lately." His father seemed lucid but in another dimension. He spoke with such conviction that it was hard to believe he was still unconscious. His forehead knotted. "It's not your fault, son. It's not your fault. It's mine. I didn't mean to hurt her. I didn't mean to disappoint your mother." He groaned and tilted his head as if he were trying to look away. "She's not been feeling well lately, but it's not your fault. She's not been the same since . . . She's not been the same . . ." His voice trailed off.

Carter leaned forward and whispered, "What, Daddy?"

His father looked startled, and his eyes widened. "Katharine?" he called. Then his brow furrowed, and he sank back into his pillow and mumbled, "She was so hurt. She was her best friend." And his eyes slipped back into the middle distance.

"Daddy!" said Carter sharply.

His father started and looked at him. The dreamy look in his eyes melted. He answered in a weak but clear voice. "Son?" This time he seemed wide-awake and alert.

"Dad, you were talking in your sleep."

"What's going on?" His father was definitely coming out.

"You're in the hospital. You had a heart attack."

"I know, son. I know." He closed his eyes and said with a half smile, "It hurts." Though short of breath, his father spoke clearly. "What were we talking about?" He sounded like his old self. Carter wanted to rush out and alert the doctor, but he was afraid to break the spell.

"Something about Mama."

"What about her?"

"About her being sick. You sounded upset."

"Your mother was . . ." He paused to catch his breath. "She was fragile."

"Can I get you something, Daddy?"

His father shook his head.

"What can I do for you?"

"Just talk to me. I swear I thought your Mama was here."

"You were talking to her."

"What did I say?"

"You said you didn't mean to hurt her. You said something about her best friend. Who were you talking about? Sheppy?"

His face showed very little.

Carter pressed on. "What about her? You told me you didn't have an affair with her."

His father's voice sounded strained and weak, but he seemed eager to talk. "It wasn't an affair. Just a tragic moment of weakness a long time ago."

————

MITCHELL RANSOM AND SHEPPY GRAYSON GLIDED around the dance floor at the Troy Country Club. They made a striking couple. The rest of the genteel revelers surrounding the dance floor couldn't take their eyes off them—he, tall, lean, and handsome, and she, slender, graceful, elegant. Though they were dancing as if they were a couple, they were just friends. Sheppy was engaged to be married. Her fiancé was missing in action in the Pacific, but there was hope that he was alive. Mitchell was already married, his wife still in school back in North Carolina, and he was headed off to Harvard Law that fall on the GI Bill. They had enjoyed each other's company all summer, more than enjoyed, perhaps: craved. But they had kept it at that level of innocent companionship.

Sheppy smiled up at Mitchell as they swayed and twirled to the big-band sounds of the Jack Hartley Orchestra up from New Orleans. "Are you looking forward to seeing your wife and son, Mitchell?"

"Sure I am. But I was lucky Ray found me the job down here."

Sheppy seemed to understand that he meant more than just the money he had earned to pay for living expenses in Cambridge for the coming school year.

Mitchell had not told Sheppy about the claustrophobia he had felt after only a few days at home, living with Katharine and her sister and the baby in that tiny millhouse in Eno, North Carolina. And the guilt he felt about it. It was hard enough to explain to himself: how he could come out of a Nazi prison camp and after only a few days back home feel like he missed it. Katharine would never understand. Ray Renfro was the only person who would, the only one who knew what it had been like, and how jarring it was for a POW to move out of the war experience into civilian life and be expected to adjust without a hitch.

The swing music they had been dancing to segued into a ballad, and Mitchell drew Sheppy close. He had been reluctant to talk to her about his bind, but something about the night, the smell of her hair, the closeness of her ear to his lips as she laid her head on his chest, and the close of the season led him to open up.

"In the POW camp I sometimes wondered if I had ever gotten married," Mitchell said. "By then, Katharine and I had been apart longer than we were together, and I sometimes had to actually relive our wedding to make myself believe I was a husband. You know how it is."

"I do."

"We married just before I shipped out. It was kind of a rash decision. You don't know if you'll ever see the other person again. You make vows you maybe wouldn't have under normal circumstances."

"Glen and I got engaged sort of like that. And it didn't help living in a fishbowl like Troy, or to feel the disapproval of my family. I sometimes wonder if I wasn't caught up in some childish defiance of my parents when I got engaged."

Mitchell said, "Katharine had a tough time as a child. Her old man was a no-account—abandoned his family when she was small. Her mother had to work in the cotton mill to support her children. Katharine came up hard. I think I may have been playing the knight in shining armor a bit."

The song they were dancing to ended, and Sheppy led Mitchell to the moonlit terrace. They remained silent, looking out over the knolls of the golf course. When his hand touched hers as they leaned against the stone balustrade, she did not move it away.

"Sheppy," came a voice from the double doors that opened out onto the terrace. They turned to see Ray Renfro. "Rose and I are heading home. Do you want us to drop you off?"

Sheppy looked at Mitchell. "I'll drop her off," he said. "Hey, Doc. Thanks again for the send-off." Ray and his wife, Rose, had thrown a going-away barbecue for Mitchell at their house before the dance at the club. Ray had been hunting that weekend and cooked up his venison.

"Oh, you'll be back." Ray Renfro laughed. "Or old man Grayson will send me up to Cambridge to hunt you down like that six-point buck y'all ate for dinner." Ray had gotten Mitchell his clerical job in the legal department at Graysonite that summer. They had taken a liking to Mitchell, and Mr. Grayson promised to pay for his rent through law school on the condition that he would come back and practice in Troy.

"I'll see you in the morning before I ship out," Mitchell called to Ray as he turned back inside to the ballroom.

"Behave yourself, you two," Doc called over his shoulder.

"It's such a beautiful night," said Sheppy, tilting her chin up while leaning against the stone wall. "Look at those stars."

Mitchell lifted his eyes toward the heavens. "It's hard to believe those are the same ones we looked at from Stalag Luft Three."

"Just think. This time next week you'll be looking at those stars in Cambridge with your family," Sheppy said ruefully. "And I'll still be here."

"Any word on your fiancé?" Mitchell asked.

"None."

"You'll hear."

"That's what my father's afraid of." Sheppy ducked her head, and her chin began trembling. "I feel so bad for feeling this way. My family was scandalized when I started going out with Glen Boutwell. And so was half the town." When Glen shipped out, he and Sheppy had corresponded regularly until he went missing, and now the family's comments were starting to get to her, undermining her confidence. It was almost as if they wished he wouldn't come back. Her flirtation with the charming young veteran ex-POW, even though he was married, had almost been encouraged.

"Why were they upset?" Mitchell asked. He had been curious all summer about Glen Boutwell but had thought it unseemly to inquire.

"He's not 'one of us,' " Sheppy said drily.

Mitchell felt that ineffable bond of class between them and wondered how Sheppy would view Katharine and her cotton-mill family.

"Now I don't know what I'll do when he comes back," Sheppy said. "*If* he comes back."

"You're a wonderful girl, Sheppy. You deserve happiness." He lifted her chin toward him, and the moon shone in her eyes.

"So do you, Mitchell. I'm going to miss you, Mr. Ransom. You've made this summer bearable."

"I'll never forget you, Sheppy."

"Hush," she said, pressing her finger to his lips.

Mitchell looked over his shoulder toward the ballroom and saw nobody near the double doors. Emboldened by their public, vertical intimacy on the dance floor, he pulled her to him, and they kissed. Sheppy gave a slight gasp, and Mitchell felt the two long war years of restraint and self-denial unleash and rush against the rectitude he and Sheppy had cultivated for two months. Their friendship had been a balm and a distraction from the doubts they both faced. But tonight they were on the cusp of a new phase in their lives. Tonight might be the last time they would see each other for a long time without the encumbrance of family and duty. Tonight everyone was a little drunk. Or at least that's how they both rationalized what they were about to do.

And perhaps to reward themselves for having been so noble right up to the last moment, when fate could disguise itself as a singular, inconsequential anomaly.

He took her hand and led her down the steps toward the golf course and into the shadows of the trees that lined the green.

———

"SHEPPY GRAYSON GOT PREGNANT that summer." His father's matter-of-fact, no-nonsense lack of sentimentality was speaking now. Judge Mitchell Ransom was definitely back. In his cut-to-the-chase courtroom style he said, "That's what your mother found out years later. That I'd fathered another child."

"Not Grayson."

"Lord, no." His father smiled wanly. "You would have been dating your sister."

"Who then?"

Mitchell looked at him quizzically, as if he was surprised that Carter didn't know. He stalled. "We all make mistakes, son. We never know how a decision we make will affect us and everyone in our orbit. How God will ambush us. I don't have to tell you. We make choices that can affect us for the rest of our lives, and we have to live with them."

His eyes turned tragic, and he said, "Get me some water, son."

Carter rushed to the sink to fill a water glass, but by the time he got to his father's bedside, the judge was slipping back into his slumber. "Dad?" he whispered, pressing the glass to unresponsive lips. "Daddy!" he shouted, and went to the door to summon the nurses. Waiting for them to arrive, Carter began quoting a favorite passage of his father's from Thomas Wolfe, words from a fellow Tar Heel that Mitchell had recited to Carter ten thousand times in his youth. " 'Each of us is all the sums he has not counted,' " Carter began. " 'Subtract us into nakedness and night again, and you shall see begin in Crete four thousand years ago the love that ended yesterday in Texas. The seed of our destruction will blossom in the desert, the alexin of our cure grows by a mountain rock, and our lives are haunted by a Georgia slattern, because a London cutpurse went unhung. Each moment is the fruit of forty thousand years. The minute-winning days, like flies, buzz home to death, and every moment is a window on all time.' "

THE DOCTORS SAID Mitchell had had a stroke. The likelihood of his recovery was marginal at best. Carter continued to shave his father, hoping it was the magic formula for bringing him back. He read to him from newspapers and magazines and books, played songs on his guitar. Finally, when there was nothing else he could do, Carter would just sit there rubbing his father's head along the hairline, running his fingers gently through his hair, massaging his scalp, stroking his head in a sustained rhythm. It was a tactile pleasure Carter's mother had introduced him to as a child. He knew that a son seldom gets to comfort his father this way. And he knew his father would never have asked. Since his father's rally and retreat, the anxiety Carter felt over whether he would not be there with Mitchell at the end—or, even more upsetting, the fear that he would—reduced him to a kind of numb dutifulness. Carrying out his obligations with an anesthetized volition, he operated on autopilot, waiting for nature to dictate his next move.

One evening, after Carter had relieved Sally so that she could go home and tuck Willie in, he and Doc Renfro were left alone with the patient. Doc had retired from his family practice and spent most of his time lately hunting and fishing, so he was free to drop by frequently to check on his old friend. As a gray eminence at the hospital, he kept the staff and specialists on their toes in his role as the family's medical adviser.

Doc was a thin, wiry Henry Fonda–handsome man, with sharp, angular features and a thinning shock of white hair. Like many physicians, he seemed unfazed by physical deterioration and did not alter his demeanor just because one of his best friends was lying comatose before them. "So your daddy rose on the third day, then reconsidered," Doc said, tapping the judge's wrist. "Mitch never was much for miracles."

They stood there talking in front of his father, not knowing if they were heard or not. Doc reached into his jacket and handed Carter a small photograph in a black dime-store frame. It showed Ray and Mitchell in front of the barracks in Stalag Luft 3. "I don't know if you ever saw this," Doc said, propping it against the footboard of the hospital bed.

"No," said Carter, staring at the impossibly young men in their fleece-lined flight jackets squinting at the camera. "How old were you?"

"I was twenty-eight. Your dad was twenty-three. Did your father ever tell you how we met?"

"A little. But I never heard your version."

Doc proceeded to tell the story of the mission that had led to their companionship for the rest of the war in POW camps. Ray Renfro's eyes shone with the odd pleasure grown men get when describing harrowing moments from their youth.

"Your dad saved my life, you know," he said. "We were shot down in the Mediterranean and had to ditch the plane." He then described how he had a shoulder injury and was panicked and disoriented, flailing around in the water when they couldn't get their raft to inflate. Mitchell had to knock him out to keep him from drowning them both. Doc chuckled. "Your dad packed quite a punch."

"He never told us that part."

"Probably didn't want to embarrass me."

Carter looked at the recumbent form of his father, breathing steadily in the bed before them, unable to inhibit the discussion. He wondered if that instinct for survival was still struggling to assert itself now.

"We spent the next eighteen months together in the German POW camp, until the Allies liberated the camp in April of 'forty-five." Doc seemed to come even more alive as he told the story in his soft, clipped Mississippi accent. "I'll always remember the great day when one of General Patton's tank companies roared through the main gate and the Germans surrendered the camp. We remained for several days while arrangements were being made to move us out. During our wait, General Patton visited our camp, striding through our tent—helmet, boots, pearl-handled revolvers—cursing the Germans every step of the way." Doc checked his fingernails. "Your dad got to go straight home, but because I was medical, I got enlisted to tag along with the Forty-fifth Infantry and help liberate Dachau."

Carter said, "I didn't know you were involved in the liberation of the camps."

"Just Dachau. But that was enough for me." Doc's eyes darkened. "The thing I'll never forget was the stench. You began smelling it a mile away, and it got worse as we got closer. Of course, what we saw when we got there was worse than the smell. And that's a doctor talking. Think how the rest of those boys must have felt."

Carter knew the rest of the story, how his father went home in late May 1945 and ended up in Troy, Mississippi, that summer before Harvard Law.

"Doc, I heard something during the trial about Daddy and Sheppy Boutwell. And he confirmed it last night. Do you know anything about this?"

Ray Renfro's face looked the way Carter imagined it had when he told his patients they had to come back in for further tests. "I might need a drink," he said. "Why don't you walk down to the cafeteria with me for a Dr Pepper."

They alerted the night nurse that they were stepping away, and when they entered the elevator, Doc stared at the floor and said, "What did you hear, son?"

"That Daddy had an affair with Sheppy Boutwell."

Doc looked pained. "All I know is, your father loved your mother very much. Where did you get your information?"

"Doc," Carter said, "it's not right for the Sovereignty Commission to know something about a man that his own son doesn't know. Daddy told me Sheppy became pregnant."

"That summer, when your father came to Troy for the first time, he and Sheppy hit it off. It all seemed innocent—he was married, she was engaged." Doc's eyes were glistening. "They were both young and attractive and lonely. Nature took its course. Mitchell went away. Sheppy discovered she was pregnant."

"That much I now know," said Carter.

"Glen comes home right after your father leaves. He and Sheppy elope, and soon she announces she's with child."

Renfro had monitored the pregnancy and became concerned that something was amiss. Sheppy was not gaining enough weight.

"Did you have a hunch about who the father was?" asked Carter.

"Sheppy seemed ambivalent about having a baby," Doc hedged. "But my medical opinion would have to be that the pregnancy was affected by some venison she ate."

"At Dad's going-away party," Carter said.

"We ate that buck into fall." Doc seemed to deflate slightly.

The newborn infant had the classic symptoms of congenital toxoplasmosis—jaundiced skin and an enlarged head. Glen, still coping with a hostile new social milieu, wanted to place the baby in an institution.

Renfro took a deep breath. "Sheppy's Catholic, of course, and so is my wife. Sheppy couldn't go through with having her baby put away. Rose and I had been trying to have a child for several years. She wants to adopt Sheppy's infant, so I agree."

"But what about the timing?" Carter said. "Wasn't it pretty obvious to the community what had happened?"

"I had privileges at the hospital in Jackson, and because of the complications with the pregnancy, Sheppy gave birth there. The staff didn't have any reason to check up on what happened once he was discharged." As far as Troy was concerned, the Boutwell baby was stillborn.

Rose had taken Hugh to the Renfro's cottage in Panama City for the summer, and they "adopted" him the following fall.

Carter's entire sense of his family history and that of the town jumbled and rearranged itself kaleidoscopically. Doc continued the story of how Mitchell returned to Troy and started his practice. Years later, Glen was coaching Little League one summer when some viral epidemic required team physicals, and he noticed that his and Hugh's blood types didn't match. His guilt for giving up Hugh and his wish that Hugh had never been born had festered over the years and congealed into a suspicion that Hugh was not his child, which was then confirmed. He pummeled Sheppy with questions until she broke down and confessed it was Mitchell Ransom's baby.

"Of course, this is news to Mitchell," Doc said.

Carter felt the kaleidoscope turn again. "How could that be?"

"Sheppy had never told him the consequence of that last-night tryst. As it turned out, Glen had always been jealous of Mitchell. Over the years, Mitchell had advised Sheppy on some legal matters." Doc doubted that the physical relationship continued, but Glen suspected that she was confiding in him about problems in their marriage. He accused Sheppy of sleeping with Mitchell.

"None of us knew about Glen's Klan activities at the time," said Doc Renfro. "Apparently he got drunk one night with Sam Bohannon and Peyton Posey and spilled the beans about his suspicions about the judge. I guess they had been griping about Mitchell being un-American, and whatnot . . . Posey reported it all to the Sovereignty Commission. That was when they began putting pressure on the judge, trying to blackmail him about an affair with Sheppy and about his illegitimate son."

"So Daddy was afraid that all this would come out if Hugh testified?"

"He thought the Klan would kill Hugh if he was allowed to testify, and so did I. But I'm sure he also worried about what else would come out. For starters, that Glen Boutwell was a leader of the Ku Klux Klan. That much alone would have hurt Sheppy and Grayson, and then you're off to the races."

Suddenly, to ask whether or not Mitchell threw the case seemed to be the wrong question.

"Knowing your father," said Doc, "he was simply acting on the rule of a higher law than those written by the state of Mississippi."

Carter was only beginning to compute the various exponents contained in Doc's revelation. Maybe, Carter thought to himself, there was still another reason Mitchell had no stomach for revisiting the Shiloh Church bombing. He could not face the fact that one son helped murder his other son's girlfriend—and his own grandchild.

The next morning, Sydney arrived from Jackson. Carter had woken her up in the middle of the night to tell her about his conversation with Doc

Renfro, and she had driven to Troy first thing. Carter had gone sleepless on the cot outside his father's room, his mind having dredged up every single instance when he had been unkind to Hugh Renfro.

"Talk about the sins of the fathers." Sydney was rubbing his wrist-bone as they sat in the hospital cafeteria after their lengthy debriefing.

"Not to mention the sins of the mothers, and brothers," Carter said. Then he felt a surge of anger mixed with class pride. "Goddammit, that fucker Bohannon knew more about me than I did. To think the Imperial Wizard would have had that kind of power over my family."

"I'm sure he saw himself as a kindred member of the Southern aristocracy. He did, after all, keep the secret, no?"

"Ah yes, the 'our crowd' of Mississippi."

"Speaking of Bohannon," she said, reaching into her briefcase. "Wentworth overnighted the proof for next Sunday's *Tribune Magazine* cover."

"Did they use any of Lacey's shots?" Carter said with an uncharitable smile. He took the photographs: Sydney and Lige gazed into the distance against a cobalt-blue sky pierced by the steeple of Shiloh Church. The cover line read: "New South Siblings." It was somehow reassuring to Carter that she continued to function in the known world while he made one of his visits to the foreign country of Thanatos.

"You look like you belong on Mount Rushmore," he said.

"Thank you," Sydney said, not taking the bait. "You'll note that they didn't use Lovelace on the story. He seems to be on some kind of probation, pending investigation."

"I know. Dennehy called," Carter said. Apparently, the internal investigation into Lovelace's "payment" of Hullender for information had uncovered other examples of journalistic fraud and plagiarism. The *Trib* was said to be working on an unprecedented story-length apology. Wentworth's job might be on the line.

Carter composed his sincerest look for Sydney. "Hullender was right—there is a God."

Sydney popped him with the magazine.

"Speaking of whom," he said, "what are you turning up in the Dexter

Washington investigation?" Carter assumed that most of the principals were dead, except for Strawberry, who was turning state's evidence.

Sydney studied him for a moment. "Well, neither of us would ever be accused of claiming things are simple in the South, right?"

Carter raised his eyebrows to signal that nothing could surprise him, but it turned out that he was wrong. Strawberry had told Sydney that the rump group of Klansmen who lynched Dexter had decided, after the fact, to implicate the so-called higher-ups as co-conspirators, partly to make sure that the case would never be "solved."

"I think this should wait till we finish lunch," said Sydney.

"I'm done," Carter said, putting his plate of egg salad remnants on the tray to his right.

Sydney had further endeared herself to Sheppy Boutwell by sending investigators over to the house to look for evidence of Glen's involvement in the Dexter Washington case. Glen had, Strawberry assumed, been brought in only after the murder, to dispose of the body. The detectives found what they were looking for on a shelf in the basement: an old jar of Sambo's famous baby gherkins.

"So?" Carter said.

"My guys opened it up, and it smelled funny," Sydney said. "At first they thought the vinegar had turned."

"What was it?"

"Something in the jar besides little cukes."

"Tell me."

"A finger."

A souvenir of Dexter Washington's lynching had been stuffed in among the baby gherkins. That had prompted Sydney to get a warrant to seize all jars of Sambo pickles at the home of the living suspect in the case: Sheriff Lawrence Mizell. She had—correctly, it turned out—assumed that Peyton Posey had presented his boss with a jar of gherkins as insurance against future prosecution.

"Mizell reformed," Carter said.

"Maybe that was the cause of the conversion," said Sydney. "But he was in charge of the investigation into Dexter's disappearance." She sighed. "Like I said, nothing's easy."

•

That evening, Sally insisted that Carter take a break from his bedside duties so he and Sydney could go out on their official first date. Carter drove her up and down the strip he and his friends used to cruise in high school—from the football stadium, through town, around and around the courthouse square to the Dairy Queen and the icehouse. But instead of winding up at Wad's, they ate fried Gulf shrimp at Knotty's and slow-danced to Hank Williams on the jukebox, staking out a private dance floor between the pool tables. Then they went to a drive-in movie, to resume their positions in the backseat.

"You know I could never get involved with a shiksa like you," said Carter, writing Sydney's name on the fogged-up window above them. "I only go for Jewish girls."

Sydney laughed. "You're stuck, buddy."

"What?" Carter said.

"You're going to think I'm making this up. You know the grandfather I was so close to?"

"Even though he worked with the Klan busting the heads of labor organizers during the Depression. I'm familiar with the type."

"He was half Jewish," Sydney said. "I guess he wanted so badly to pass that he did the country-clubbers' dirty work." She had found this out at his funeral, when some of his long-lost cousins showed up from Greenville, South Carolina. She gave him a mock coy look and said, "Finally, I've earned your respect."

Carter had begun to unbutton her shirt. "Respect is not the feeling I was going for tonight."

It felt surreal to be having an adolescent hormonal indulgence after what seemed like a lifetime in the crepuscular world of intensive care. But Carter and Sydney didn't pass much more of the evening groping each other in the backseat. They retired to the Pinehurst and spent their first night together as a couple, naked in Sydney's bed.

On the morning of the sixth day after his father was admitted to the hospital, the neurologist checked in and asked Carter the question he had been dreading. "Do you want to unplug life support?" When he hesitated, the doctor said, "Why don't we do it this evening?"

"No," Carter said.

"His brain functions have deteriorated. There's no need to prolong this."

Carter said irritably, "I need to talk to my sister. This can wait till tomorrow."

The next day, Carter and Sally informed the doctor that they would do it in the morning. Carter called Grayson and told her she might want to bring Sheppy by.

The Boutwell women arrived at the hospital that evening with a bouquet of roses. Carter felt some relief on Grayson's behalf when she told him that she had decided to take Sheppy with her and the girls to Jackson, where she was going to finish her degree at Millsaps. On top of everything else, Carter was not going to assume the task of informing Grayson that they shared a half brother.

Sheppy seemed distraught seeing the judge, and the Boutwell women didn't stay long. Grayson stood at the door with Sally and Carter as her mother approached Mitchell's bedside and held his hand, softly weeping. Sheppy, still regally beautiful, all cheekbones and smooth white skin, leaned over and kissed Mitchell's forehead. When she withdrew from him, a tear moistened his brow.

On a brisk, sun-dappled October day, most of the population of Troy filled the First Baptist Church for the funeral of Mitchell Ransom. In front of the altar was the mahogany casket, draped with the traditional American flag of a military funeral.

Carter sat in the first row with Sally and Willie and the North Carolina relatives. Directly in front of the family, Stephen Musgrove commanded the helm of the Skinner pipe organ playing a Bach prelude. At the far end of their pew sat Stephen's mother, Nell Marie Musgrove, dolled up in lipstick and pearls and, despite her black dress and veil, looking as if she were at a debutante ball for the first time in years. She beamed at her son, perched on the same mahogany bench whence she had prevailed for so many years. Glancing discreetly over his shoulder, Carter saw Nettie and Lige and their extended family filling an entire pew, and behind them Sheppy Boutwell, Grayson and her daughters, and Governor Tom Wheaton. The array of dignitaries, including jurists from around the state, made the congregation look like a plenary session of the Mississippi Bar Association.

The eager young pastor of the First Baptist Church, whom Carter met for the first time that morning, had the sense to realize that the occasion transcended the prescribed rituals, and after a minimum of Baptist funeral boilerplate he turned the pulpit over to Congressman Elijah Knight. Lige summoned his "preacher voice" to describe what the judge had meant not only to the community, the state, and the nation but to him personally. He conveyed the same prophetic conviction with which—as young lawbreaker so long ago—he preached the Constitution from the courthouse steps to the sheriff who now sat among the congregants, facing his own day in court. Lige ended with one of the judge's favorite passages, from Romans 14:11. " 'For it is written, as I live, saith the Lord, every knee shall bow to me, and every tongue shall confess to God.' "

Carter meditated on that Scripture verse. As a child, he had heard Nettie proclaim it in humility whenever she was confronted with disaster in the kitchen or on the evening news: "Every knee shall bow, every tongue confess." He thought about how life had a way of bringing us to our knees, bowing us low before eternity, and forcing confession even from those with the most withholding of tongues. Confession had been commodified in recent years by televangelists parading their disgrace in exchange for donations, and by their secular counterparts, the moral freaks and grotesques of the TV talk shows. The sacred and the profane were now Siamese twins on the gaudy midway. Even Magic Time had become a prop for a photo op. But there were still sins worth confessing and personal truths that transcended vanity.

Lige's sermon was followed by eulogies from old friends—Pete Callahan, Raymond Renfro, Mayor Otis Jameson, Lonnie Culpepper— some of whom had spoken at the highway dedication only months before. After the minister offered his prayer of benediction and the people began their slow way out of the church toward the cemetery next door, Carter took in the size and makeup of the congregation and saw that even the second tier of the balcony was full. That's when he spotted Sydney Rushton, standing by herself off to the side, flashing him her motionless wave.

At graveside, under a white canvas tent, Carter read from one of his father's sacred texts, the speech that Oliver Wendell Holmes, Jr., a fellow judge, delivered in May of 1884 to commemorate the anniversary of the end of the Civil War. "'Through our great good fortune, in our youth our hearts were touched with fire,'" Carter read. "'It was given to us to learn at the outset that life is a profound and passionate thing.'"

Carter thought of Sarah and those brave and luminous young men and women who came south to his home one hundred years after that terrible conflict and offered themselves up in fiery sacrifice to a truth greater than themselves, who transformed his own young manhood while setting out to save a nation. Until now he had never connected their fateful bravery to the heroism of his father's generation in defying a holocaust on foreign soil. Like Holmes and his generation of veterans, they all had been "set apart by the experience." But it had never occurred to Carter that his father's own heart had suffered a wound even more intense than patriotic gore.

The meaning of what he was reading opened up to him like the autumn sky above. "It is required of a man that he should share the passion and action of his time at peril of being judged not to have lived," Holmes wrote. Carter grasped what Sarah had understood instinctively, what she had been willing to die for because it affirmed that she had lived. "'To fight out a war,'" Carter read, "'you must believe something and want something with all your might. So must you do to carry anything else to an end worth reaching. More than that, you must be willing to commit yourself to a course, perhaps a long and hard one, without being able to foresee exactly where you will come out.'"

Sydney, too, had found a way to be part of the experience and had rescued Carter from the anguish of having been set apart. Zealous, Carter thought, with admiration. Sydney did not yet know what it was like to lose, but Carter looked forward to exploring with her Holmes's

century-old truth: the meaning is in the struggle, and whatever its outcome, whatever its legacy for future generations, "it is enough for us
that this day is dear and sacred."

Lonnie, Stephen, and Jimbo rose and beckoned Carter to a reunion of
the Boys of Troy, to sing an a cappella version of Mitchell Ransom's favorite song from the *Broadman Hymnal*, "Just as I Am." Carter sought
out Lige's face in the crowd and extended his hand to him. The five of
them stood in the golden autumn sunlight, the faint scent of woodsmoke
on the morning breeze, and harmonized to the lyrics of that old gospel
standard:

> *Just as I am, without one plea,*
> *but that thy blood was shed for me,*
> *and that thou bidst me come to thee,*
> *O Lamb of God, I come, I come.*

Sydney, in black, stepped into view. Their eyes met as he sang, and
Carter was taken back to the early days of high school when he and the
Boys of Troy had made their debut at the sparsely attended Sunday
night services in the church next door. His parents had been seated in
their usual place near the front, and he remembered the pride in their
eyes, caught out of the corner of his own, the paternal gleam that he
would avoid at all costs.

On that glorious fall morning, Carter soaked up the gaze of the
woman he loved. She smiled slightly in encouragement and placed her
hand over her heart. Carter's eyes filled up as he sang the words he had
uttered so many times before without understanding:

> *Just as I am, and waiting not*
> *to rid my soul of one dark blot,*
> *to thee whose blood can cleanse each spot,*
> *O Lamb of God, I come, I come.*
>
> *Just as I am, though tossed about*
> *with many a conflict, many a doubt,*

fightings and fears within, without,
O Lamb of God, I come, I come.

Carter returned to his seat. The casket rested on a scaffold in front of him, adjacent to Katharine Ransom's grave. The sound of taps cut through the air, and the color guard from the Keesler Air Force base in Biloxi advanced from the edge of the crowd. Six young men in their dress blues approached the casket in slow-motion precision, each touching the flag draped over it with crisp white gloves as they passed. Then two of them stepped forward, lifted the flag, and folded it into a tidy triangle of red, white, and blue. They handed it to the officer in charge, who saluted, turned, and approached Carter and Sally. Solemnly he dropped to one knee, head bowed, and presented the folded flag to Carter. As the tall black officer stood at attention and saluted, Carter accepted the flag of his father and took it to his heart.

Epilogue

M ITCHELL RANSOM LEFT the family home to Sally, along with
a considerable inheritance, much of which she intended to plow
back into her bookstore. Carter was given the beach house at Gulf
Shores and some acreage along the Little Chickasaw. The most surprising outcome of the will was that Carter now owned the judge's control-
ling interest in *The Troy Times*.

"Congratulations," Dennehy said when Carter informed him that
he was resigning as the *Examiner*'s columnist-on-sabbatical to become
editor and publisher of the local newspaper. "I can't say as I blame you.
Big-time journalism is all corporate bullshit now—profit margins, market penetration, and meetings about sexual harassment guidelines and
carpal tunnel syndrome. Human Resources has taken over, and it's no
fun anymore. I'm up for retirement soon. Let me know if you ever need
a managing editor down there."

The *New York Examiner*'s coverage of the bombing of the Institute
of Modern Art, including Carter's columns, won a Pulitzer Prize in the
Breaking News Reporting category.

While going through their father's personal effects, Carter and Sally
found—among the trove of memorabilia in a trunk in the basement—
virtually every story or column ever written by or about his son, from

faded yellow clippings chronicling his high school athletic exploits, to early articles Carter had written on the civil rights workers at Magic Time, to pieces for the Nashville, Atlanta, and New York papers.

Another item Carter and Sally came across, in the bottom of an old toolbox in a cabinet in his basement workshop, was a letter addressed to Mitchell in care of the Harvard Law School on Massachusetts Avenue in Cambridge. It read:

> Dear M.,
>
> I am sending this to you in care of the law school. I hope it gets to you. Glen got home safely and we have gotten married. You may disapprove, given our discussions, but you must understand it's for the best. I will never forget our special time together last summer. You must accept the Graysonite offer when you finish law school. Don't let any of what went on between us affect your decision. I couldn't bear it if you did. I will make sure that your wife is comfortable in Troy. Please do not worry or feel guilty. I only wish we could have met earlier and under different circumstances. I hope you have a wonderful life. You deserve all the best.
>
> Destroy this letter after you read it.
>
> Love always,
> S.

Sally looked at Carter and said, "I don't want to know."

Jimbo Stein finally got the answer he had been waiting for. On a lonely pilgrimage up the Little Chickasaw in his Boston Whaler, he rigged up his boom box for the umpteenth time to play his birdcall recording. He was reading *The Troy Times* as the early morning sun set the treetops ablaze in yellows and reds, and then he heard it. The distinctive *"Yank yank, srrrripp!"* of *Picoides borealis*, the red-cockaded woodpecker.

A couple of weeks before the November election, Jimbo, Carter, and Congressman Elijah Knight paid a visit to WunderCorp's Helmut Schlank in his penthouse presidential suite at the Pinehurst.

"Come in, Congressman," said Schlank, who was going over some spreadsheets on his laptop when they were ushered into the seating area by his assistant. "What can I do for you?"

"Mr. Schlank, I believe you know Mr. Stein," said Lige. "He's with the Nature Conservancy, and he chairs my reelection campaign. And this is Carter Ransom."

"Of course," said Schlank. "The journalist." He nodded and extended his hand to Carter, while barely looking at Jimbo.

"We're here to talk with you about your project on the Little Chickasaw," Lige said.

"Good," said Schlank as he offered them seats on the divan in the receiving area of his suite. "I hope you've finally come to your senses."

"Yes, I think we may have done just that," said Lige. "Jimbo, why don't you tell him about it."

"Mr. Schlank," said Jimbo, "we thought you'd like to know that we've found evidence that the Chickasaw River basin, as we've long suspected, is the habitat of the red-cockaded woodpecker."

Schlank's perpetual look of condescension bordered now on pity. "And?"

"The red-cockaded woodpecker has been thought to be near extinction. I identified one a few days ago on the Little Chickasaw not far from the Magic Time and Shiloh Church sites that you have targeted for development. I have since had it verified by ornithologists with the Audubon Society and the Fish and Wildlife Service."

Schlank appeared unfazed. "We have very sophisticated land-management plans that ensure that such rare species, if confirmed by our experts, are not further threatened or, worse, driven to extinction by any of WunderCorp's activities. I will notify my environmental resource people immediately."

"You don't understand," said Jimbo. "This puts the kibosh on your land-management plans."

Lige raised his hand to calm Jimbo. "The costs of single-species rescue programs can be prohibitive."

"Yes, well, in our experience with these matters, we've found that, with early intervention, a few simple and relatively inexpensive adjustments can often allow natural systems to stabilize and maintain their constituent plants and animals." Then, to Jimbo, "We also have a legal department with vast experience contesting such habitat designations."

Jimbo smiled in acknowledgment. "We're prepared to get a court order."

"Go ahead," said Schlank. "Your Fish and Wildlife Service's list includes many of the most controversial habitat designations, some of which have already been litigated by us several times. We always win. Now, gentlemen, if you have no other business."

"But I think you might be interested in some of our other findings," said Lige. He looked at Carter.

Carter cleared his throat. "Yes," he said, "there's another little environmental concern. I've been working on a story on the Chickasaw land deal." Carter got out his notebook and began thumbing deliberately through its pages. "I was wondering if you have any comment."

"On what?"

"Tomorrow the *New York Examiner* is running the first article in a series on hazardous waste disposal in the lower South. WunderCorp's plans for Ellis County is my peg."

"What does that have to do with this?" said Schlank, showing a slight shift in gravity. "I hope you're not allowing yourself to become a mouthpiece for extremists like Mr. Stein here."

"Actually, I wrote it without the help of Mr. Stein. I've been able to do some research of my own with the help of the Internet. WunderCorp has quite a history."

Schlank's voice dropped into the register of a television infomercial announcer. "Yes, we are proud of our heritage as one of the world's largest and finest petrochemical companies."

"Yes, I know." Carter began reciting from his notebook. "Plastics and polyurethanes, crude oil and natural gas, agricultural products, food processing, pharmaceuticals . . ."

"Insecticides?" said Jimbo.

Schlank wouldn't look at him. "Yes."

"You have quite a history of manufacturing chemical agents, don't you, Herr Schlank?" said Jimbo.

"Of course, we have been in business a long time."

"Yes, we've traced your heritage back to before World War Two," Carter said, and again read from his notebook. "In 1925 you became part of IG Farbenindustrie AG. For the next decade, it says, 'advances in technology led to important synthesis processes.' On your Web site you say, 'The outbreak of World War Two forced the company to switch to a war economy, beginning a chain of events which saw IG Farben, too, entangled in the toils of the Nazi regime.' Interesting phrasing."

"So what?"

"One of your insecticides—you know—exterminators," said Jimbo. "The world has heard of it before. Even in a little old backward place like Troy, Mississippi."

"Farben manufactured Zyklon B," said Carter. "Can you clear this up for me? I know that was the gas the Nazis used at Auschwitz. But did they use it at Treblinka, too?"

"And now you're planning to use the land in Ellis County for dumping hazardous waste," Lige said. "Or is there some other use you have in mind for the thousands of acres you've bought up?"

"We offer nothing but economic prosperity for Troy," said Schlank, his face reddening.

"Your economic prosperity seems to be a Trojan horse, Mr. Schlank," said Lige. "As you can imagine, sir, when this story breaks, my constituents are going to have a lot of concerns beyond the fate of the red-cockaded woodpecker."

Carter's farewell piece for the *Examiner*, on WunderCorp's plans for dumping toxic materials on rural Ellis County, was picked up on a TV newsmagazine show, sparking citizen protests and legislative inquiries. Schlank checked out of his penthouse suite in the Pinehurst, where he had been ensconced for more than a year, announcing that the Wunder-Corp development, including the plans to turn Troy into a civil rights mecca, would be put on hold. He returned to WunderCorp's American headquarters, at the World Trade Center in New York City. Jimbo regaled everyone with the story of their meeting and swore that Schlank's last words to them as he ushered them to the door was, "I was just following orders."

Carter received a handwritten note from Sam Bohannon in Parchman prison congratulating him on running WunderCorp out of Ellis County and offering his condolences for his father's death.

Lige was reelected that November. The Reverend Charles Lloyd, who was defeated in his mayoral bid that fall, moved back to Mississippi with his wife to work for Congressman Knight as his constituency liaison in Ellis County.

The Simon Lester documentary on the Shiloh Church case aired on PBS's *Frontline*. Smitty Crawford wrote a fictional version of the church bombing case, in which one of the victims was a local debutante who was moved by the plight of her maid to join up with the SNCC outsiders, in defiance of her Junior League mother; she survived the church bombing and testified against the perpetrators, who included her father, a minister.

The film rights were optioned by Michael Solomon at Warner Bros. When the screenplay was not assigned to Bradley's husband, Harold Bernhardt, he accepted a high-paying job in public relations with a WunderCorp subsidiary that had bought up abandoned tar-paper shacks around the state, once owned by actual sharecroppers, with a plan to remodel them as bed-and-breakfasts for tourists. "We re-create actual 'blues conditions,'" as Bernhardt put it in the glossy brochures he produced, "for anyone interested in reliving the actual 'blues experience.'"

Magic Time was saved and, along with Shiloh Church, was put on the national historic register. The young folklorist from Troy University, Tom Thames, received backing from Eric Clapton for his dream of providing relief for aging blues pioneers, involving assisted-living care, medical coverage, alcohol and drug rehab, relationship counseling, and state-of-the-art studios to record and preserve their music. Magic Time became headquarters for Tom Thames's Living Blues Project.

Carter took over the newspaper that had first published him, and Sydney was in Troy starting up a unit to work full-time on old civil rights cases.

One Saturday morning in June, twenty-eight years after Carter came to Magic Time during Freedom Summer, he took Sydney and Willie and Josh, who was down on one of his frequent visits from New York, on an outing to Naked Tail. As they drove through town and past the court-house and the statue of Hugh in front of the Starlite Cafe, Josh asked from the backseat, "Who's that?"

"He's a local legend," said Carter.

"He was cuckoo," said Willie, circling his temple with his forefinger.

"He had more sense than a lot of people around here," said Carter. "He was just born with problems." He told the boys about how Hugh had directed traffic and talked in rhyme and done impressions of José Jiménez, and about the day he broke up the attack on the demonstra-tors on the courthouse steps.

"That's pitiful," said Josh.

"Hugh didn't know that," said Carter. "Sometimes life is lived more fully by those who have to fight for it than by those of us who can take it for granted."

They got on the newly completed Mitchell Ransom Expressway for a short distance until it emptied them off onto Front Street and the city marina on the Chickasaw River. They piled into Jimbo's Boston Whaler, which Carter had borrowed for the day, and sailed up to Naked Tail for a picnic and a swim.

He and Sydney lay on a blanket on the shore and watched the boys laughing as they took turns on the brand-new rope swing he had rigged up on the oak tree. "Do you miss your cigarettes?" she asked.

"Sometimes. Usually when I'm writing my column." Carter had stopped smoking the day he learned that Sydney was pregnant.

"You're so sublimated," she said. "You take all the sound and fury within and turn it into rectitude and restraint and words."

"Just doing my part for civilization," Carter said. He traced her pro-file with his finger. "Besides, somebody had to have the moral fortitude to make a married woman of Sydney Rushton."

"Only because you're so much fun to un-sublimate," Sydney said. She turned to him and hooked her finger on the waistband of his bathing suit.

There would be no skinny-dipping this day, however. Carter had brought Sydney in the late spring to Naked Tail after returning from their small wedding in Birmingham, and they had swum naked together and made love on the shore. It was there that they had conceived their child.

Carter had finished his weekly column early that morning so they could have the whole day together. It was a piece comparing the old Klan to the Islamic extremists in the Middle East.

"Ah," Sydney said sympathetically when he described it to her. "Your life story." Then she intoned the headline. " 'Terrorists Past, Present, and Future.' "

" 'Broke-Dick Men Wreak Havoc All Over,' " Carter said.

" 'The Awful Responsibility of Time,' " Sydney said.

Carter looked at the gnarled trunk of the oak tree now resurrecting the pale green leaves of early summer and said, "I never really understood what that meant."

"God. What a world of hurt we've arranged for baby Katharine."

Carter put his ear to her belly. She clasped him close, gliding her hand around his temple and covering his eyes.

"I would not have missed it for the world," he said.

Acknowledgments

Of the many excellent nonfiction accounts of the civil rights era, the ones to which I am particularly indebted for the historical details in this novel are *Walking with the Wind,* by John Lewis, with Michael D'Orso; *God's Long Summer* and *The Last Days,* by Charles Marsh; *Carry Me Home,* by Diane McWhorter; *Terror in the Night,* by Jack Nelson; *Letters from Mississippi,* edited by Elizabeth Sutherland Martinez; and *Dixie: A Personal Odyssey Through Events That Shaped the Modern South,* by Curtis Wilkie.

I was inspired by personal encounters with John Lewis, Fred Shuttlesworth, Carolyn Goodman, Ellie J. Dahmer, Douglas Stenstrom, Jim Wann, Judge James B. McMillan, and Dr. William Blythe.

For their expertise on matters ranging from courtroom proceedings to hog dogs, I am grateful to Doug Jones, Jerry Mitchell, Andy Sheldon, Karen Scott, Erica Berger, Janis Owens, Richard Maschal, Lew Powell, Bland Simpson, Myrna Harris, Greg Massey, Lisa Vail, Martine Bellen, Esther Newberg, and Sarah Crichton.

A NOTE ABOUT THE AUTHOR

Doug Marlette has won every major award for cartooning, including the Pulitzer Prize. His award-winning first novel, *The Bridge,* was published in 2001.